'A topi
for a w

'The au
by a
her ch
empat

'The st
intens
acters

'The
recon
up wl

'Each
between the lives of two women ... Sarah Rayner has got
the balance just   vening News

'A must read! T   ompelling –
a real page-turn   g3 magazine

'I finished the   a great read
and you won't

Kate   Guide to IVF

Sarah Rayner grew up in London and now lives in Brighton. She is the bestselling author of *One Moment, One Morning*, which has been translated into eleven languages. She worked for twenty years as an advertising copywriter, and now writes fiction full time.

Sarah loves hearing from her readers, and you can visit her website at: www.thecreativepumpkin.com.

The
Two Week
Wait

SARAH RAYNER

PICADOR

First published 2012 by Picador in paperback

This edition published 2012 by Picador
an imprint of Pan Macmillan, a division of Macmillan Publishers Limited
Pan Macmillan, 20 New Wharf Road, London N1 9RR
Basingstoke and Oxford
Associated companies throughout the world
www.panmacmillan.com

ISBN 978-0-330-54410-8

1 3 5 7 9 8 6 4 2

A CIP catalogue record for this book is available from
the British Library.

Typeset by Ellipsis Digital Limited, Glasgow
Printed and bound by CPI Group (UK) Ltd, Croydon, CR0 4YY

Visit **www.picador.com** to read more about all our books and to
buy them. You will also find features, author interviews and news
of any author events, and you can sign up for e-newsletters
so that you're always first to hear about our new releases.

I

The water is getting cold; Lou has been in the bath a while. Whilst usually she prefers the swiftness of showers, very occasionally she likes to bathe, to linger and relax, surrounded by bubbles. She is shaping them into miniature mountain ranges, like she did as a girl. She laughs to herself as she sculpts two extra high peaks from her breasts, Everest and K2.

She slides forward to twist on the hot tap with her toe. It's a manoeuvre she's done countless times: this is the bathroom of her childhood home, though only her mum, Irene, lives here now. The foam – given a second burst of life by the running water – billows in candyfloss clouds at her feet. Lou closes her eyes, inhales. Even the scent is redolent of her past: Lily of the Valley, her mother's favourite.

It is late evening and, after a long drive down from the Lakes, the worn avocado suite beckoned like an old friend. Lou lies back, warmth easing up her body and loosening her muscles. She listens. The sounds of the house are familiar: the wind in the trees outside – she misses those, her Brighton flat has none nearby; the plaintive hoot of an owl, so much less raucous than gulls. Through the faded pink shagpile carpet she can hear a deep male voice; her mother is watching television. Lou pictures Sofia sprawled on the counterpane in the next room, flicking through Sunday's supplement, having discarded the paper that Irene gets delivered with a huff, unable to endure its political leanings.

Lou would like Sofia to be in the bathroom with her, perched on the Lloyd Loom laundry basket, nattering. But it makes Irene edgy when she's confronted with physical intimacy of any kind – Lou doubts her mum ever allowed her father to sit there when he was alive. Lou and Sofia's displays of affection seem to make her mother especially tense, so they tend to avoid expressing any tenderness when she's around.

Lou shifts position; the bubbles float to the edge of the bath, revealing the slight dome of her belly. 'Your little pot', Sofia calls it. It galls Lou that her tummy is not as taut and flat as Sofia's, when she's the one who's into exercise. But whilst the rest of her body is reasonably toned, it seems that no matter how hard Lou works out, the pot remains. If anything, it seems to be getting bigger.

That's odd, Lou thinks, I'm uneven. One side doesn't match the other, close to my pubic bone.

Maybe she's not lying flat. She shifts again, carefully places one foot beside each tap to ensure she is symmetrical.

But if anything it's more marked. There, to her left, a bulge.

A flutter of anxiety.

Don't be silly, she tells herself, it's probably something

you've eaten. But her stomach is up towards her breastbone, and it's hardly as if she swallowed her roast potatoes whole at dinner.

Maybe I just need the loo? she wonders. But she's unconvinced, so she presses the area with her fingertips.

Hmm. She *can* feel something. She presses the other side. It seems softer, less resistant. Perhaps the angle is different; she's using her right hand. So she swaps to her left.

She can even detect the shape, rounded, like an orange.

Deep breaths. Don't panic.

She lies a moment longer, trying to take stock.

She jumps out of the bath, half-dries herself, and runs into the bedroom with a towel clutched round her, not caring that her mother might catch her undressed in the hall.

Sofia is lying on the bed, listening to her iPod. Dark curls scooped in a makeshift topknot, lace-ups discarded on the floor, hoodie slipping off one shoulder.

Lou gestures at her to turn down the music.

'I think I've found a lump,' she declares. No point in softening it.

Sofia sits up, unhooks her earphones. '*Si?*'

Lou repeats it. 'Here,' she indicates.

'Your pot?'

Lou nods. She hopes her girlfriend will be able to provide a rational explanation. Though why she would have more insight than Lou Lord knows: she's a web designer, not a doctor.

'Can you see?' Lou turns, drops the towel.

Sofia inspects her belly. 'Er . . . no.'

'It's bigger on one side than the other.' Lou stands there,

3

shifting from foot to foot. Even though they've been naked together countless times, the worry makes her self-conscious.

Sofia squats down, twisting her head to examine fully. 'It looks the same to me.'

'Here.' She takes Sofia's hand, guides her to the spot. 'No . . . Not like that, you won't be able to feel anything. Prod harder.'

'It will hurt.'

'OK, I'll lie down.' Lou stretches out on the fleecy counterpane. She's still wet from the bath, but no matter. 'Now, look from here,' she instructs, yanking Sofia down by her sleeve to her own eye level. 'As if you're me.'

Sofia crouches down, rests her chin on Lou's shoulder. A wave of her hair brushes against Lou's cheek.

'There,' says Lou. 'See?'

* * *

Cath is trapped in another world, lost in a vast public building, desperate to get somewhere, fast. Time is short – it's a race against the clock – but there are hordes of people in her way, moving frustratingly slowly.

'I've got to get through,' she tries to explain to those around her, struggling to push past the throng, but no one acknowledges her pleas. Instead people leer at her, pale-faced and ghoulish, or turn their backs, unyielding. Eventually she reaches a barrier, guarded by a man in a white coat. Perhaps he can help her. He's carrying a clipboard; he appears to be some kind of doctor – he has a stethoscope round his neck.

'I must catch it,' she begs. 'It's terribly important. It's—'

4

She wants to tell him it's a matter of life and death, yet can't seem to get the words out.

He blocks her path. 'I'm afraid it's too late,' he says.

She jerks awake with a gasp. Her heart is pounding; it takes a moment to ground herself, realize she is safe here in her room. The cat is wedged behind her on the pillow, as she often is; the gap in the curtains is at the end of the bed, as usual. Cath snuggles in tight to her husband, feeling her breasts and tummy against the smoothness of his back, easing her knees into the parallel Vs of his larger ones to calm herself, careful not to disturb him. Outside the warmth of the duvet the air is chilly; her arm is cold. She slides it under the covers too, inhales the comforting scent of his naked flesh as she does so; slightly honeyed, lemony. Beneath her palm she can sense the hairs on his chest, soft and curled. His breathing is deep and slow, it feels solid, just as he is. Gradually she feels her panic subside. It must be worry about the journey ahead, that's all.

Just then, Rich's mobile goes off beside him, a frenzy of buzzing and vibrating. He stirs beneath her touch.

'Bloody hell, that's a bit much.' She is jangled again.

'Sorry.' He reaches to switch it off. 'I was worried we'd sleep through.' He's bleary. 'I was having the weirdest dream . . .'

'Me too,' says Cath.

She's just about to tell him about her nightmare when he says, 'Amy Winehouse was in our kitchen, loading the dishwasher.'

'Really?'

'Yeah . . . There she was, in one of those tight little dresses she used to wear, with her beehive piled high . . . Stacking plates. Very odd.'

'Mad,' says Cath.

'Mind you . . . ' he chuckles. 'When did anyone ever have a dream that *wasn't* strange?'

'Yeah, it's not like you wake up and say, "Ooh, last night I had a very *conventional* dream."' She laughs. Bless Rich for lightening her mood. She flings back the bedclothes. 'Come on then, let's get up.'

Normally they emerge from sleep gradually. Cath wears earplugs to block Rich's occasional snoring; he wakes to the muted talk of the radio, nudges her, and they both snooze a while before getting up for work. But not today. Their plane leaves in three hours; before that, they must drive from Meanwood in Leeds to Manchester Airport, over fifty miles away. They pull on clothes left out the night before, Rich gulps down coffee, Cath tea, and Cath puts down food for the cat.

'No sign of sunrise yet,' she says, as they lug their suitcases down the front steps. It's mid-December; in a few days it will be the longest night of the year. Rich heaves the cases into the boot of the car and Cath gets into the passenger seat. The windscreen is icy. Rich removes the worst with a gloved hand while she waits for him inside, breath steaming white and cold.

'Right,' he exhales, getting in. He starts the ignition, turns to her and grins. 'Ready to roll.'

Cath waves goodbye to their red-brick terrace as Rich edges the car with a *bump bump* over the potholes that have been deepened by a succession of freezing winters, and out onto Grove Lane. They've barely gone half a mile past their local shops on the Otley Road when he suddenly brakes. Luckily, there's no vehicle behind. He swivels to face her. 'Did you feed Bessie?'

'Yes. *And* I left the keys out for your sister. Now, come on. We'll be late.'

The ring road, frequently nose-to-tail with traffic, is ghostly quiet as they head past warehouses and budget hotel chains out of town. Presently they're speeding across the Pennines. The M62 never sleeps, it seems; even though it's not yet 6 a.m., lorries thunder down the inside lane, spewing spray from overnight sleet. Alongside, their hatchback feels small and vulnerable; Cath can feel the wind buffeting the side of the car. She rubs mist from the window so she can see: spies a cottage on a remote hillside, whitewashed and pale against the dark heather. She wonders who lives there, on the moor, whether they're lonely with no one nearby. She tries to imagine her own life away from the city, their little house, the shops and park, far from anyone. It might be good for her artistically – she imagines she'd be so bored she'd have to occupy herself somehow – but she would crave company, miss her friends.

She reaches for Rich, appreciating his presence, strokes the back of his neck where his hair is downy, going grey. He hates his neck, thinks it's too thick and makes him look stupid, no matter how often she tells him it's manly. 'It's almost fatter than my head,' he claims.

As if he can read her thoughts, he glances at her and smiles.

She smiles back affectionately, pulls down the mirror on the back of the sun visor to check her own appearance.

At last her hair is growing back properly. Initially it was a different texture entirely; still mousy, but curlier and thicker than it had been; a small consolation for everything she'd been through. But now it's returned to its familiar form: thin, wispy, infuriating. She has to wear it short and layered, it won't 'do' any other style. Nonetheless, she is pleased; at least she looks herself again. Though her skin remains grey and drawn and her eyes have lost some sparkle; she seems older, somehow. Worn.

She hopes this trip will help. After the tsunami of emotions they've experienced in the last two years, they both deserve a good time.

She thinks of the mountains that await them, dazzling whiter than white beneath bluer than blue. There will be dramatic peaks, there will be sun, there will be crystal-clear air . . .

At once, a burst of excitement. Soon it's Christmas, then New Year, and she can kiss goodbye to this vile twelve months forever.

'We're going on holiday!' she says, and claps her hands.

* * *

Lou resists an impulse to wake Sofia. It's 5 a.m., wouldn't be fair.

It's all very well telling me not to worry, she thinks. If only it were that easy to switch off my mind.

She rolls over onto her back, eases down her pyjama bottoms, checks her abdomen. Is it her imagination or does

8

it feel tender? Though she could just be bruised from all the prodding.

The previous evening they had scoured the Internet for possible diagnoses. Sofia homed in on less dramatic conditions (including, to Lou's irritation, constipation), but Lou is still convinced it's something worse. They'd wondered about calling a medical helpline, then decided it was too late and not really an emergency. 'Let's go to bed,' Sofia had urged. 'We can ring the doctor in the morning. We'll get you an appointment as soon possible.'

So Lou is here, in one of the twin divans her mother insists on giving them. These days Irene runs the family home as a B. & B., and this is the room they've been allocated, even though her mother doesn't take guests over the Christmas holidays, so there's a much larger double free next door. 'She is like a woman from the 1950s, your mum,' Sofia had moaned. 'Even in Spain, most mothers are not so strict. Does she believe it will stop us having sex?' 'It'll stop her having to admit we do,' Lou had replied. Her mother's propensity for denial would be laughable had not vast swathes of Lou's life gone painfully unacknowledged as a result.

Lou continues the exploration. She knows she's being obsessive, yet she's vaguely hoping it will ease her fear, and at least in the dark, in the silence, she can concentrate. With both hands she locates the lump again. It feels huge. How can she have missed it until today? She presses it; it makes her need to pee.

Sofia stirs and rolls over. Lou holds her breath – she could do with Sofia to murmur sleepy consolation, soothe her – but she doesn't wake.

Lou persists with her mission, fingertips slow, ominous, tarantula-like. If the lump were in the middle, she'd concede it was just the way her body is made. It's the alien asymmetry that most alarms her. She swallows her fear. She can't – she won't – allow *that* notion to gain hold.

She puts her counsellor head on, thinks what she would say if she were a client. She is better at giving advice than receiving it. Perhaps she should make a list of symptoms to report to the doctor.

1. *I need the loo quite a lot – more than Sofia.*
2. *My periods are heavier than they used to be.*

She's made allowances for her bladder – sitting on the end of a row in the cinema, snatching any opportunity to go to the toilet on protracted journeys lest she get caught short – for as long as she can remember. But she's hardly incontinent and her periods aren't that bad. Many women suffer from much worse.

Otherwise, she's pretty fit. She can do a hundred sit-ups in succession, easy, so there's nothing wrong with her muscles. She doesn't drink much; her diet is almost exemplary. So what on earth is it? If something major were wrong, wouldn't she be in some kind of pain?

None of this is helping. It's only raising more questions, sending her thoughts spinning. And whichever way she turns them, she ends up with the same answer, like a ball on a roulette wheel that lands on the same number, time and again.

* * *

The plane rumbles along the runway, gathering speed. Cath watches the airport blur past, grips the seat arms with clammy palms, waiting for the wheels to lift from the ground. In the seat in front of her a toddler is crying.

Poor thing, she thinks. I hate take-off and landing, too.

That's when she has heard most accidents happen, and certainly it's when there's no escaping the absurdity of spewing a vast metal object into the sky. When they're cruising tens of thousands of feet up, Cath can suspend disbelief, imagine she's just in some strange tube-shaped cinema, watching the sun and clouds through the misty porthole like a film.

Faster and faster they go: she can't believe they're not yet airborne . . .

Finally – *whoooosh!* – they're up.

Phew.

She's been holding her breath the entire time.

She sits back, relaxes. Shortly the 'Fasten seatbelts' sign goes off, and the child in front stops wailing. Cath can feel him jolting the chair, wriggling, restless, so she scratches the white antimacassar above his head to get his attention. He peers round the gap between the seats. His face is tear-stained.

'Hello,' she says, and smiles.

He ducks away, wary. Shortly he re-emerges, wide-eyed, curious.

'Boo!' says Cath.

Again he disappears, and a few seconds later he's back.

She hides her face behind her hands, then quickly removes them. 'Boo!'

He giggles.

What a sweetie, Cath thinks.

So now there's just landing, then her first skiing lesson, to get through. She's dreading that. Cath was never good at PE; she was the girl at school who took every opportunity to skive and sit on the bench, and skiing will require not just aptitude but bravery too.

Still, having stared at her own mortality in the mirror, nothing frightens her quite as much as it did.

* * *

It's no good: Lou can't rest, and now she can hear birds – at this time of year it must be a robin, laying claim to its territory. Perhaps she doesn't miss those trees after all.

She gets up, impatient, throwing back the sheets. At least with Sofia in a separate bed it's easier not to wake her.

She raises the blind a touch to help her see, rummages through her holdall for appropriate clothes, retrieves her trainers from the floor and tiptoes into the bathroom to pull on her tracksuit. She has to do something with this nervous energy.

Down the stairs, softly, softly. Her mother is the lightest sleeper; Lou can't face a dressing-gowned inquisition on top of her own anxiety. She eases back the bolts on the front door, praying they won't clank, and then she's out and on the drive.

She inhales fresh air deep into her lungs, and, without stretching – the desire to get moving far outweighing any concerns of injury – she's off down the lane.

The house is on the outskirts of town. Bare, tangle-twigged

hedgerows rise on either side of her. In the distance are gently undulating fields, ploughed and ready for planting. Dawn is approaching; mist rising from the valley, spectral grey on brown.

It takes a minute or two for her muscles to warm up and to hit her stride. Ah, that's better – the rhythm helps calm her, each footfall brings with it increased lucidity, shaking down thoughts like rice in a jar so they no longer crowd her.

Sofia must be right. Would she be able to sprint like this if she was really ill? Of course not.

It's just, things have been going so well lately. The two of them are looking to buy a place together; her job counselling kids who've been excluded from school is easier now she's no longer such a novice. It would be typical if something were to trip her up.

As if to comment on her thoughts, a driver toots, forcing her into the kerb, then overtakes at speed in a glistening Audi.

What's the hurry? thinks Lou, annoyed.

She decides to get off the main road. Hitchin is commuter-belt territory; even this early, people are heading to work.

She turns left through a kissing gate and onto the common. The riverside path weaves through alder trees and the arching stems of pendulous sedge. In the reed beds frogs will be mating come early spring, then there will be tadpoles just like the ones she and her sister used to collect in jam jars when they were small. And there in the grazing pasture are the cattle: English Longhorns, an ancient, placid breed. They raise their heads from the vegetation to gaze at her, bemused.

She takes her cue, reduces her pace.

You can run but you can't flee, she tells herself.

Two laps later, she's feeling less agitated. As she jogs out onto the road once more, she has an idea. Yes, why not? She'll go back that way, through town.

She slows to a walk as she approaches the entrance, a mark of respect. She briefly wonders if anyone will mind that she's in her exercise gear, then remembers it's most unlikely there will be other visitors at this time.

It's been a while, but she finds the spot quickly and kneels down. The ground is damp with frost.

How strange to think of him beneath this soil.

Even after all these years, she still misses him. She wishes that she could talk to him; so much has happened since he died. She's finished her training, moved to Brighton, come out to her mother . . . And now, this lump. What would he say about that?

In part he's what's made her so jumpy. She's thrown right back to the experience of his illness: the protracted demise, the pain and fear, the loss of dignity. He became so thin and fragile, a ghost of his former self. The prospect of going through anything even remotely similar to her father terrifies her.

Lou plucks at the grass, struggling with her memories. Although most plants have withered in the cold, the hump still needs weeding, she thinks abstractedly. It can't have been done in a while. She's surprised her mother hasn't tended it – Irene's garden at the B. & B. is immaculate: every pot diligently planted with winter pansies, the drive lined with snowdrops, just beginning to push through. Maybe she doesn't come here much, can't face it. Lou finds that notion strange, but that's her mum all over.

She yanks at the weeds more deliberately, uses her nails to prise them from the cold soil, working from the front of the plot to the back. Soon she's collected a little pile of wilted leaves. She smoothes the earth with her palms, sits back to check her handiwork. The couch grass will need a fork, but it's a start.

2

'That'll be Mummy,' says Lou. 'Do you want to buzz her in?'

She follows Molly to the intercom. Small fingers reach up to hit the button.

'Let's watch her come upstairs,' Lou suggests. Together they go to the landing; she lifts Molly so she can see over the banister.

Lou and Sofia live in a studio flat on the top floor of a three-storey house – she and Molly hear Karen's footsteps before they see her. Eventually she comes into sight: chestnut hair and anorak soaked from the rain.

'Mummy!'

Karen looks up from the floor below, her cheeks rosy from being outside. 'Hello, Molster,' she smiles. When she reaches them she bends to kiss her daughter.

'Ew, you're wet,' says Molly. 'And don't call me Molster.'

'Sorry.' Karen glances at Lou. 'Everything OK?'

Lou nods. 'We've had a great time, haven't we?'

'We've done a funny drawing,' says Molly.

'Ooh,' says Karen. 'Why is it funny?'

'It's a plan for the allotment,' says Lou. 'She wanted to plant seeds – she saw the ones I'd ordered from the catalogue – but I told her it wasn't the right time of year. So we did a plan instead.'

'Come and see!' says Molly. The three of them head into the kitchen.

'It's really great of you to have her,' says Karen, peering at the drawing.

'No problem at all,' says Lou. She looks at the combination of her own adult handwriting alongside Molly's enthusiastic colouring-in and smiles. 'I've enjoyed it.'

'Well, you know Molly's your number one fan.'

That pleases Lou. The feeling is mutual. 'Have you time for a cup of tea?'

Karen pushes damp tendrils from her face. 'I guess I have – just a swift one.'

'Here, let me.' Lou takes Karen's coat, hangs it on the radiator to dry.

Karen stands gazing out of the window. The street of Victorian terraced houses looks tired and tatty, a hotchpotch of mismatched dirty pastel frontages. Beyond it the sea is dark and dreary. Even the pier seems to be struggling to remain bright and cheerful with its gaudy lights flashing in the drizzle and fairground attractions empty.

'So how are you?' says Lou, catching Karen's wistful expression.

Karen sighs. 'OK, I guess.' Molly is winding herself round her legs like a cat. Karen glances down at her daughter, strokes her hair. She looks up and smiles wanly at Lou. 'I've been worse.'

Lou nods, recognizing Karen's sadness. She pauses, unsure whether to make this observation, decides it's better to do so: 'It must be tough, the run-up to . . . well, you know.'

Karen swallows. Lou can see she is fighting back tears, which must have been near the surface. Oh dear, she thinks, perhaps I shouldn't have brought it up with Molly here. But there are enough people scared of mentioning what Karen's been through; Lou doesn't want to be one of them.

Karen struggles to keep her voice steady. 'It's our first Christmas without him.'

'I'm so sorry,' Lou says. 'I should have thought.'

'Don't worry,' says Karen.

But Lou feels dreadful. She's been too wrapped up in her-self; first enjoying the Lakes with Sofia, then preoccupied with this wretched lump. Yet she, more than anyone, ought to have remembered how her friend would be feeling. Lou was with Karen when her husband died the previous February.

The kettle has boiled. Within seconds Lou is handing over a steaming brew. It seems inadequate but Karen takes it gratefully.

'Molly, love,' Lou says gently. Molly has stopped entwining, is eyeing her mother. 'Would you like to watch *Princess Aurora* for a bit while Mummy and I have a chat?' Karen brought the DVD when she dropped off her daughter; it's Molly's favourite.

'I've seen it already,' says Molly.

'It's all right,' says Karen. 'Don't worry. I'll be fine.' She goes over to the sofa, adjusts a couple of cushions so she can sit down. Molly clambers onto her knee, all pink and pastel against her mother's olive greens and browns.

Karen continues stroking her daughter's hair, running comb-like fingers away from her forehead. Molly wrinkles her nose and pouts. Karen, lost in her thoughts, doesn't see; the motion seems more to comfort herself than Molly. Lou switches on the TV anyway, flicks it to a children's programme. Soon Molly is transfixed by the antics of a giant-eyed CGI bunny, so when Karen clutches her tight and kisses the top of her head repeatedly, she barely registers.

'Biscuit?' Lou reaches for the tin.

'Why not?' Karen takes a digestive and breaks off a chunk for Molly. 'Actually, we're having a little family gathering on Christmas Eve, in the day, to remember Simon, you know. I thought it would be nice for the children. As well as for me and the grown-ups, obviously.' She's regained her composure; Lou can't help but feel relieved. 'I'd love you to come if you'd like?'

Although Karen has become a good friend in the last ten months, Lou hesitates. 'If it's just family, I'm not sure . . . I wouldn't want to intrude.'

'It won't be entirely relatives – you can bring Sofia, and Anna's coming as well. There's no ceremony or anything formal – it's a party. We're having bubbly. And cake . . . '

'OK.' Lou grins. 'Thank you. That would be lovely.'

When Karen has gone, Lou checks the clock: it's a while before she's due to leave for the doctor's, where she's been promised an appointment last thing.

Lou had been hoping to tell Karen about the lump, but it didn't seem appropriate in the circumstances. It's been good having Molly to look after, kept her worries in perspective. She bends to pick up the cushions she and Molly used to make a train on the floor.

Poor Karen, no wonder she was so tearful, she thinks, plumping the sofa. I can only begin to imagine what it's like, losing your partner that suddenly. Simon died of a heart attack one morning on the train. Karen was with him, Lou witnessed everything. She is haunted by the memory of the 07:44 to Victoria. One moment she was half watching people as she dozed; across the aisle was Simon, stroking Karen's hand. The next: *boof!* He was gone, and there was nothing anyone could do to revive him. If there's one thing Lou has learned, it's that you never know what's coming to knock you off course.

*　　*　　*

Down, *swish*, down, *swish*, down, *swish*; Cath is gaining confidence, becoming more stable on her skis, able to go faster. The instructor is ahead of her; she's following in his tracks, her first blue run. Here's the scary bit – the steep gradient she has been dreading. From the cable car she's seen more proficient skiers fall foul of it. They're early in the season and even though they've chosen a resort at a particularly high altitude, it's not snowed in days, so it's icy in patches. But she hasn't the time to get really nervous; she's in the present, eyes on Claude, carving the same sweeping curves as best she can.

Along, turn, bend the knees, swoosh; along . . . and *swooooooooooosh!* She pulls up beside him with a spray of powder, triumphant.

He lifts his goggles and beams at her. 'Well done, Cathy!'

Her name isn't Cathy, it's Cath, but she lets it pass because he's young and good-looking and it sounds extremely charming with a Gallic accent.

She beams back.

'Much less snowplough and more skis parallel. You are getting so much better!'

Her grin broadens.

'Now, once more up in the lift and we do it again.'

Damn. She thought that was it for the day and wanted to finish on a personal best. Next time she's bound to fall. Dutifully, she staggers after him, skis skidding diagonally like a clumsy duck, and joins the queue to return up the mountain.

Rich was right, she realizes as she edges forward in line, it's taking her out of herself, learning to ski. She's been so focused, so determined to master at least the basics, she hasn't had time to worry or analyse anything else, and that's been such a change, a joy. For the first time in ages her nervousness has been excitement, not fear, and her muscles have ached as the result of exercise rather than chemo. She'd not been at all sure beforehand; she'd had moments of believing the holiday was just a ruse for Rich, a skier since childhood, to indulge his own passions. But her husband isn't so self-centred, and he is aware how fragile she's been.

Later, she and Rich are sitting on a wooden bench by their locker, struggling to remove their boots, when Cath has an urge to say, 'Thank you for making me come.'

'No worries,' says Rich. But he remains focused on clasps and Velcro – she doesn't think he's taken it in. She wants him to know he understood what was good for her better than she understood herself.

She places a damp gloved hand over his. 'No, I mean it. I appreciate your persuading me. I'm having such a good time. I feel much better, really I do.'

'That's great,' he says, swapping his hand so it's over hers, and squeezing it.

3

The party seems well under way; Lou can hear voices as she and Sofia lock their bicycles to the drainpipe of Karen's 1930s semi. Lou rings the bell: it ding-dongs like the 'Avon Calling' ads of her youth.

'Get that, will you, someone?' she hears Karen call.

Anna opens the door. She's dressed in a slim-fitting black shift dress that emphasizes her height and figure. Her make-up is perfect, dramatic as always, her bob sleek. Although Lou has washed her hair and has her favourite T-shirt on, she feels hot from cycling and scruffy next to Anna.

'Lou! Sofia!' Anna kisses each on the cheek vigorously. 'Before we go in' – she leans in to Lou – 'tell me. How was the doctor?' Lou had confided her concerns on the phone the night before.

'He couldn't really say much,' says Lou. 'But let's get a drink and I'll tell you.'

They squeeze past a cluster of grown-ups standing in the hall, chatting. One is Karen. She's in a chiffon blouse and surprisingly trendy jeans. Lou can tell she's made an effort to look her best – it's strange to see her wearing lipstick. 'Hello, hello,' she says when she sees them. 'Glad you could make it.' She turns to the people she has been talking to. 'Excuse me, just want to have a quick word with these friends.' They head through to the kitchen.

'Pop your cycling stuff under the table if you like,' says Karen.

Lou and Sofia do as she suggests, one helmet atop the other.

'Bubbly?' offers Anna.

They both nod, and Anna deftly pours them each a glass.

'Anna tells me you've had a bit of a scare this week,' says Karen.

Lou is taken aback that they've plunged straight into the subject, but perhaps she shouldn't be – the fact that she met these two women on the day Karen's husband died has fast-tracked their intimacy. They've shared so much, why not this?

'Mm,' she says. 'I've found this lump in my lower abdomen, so I went to the doctor.'

'What did he say?'

'He couldn't be that specific.' Lou is about to elaborate when she recalls the occasion. 'Anyway, it's OK. I'll be OK. I'll tell you another day. You go and mingle.'

'No, no,' says Karen. 'I want to know.'

Typical Karen, thinks Lou, always more interested in others than herself. Having started, Lou will have to finish. 'It seems I have some sort of tumour in, er . . . ' – she checks no one else is listening – 'my uterus.'

Karen frowns. 'Nothing serious, I hope?'

'You told me the doctor said it was probably . . . what is the name . . . ? A fibroid,' Sofia offers.

'Or cyst,' adds Lou. 'But we don't know yet.'

Karen continues to look perturbed.

Lou is still afraid it's something worse but knows she mustn't bring her private gloom into such a difficult occasion. 'Don't worry. Whatever it is, he said it's most unlikely to be malignant.'

'Oh, that's a relief.'

'I've got to go for a scan on Monday.'

'Your poor thing,' says Karen. 'That's no fun.'

'I'll be all right.'

'I had scans when I was pregnant and they can be a bit daunting.'

'Really?' says Lou.

'Depends how you are with . . . um . . . hospitals.' Karen gulps. We really ought to change the subject, Lou thinks. 'I mean, usually doctors are fine, but sometimes, and I'm sure they don't mean to be, they can be a bit brusque. And, you know, it can be hard to take everything in.'

'I must come with you,' says Sofia.

'But you've got work,' says Lou.

'Take her,' urges Karen. 'She can listen too, in case you miss something.'

'If you insist.' Lou relents. She's used to counselling others, is not entirely comfortable with the notion of needing her own hand held, but it seems good advice. 'Enough of me. Did you hear Sofia got promoted last week?'

'No! Sofia, well done!' says Anna. 'So what does that make you now?'

'I'm a partner,' Sofia grins.

'Wow.' Anna stands back, impressed.

'I will be doing less of the web design work and more consultancy,' she says.

As Sofia continues talking about her job, Lou takes a look around her. Karen's place is such a contrast to their little attic and she wonders if she and Sofia will ever live in a proper house like this, filled with Christmas decorations and cards from other families. Nevertheless, there are similarities. The kitchen walls bear witness to years of fingerprints and spillages. They need painting as badly as hers and Sofia's do. Outside the window, the patio garden looks badly in need of some TLC. But it's just not possible to do it all with kids as young as Karen's; nor, in Lou's opinion, should it really matter. Pristine homes be damned. Karen has had a hideous year, it's incredible she's not sunk under the strain, yet she's still here, smiling and welcoming guests.

Even if it's a front – and Lou has seen Karen weeping often enough to know that in many ways it is – it's laudable. Fleetingly, she wonders what's kept Karen going. And then she remembers the way she was with Molly, the comfort she has gleaned from her daughter. Though Lou is not a mother, she does work with kids. It's another way her life echoes Karen's; the way children both drain and sustain them.

*   *   *

After a morning of fresh air, concentration and exercise, Cath is so hungry she devours her lunch in minutes. The menu is nothing to write home about – baguettes filled with rubbery cheese or ham, too-dry toasted sandwiches, slippery omelettes and chips: only the hot chocolate is exceptional. Doubtless the owners know they have a captive audience; the cafe is at the hub of the resort. Rich has had to dash off to his lesson for advanced skiers, but Cath is in no hurry to leave. The terrace is perfectly situated to take in the Alpine views and people-watch.

Climbing up the mountain to the left of her is a red run, 'a cinch' according to Rich; Cath finds it intimidating merely to look at. She watches a group of young snowboarders with a mixture of envy and awe. Such agility and assurance, such recklessness – she can't imagine ever being that bold. They are laughing and joking, poking fun at each other and the world. With their array of headgear – a court jester, a black bowler with devil's horns, a Mad Hatter, a furry pig's head – they remind Cath of a band of travelling players.

To her right is the top of the lift that returns skiers from the blue run she conquered for the first time last week. Round and round it spews endless brightly coloured holi-daymakers back onto the snow, as if they were sweets on a factory line. Most head straight back down the slopes again, dogged and purposeful, but one couple fail to cope with the speed at which they are ejected, and tumble giggling and inept, skis zigzagging madly.

Sweeping close by her is the gentle gradient of the nursery slope. It's here that dozens of children follow in the wake of instructors, diminutive trains of helmeted focus. Some are so small Cath is amazed they can walk, let alone ski. Yet ski they do, limbs constrained by padding, with a fearless-ness and enthusiasm that exceeds that of their adult counterparts. Cath wishes she'd learnt when she was as young and open; the dread of falling seems to mean nothing to them. There's something about the way they form a succession of triangles, legs angled outwards one way, skis to slow their speed another, that she finds touching. She's just thinking of her nephews, eight-year-old twins Alfie and Dom, and how much they would love this – they are such physical boys, and they've not yet hit that age when cynicism sets in, when it's important to be cool, not to be caught trying – when, *WHOOPS!* a little girl, right at the back of one of the trains, loses her balance and falls over.

Ouch! Cath says to herself, then sees the child struggle to get back up whilst keeping her skis on her feet. But she slips and falls again.

It takes a moment for the instructor to notice what has happened. *'Ici, Angeline, lève-toi!'* he shouts up at her from the bottom of the slope.

Angeline tries again, to no avail. Cath feels her distress and fear; she's fallen herself many times. Oh, the confusion over what limbs to move, how to push up on the skis with gravity pulling you downhill.

'Comme ça!' The instructor tries to show Angeline how to raise herself to standing, but he is a long way from her, powerless to really help, and his encouragement only makes her more flustered. Cath can tell she feels the pressure of a dozen impatient classmates, waiting. She is much nearer to Angeline than he is. As hurriedly as she can, she clumps across the snow – darn her ski boots, they're so stiff and difficult to walk in, she's like a slow-motion storm trooper. Presently she is standing over the little girl.

'Here,' she says, and holds out a hand.

The child looks up, worried.

'It's OK,' says Cath, softly. She wishes she spoke better French.

Grateful, the little girl reaches out, and Cath braces her legs so that Angeline can yank herself up.

'*Merci.*'

Cath steps back and watches her shoot off down the hill, wobbly and precarious on her skis, but upright.

She returns to the cafe, sits down again.

Then, suddenly, like a gale-force wind whooshing over the mountains onto the terrace, it hits her, right in her lower abdomen.

A longing, primal and powerful, so overwhelming she nearly falls from her chair.

She's put her desires and hopes on hold for such a long while – she had no choice but to do so – but now it seems a familiar yearning is making itself felt once more.

※

She'd still been woozy from anaesthetic when the oncologist had finally come to her bedside. Rich had been sitting next to her, on one of the hospital plastic chairs, waiting in trepidation for the doctor to do his rounds.

'So how did it go?' Cath had asked. She'd tried to prop herself up on an elbow, but hadn't the strength; there were stitches across her abdomen. She was forced to lie back on her pillow.

'Good,' the oncologist had nodded. 'The chemotherapy

shrank the tumours enough so we could operate much more easily.'

'That's great,' Rich had said and smiled at her.

But Cath had remained uneasy. 'And my ovaries?'

'We wanted to be sure we'd removed all the cancer,' the doctor said.

'So . . . ?'

'The good news is it hasn't spread. We have caught it in time.'

'But my ovaries?' She *had* to know.

'We had to remove them.'

'Completely?'

'Completely.' The word stabbed more than any scalpel. Cath closed her eyes as if shutting out the world might obliterate her pain.

*

She buttons her jacket up fully, ready to leave. She should talk to her husband soon; this holiday is a good moment, surely. It's an uncomfortable conversation to have to have, but eighteen months have passed since the surgery, and there is no point in putting it off any longer. Time is ticking; they can't afford to.

4

'Louise Burgess?' calls a man in a pale-blue coat.

Lou rises from her chair. 'That's me.'

'This way, please.'

He leads Lou and Sofia from the hospital waiting room.

'I take it you're a friend?' he asks Sofia, over his shoulder.

'Partner.'

'Oh. Well, I'm the radiographer.' He addresses Lou. 'Please would you mind taking off your clothes and putting on this hospital gown?' He draws a curtain so she can do so in private.

Lou is desperate for a pee. She's been told to come with a full bladder, and wriggling out of her jeans and knickers makes it worse. She needs to go so badly she can't even worry about the scan – she can only focus on getting it over with. She flings her clothes on the floor and doesn't bother doing up the ties of the gown.

'Could you lie down here?' The radiographer pats the couch next to the ultrasound machine. 'Now I'm going to spread some of this gel onto your tummy.'

Lord, it's cold.

'What's that for?' Sofia steps closer to look.

'It helps transmission of sound waves to and from the microphone. They bounce off the organs inside your body. In this instance the womb. This computer' – he gesticulates – 'then turns the reflected waves into a picture.'

Sofia peers at the screen. 'Fascinating.'

Lou wishes they would shut up so he can get on with it. She's going to wee on him otherwise.

'Do you want to see?' he asks her.

'I guess,' says Lou, though the prospect fills her with dread.

He turns the monitor towards her and as he moves the microphone back and forth, Lou can make out fuzzy black-and-white shapes, like a TV with its aerial missing, picking up a ghostly channel. What they indicate she has no idea.

Sofia steps closer and takes hold of Lou's hand. 'Are you OK?'

Lou nods. 'Can you see what's wrong?' she asks the radiographer, and grips Sofia's palm.

*　*　*

In the evening, the sanctuary of the chalet is a well-earned antidote to the challenges of the slopes: if daytimes are marked by bright sunlight and views stretching for miles across mountaintops, nights are cosy and burrow-like. There is soft lighting, a log stove, and the warm hues of pine-clad walls offset by the deep reds of the local Savoie decor. A chicken casserole is stewing in the oven and Rich is flopped on the sofa in his favourite tracksuit, his face pink and shiny from hours in the fresh air followed by a bath. He looks so healthy and happy, Cath feels a surge of love for him. She's proud of him, his physical ability, his sportsmanship.

'Can I get you a beer?' she offers.

'I think I'd prefer wine.'

She'll have a glass too; it might help lubricate their conversation. She fetches two glasses and the bottle from the kitchen. 'There's something I want to talk to you about,' she says.

'Oh?' It's a lousy corkscrew. He sees her struggling. 'Here, let me.'

She passes over the bottle. 'It's just I was thinking today, about . . . Um . . . ' Lord, how should she tackle this? She should have planned it. He looks up, concerned. She adds, 'It's nothing bad, though.'

'Thank goodness.' A defiant pop and the wine is open.

'Obviously the treatment finishing and being told I don't need to go back to the hospital for another six months is great news. I'm still so relieved I can hardly believe it.'

Rich nods. He fills their glasses and raises one to toast her. 'Fantastic.' He moves his legs to make room for her. 'It's a real milestone.'

Cath sits down. 'But I know, well, you know, the cancer could come back, at some point. Maybe not now, maybe not for years. We don't know. Being free of it only means I'm clear at the moment, not forever.'

'Yes, I suppose, but I don't think we should think like that.'

Cath flinches. This is as hard for her to say as for him to hear. 'But we *do* have to think like that, honey, really. In terms of the big decisions we make, we do.'

Rich frowns; she is aware he doesn't like her talking like this. He's said he finds it hard because he loves her; nonetheless they can't deceive themselves.

She hesitates, then, out of nowhere, she starts to cry. Giant tears plop forth, unstoppable. It takes her aback as much as it does Rich; she puts down her glass so she can gather herself.

Rich moves closer to her. 'Oh love, don't. You've been so happy this week, it's been such a wonderful end to such a rotten year, don't bring yourself down. It's OK, you're OK . . . You've made it. You're out the other side, you did it.'

'Sorry.' Cath sniffs loudly. 'I don't know where that came from.' She wipes her eyes on her sleeve.

Rich smiles at her. 'Well, you've not cried all week, so the tears were probably bursting to get out, wondering why they'd not been given an airing.'

It's true; ever since her original diagnosis, Cath has cried an awful lot. But they're still not talking about what she's been trying to say. 'It's not the cancer that's getting to me, it's something different.' She stretches her legs out on top of his and gently nudges him, a signal to stroke her feet. Rich obliges. Perhaps she'll start at the end, not the beginning. 'After you'd gone to your lesson yesterday, I was watching the children on the nursery slopes . . . Anyway, since then I've been thinking . . . ' She checks her husband's reaction. He has stopped smiling, appears curious, uncertain. 'Ever since I was ill, it changed my perspective. My priorities shifted, I re-evaluated what matters.'

'Me too,' he says. They've spoken of this before.

'It made me see how important my friends and family –

and you, especially – are to me. I want to make a fresh start next year, and you know I don't find my job at the gallery that challenging . . . ' Another deep breath, then she bursts out, 'I want to have a baby.'

He looks perplexed. 'But I thought . . . We were told, after the treatment, that, um . . . it wouldn't be possible.'

'I *know!*' Now she is sobbing so loud, she can hear she sounds ridiculous. She hopes Rich doesn't see her tears as blackmail, yet is powerless to stop. 'You don't have to remind me they've removed my stupid ovaries.'

Rich winces. 'I know it's rough, I can only begin to imagine how rough – you've been so strong; you've been brilliant; I'm so proud of you. I thought over time that we'd both come to terms with the situation. We've talked about it before, and I'm OK with it, love.'

'I know that too.' Cath reaches for her wine again, takes a big gulp, trying to stave off her weeping. 'Or that's what you say, anyway. But either way, it's not OK with me.'

Rich stops stroking her leg. She knows him so well, the way his face falls; she can see him assimilating. 'What are you saying . . . ?'

'I don't know.' She thinks of the train of toddler snow-ploughs, the little girl who fell over, of Alfie and Dom, and again feels an enormous tug of yearning. 'I've changed my mind. Last time we talked about it I was in the middle of my treatment – I had to block it out. But I'm in a different place now. We were trying for a baby before I got ill, remember.'

'Of course I remember.' It was because she was finding it hard to conceive they discovered the cancer in the first place. Eventually he says, 'Do you think we should consider adopting?'

She's thought of that. 'I'm not sure we can. We're pretty old, aren't we? Or I am . . . I think you have to be under forty . . .' The tears continue falling, though not as heavily.

Rich gets to his feet, fetches some tissue from the bathroom. 'We could find out,' he says, handing it to her.

'I guess.' She blows her nose, wipes her eyes. The tissue is covered in black smears from her mascara. She must look a right mess. The wood crackles in the stove; a log tumbles into a new position. 'Are you sure?' she says, presently. 'I don't want to pressurize you or anything.'

'You're not pressurizing me.' But Rich is still frowning. 'I do think you might be right though, that we wouldn't be eligible.' He resumes stroking her leg.

'Maybe there are alternatives to adoption.'

'Oh?'

'Where we use, you know, your sperm . . .'

'Mm?'

'With someone else's eggs.'

'Right.' He sits back, lets out a slow breath, runs a hand through his hair. 'Oh love, I don't know about that.'

'It's just a thought.'

'A surrogate, you mean?'

'Um, yes, perhaps—'

'Blimey.' He raises his eyebrows. 'Hmm . . . I'm not sure . . .'

Her shoulders slump. 'Why not?'

'I dunno . . . I'm not saying no, definitely. I'd need to think about it. It's just the whole idea of it. Paying someone to have our baby . . . putting them through the whole stress of pregnancy . . . ' He shakes his head.

Cath feels a mixture of exasperation and appreciation. If Rich weren't so kind and principled, he might not baulk at it; yet she loves him for precisely these qualities. She says, 'But wouldn't it be better if at least the child was yours?'

'I guess . . . I'm sorry, love, you're a bit ahead of me. You need to give me a while to catch up. You know, I'd kind of put all this on the back burner and now—'

She jumps at his words. 'The "back burner" – there you are, see? You hadn't given up on the idea.'

'Sorry?'

'It's still there, simmering away.'

He seems spooked by the speed of her interpretation. 'Maybe . . . '

'I know you need to think about this further, and so do I. I only wanted to open up the conversation.'

'I'm just not that sure about fathering a baby with someone else. You're my wife. I mean, how would you feel about that?'

'I don't know . . . A bit odd, I guess.'

'Exactly.' His face clears: he's come to his conclusion. 'It's not a matter of whether we could afford it or not – though I'm not sure we could – I reckon using a surrogate could cost tens of thousands of pounds. I'm not sure it's legal here to pay someone, I think you have to go to America. But, anyway, it just doesn't feel right, using another woman's body like some sort of incubation chamber.'

Cath is disappointed, but she understands. She's not happy with that idea herself.

He pulls her towards him on the sofa to give her a hug. 'I'm sorry.'

She snuggles into his chest for solace, inhales the scent of his sweatshirt: it smells of Rich himself. She strokes the velvety fabric; she likes this top, it makes him especially cuddly. Before them the fire is burning low; it could do with another log. The casserole should come out of the oven, too. 'It's just I love you . . . ' she says, lifting her head. Next is the hardest bit to say. But she's brought the discussion this far; she has to. 'And I don't want to deny you the chance of becoming a father—'

'But you're not—'

' – just because I can't have children,' she finishes.

'I've had time to come to terms with it – all the time you've been ill, you know.'

'But still, you're younger than me, you're healthy.' Does she really need to point this out? 'I just don't think it's fair . . . '

He pulls away from her. 'What are you saying now? That I should leave you and go off with someone else? Hell, Cath, you're my wife and that's it. Or perhaps you'd like me to?' His lips form an angry line.

'That wasn't what I meant.' She is floundering, still trying to get a handle on the issues herself. Still, at least he's made her stop crying. 'No, I was talking about *us* having a child, silly.'

'Oh.' A tad sheepish. 'But how?'

'I don't know.' She throws up her hands. 'I just wanted to bring it up, because I haven't. Not since I was ill. It's not been something I've been able to really think about again

38

till now. I thought I might die, for Christ's sake, so I was kind of focused on that. But I didn't. I'm still here. And I know my insides have been blasted by effing chemo, but you never know, with modern medicine . . . Perhaps when we get home we could explore some of the options, rather than write it off completely?'

Rich sighs, and reaches to pull her close again. 'It's only I don't want you to get your hopes up.'

'I know, I know.'

He strokes her hair. 'You've been through such a lot already.'

Cath knows he's right, and that he's trying to protect her. But she feels tears prick behind her eyes again; in her heart, she knows those are not good enough reasons not to try.

'It's just I want to be a mum,' she says.

*   *   *

Rich's mind is buzzing. Cath went off to sleep almost the moment her head hit the pillow, and she's curled up beside him, like a child exhausted by emotion. Meanwhile he is still trying to get his head round their conversation that evening.

Everyone says how brilliant he's been about his wife's illness: what a rock, a treasure. Only last week her mother, Judy, said, 'Cath couldn't have got through it without you,' which was over the top, Rich reckons. He might have helped make the experience a little less awful, but her getting through it was down to the doctors and Cath herself. He was simply there. As for being rock-like, he often felt more like a piece of jelly, though he never said so. With Cath all over the place

39

– despairing one moment, defiant the next – the last thing she needed was to see how distraught he was too.

In truth, beneath his calm exterior, he has spent much of the last two years terrified. Terrified of losing her, terrified of hearing the words 'there's nothing more we can do', terrified of mishandling the situation or asking the wrong questions, terrified of saying inappropriate things to her family, terrified of letting Cath down. Moreover, he's had to adjust his vision of the future completely. Before her illness, he thought he knew where his life was going. He didn't have a very precise map, but the route forward was there, in pencil to allow for the odd bit of rubbing out and redrawing, in his mind's eye. Maybe they'd move further from the city centre of Leeds, to Ilkley or Guiseley – somewhere closer to the Dales. He'd like more time for exercise, and a new car. Ideally his job in the music industry would evolve: he'd prefer more security, money and responsibility, though compared to some of his friends, he wasn't doing badly. But one thing he was clear about, because Cath was already 'getting on a bit', as she put it, when they met: children were in the picture. Soon.

Then came the cancer.

Initially they'd been existing day to day, getting over each hurdle as it arose: the operation, the chemotherapy, the susceptibility to infection, the hair loss. Then, post-treatment, they faced the new reality; he's permitted himself to look further ahead, but the vista has changed. No longer does he assume with naive certainty he'll grow old with Cath, nor does he think – as he did when they first discovered she was ill – that she might die at any minute: he simply does not know. His job has got more precarious; he's seen colleagues laid off, he's had to travel more, work longer hours. So he's reined in his expectations; the view is not as panoramic as it once was. It's mistier, more lightly pencilled. And children, if he is to stay with Cath (and there have been moments, fleetingly, when he has wondered if he's got it in him to do so), are no longer a part of it. Are they?

Rich isn't as fast at processing information as his wife. He might be a swifter skier, but mentally, she's a hare to his tortoise and lately he's been so focused on putting her needs first, it's underlined this difference between them. Occasionally he gets frustrated with himself, but she says it's what balances them out: she needs him to ground her, and he believes her – if they were both as stubborn and impulsive as Cath, their relationship would probably explode. Nonetheless, sometimes he needs to take time out, to work out where he stands.

Lying awake isn't helping, and he wants to be alert tomorrow; he has been relishing discovering his skills on the snow again. Maybe getting up will stop his mind churning. Carefully, he eases himself out of bed, pads to the bathroom, closes the door, pulls the string of the light.

It takes a few seconds for his pupils to adjust. He scrunches his eyelids together, slowly opens them, looks at himself in the mirror.

His hair is standing up in crazy tufts. He is bleary, needs a shave. Otherwise, he appears just the same as always.

5

'I feel like a freak,' says Lou.

'Why?' asks Anna.

Lou drops her voice; there's a man sitting across the aisle. 'This horrible lump: I went and had my scan yesterday, and apparently it's a cyst.'

'What sort of cyst?'

'A tumour – a fibroid. I'd never even heard of them before.'

'I have,' says Anna. 'They're quite common when you get into your forties. I've got a couple myself.'

'Really?'

'Mm. They're tiny, so the doctor said it's best to leave them alone, unless they're causing me a problem. And they're not. They're harmless.'

'Oh.' That makes Lou feel slightly better. 'But mine's enormous.'

Just then Sofia arrives with coffees wedged into a cardboard tray.

'Hello, Anna,' she says, sliding into the seat they've been saving opposite.

They're on the 07:44 to London, heading to work. This is their morning ritual. Anna is the best timekeeper and lives nearest the station, so she boards first and reserves a table, third carriage from the front. Lou and Sofia cycle from Kemptown: they lock up their bikes, Lou hurries to join Anna so other commuters don't get miffed by her hogging seats, and Sofia buys coffees from the man-with-a-van on the forecourt.

'I was just telling Anna about yesterday,' says Lou, her voice still hushed.

'The hospital?'

Lou nods.

'It is good news, do you agree?' Sofia says to Anna.

'I suppose it is.'

'At least it is not malignant.'

Lou flushes, irritated: Sofia sounds blasé. Doesn't she appreciate how upset I am? Lou thinks. Maybe she's avoiding making too much fuss lest it alarm me further. 'Still, I feel like a freak.'

'How big is it, then?' asks Anna.

'About the size of a grapefruit.'

'Blimey.'

'Exactly. I'm a freak.'

'You are not a freak,' says Sofia.

'If you're a freak, I'm a freak,' says Anna.

Lou laughs. 'I guess.'

The train is filling up; a woman asks to sit beside Sofia. The three of them huddle across the table.

'Anyway, they say I ought to consider having it removed.' She lowers her tone still further.

'Why?'

'Because it's so big, and it may well get even bigger. Who knows, if it's grown to the size of a grapefruit already, it'll be a blooming watermelon next . . . ' Lou shivers. 'Then it'll be trickier to operate on – and I'm told it's not that easy as it is – but also if I want to have children, it could make it difficult to get pregnant.' The man across the aisle straightens out his broadsheet with a flick of his wrists. Lou could swear he is eavesdropping. She whispers, 'It's right in the middle of my womb.'

'I see,' says Anna. 'So, you want children then?'

Lou glances up at Sofia. The subject is not one they've ever discussed in detail. She thought they had plenty of time to think about babies. They've been together less than a year, are in the first flush of love.

'I think so. And if I want to have them, I should have surgery, and then, apparently . . . ' She pauses, aware this will be news to Sofia. 'I read online last night that I – um, well, we – shouldn't hang about.'

'And how about you, Sofia?' asks Anna. Once more, that disarming frankness.

Sofia hesitates, and Lou holds her breath while she waits for her answer.

Finally she says, 'To be honest, I don't think I do.'

* * *

It must be coincidence, but when Sofia gets off the train at East Croydon, everywhere she looks there are mothers and babies. At the newsagent where she picks up *Design Week,* there's a woman with a pushchair at the counter. In the queue at M&S, as she waits to buy a sandwich for her lunch, there's a customer with a tiny newborn in a papoose strapped to her chest. There are even two women taking up the entire breadth of the pavement with their brood of thigh-high offspring, chatting in the street she cuts through to the office.

It's as if they have been put here to make me feel bad, she thinks.

Sofia is doing her best to support Lou, but it's so hard. She knows how tense Lou is about cancer; losing her father was devastating. Nevertheless, the conversation on the train alarmed her. Becoming a parent is not something she's had to focus on before, and it all seems very strange and very sudden.

Before this, Sofia thinks, if Lou had asked how I felt about having a baby, I would have said it was not something I was going to do: not now, certainly; probably not ever. I don't see it as likely to happen – and lots of my gay friends feel the same, the men especially. It is not how we imagine ourselves. Perhaps if I was straight and had stayed in Spain, I could have fallen into having children . . .

But it was largely to escape from those pressures that brought Sofia to England in the first place. Finding a sperm donor, arranging insemination, answering everyone's questions . . . The childcare issues, the bullying a kid might experience at school, the financial burden . . . She shudders.

It is a massive commitment.

It's not as if I don't see myself with Lou long term though, she reasons to herself. I love her – I wouldn't be looking at buying a flat with her if I didn't. But I want to go to parties,

45

travel, play – yes, with Lou. And until all this, I'd assumed she felt the same . . .

Given we tend to discuss so much, I suppose it's surprising the subject hasn't come up; we've moved fast in other respects. But cohabiting can be undone, having a child can't. Maybe deep down I've been wary of uncovering such a difference between us. And now it seems there's no room for being blurry; apparently we have to decide one way or the other, soon.

Maybe *I* could have a baby? she wonders, as she waits at a pedestrian crossing. But at once she rejects the idea. She can't countenance taking months out of her job when she's just been promoted, and she can hardly promise Lou that she will do so for sure in the future.

What a mess: rarely has Sofia felt so guilty and inadequate. When she pushes open the door to the office there's a blast of warm air, the sound of phones and chatting, the smell of toast. Work beckons. For the time being, at least, she can lose herself in that.

*　*　*

'You OK?' asks Anna. 'You've gone very pensive.'

Lou is leaning against the train window, watching the gardens of south London whoosh by. 'Mm. I was thinking.'

'You'll be all right.'

Lou wonders if she should admit what's upsetting her. It's just the two of them and Anna has confided in her often enough.

'Is it what Sofia said about children?'

Lou nods.

'She might come round.'

'I thought we'd have quite a while before we had to think about it seriously.'

'Finding that you don't must be quite a shock.'

'It is.'

'For both of you. She's probably still coming to terms with it.'

'Though she sounded pretty adamant, didn't she?'

'It's not surprising. She's young. What is she – twenty-eight? Twenty-nine?'

'Twenty-eight,' says Lou.

'I certainly didn't think about having children at her age.'

'So . . . Can I ask?' Lou turns to face her friend. 'What about you?'

'Sorry?'

'Did you ever want kids?'

Anna shrugs. 'It just didn't happen for me. That's it, really.'

'Do you mind?'

Anna fidgets with her empty coffee cup. 'Um . . . A *bit*, I suppose. But I was never the kind of person who was so eager to have children I'd have gone and done it on my own – like those single women who just feel a burning desire to be a mother no matter what. And somehow, none of the men I've been involved with seemed appropriate father material.'

'I can see Steve wasn't.'

'No,' she laughs ruefully. 'He was rather a child himself – imagine trying to get him to change nappies and things, drinking like he did. But as it is, I was forty by the time I

47

met Steve. The guy I was with before that wanted children, but I could never imagine us as a family, which is why we split up. I guess if I'd *really* wanted them, I would have picked a man I could see myself being a parent with.'

'But you're so good with kids.'

'Thank you. Though not as good as you.'

'I'm not so sure.'

'No, I'm only good with kids I like. I'm good with Molly and Luke because they're Karen's children and I love Karen and I've known them since they were born and they're adorable. But you – you're good with kids who frankly, I couldn't bear to be around. You work with the kind of kids who listen to music on their mobiles at full pelt on the top deck of the bus just to annoy other people. I brush against them for ten minutes a day and that's too much. You counsel them. I want to kill them.'

Lou laughs. 'I suppose.'

'You definitely *definitely* want them?'

The train is coming into Victoria – all around them people are shuffling papers into briefcases, putting away books and magazines, shutting down their laptops. The man across the aisle gets to his feet, the woman opposite pulls on her coat. There's no time to contemplate.

'Yes.' Lou goes with her gut. 'I do.'

6

Lou is curled up on the sofa under a blanket when her mobile bleeps. A text:

Sorry. I forgot to tell you that I've a leaving drink tonight so I'm going out to Soho with colleagues. Please eat without me. Sx

Sofia could have told me before, she thinks.

Lou has been alone all day so was looking forward to some company, and she's made a special effort with dinner: green curry with wild rice. Getting the ingredients wasn't easy: she's still recuperating from her operation. She's not supposed to drive or lift anything heavy, and she had to edge her way round the local shops like an old lady, wary she might get knocked or jolted any moment. Now, without someone to share the experience, it's hardly worth bothering to cook.

Damn Sofia! Lou throws her mobile to the far end of the sofa.

A few seconds later it is still blinking up at her. Perhaps I'm being oversensitive, she tells herself.

Maybe it's hormones, and she has had major surgery; that

she's so physically and mentally vulnerable is probably inevitable. Certainly, her tummy is still sore and if she does anything other than lie around watching telly or reading she gets exhausted. She also appears to cry very readily, neither of which she is used to. Lou usually expels emotions through exercise – she'll bash a tennis ball or pound the streets if she's feeling angry or upset – so being forced to take it easy is doubly hard.

Sod sitting around waiting, she decides eventually. What I need is a blast of fresh air.

The flat is only yards from the seafront, but before she's even reached the bottom of the stairs, she starts to feel the strain of getting there. A few paces later, she is obliged to stop and rest against the wrought-iron railings of a B. & B., and at the end of her street she has to pause again before crossing the dual carriageway of Marine Parade.

It's not fair, she thinks. It's the weekend – I bet everyone's having more fun than I am. Then she chides herself for being self-pitying and scans the prom to see who else is out.

On the corner, lit by the orange glow of streetlights, is a group of young women in short skirts, high heels and T-shirts replete with fairy wings. In their midst is a white-tulle-clad bride-to-be. It's so cold and blustery, they should be freezing, but their whoops and guffaws suggest they are too tipsy to feel chilly. Two sprucely dressed men are waiting at the roadside with a Jack Russell; the dog is straining at the leash, scenting the salty air of his beach playground. And half sitting on the balustrade opposite, a young man is hunched over and blowing on his hands to keep warm. He looks up and down the seafront and gets to his feet as he sees someone headed towards him. The two come together, there is a quick glance to ensure no one is watching, a shuffling of hands and pockets, then they part and go their separate ways. Lou can read the signs; a drug deal.

She waits until they've gone, then cautiously heads down the steps and onto the beach. With a crunch of trainers on stones she makes her way towards the sea, sits on the shingle, as close to the water as she dares. The waves are up, crashing in giant furls of white spray, rolling back pebbles with a clatter. It's dark; the lights of the pier barely illuminate the slate-coloured water, and purple clouds form strange and sinister shapes at the horizon like vast uncharted mountain ranges. The air is damp and soon so is Lou's hair; she can feel salt on her fingers, sticky. Even in her parka she is cold, but she doesn't care.

How different this feels from the beach of summer days, when the seafront is full to the brim with excitable children and put-upon parents, youths full of derring-do and pink-skinned pensioners; where the sounds and smells of beatboxes, different languages, barbecues and picnics assault her senses. Down here she feels a thousand miles from the seaside resort of dirty postcards and Day-Glo rock, drag queens and dubious assignations. And yet she loves this Brighton as much as, if not more than, its alter ego. The elements are what give the place its *gravitas*; they remind the inhabitants they mustn't go too wild, get too big for their boots, for they are, after all, only humans perched on the edge of the ocean, and the sea is bigger and more powerful than any of them.

She digs her hands deep into the pebbles, feels the cool round hardness against her fingers; recalls the earth, soft and malleable by contrast, of her father's grave. And she thinks yet again of Anna's question: does she want children, *really*? She can't stop mulling it over. If her father's death, then witnessing that of Karen's husband Simon, has made Lou understand something of the fragility of life, this recent operation has forced her to confront her own mortality, and alongside it the nature of her being, her womanhood. Sitting here on the beach brings home to her why she wants to be a mother; she wants to be part of the earth, the cycle of things, to help give meaning to her place on the planet.

* * *

Rich opens the door of the hotel suite. Cath steps inside, he follows.

'Bit posher than home,' he says.

'That's an understatement.' She paces the carpet, a lioness exploring new territory. She runs her fingertips over the cool glass of the coffee table, strokes the velvet of the sofa and the heavy silk brocade of the curtains.

'My colleague George puts so many clients up here, he got us a special deal, just for tonight.'

She circles the suite again – it must be twice the size of their bedroom in Leeds – then returns to the window, slides open the double doors and steps out onto the balcony. The night is notably warmer than it has been in Yorkshire; the tightly packed buildings trap the heat, and the air-con units on neighbouring rooftops doubtless contribute, too. It's a strange vista: a mixture of chimney pots and TV aerials, fire escapes and the backs of theatres; not exactly Covent Garden at its most beautiful. It reminds Cath of an article she saw in a magazine, where two photographs were placed side by side. One showed the front of a model: tall, slim, elegant, hair immaculately styled, clothes fitting like a dream. Alongside was the same model in the same outfit, but this time from the rear, revealing the back of the dress pinned by a dozen bulldog clips to make it fit her, hair a ghastly tangle, shoes too big and clearly uncomfortable. Here she can see the machinery behind the myth-making, what it takes for the capital to put on its show for the people at street level.

Rich interrupts her thoughts. 'Have you seen this?'

She steps back inside but she can't see her husband anywhere. Maybe he's hiding behind the drapes of the four-poster.

'I'm in here.'

She follows his voice to the bathroom.

'Wow.' The walls are floor-to-ceiling caramel marble; there's more beneath her feet. The lights, the mirrors, the taps, the toothbrush holder – every fixture oozes luxury. The shower-head is the size of a dinner plate.

'Quite something, eh?'

'You're telling me.'

'George did say he sends all his prima donna stars here.'

'The size of that tub!'

'I know.'

'And don't you just love the way hotels do this with towels?' She fingers the soft downy row. 'Why can't we ever get ours lined up like that?'

'Love, if you ever did anything so pathological, I'd have to leave you.'

'Says the man who never picks his up off the floor.'

'Anyway. Fancy a bath, madam?' He bows with a manservant flourish.

'Madam might be persuaded.' She lifts her nose, mock prim.

'Together?' He raises an eyebrow, teasing.

'Be rude not to.'

While Rich sets the water running and gauges the temperature, Cath locates a bottle of bath oil and adds a far bigger gloop than she would at home.

Minutes later she and her husband are toe to toe. She lies back, eyes level with his chest. The hairs are greying but she rather likes that. He's still very attractive, and his stomach is so pleasingly taut . . . More than can be said for me, she thinks ruefully, all too aware of the rolls of fat on her midriff.

Compared to when they first met, it's rare for Cath to feel sexy; lately she's been inclined to recall the days she felt hungry to make love with sadness and more than a touch of guilt. When she was very ill, she didn't feel remotely attractive – having her ovaries removed was hardly conducive to swinging from the proverbial chandeliers – and she still gets more tired than she used to. Rich has been supremely patient; nonetheless, his healthy libido is one of the reasons Cath fell for him initially, so she can hardly expect him to change on that score. He travels a lot for work; she fears he must be tempted occasionally – she'd hate to lose him because he isn't sexually satisfied at home. So whilst she's never faked an orgasm or gone along with lovemaking when she *really* couldn't bear to, she has found herself yearning for the self-confidence and sheer animal lust she once had.

Yet here, in the warmth of the water, in such sumptuous surroundings, Cath feels so relaxed and sensual that her consciousness of her imperfections – the rolls on her scarred tummy, her cellulite-ridden thighs, her wispy hair – ebbs away. So what if she's no supermodel? Instead, it's as if she sees herself through Rich's loving gaze: her breasts, still pert and full; the curve of her hips, feminine and inviting; the arch of her throat, smooth and seductive. She reaches under the water and finds to her delight that Rich is full of desire too. Slowly, with practised strokes, she massages him. The water makes soft splashy noises in rhythm with her movements.

Lucky the taps are in the middle, she thinks, as he stretches back, rests his head against the end of the bath, closes his eyes and gives in to the pleasure.

*   *   *

It's nearly midnight. Unless she leaves any minute, Sofia will miss the last train.

'Fancy another?' Malene jerks her head towards her vodka shot. The bar is heaving, music blasts from speakers beside them; Sofia can barely hear her. What the hell. It's been ages since she's done this. And Malene is hot – blonde and slim and pretty: exactly the kind of woman Sofia likes. Swedish or something. Strobe lights flash, dry ice pours from the stage, an other-worldly mist of fluorescent pink and electric blue.

Dada, dom, dom, dom – the beat segues into a different intro; it's a track she loves.

'No. Come on, let's dance.'

She steers Malene through the crowd and they find a tiny spot on the floor. Sofia sashays her hips, Malene gyrates against her – whether deliberately or because there's no room to move otherwise, Sofia doesn't care. She's been madly busy at work; these days she has to act like the boss, restrain herself from confiding in colleagues she used to be intimate with. Plus Lou's been in hospital; she's been so fragile and needy, Sofia could hardly offload onto her. But now her girl-friend is sixty miles away, her workmates have gone.

The rhythm shifts up a gear, lights whirl. A sci-fi rainbow colours a hundred faces, bodies, the ceiling, the walls. The track reaches its crescendo: a chorus that begs to be chanted en masse. The floor beneath Sofia's feet judders. All around people are sweating, writhing, cheering, so tightly packed they're keeping one another upright. It's impossible not to be caught up in the sheer hedonism.

Sofia raises her arms in celebration.

Aah, Soho . . .

This is where she belongs.

7

'Anna?'

'Speaking.'

'I'm sorry to bother you so early.'

'Mm . . . ?' She is croaky; Lou has woken her. 'What time is it?'

'Seven thirty. I can phone back—'

'No, it's fine. Is everything all right?'

Lou badly needs to talk to someone. She's had a dreadful night, jerking awake at intervals, expecting to hear Sofia stumbling round the room: drunk, but home. Yet there's still no sign of her.

'It's Sofia.'

A rustling of sheets as Anna sits up. 'Has something happened?'

'I don't know. She didn't come back last night.'

'Oh Lord. Do you know where she went?'

Lou has imagined all sorts, but she decides to stick with the facts. 'She texted to say she was going into London with her colleagues. It was someone's leaving do.'

'I see . . . And she didn't come home?'

'No.'

A pause, then, 'I wouldn't worry too much, not yet. She probably got drunk or something, crashed at a friend's. Was it a good mate who was leaving?'

'Not as far as I know.'

'I presume you tried calling her?'

'It goes straight to answerphone.'

'Maybe it's run out of juice.'

'I guess, but she could have borrowed someone else's to let me know she was staying in town, don't you think? I've been worried sick.'

'Mm, she must have known you'd be anxious, and she isn't normally that thoughtless. What are her colleagues like?'

'I don't really know them, though they seem a nice enough bunch. They're fairly tame, most of them, from what I gather. They all live in London though, other than Sofia.' Lou endeavours to control her panic. 'I'm sure something has happened.'

'It does sound a bit strange for her not to have got herself home. Maybe she just lost track of time. Has she ever done this before?'

'Stayed out all night, you mean? No. Although . . . ' Should Lou confess this? It seems unfair to interrupt her friend's Saturday lie-in and not tell her the truth. 'She has been a bit distant lately.'

'Really? Why's that?'

'I guess . . . Oh, I don't know. This operation . . . Though maybe I'm being unreasonable.'

'Tell me.'

'It seemed to freak her out rather – so she's not been quite as supportive as I thought she would be.'

'Oh dear, Lou, I'm sorry. I had no idea.'

'It's not your responsibility.'

'No, but, well, I'd have been more hands-on myself, if I'd known. You've always been there for me.'

'I didn't want to make a fuss.'

'So in what way wasn't she supportive?'

'It's hard to describe . . . ' Lou is torn between wanting to share her fears and loyalty to her girlfriend. 'I hoped she'd take more time off work to be with me, perhaps.'

Anna harrumphs.

'Well, no, she did . . . She collected me from the hospital.'

'So I should hope!'

'And she took the rest of that day off.'

'Big deal! It's a major operation you've just had.'

'She is pretty busy at the office.'

'I think that's pathetic, if you want my opinion. God knows, you're hardly demanding. If I was in your position, well, she'd never have heard the end of it. But you're so good at caring for yourself – you never ask for people to look after you.'

Though she knows Anna means well, this isn't entirely helping. 'I'd feel so much better if I only knew where she *is*,' says Lou. She pictures where Sofia might have stayed, and with whom, and shudders. 'I think you're probably right; she's got drunk.' She hesitates, then admits, 'I guess she might be having some sort of wobble about us.'

'She doesn't know how lucky she is!'

Lou laughs.

'Look, I don't think you should just sit there, waiting for her to come home. Unless you really believe she might be in some kind of trouble?'

'No.' Given Sofia's recent behaviour, the evidence suggests she is not in actual danger.

'Why don't you come round here for coffee?'

'Erm, that would be nice, but—'

'Oh no, of course, you're recuperating – how thoughtless of me. Do you want me to come to you?'

'Don't worry, I'm not that bad.'

'Still, I thought you were supposed to take it easy?'

'It's been over a fortnight . . .' There is another issue, and if Anna is going to help Lou see everything more clearly, she'd best explain. 'The thing is, Sofia and I were supposed to be going to this show in London today.'

'Oh?'

'Now we're talking this through, I think that might be why she's not come home.'

'Really? What sort of show could possibly make her do that?'

'Well, it's the Alternative Parenting Show, you see.'

Silence. Eventually, 'I'm sorry, but you've lost me.'

'It's an exhibition, with stands and stuff, for people who are considering having children.'

'Ri-i-ight . . .'

'You know, lesbians and single women and gay men – people who want to adopt or foster – alternative parents, if you will. And I wanted to go with Sofia so, well, we could find out about the options.'

'Ah. So you think Sofia's running away from that.'

'Possibly, yes. Probably, in fact.' Lou has a flush of anger. How dare Sofia jeopardize this day of all days? This show is important to her. Sofia knew that.

'Are you really recovered enough to go?'

'I'm fine. Honestly.'

'It sounds a lot to take on.'

'Sofia was going to drive us so I didn't have to walk much.' As fast as it hit her, fury dissipates, gives way to disappointment.

'Can't you go another time?'

'It only happens once a year, and there are all sorts of exhibitors there: fertility clinics, fostering agencies . . . '

'Where is it exactly?'

'Covent Garden.'

Another pause. 'What time?'

'It starts at 10.30. But it's on for the whole day.'

'Fuck it.'

'Sorry?'

'Can you get yourself dressed OK?'

'Yes. It takes me a while, but—'

'Right. I'll take you. Give me forty-five minutes and I'll be round.'

'Are you sure?'

'Of course I'm sure. We'll go in my car. Be ready at quarter past, I'll toot outside, save me parking – your road is a nightmare. But don't rush. I don't want you doing yourself an injury coming down the stairs.'

'Thank you.' Lou feels like crying.

* * *

'So where is it, did you say?'

Cath swivels her smartphone so the map tallies with the direction they are walking. 'This should be Drury Lane . . . Then it must be first left.' She looks up. 'Yes. Now, the Assembly Rooms are number 61–65.'

'Over there.' Rich points. 'I can see the sign.'

'Great. We're on time.'

'Clever old us,' says Rich.

'Where's our programme?' Cath rummages in her hand-bag. 'So, the talk I want to go to is at eleven . . . We've got a few minutes for a coffee. Let's see if we can find one inside, shall we?'

Rich nods, but in the lobby they are brought to a halt by a woman with a clipboard.

'Homes Show or Alternative Parenting?' she asks. There are two queues, one short, heading off to the left; another snaking all the way up the stairs and onto the next landing.

'Alternative Parenting,' says Cath.

'That's this one.' The woman waves her arm at the snake.

'But we've got tickets.'

'Still got to queue, I'm afraid.'

'Bollocks,' murmurs Rich, joining the back of it.

'Tell you what, you wait here, and I'll see if I can get us a coffee. I think we passed a place on our way.' And before Rich can ask what he should do if he gets to the front of the queue before she returns, Cath has gone.

While he waits in line, Rich assesses the people around him. There are a lot of women, he notices. In fact, there are hardly any men. He sees that one guy waving to catch the attention of another is wearing a *Stonewall: Working for Equality* T-shirt and puts two and two together.

He glances behind him; there's a woman with sleek hair in a bob. She is wearing crimson lipstick and her eye make-up is quite pronounced. She is with another woman dressed in jeans and a parka. They are chatting intimately, so must be a couple.

He feels a touch uncomfortable: he and Cath seem to be the only straight people here.

* * *

'I'm the only straight woman here,' Anna is muttering.

'Hold on . . . ' Lou is sending another text to Sofia. *Where are you? I'm worried. Please call me. I'm at the show.* Then she looks up, scans the queue. 'Actually, I reckon you're right. Ha – now you know what it feels like.'

'Fair point. So, what's first?'

'There's this talk at eleven.' Lou pulls the programme from her pocket; she's folded it to the right page. 'I definitely want to go to that.'

Anna peers over her shoulder. 'Mm, sounds interesting . . . '

At that moment someone coughs behind them. Lou turns, sees a slightly plump woman with wispy brown hair and an anxious expression.

'Sorry,' says the woman and nods in explanation at the two coffees she is carrying. 'Can I squeeze through?'

'Oh, sure.' Lou and Anna part to make room. Lou is careful to protect her tummy, in case she gets jolted.

The woman hands the man in front of them one of the drinks and he smiles at her. 'Thanks, love.'

His hair is greying at the temples; he has the sort of face that Lou instinctively warms to. There is an intimacy to the way he looks at the woman.

She leans in close to Anna. 'Well, you were wrong,' she whispers and jerks her head towards the couple.

* * *

Sofia has been vaguely aware she is not in her usual bed all night. The mattress is lumpy and narrow and she has almost no room to move. When she wakes more fully, she realizes why: she's in a sleeping bag, on a sofa. But whose? There's a bamboo blind opposite, letting in far too much light – it makes her head hurt. The carpet is covered in ghastly orange and brown swirls – if she'd seen it before, she knows she'd have remembered. On the table next to her is an ashtray, overflowing with cigarette butts. Ugh. She heaves herself up onto her elbows to push it away. Her throat is parched; she badly needs some water.

Then she remembers.

Malene.

Oh no . . . They were dancing in the club when Malene asked her back to her flat, Sofia recalls that, though where they are in relation to Soho now she has no idea. It was late, and she was drunk; presumably they got here in a taxi.

The rest is blank. She fervently hopes she didn't sleep with her – that she's not in Malene's bed might be a good sign . . .

Gradually she pieces events together. She remembers kissing Malene, here on the sofa, the room spinning. Yes, she was so giddy, it was like being on the waltzer at the end of Brighton Pier. At one point she actually thought she might vomit. She remembers that in the brighter light of the living room, Malene had terrible skin, and looked about nineteen. Then there was the smoker's breath – what a contrast to Lou . . . Sofia had had a pang of conscience, and backed off.

Still, now she's stuck who knows where, and she has no clue what the time is.

Where's her mobile?

Ah, here: by some miracle, it's still in her breast pocket. She's amazed she didn't take off her denim jacket when she fell asleep. She must have been in a very bad way.

She tugs out the phone. It's completely out of battery, and Sofia never carries her charger around.

Then she sees a familiar thin white wire trailing from a socket to the table with the ashtray. What luck – Malene must have an iPhone too.

The mobile will take several minutes to acquire a basic charge. She'll get ready meanwhile. She feels bad enough about her behaviour already; the last thing she wants to do is hang about.

*　*　*

'Well I never,' says Anna, as they step inside the hall of the show. 'Marketing babies. What a weird world we live in.' Everywhere there are pictures of wondrous newborns, clear-skinned, bright-eyed and rosy-cheeked; there's not a runny nose or cradle-capped scalp in sight. 'All these billboards are a bit tactless, surely. I mean not everyone can have a baby, can they?'

'You'd be amazed what's on offer,' says Lou. 'Many people will do anything to have a child.'

They are surrounded by the evidence: there are stands promoting every imaginable aspect of becoming a gay or 'alternative' parent. There's the North London Lesbian Midwifery Clinic, the Birmingham Sperm Bank, the Pink Adoption Agency, the Centre for Surrogate Parenting, not to mention umpteen family law specialists and lobby groups campaigning to stamp out homophobia. There are products too – assisted conception kits so you can inseminate yourself at home, vitamins and minerals to help. You can even buy a blow-up birthing pool to take away the same day.

It's a lot to take in, and after weeks of barely seeing anyone, Lou finds it a shock to be amongst so many people. Her head is swimming.

Anna slips a protective arm around her. 'Hey, how are you feeling? You've been standing quite a while.'

'I'm OK.'

'Hmm. You look a bit pale. Shall we go and find the room where they're having the talk, so you can sit down?'

'Good idea.' Lou allows Anna to guide her carefully through the throng.

* * *

'That coffee's gone straight through me,' says Cath. 'Find us a seat while I nip to the Ladies?'

Once again Rich does as he is bid, but as the conference room fills he feels increasingly uneasy; he must be outnumbered by women a hundred to one. He can only see one other guy, and he is busy making notes in a pad so is probably a journalist. It brings home to him something that's been playing on his mind; it's one aspect of having a child that he and Cath haven't spoken of. It's fundamental, yet he has no idea how to broach the subject.

What if she were to get ill again? he worries. Has he got it in him to be a single father? Because should the worst happen, there is the distinct possibility that this – a world where he's constantly surrounded by women – might be his future. Parenthood is a huge commitment anyway; for him it could be gargantuan. He tries to imagine whether he could be the kind of person – that strong, that wise, that unselfish – who could bring up a kid alone. What would happen about childcare? His job? Money?

He struggles to bring his focus back to the room. Before him is a panel of speakers; to their left, a podium. It all looks very formal and intimidating, and he's not even sure why Cath was keen to come to this particular talk. He slumps down in his chair, hoping to make himself less conspicuous.

Shortly his wife returns, sits down next to him, and the lights dim.

Oh well, he thinks, I guess it does no harm to get clued up about our options. Hopefully the answers will come in due course.

Next, a tall man with white hair, deep-brown skin

and wearing a well-cut suit gets to his feet and goes to the stand.

'Good morning,' he says. 'I am Dr Khalid Hassan. I am the Managing Director of the Marylebone Fertility Clinic, and it is an honour for me to join you today to tell you about a very special form of IVF. It's a subject close to my heart, a treatment with remarkable success rates which is helping many couples – both gay and straight – and indeed single women' – he smiles at the audience – 'to have children.'

He flicks up a slide. A giant toddler now beams at Rich too.

'Parenthood is the right of everyone,' continues Dr Hassan. 'And we have the technologies to achieve that dream.'

Is it? thinks Rich. I'm not sure I think of it as my right, not any more . . . And what if you're sixty-five? Or a psychopath? But before he has time to analyse, he's swept up again. Dr Hassan's voice is assured but gentle, his whole demeanour exuding avuncular geniality.

'In particular, I'm here to speak to you about how two women can make babies together.' The doctor chuckles.

Blimey, thinks Rich. Then wouldn't that make me redundant? He's finding it hard to keep pace already.

'Yet these two women will never meet each other. At our clinic, we go to great lengths to ensure that. Though whilst they will never come face to face, they will arguably make more of a difference to one another's lives than any other single individual.'

What about me? protests Rich inwardly. I hope I make a difference to Cath. He can feel her beside him listening intently. I must get a handle on this for her sake, he says to himself.

The doctor says, 'We will synchronize these two women's cycles, and their pregnancies may well happen simultaneously. Their children will even be genetically linked.'

Another slide flicks up: two flowers, heads bent together, bloom in unison.

He leans in to the microphone. 'As many of you will doubtless already know, for some women there is a shortage of ova – or eggs as we think of them – for use in IVF. And yet many women undergoing treatment produce a surplus. So we've devised a programme designed to bring these two sets of women together. The name of this programme is *egg sharing*.'

Aah, thinks Rich, catching up at last. So *that's* why Cath was so keen on coming to this particular talk.

8

Slowly, Sofia opens the door to the auditorium. She winces as it squeaks – the presentation she recalls Lou wished to attend has already begun.

'If you are under thirty-six and able to produce healthy eggs, you can donate some to a potential mother in need of them,' the speaker is saying.

She tiptoes inside, feels people turn to stare and leans against the wall to make herself as thin as possible. She scans the rows of seats in front of her, but the lights are dimmed and it's hard to make out people's faces.

The speaker continues, 'In return, the clinic will provide basic IVF treatment, for free. You'll also have the satisfaction of helping another woman become a mother.'

A woman with a clipboard swiftly pads over to Sofia, puts a finger to her lips and mouths, 'Wait here.'

Sofia does as she is told. Given how bad she feels already, it seems fitting to be treated like a naughty child.

A diagram flashes up, illustrating connections between egg sharers, and the speaker continues. 'But there are many other advantages to sharing eggs. Because of the shortage of eggs in this country, many women and couples are forced to travel abroad to find donors. This can be expensive, time-consuming and stressful. Even though recent legislation means increased financial compensation is now available to donors here in the UK, it's only designed to cover expenses; you can't pay a woman specifically to donate. And whilst many clinics overseas offering donor eggs are perfectly reputable, some aren't. Donors are often less thoroughly vetted, and because they have been paid large sums for their eggs, their motivations are compromised. They may be less suited psychologically to dealing with the long-term implications.

'I should also point out that since 2005, every child conceived by egg or sperm donation has the legal right to find out who his or her donor parent is when he or she hits eighteen years of age. Clearly, this can have a big impact on a donor's life, not to mention the young adult involved. But you can rest assured that on our egg-sharing programme, our donors are thoroughly checked out. They also undergo counselling to ensure they are fully aware of this risk and are prepared – insofar as is humanly possible – to take full responsibility should a child come knocking on their door in two decades' time.'

Sofia's eyes are growing accustomed to the dark. The auditorium is nearly full, but even so she thinks she can make out the familiar spikes of Lou's crop silhouetted several rows in front of her, and, unless Sofia is mistaken, the smooth, sleek bob of the woman she is leaning towards looks like Anna. Of course, Lou wouldn't have been able to get this far by public transport, and she's not allowed to drive. Sofia has another stab of remorse. It would be typically generous of Anna to step in. Sofia can't suppress a touch of jealousy.

Meanwhile, a slide of a Petri dish under a microscope appears on the screen.

'Another benefit of egg sharing,' says Dr Hassan, 'is that it reduces strain on the National Health Service or similar public funding bodies in other countries.'

Anyone would think this old man was running a charity, Sofia thinks, not making thousands of pounds from each woman he treats.

At that moment, as if spooked by her inner criticism, the speaker drops his microphone. While he retrieves it from the floor, Sofia acts fast.

'I'm just going to find my friends,' she whispers to the woman with the clipboard, and scoots down the central aisle.

*   *   *

'Excuse me.'

Cath looks up. There's a woman standing at the end of the row, a few seats away. In the half-light, Cath can just make out dark hair and a denim jacket.

'Do you mind if I squeeze in?' The woman points, clearly embarrassed, and Cath sees there is an empty chair on the far side of Rich.

All the people in the row stand to make room, Cath included. As the woman passes (treading on Cath's toe) Cath observes she is quite young and pretty, with the sort of thick, wavy hair Cath would dearly love to have herself. Once the

72

woman is seated, she taps on the shoulder a parka-clad woman directly in front.

'Lou?'

A swivel of a head, a gasp: 'Sofia! Thank God you're here!' and Cath recognizes Lou from the queue. 'What the bloody hell happened to you last night?'

'I'll tell you later. Don't want to interrupt the talk.'

Dr Hassan is reunited with his microphone and is poised to resume.

'Humph.' Lou turns to face the front again. There's something about the line of her shoulders and tone of voice that make Cath conclude she is annoyed in the way a partner would be. What is the story there? she wonders. I thought she was with the woman with the bob. But much as she savours working out the dynamics of strangers' lives, she wants to hear what Dr Hassan is saying.

'So, as I've mentioned, with egg sharing, the egg recipient bears the cost of treatment for the donor. It's here I'd like to explain more about the benefits of IVF. It goes without saying that if you're looking to get pregnant without a male partner, you'll need a sperm donor. Many gay and single women might therefore think that a sperm donor is all they will need, and there's no requirement for IVF. Whereas IVF can play a big part in making it easier – and surprisingly less expensive – to conceive in the long run.

'Let me take you back a stage. IVF or "in vitro fertilization" means the egg cells are fertilized by sperm outside of the body. "In vitro" literally translates as "within the glass" and involves hormonally controlling ovulation, removing eggs from a woman's ovaries and letting sperm fertilize them in a fluid. The fertilized egg is then transferred to the uterus to try and establish pregnancy. Every time a woman undergoes IVF, several eggs will be harvested from her ovaries to maximize the chance of success, some of which will not be used. With egg sharing, she will donate these eggs to another woman whose eggs are too poor to be used in her own IVF cycle.'

That's me, thinks Cath. I don't have any eggs at all.

'Next, let me show you what I find to be a very interesting chart.' The doctor points at a fresh slide. 'If we take a closer look you'll see donor insemination has a success rate of just over 25 per cent. However, if you combine donor insemination with IVF, the success rates go up to 69 per cent. That's quite a difference. Moreover, if you're a gay or single woman looking to become pregnant, if you choose to go the egg-sharing route, in return for donating some of your eggs you can enjoy *free* IVF. Which means a greater chance of conceiving a baby, and for egg donors, no extra expense at all.'

Doesn't sound as if it would be cheaper for us though, thinks Cath, if we have to pay for someone else's treatment as well as our own. Privately funded IVF is hideously expensive as it is. She shudders at the prospect. She and Rich have virtually no savings . . . Focus, Cath, focus, she tells herself, you can work that out later. She peers at the screen. She had been confused as to why an egg donor would put herself through the trauma of IVF if she didn't have to have it, even if it were free, but if the conception rate with IVF is nearly three times higher than without, that explains it. She's beginning to see how it works, but figures aren't her strong point, and when the woman with the bob swivels round to shoot the woman next to Rich – apparently named Sofia – an unmistakably vicious look, she is distracted again.

'We've been so worried about you!' the bob woman hisses.

'I'm sorry, Anna.' Sofia looks guilty.

'Where have you been, for crying out loud?'

'Shhh!' hisses another member of the audience.

Wow, she's scary, thinks Cath. I'd hate to be on the wrong side of her. She reaches for Rich's hand, appreciating how even-tempered he is. They've had their share of tough times and painful conversations, but their lines of communication are relatively untangled, and given the journey they may be about to embark upon, she is hugely grateful for that.

*   *   *

'So where *have* you been?' Lou asks Sofia the moment the talk finishes. The people around them are yet to leave, but she doesn't care if they hear. After what Sofia has put her through, she actively wants to humiliate her. She is pleased when Sofia blushes.

'*Lo siento—*'

'Yes?'

'I got drunk so I stayed with a friend.'

Anna touches Lou's shoulder. 'Told you. Er, I think I'll go and have a look at the rest of the exhibition for a bit. Give me a buzz when you've finished telling her off.' Sofia blushes a deeper crimson. 'You're bloody lucky it's not me you're dealing with,' Anna says to her. 'Lou is more of a softie than me, but I hope she gives you a tough time.'

'Sorry, Anna,' says Sofia. 'And thank you for bringing her here.'

'I did it for Lou, not you,' says Anna.

Lou watches as Anna pushes past the people in front of her, then turns to her girlfriend. Sofia looks dreadful, thinks Lou, far from her usual confident self. Not only does she appear hungover and tired, she's sheepish. Yet Lou is not going to let up. 'So?'

Sofia can't meet her gaze. 'We went out to Soho, like I said. Some colleagues went with me to a club by Old Compton Street. When I saw the time, I had missed the last train. I am very, very sorry – it was an accident.'

'*Accident!* An "accident" is what happens when you can't control your circumstances. You could have rung me.'

'My phone ran out of charging.'

'Why didn't you use someone else's?'

'I did not know your number.'

'Jesus!' In truth, Lou doesn't know Sofia's either; it's a hazard of technology, precious contacts on speed dial. But that's not the point. 'Couldn't you have rung the landline? You know that.'

'I suppose so. I'm very sorry, really.'

'You made me feel such an idiot!' Now Lou is fighting back tears. Damn her topsy-turvy hormones. 'You knew how important today was to me.'

'I don't know what else to say.'

'Nor do I, frankly. Who were you with, some girl?'

'No, no.'

'Well, who?'

'A friend from work hosted me.'

'Who?'

'Her name is Rosetta.'

'Is she gay?'

'No! She lives with her boyfriend. They share a flat. You can ring her if you do not believe me.'

'Hmm.'

Presently Lou is aware there is still a man sitting next to her, busy writing notes. She noticed him earlier. She reckons he is some kind of journalist. This should give him good copy, she thinks.

She shakes her head, despairing. 'I'm not stupid. It's clear you've got some kind of issue with this whole thing. It's classic avoidance.'

'I wish you would not . . . be like a counsellor with me,' mutters Sofia, eyes fixed on the floor.

'What else am I supposed to do, when you can't be honest enough to tell me what you're really thinking? You won't even look at me, for God's sake.'

Sofia glances up. Those big brown eyes . . . Lou is so susceptible to them, but she's determined to resist.

'Why do we not go to look at the show?' suggests Sofia. 'We are here now.'

'Yeah, guess we could.' Lou picks up her bag, feels a twinge across her tummy. 'I want to find out more about sperm donation.'

'*Si, si.*'

There's a limit to how much Lou can deal with in such a public place.

9

'So, do you seriously think you're going to do this egg-sharing thing, then?' asks Anna.

Lou doesn't wish to commit so fast. 'Maybe.'

She is sitting in the passenger seat of Anna's Saab: a spacious convertible with an expensive stereo and upholstery that still smells new. The dashboard before her is so futuristic Lou can't begin to work out what all the lights, dials and numbers mean.

Sofia leans between the two front seats to join in the conversation. 'Your mother will . . . what is that word you use to describe when she gets upset?'

'Freak,' says Lou. You seem pretty freaked too, she thinks, but lets it go.

'Would you tell your mother?' asks Anna.

'I don't even know if I'm going to go that route.' She wishes Anna hadn't brought the subject up.

'I think it's a weird thing to do,' says Sofia.

'I don't think it's weird at all,' says Anna. The traffic has been stop-start since they left the West End; they've come to another halt at the junction by Harrods. Dozens of people hurry to cross the road while the lights are red. 'I think it's rather lovely.'

'OK, maybe "weird" is not the right word, sometimes my English is not so good . . . But imagine if you share your eggs then a child comes to find you when they are eighteen.'

'That's a long way in the future,' says Anna. 'What about the here and now?'

Lou fights to keep her voice steady. 'Exactly. I like the idea of helping another woman have a baby.' She wants to tackle her issues with Sofia once they're alone, not heading home on the A4 with Anna driving, yet she feels too strongly to keep silent. 'Imagine what heartache some women must be experiencing if they can't have a child. My eggs could change someone's life.'

'I think you're romanticizing it,' says Sofia.

Lou is hurt. That she's romantic is not something her girl-friend should object to.

'Having children is not everything,' Sofia continues.

'I know it's not the be-all and end-all, but nevertheless, for many women – and men – it's a major part of being an adult.' Lou uses the word pointedly.

'Even if you don't believe having children is the most important thing in life, and I don't, actually – I mean, look at me – surely you can appreciate that for some people it really matters?' asks Anna. She edges the car forward to the next set of lights, where yet more shoppers are crossing the road. 'You can't write it off just because it's not *your* priority.'

'I'm not,' says Sofia.

'It sounded like that,' says Anna. 'I think sharing eggs seems very altruistic.'

Perhaps the fact she initiated this conversation isn't so awful, Lou thinks. Anna's expressing what I feel without my having to say it myself.

'It is still about the cost,' says Sofia. 'The donor may not be taking the money, but it means treatment that would otherwise be very expensive is free. Who is to say that doctor is objective? Of course he is not. His suit looked very nice, yet there he is standing and telling everyone how wonderful this IVF is, whilst he's getting richer himself. Sounds like a good way around the law to me. It cannot be this simple.'

But this isn't some intellectual debate, thinks Lou. It's my body – *our* future – we're talking about. Again she tries to keep the emotion out of her voice. 'After having this fibroid removed, IVF would make it far easier for me to get pregnant, so it'd be to my benefit, too.'

'Are you sure about that? How do you know?'

'Yes. I talked to the surgeon about it when I went for my post-op check-up,' Lou confesses.

'Oh. Why you didn't tell me?'

There's an awkward silence. They both seem to have secrets. Lou is convinced Sofia isn't being entirely honest about last night; equally, her own research was underhand. For the last few weeks they've seemed to be growing away from each other; now they seem in danger of completely snapping apart. Yet she feels compelled to be honest: 'Because you didn't seem at all interested.'

'Well, it's great you wouldn't have to pay for IVF.' Anna's tone is forcedly bright.

'I couldn't afford it otherwise. I can't just drum up several thousand pounds like that, on my salary. It would take me years. And years are something I don't have, apparently. Not only because of this stupid fibroid, but also, if I'm going to do egg sharing, I've got to hurry.'

'I am very surprised how expensive this treatment is here,' says Sofia. 'I am sure IVF is a lot cheaper in Spain.'

'It is – much,' says Lou. 'Though you'd still have to shell out for the flights, and take extra time off work.' Oh dear, yet more research she's done on the quiet. She explains, 'Women abroad getting paid to donate their eggs isn't something I'm happy about. You don't know why they're doing it – to get out of poverty, fund degrees – who knows? And it's a massive thing to put your body through, the hormone injections, and the removal of eggs is invasive in itself. At least with me, I'd be having all that treatment anyway.'

'Who would father the baby?' asks Sofia. 'Are you going to pay for a sperm donor through that clinic, too?'

Lou can't help noticing she says *you*, not *we*. 'I don't know for sure. From what they said at the stand, I can see there are advantages to using one, yes, but I was only going to find out the options today, not make any definite decisions.'

'Then that will mean more money, too.'

'It's not much,' says Lou. 'Weren't you listening to what that guy told me?'

'Not really, no.'

Lou flinches, bruised. 'The men don't get paid to donate sperm – they can't, here. We're not like America. I'd just be paying a few hundred pounds to cover vetting the donor.'

'So more profit for the doctor in the nice suit.'

They've hit the dual carriageway: finally Anna can accelerate. Giant advertisements line the Cromwell Road, campaign showpieces that are bigger and brasher than any they might see in Brighton.

Sofia continues, 'You're not allowed to sell other parts of your body, like your kidneys or blood, here in England though, are you?'

'But a donor wouldn't be selling his sperm, and I wouldn't be *selling* my eggs. That's the whole point.'

'You'd be exchanging them. Like in a market. Treating a potential child as a thing that can be bought.'

'I think you're being a bit harsh,' Anna chips in. 'For sperm donors it's easier – physically at least. But it's a lot to ask a woman to give up her eggs. It's practical, that's what. Two women need something – they swap it. Both benefit. Where's the harm?'

'You would say that,' says Sofia.

'Excuse me?'

'You work in marketing.'

'Meaning?'

'So clearly you think it is OK to sell almost anything.'

They're brought to a halt by yet another set of lights. Since Lou was last here, a purpose-built supermarket appears to have landed right by the junction like a giant spaceship. Anna takes the opportunity to turn to face Sofia.

'Do you want to walk home?' She grips the steering wheel, knuckles white.

'No . . . '

'Then I suggest you watch what you say.'

Lou winces. Sofia is clearly using Anna's presence to express beliefs too loaded to air one to one.

'Sorry. It's my English . . . '

'But you can't *get* eggs on the NHS,' interrupts Lou. Doesn't Sofia understand? 'Not easily, anyway. There are hardly any available.'

'And it's not like you'd be helping just any woman to have a baby,' says Sofia. 'You would be helping a *rich* woman.'

'How do you work that out?'

'If someone can afford to pay for you and for themselves, they must have a lot of money.'

'You can't be so certain,' says Lou. 'But doesn't a rich woman deserve help too?'

The car moves forward again. 'I've heard of people sacrificing a great deal to pay for IVF,' says Anna. 'They could be going into debt, remortgaging their home, forfeiting holidays – you have no idea what another person's circumstances might be. You're being a bit unsympathetic.'

Sofia shrugs. 'As I said before, it depends if you believe having children is the most important thing.'

'Sofia's not being unsympathetic.' Lou is so upset she can't address her girlfriend directly. 'She's defensive because she doesn't want children herself. Can't you tell? She just thinks I should accept my lot, like some Victorian spinster.'

'Plenty of people cannot have children, and they have to learn to live with this. Until recently that was true for us all if we were lesbians unless we want to . . . well, fuck a man.'

Anna almost swerves the car.

'And still it is only in the rich world a woman can afford to have a baby like this. In Africa—'

'Don't pull the poor-women-of-the-third-world card on me,' snaps Lou. 'Since when did you get so PC? You've a nerve lecturing me on global issues when you couldn't even call your so-called nearest and dearest to let me know you were alive.'

'I said I was sorry.'

'Like hell you are.'

By now the car feels extremely small and uncomfortable. It's impossible to force such resentments back inside Pandora's box, undo what's been said. They spend the rest of the journey in silence.

* * *

'I wonder what sort of woman would give up her eggs?' asks Cath.

She and Rich are facing each other on the train home to Leeds. There is no one nearby – just a table of lads at the far end of the carriage on their way home from a football match, and an elderly couple a few seats in front.

Rich looks up from a brochure. 'According to this, they might have some sort of fertility problem themselves.'

'But not necessarily.'

'I reckon they're likely to be gay. Judging from today.'

'Though not definitely that either. I suppose the only certainty is they'll be younger than me.'

'Under thirty-six, didn't that doctor say?'

'And not that wealthy. If you were wealthy, you wouldn't need to share your eggs. You'd say never mind the money, and pay for the IVF.'

'Don't you think some women might do it anyway?' says Rich.

'Out of the goodness of their hearts? Unlikely. That's why there's such a shortage – people aren't that generous.'

'I guess.'

'So, we've got poorish, possibly gay, and under thirty-six.' Cath allocates a finger to each point. 'And healthy, I presume. How would you feel, having a baby with someone like that?'

'I'm not sure . . . ' Rich pauses, evidently doing his utmost to keep up. 'I wouldn't really be having a child *with* them, would I? I'd be having a child with you.'

'Except it would be their genes.'

'It's only an egg you'd be having. The cells would be so small. It's not like we'd be getting a fully grown newborn baby.'

'I feel that as I'd be the one carrying it, it would be mine too. The egg would grow inside me. It'd be my blood supply. The baby wouldn't exist if it weren't for me. So it'd be a sort of three-way baby. Hmm . . . I wonder what it would look like?' She appraises her husband across the table: his blue-green eyes, his slightly lopsided mouth, his broad fingers with their distinctive square-shaped nails, his purportedly too-thick neck . . . She's so fond of him, it's impossible to be objective. 'I hope it'd be like you.'

Rich leans over towards her and gently takes her hand. 'Love, I think you're racing ahead a little. We've got a long, long way to go before then. We haven't worked out how we'd begin to pay for all this – and it doesn't sound as if it would leave much change from ten thousand pounds. That's a lot of money, and we've only just come back from holiday.'

Cath is crushed. 'I didn't think it was *that* much.'

'I think you'll find it is. By the time we've paid for their treatment, and ours.'

She bites her lip. It seems so unfair that at forty-two she's too old for treatment on the NHS. She would have qualified before her cancer diagnosis – it's as if she's being penalized for being ill. And Rich is only in his mid thirties – they're hardly OAPs. Not for the first time Cath wishes she'd been more successful professionally. Her job at Leeds Art Gallery is poorly paid and she'll have to rely on Rich to contribute the greater share. It was one thing his treating her to the ski trip; it's quite another expecting him to fund IVF almost single-handed.

She says, 'Surely we're talking about something money can't buy? It's impossible to put a price on a baby. We'll find it somehow, won't we?'

'I hope we can work something out. Perhaps we can apply for a loan. Besides, you haven't even had a chat with the specialists at the clinic yet.'

'I suppose, but we have to talk this through together, don't we?' She glances down at the brochure Rich has pushed aside. The image of two flowers bent towards each other calls out to her. 'I like the idea of egg sharing. I imagine it means just as much to someone else to have a child as it does to me, and it would be lovely to help another woman become a mother.'

'They made it sound relatively easy this morning, but you know, and I know, that a lot of the time, for, er . . . older women, IVF doesn't work.'

'Mm.'

'And . . . well . . . with all your, um, history . . . '

She holds up a palm. She doesn't want to talk about her illness right now. She appreciates that the odds are stacked against them, that even without her medical history it would be likely to take several attempts for IVF to succeed. But she can't forget Angeline and the train of skiing children . . . She's had her fill of pragmatism.

Cath tucks her jacket against the windowpane so she can rest her head more comfortably and look at the flat green fields flashing by. It's strange to think that somewhere out there is someone else, possibly carrying the eggs of their baby.

I wonder where she is? Cath asks herself. What she is thinking, what she is doing?

10

'I am going to have a beer,' says Sofia. They've just arrived home, not yet removed their coats.

Great, thinks Lou, but she doesn't try to stop her.

Sofia opens the fridge. Lou sees carrots, lettuce, half a tin of sweetcorn, juice, last night's uneaten curry. No beer, no wine. Lou is off alcohol, Sofia's been at work all week; neither has stocked up.

'I'm going to get some.'

'I thought you were hungover?'

Sofia picks up her purse and keys again. 'Do you want anything?'

Lou shakes her head. Sofia heads out, slamming the door.

Lou sits down on the sofa. Her limbs are heavy, her head aches, the stitches across her abdomen are throbbing. She hasn't even the energy to take off her parka. And now she has to brace herself for another set-to. Worse, it looks destined to be clouded by alcohol. Lou has worked with alcoholics in her role as a counsellor; she also helped Anna when things came to a head with her ex-boyfriend, Steve, who was a heavy drinker. Sofia's nowhere near that bad, but this time Lou is not one removed.

I've not even had the chance to work out what I feel myself about trying to have a baby in the near future, she thinks, bending to remove her boots. I'd hoped the exhibition would enlighten me about the options. Instead the drama with Sofia has taken over.

She rotates slowly on her bottom – ouch, her tummy really does hurt – and carefully hoists her legs up so she's able to lie down. She dangles her feet over the arm of the sofa and pulls a cushion under her head.

* * *

Sofia sits on the armchair at right angles to Lou, beer bottle in hand, watching her girlfriend slumber. It's hard to be angry with her when she's so vulnerable. She watches Lou's eyelids flicker, dark lashes against pale cheeks, and wonders what she's dreaming of. Sofia's own mind is full to bursting of all sorts: guilt and rage and upset and resentment and jealousy and . . . oh, yes, love.

Looking at Lou there, with her parka half unzipped and her boots hanging off the end of the sofa, with her lips slightly open so she can breathe more easily and her brow furrowed as if she's concentrating hard on something, Sofia remembers that she loves her. There's something so innocent about her, childlike.

What would a little Lou be like? she wonders. A smaller version crawling around this flat?

She imagines a baby – it's difficult, she's not used to

thinking about babies. At first she just hears it crying, needing milk, winding, its nappy changing, being put to sleep. But eventually she has a different sense of it: the scent of its skin, its soft downy hair, the folds of plump flesh . . . Its gaze as it learns to focus for the first time, its smile as it looks up at its mother . . .

She can't deny Lou that.

Nor, when Sofia pauses to think about it, does she want to. It's just she can't do it alongside her. Not right now, at least, and it seems that it's now, for Lou, or not at all.

* * *

Lou is hopping from foot to foot on the sand, eager to play in the sea.

'Hurry up, Daddy,' she is saying.

Her father is blowing up a lilo, cheeks puffed out; he looks funny. Finally, he pinches the valve shut with two fingers, pops the tiny plug in. 'Right then, Louloubelle, we're ready!'

'You coming, Mummy?' she asks.

'No, I'll stay here,' says her mother. She's busy laying out the picnic on the rug. Irene never comes in the sea; the water's freezing, she claims. Just for once Lou would like her to.

'I'll stay with you,' says Lou's sister, Georgia.

'Race you, then!' says Lou's dad, and before she can get to her feet, he's off across the sand, airbed bouncing in the wind behind him. 'First one in!' he yells, his voice diminished by the breeze.

He's got a good head start, and he's a decent sprinter, but Lou is good at running. Faster, faster, faster she goes, and, though her legs are much shorter, and she can feel her lungs pressing against her chest, soon she's closing in on him, then she's abreast of him, and – hurray! – just before they reach the shallows, she overtakes. With a triumphant *sploosh! sploosh! sploosh!* she keeps on going into the sea. Before she realizes it, she's up to her thighs, in over her waist – cold, excited.

She turns back to face her dad; he's wading in more slowly, pushing the lilo into the waves ahead of him, grinning broadly.

'Me on the front and you on the back?' he says, patting the tubing.

'Me on the front!' says Lou, and with a squeak of plastic, hoists herself aboard.

*

Lou wakes, disoriented. It takes a moment to work out where she is. The lights are dimmed and the TV is on. The volume is down low; a woman in a skimpy outfit beckons viewers to gamble online. Sofia is asleep in the armchair opposite, head back, snoring faintly. In her hand is a half-drunk bottle of beer, tilting precariously.

Slowly Lou raises herself to a sitting position, stands up, tiptoes over. Gingerly, she tries to ease the bottle from Sofia's fingers.

Sofia stirs, opens her eyes, looks up at her, surprised.

'*Hola* . . . ' She realizes what Lou is doing. 'Oh, sorry.'

'It's OK. I was worried you'd spill it.' Lou puts the bottle on the floor.

'Yes, sure, you are right. Ooh, I fell asleep. What time is it?'

'Just gone midnight.'

Sofia yawns. 'I am so tired.'

'Me too.'

Lou turns off the television, returns to Sofia, arms outstretched. 'Come on, let's get you to bed.'

Sofia reaches up, grabs her hands. 'Thanks.'

Ow. She's quite a weight. They've both forgotten Lou isn't supposed to lift anything, but she's done it now. She sits down on the duvet – their studio is small; the bed is close by. 'Can you help me take off my boots?'

'Sure.' Still bleary, Sofia crouches to undo the laces, carefully slips them off Lou's feet. She puts them aside, neat; catches Lou watching her. 'I'm sorry,' she repeats.

'It's OK.'

'No, it is not OK. I have been horrible.'

Lou half smiles, appreciative. 'Yes, you have.'

'I don't know what has happened to me. I have been like an idiot.'

'Yup.' Maybe, thinks Lou, everything will be all right.

Then Sofia rubs her eyes, ferociously, as if it will help her see more clearly, sighs, and sits back on her haunches on the floor, a few feet from Lou. Her voice is small, woeful. 'I can't do it, the baby . . . you know.'

Lou exhales. 'I know.'

Sofia starts to cry. Lou moves to sit cross-legged with her – even though it tugs at her stitches to get herself there and the wooden floor is hardly comfortable. Again she reaches for Sofia's hands, takes them both in hers.

This is the wrong way round, she thinks. She should be comforting me, but no matter. This is what happens.

'I am not ready,' says Sofia.

Lou laughs, almost bitterly. 'I'm not sure I am.'

'You know what I mean.'

Lou nods.

'And I cannot . . . get in your way.'

'No.'

'It would be terrible, you'd always hate me.' Sofia looks up; it's those big brown eyes again, only this time they're filled with tears. If Lou's heart weren't breaking already, this would smash it to pieces.

'Hate you?'

'Yes, you would. *I* would. I would hate myself. It just wouldn't work.'

They are quiet a moment. Lou knows Sofia is right. The evidence is there: she's only to consider Sofia's behaviour of the last twenty-four hours. Sofia will get more self-destructive, crueller, if they carry on.

'It's rubbish, isn't it?' Lou says. For some reason she can't cry, maybe because Sofia is.

'Yes.' Sofia giggles for a split second through her weeping. She strokes Lou's fingers. Her touch is feathery, delicate. 'I wish life is not . . . was not . . . so complicated.'

'Me too.' Lou strokes Sofia's fingers back.

'And it's worse sometimes, for us.'

'Eh?'

'Well, if we were straight, you would probably have got pregnant by accident.'

'Mm. Maybe you're right. Though I've always disliked women who do that. It seems so manipulative.'

'*Si* . . . We do not have that luxury.'

'We have to plan it all, think everything through.'

'Be rational.'

'Not blurry.'

'I feel blurry,' says Sofia.

'So do I,' says Lou. They smile at one another. 'Listen to us. Agreeing on everything . . . How ironic, eh?'

'Very.'

'Though we always did agree on most stuff.' *Did*, Lou thinks. Past tense. She used it without meaning to. She says, 'I'm not even completely sure I want a baby.'

'I know,' says Sofia. 'Though I think you do. And I really don't. Not yet, not this fast. I feel rushed – what is that word you use sometimes? *Bamboozled* . . . But you . . . You love kids. You *should* be a mother. You deserve to be, and I can't ask you to wait, when I might never be ready.'

'Though it might not happen,' says Lou. 'I may not be able to get pregnant.'

'Still, you have to try.'

'Yes,' says Lou.

It's becoming clearer. Lou has no idea how she'll cope with a baby all on her own. Being a single mum is not a situation she ever thought she'd find herself in. She can only begin to imagine how people will react, what her family will say. Her mother will be a nightmare for a start. Lou can't see Irene liking the notion of a baby conceived by sperm donation any more than she has liked the fact that her daughter is gay. But whilst she's still undecided about egg sharing, now Lou is up against it, she is certain that she has to give having a baby a go. Even though it means forfeiting her relationship – probably the best relationship she's ever had – to do so. That Sofia has at last been honest has helped her see this.

'Thank you,' she says.

Then very gently, a little tentatively, she leans forward and kisses Sofia. Sofia kisses her back, and helps her get to her feet, and they go to bed, and make love, tenderly, sweetly, sadly, one last time.

11

'We're here to see Mr Edwards,' Rich says.

The cashier looks mystified.

'About a loan? It's Mr and Mrs Morris.'

She checks a screen. 'Ah, yes. If you'd just like to take a seat at the desk over there, I'll call him.'

Shortly there's the click of a lock, and a young man in a suit comes to join them. His hair has too much gel in it, thinks Rich, and his shirt is pink and stripy. He shakes their hands in turn. His grip is not as firm as Rich's and he looks at least ten years his junior. 'Thank you so much for coming in.'

Rich shifts in his chair. Even though he's a fully grown adult, he doesn't feel any more comfortable in this environment than he did as an overdrawn student, despite the posters of smiling staff with slogans claiming they're listening and helpful.

Mr Edwards says, 'I thought it would be better to meet face to face in this instance, because I wanted to run through a few things with you.'

'Sure,' says Cath.

Rich says, 'I had hoped we could have sorted this out on the phone.' They've yet to see the specialists at the clinic – they simply want to know they can find the funds, if they have to.

Mr Edwards beams at Cath. 'Sometimes we can. But I'm sure you appreciate we're having to be a little more, um . . . ' – he hunts for the word – '*discerning* in who we give loans to these days.'

'Of course,' says Cath.

Rich wonders why she is agreeing with him.

Mr Edwards consults a form before him. 'So, to clarify . . . I see that you borrowed two thousand pounds in November. Can I ask what you're wanting the money for this time?'

'The first loan was to take my wife on holiday just before Christmas,' says Rich. 'I don't know if you're aware but she's not been very well, and we wanted to celebrate making a fresh start. We even chose to go before peak season so as to save on the cost.'

'Ah, right,' says Mr Edwards. Momentarily he looks disconcerted, as if illness was not something he'd factored in. But then he beams again at Cath. 'Go anywhere nice?'

'Skiing,' she replies.

'I hope you had a good time.'

'Yes thanks, it was lovely.'

Mr Edwards nods. 'So . . . I gather you'd like to borrow another ten thousand pounds.'

'Yes,' says Rich. He tries not to sound annoyed. 'Though not to go on holiday.'

'OK . . . So what are you wanting this new loan for, then?'

Rich finds this intrusive. He's worried about the money already; he doesn't need some guy with a different agenda making it worse. 'Do you need to know?'

'I'm afraid so.'

Perhaps they should say it's for a car. But before Rich has worked out a plausible fib, Cath volunteers: 'It's for fertility treatment.'

'Oh.' This time there is no concealing Mr Edwards' disconcertion. For several seconds he appears not to know what to say.

'My wife has had cancer,' says Rich. If this man is going to be so nosy, he might as well embarrass him in return. 'So we need IVF if we want to have a baby and be a family.' He's surprised: he hadn't realized he felt so passionate about it. Evidently he's in less of a quandary than he thought.

'Ah.' Mr Edwards blushes.

Rich has a flush of caustic pleasure. For a spontaneous tactic, it's shrewd: hopefully Mr Edwards will feel too guilty to turn them down.

Mr Edwards directs his attention back to Cath. 'So, your illness, um, is that the reason your income has been a bit . . . sporadic, Mrs Morris, over the last couple of years?'

'It is,' says Cath. 'I was on statutory sick pay for quite a while.'

Another pause. 'Which made you, Mr Morris, the main, um, breadwinner, I take it.'

'For a while I was, yes.'

'And you're in the music industry?'

'That's right, I'm a product manager.'

'Must be a lot of changes in that at the moment . . . ' He

smiles, as if out of sympathy, but Rich can discern the implication. Only last week there was another round of redundancies at the label's head office; Mr Edwards has tapped directly into one of his most prescient concerns.

Mr Edwards drives the point home. 'You'd say your job was secure?'

Surely no one's job is safe these days? thinks Rich, but instead he lies, 'Yes, I'd say so.'

'He's very popular with clients,' interjects Cath. 'And the bosses like him.' She squeezes Rich's knee under the table.

'And your monthly outgoings . . . ' says Mr Edwards. 'You think you could manage another three hundred and fifty pounds?'

'Yes.' He's still struggling not to lose his temper.

'You have been overdrawn . . . ' Again, that obsequious smile.

Rich has half an urge to punch him, but of course he won't. 'Hardly by much, and it was with prior agreement. It was because Cath was unable to work: with her full-time, we'll be fine.'

'Though should you have a baby, then I'm assuming, Mrs Morris, you'll take maternity leave . . . ?'

'She would take some time to spend with a newborn, yes.' Again, Rich is surprised by the force of his feelings.

'And you're wanting to pay back this loan over thirty-six months . . . '

'We'll manage.'

'I think you understand why I needed to run through this, though . . . ?'

No, I bloody don't! Rich wants to shout. He senses Cath

beside him, full of expectation and hope. He can't bear to think how upset she'll be if they are declined. She's been through such heartache already.

Suddenly she leans across the table. 'Please, I know it's a lot of money. I know you're under pressure not to lend so much these days. But this isn't a new BMW we're talking about, or even a holiday – if we'd known we'd need this loan, we'd have forfeited the trip abroad, just like that, even though we really needed a break. We've only recently found out it might be a possibility for us to do it this way. This is a *baby* we're asking for help with. A child. We want one so very badly.' She glances at Rich. Inside he is cringing at her forthrightness, but he nods – increasingly he's realizing how much he wants this too. She continues, 'We'd rather it wasn't going to cost us anything to conceive, of course we would. For lots of people it wouldn't cost a bean – probably it won't for you when the time comes. Do you have a girlfriend – a partner?'

Mr Edwards blushes. Rich notices he's wearing a wedding band. For the first time Rich feels for him – they both find this excruciating, it seems.

But Cath doesn't hold back. 'Well imagine, in the future, if *you* wanted a child, and you'd both been trying for years, and then found out she couldn't, or you couldn't, for what-ever reason—'

Mr Edwards coughs and looks sheepish. 'Actually, we've got two children,' he mutters.

Cath gulps. Of course she'd assumed he was too young to be a father, just as Rich had. Though it merely appears to make her more passionate. 'Well, you're lucky. But it's not the same for us – this is the only way we can do it. If we have to, we'll offset it against the house, our mortgage. Whatever. I'll work harder, my husband will bust a gut; crikey, I'll walk the bloody streets if I have to.' Rich can hardly believe she's just said that, although he's impressed by her honesty. At least she's broken through the phoney smiles and platitudes. 'Don't turn us down. I'm begging you.'

Mr Edwards looks at his form again.

Rich swallows his pride. 'Please,' he adds.

Mr Edwards reaches for a calculator. 'I'll see what I can do.'

There's another long silence, while he taps in a succession of figures. Finally, he lifts his head.

'OK . . . We can do it. But this is the last loan we can grant you until the ten thousand pounds is paid back. That is our absolute limit, I'm afraid.'

12

It's past midday and Lou is not even dressed. Several weeks have passed since her operation and she'd been planning a run to help her get fit again. At the very least she should shower, but this online forum is fascinating.

Hello everyone, After years of assuming our problem was my husband's low sperm count, we went for a review of our second failed IVF to be told apparently my eggs are 'very, very poor quality'. I am absolutely devastated. I don't understand how it's taken them this long to find out. I thought I was fine. The doc basically said there is only a 5% chance of IVF working and he did not want us to waste £5k, so suggested we go away and think about egg donation. Enquired if I had a friend/sister who might donate. But I don't know anyone! I feel sick and can't stop crying. I can't believe I am never going to have my own child. Annie33

Annie, It must be such a shock to find out there's an issue with your eggs. I've been an egg donor, and I took part in an egg-share scheme. The idea is someone like me, who's already going through IVF, shares their spare eggs. Might such a scheme work for you? If you look at the egg-share thread, you'll see that you're not alone. There are many women who have had babies from donor eggs and they are in NO WAY NOT THEIR CHILDREN. Yes, you may need help getting there, but when that egg has been fertilized by your partner's sperm, grown inside you for nine months and it's you who has carried it, nourished it and felt every movement, it is most definitely your baby. I also believe a child is what they become because of the love they receive from their parents and the experiences and lifestyle they are given. I hope with time you start to feel the same and can have your own child even if it's not genetically 'yours'. Shadow

Hi Annie33, I believe it takes real bravery to accept egg donation from someone you don't know. Due to my ethnic background, it took many months to find someone suited to my eggs but now they have found a woman who is. I really think it's God's will that two strangers can have such a magical relationship, and one day your child will understand how much you want to be a mum, and thank you for the journey you have been through. Rainbow Girl

I wish Sofia could read this, Lou thinks. Then she might not be so cynical.

*   *   *

'We'll see you back at the house, shall we?' says Cath.

Rich turns to his father-in-law. 'Fancy another, Peter? They'll be a while, I'll bet.'

Peter drains his pint. 'Same again, please.'

'Looks as if it's going to be a nice afternoon,' says Judy, as she and Cath step outside the pub. After raining all morning, the sky reveals promising patches of blue.

'Let's do the circular route by the gorge, shall we?' says Cath. Her parents have lived in the Yorkshire Dales since Cath and her brother were small, and the walk is a family favourite.

'It's so nice to have someone to go with,' says Judy, once they're out of earshot. Anything but a short stroll is too much for Peter these days, but Judy is younger and fitter than her husband.

Cath leads the way through a gate and into a field. It's peppered with sheep, heads down grazing. The gradient rises gently on either side, a stream cuts through the meadow, tall grasses dampen their legs. They stroll in companionable silence at first, getting into the rhythm. After a while, gentle undulations give way to more dramatic crags and outcrops, and as they follow the line of the stream, stepping from stone to stone, their conversation mirrors their movements, jumping from one shared interest to another. Cath tells Judy news of friends her mother is fond of; Judy updates Cath on the latest dramas involving Cath's brother, Mike, and his wife, Sukey. They share a moan about Sukey, whom they both find difficult. 'No wonder those boys are hyperactive,' says Cath. 'Their mother's an exercise junkie.'

They could natter all afternoon, but if Cath is going to tackle the subject, she'd better get on with it. She glances at her mother before she begins. Judy's expression is a half smile, eyes crinkled up in the brightness. Her grey hair is swept up in its customary bun, a few wisps fall about her still quietly beautiful face; her purple anorak is unzipped, hands swing in time with her step. She's as relaxed as she'll ever be.

'There's something I want to let you know, Mum.'

'Oh?'

'You know when they operated to remove the tumour?'

'Ye-es   '

Cath knows her mother doesn't like talking about her cancer. At the time, Judy seemed better dealing with the practicalities than talking about it openly. Presumably she found it too upsetting; nonetheless, given their closeness, Cath found it hard. She reminds her, 'Well, they left my cervix and uterus.'

'So they did.'

They're entering a narrow ravine. Great slabs of grey rise far above their heads, cut crossways and vertical by centuries of running water, like giant building blocks. Cath looks up in the hope they might lend her some of their strength. 'It means I can carry a baby.' Even saying this chokes her up, she wants it so terribly.

Judy says nothing. Cath wishes she'd react. 'I don't under-stand,' she says eventually. 'I didn't think you could.'

Cath steadies her voice and explains about using another woman's eggs. That they're walking helps her compose herself; it's as if each stride brings with it a touch more clarity, helping formulate thoughts.

When she's through, Judy says, 'Well, I suppose the same stubbornness that got you through your cancer should see you through this.'

Cath should probably ignore the criticism, but can't resist. 'Dad always says I get my obstinacy from you.'

'Good grief, Cath!' Judy bursts out. 'Have you really thought about it? You'd be going through something similar all over again. You'll be back in waiting rooms, having tests, having treatment.'

'But I won't be a cancer patient.' Why can't her mother see it?

'Having a baby, it's a lot to put your body through.'

'I'm so much better than I was.' For months following her operation, Cath's whole world shrank to her bedroom and going to the hospital for chemotherapy: the most she could take in was daytime TV; even reading was too taxing. Very occasionally between treatments, she could just muster the strength to get to the end of the street for a coffee with Rich to support her. Then when it was all over, she felt very down. Yet she pulled herself out of that too. In comparison she feels a new woman. 'Honestly. I managed skiing before Christmas, and I never thought I would.'

'But you still have days, don't you, pet, when you get ever so tired?'

Her mother has a point. Even though she's been back at work for ages, until recently Cath would find she'd overdone it somehow, get all shaky and distressed, and have to collapse into bed. The experience would send her right back to the time of having chemo.

'I haven't had a day like that since the autumn.'

Judy shakes her head. 'That's not very long. Have you any idea how dreadful being pregnant can make you feel? I was sick as a dog with both of you.'

'I've heaps of friends who've been through it. And there's Sukey.' Maybe comparing herself to her sister-in-law isn't a good idea. Sukey is super-fit and several years younger. 'Don't you want another grandchild, Mum?'

'Of course I do. You know I'd like that very much. I think you and Rich would make great parents, I've always thought that. And you've got a real knack with children.'

'Have I?' Cath is surprised to hear her mother say this. Judy is not usually one for overt compliments.

'Oh yes. When I think of you with Alfie and Dom for instance. Plus of course, I'm very fond of Rich . . . ' Judy falls quiet as she concentrates on climbing over some particularly awkward rocks. When she reaches a flat boulder, she stops to look across at her daughter. 'Though it wouldn't be genetically my grandchild, would it?'

Ouch, thinks Cath. That really hurt, especially after the mention of her nephews. 'But I'd be the one carrying it.'

'I mean biologically.'

'Well . . . it would be Rich's genetically, but the baby would still be mine. And actually, in some ways, it might be a blessing if we weren't genetically connected. If the cancer I had is hereditary, I won't pass it on to them.' Having decided to air the subject, there's little point in avoiding this detail.

'Couldn't you adopt?'

'I have thought about it, but it's so tricky in the UK, especially if you're white – there aren't enough babies.'

'What about an older child?'

But I want OUR baby! Cath longs to scream, but she must try to take this slowly, however testing her mother is being. 'I'm just not sure I could take on an older child who might have all sorts of emotional problems.'

'It might be a lot less tough than going through this IVF

treatment you seem to be planning. You'll need time off work again.'

'Mum, I don't think you understand. I want *Rich's* child.'

'And it's more drugs. You've been pumped full of so many already.'

'I'm sick of being seen as a cancer victim!' snaps Cath. 'It's not the same sort of treatment, and I wish you would stop comparing them. You know the worst thing about cancer? I felt out of place here' – she waves at their surroundings – 'in the normal world. I couldn't go for walks like this – or anywhere. I couldn't make plans – not even for the next day. I couldn't pop into town. I couldn't draw, or make pots. I couldn't even come and see you without Rich to drive me. And I certainly couldn't think about having children. Every time I did, I had to push the thought away – it was awful.' She swallows. She mustn't cry, it won't help – her mother will think she's just being over-emotional. She keeps talking. 'And all around me my friends were having babies, Alfie and Dom were growing up . . . I felt like I was living in some sort of time warp. For two years, everyone else's lives were moving on, and mine had stopped.'

Judy sighs. 'It wasn't fun for any of us.' She turns to face forward again, focuses on moving upstream.

It's the closest her mother has come to admitting her feelings about Cath's illness. But this isn't the time to work through Judy's reaction to the past; Cath is determined to convey her hopes and dreams without giving the impression they're just a fantasy. It's quite a tightrope to be walking. Presently, Judy pauses to catch her breath and Cath stops alongside her, touches her shoulder, remembering. 'It was a hideous start to married life, Rich helping me in and out of the bath, shopping and cooking for me.'

'I suppose . . .'

'He even had to clear up my sick.' Cath shudders. The physical symptoms weren't the worst of it. Once the chemo was over, she had rushes of panic – without seeing doctors and nurses almost daily, she felt adrift between check-ups. Suddenly she'd experience an alarming flurry of emotions, like bats whooshing from a cave. Her thoughts would fly this way and that, contradictory, uncontrollable: she'd be desperate to turn her mind off, but the more she tried, the more panicked she'd feel.

'Rich helped us all get through it,' says Judy.

Cath nods. Sometimes she wonders how her mother and father would have coped had Rich not been around. 'But since the beginning of this year, I guess, it's like I've wanted to set the clock ticking again.'

As they emerge from the gorge onto the hilltop, they can see the vast sweep of the landscape before them, north, south, east and west. Up here it's bleak and windswept, yet only just below are lush pastures edged with trees, and there, glistening blue in the distant sunlight, is Malham Tarn. Where else in the world offers such diversity of hill and valley, shape and scene as Yorkshire? Cath wonders. The public image of the Dales is far more saccharine than the reality: TV and postcards do no justice to the scale of the place. For all its scores of picturesque villages, from this standpoint there's barely a dwelling in sight.

'You know what, Mum,' she says. 'For thousands of years, women have been having babies. Babies have been conceived in fields and forests, just like those over there, and in beds and cars and hotel rooms. They're having babies in films, on telly, in books . . . My friends – even bloody Sukey – everyone is at it. Women conceive, carry, and give birth every day. Except me.'

Ultimately, she wants to explain, my desire for a baby is not about drugs, or cancer, or anything Rich and I or you or anyone else in my family has experienced as a result of my cancer treatment. It's about a longing so deep and intense that it's hard to express adequately out loud.

She takes a deep breath. 'I know it's difficult, Mum, but *we* need to do this, Rich and I. All that energy, all that time we spent getting through my illness. I'm fed up of being defined by what's happened to me, I want a new reason for living – and I want that reason not just to be about me. I want to put someone else and their needs ahead of mine for a change. Maybe it's selfish, but if I am, then so is half the world – they all want to have children too. Or maybe it's just I've got so much love to give and I don't want it to go to waste. I don't want to be rattling round the house in a few years just the two of us, feeling lonely and that something is missing. I want to show my child this blue sky and these dales' – she sweeps her hand around again. 'And, though he'd never say so, Rich bought into something when he married me, and he got short-changed, or that's how it seems. So I want to give him something back, after everything he's done for me. I think he'd make such a great dad. All that caring he gave me – just imagine what he'd be like with a small person.'

Judy is taking in the view, but Cath can tell from the

furrow between her brows that she is also doing her best to absorb what she has just heard. That she's trying so hard makes Cath appreciate another reason. 'You know, it's about you too. If you weren't such a good mum, I wouldn't want to be one, not with all the effort it's going to take, would I?'

By now Judy's hair is barely contained by its clip; daddy long-legs tendrils blow this way and that. As she turns briskly away and starts back down the gentler slope of hillside, Cath thinks she glimpses that her mother is also trying to mask tears. Or maybe it's just the wind, making her eyes water.

13

'She seems a lot happier, our Cath,' says Peter, settling into his armchair.

Rich takes his seat on the sofa. 'She does.'

'Looks so much better, too. Lovely to see her smiling again.'

'I know. That skiing holiday did her the world of good.'

'Fancy watching the cricket?' Peter is such an ardent fan that he subscribes to a sports channel to watch it all year round.

'Excellent idea,' says Rich.

Peter reaches for the remote, flicks on the television. It's an ad break. He turns down the volume, then says, 'You know what her mother would really love her to do? She's convinced it would help her feel better.'

Is it possible that Judy has arrived at the same conclusion they have? Cath has asked Rich to have a word with her father – Rich is unsure how to broach the subject.

'Take up pottery again.'

'Ah.' Rich struggles to catch this curve ball.

'She was always the creative one,' says Peter; Rich assumes he's also referring to Cath's brother, Mike. 'That job hardly stretches her.'

'No . . . But they were very supportive when she was ill.'

'I think Judy appreciates that.'

'And she's got some good friends at the gallery.'

'I wasn't suggesting for a moment she give that up. It just seems a shame for her talent to go to waste.'

Rich has to agree. Judy and Peter are clearly very proud of their daughter – their bungalow is full of pots and jugs and mugs and plates she's made over the years. 'I could mark the stages of my daughter's life through the evolution in her design,' Judy had said to Rich on his first visit. She'd insisted on talking him through the whole collection: the witch Cath had made at primary school, its careful sculpture marked by such enthusiastic splodges of coloured glaze that they almost hid the first signs of her gift. The tall, elegant vase she'd shaped only the second time she ever used the wheel – 'I remember her teacher was *so* excited when I came to collect her,' Judy had confided. 'He told me he'd never known a child achieve something so accomplished at such a young age.' Then there were the experiments and shocks from art school, and finally a couple of pieces in the understated whites and pale greys of the porcelain she'd made her trade-mark for the few years she worked as a professional. Cath had been mortified by her mother's showing-off, but knowing Judy better now, Rich realizes overt expression of admiration is not her usual way. For him, it merely underlined how enthusiastic his in-laws were. Yet Cath had already stopped potting by the time they met.

'She claims there's no money it,' says Rich.

'I know it's hard to make a living, but it would be wonderful to see her doing it again.'

The cricketers are coming back onto the field, so before they resume play, Rich says, 'Actually, there *is* some news about Cath. I know she's having a word with Judy, so you should probably be in on it too.'

At once Peter sits straight up. 'There's nothing wrong, is there?'

'No, no. Not at all. Sorry, I didn't mean to frighten you. It's that, well, we're going to try to have a child.'

'Eh?'

'Cath wants to have a baby.' Rich explains to Peter as best he can, but he's not fully au fait with IVF himself, so it's a struggle. It's doubly hard with a one-day international vying for his attention.

'Well, that's terrific news. I wish you both extremely good luck.' Peter adjusts the cushions in his chair and gives a satisfied huff. 'Imagine that, you a dad . . . me a grandfather again . . . Isn't modern medicine amazing?'

'It certainly is.' Rich wonders if he should confess his concerns as to how Cath will take it if the IVF *doesn't* work.

Suddenly, the England batsman sashays down the wicket and lofts a spinner into the stand.

I'll keep schtum, thinks Rich. His father-in-law seems so bucked by the news he doesn't have the heart, just as he doesn't have the heart to put the brakes on Cath.

As if to confirm the wisdom of his decision, there's the sound of a key in the lock, followed by Cath and Judy's voices in the hall.

* * *

'That'll be your godmother,' Karen tells Molly on hearing the doorbell ring. 'Do you want to get it?'

Molly gets up from the tiled floor where she's been playing with Toby, the cat, and charges to greet her.

'So, whose birthday is it . . . ?' Anna steps into the kitchen with both hands behind her back.

'MINE!' Molly jumps up and down. Toby, alarmed, scuttles out of the room.

'Yours?' Anna feigns horror. 'No way! I thought it was Luke's!'

Lou hopes Molly knows she is joking. Molly giggles. 'It's mine!'

'Oh, OK . . . so it's yours, then. But . . . I'm terribly sorry, Molly, I seem to have left your present at home.'

Molly scoots round her. 'What's that, then?'

'Ooh, I don't know . . . ' Anna swings the parcel round. 'My goodness me, I seem to have brought it after all.'

Molly gasps.

'Sit down, Molly. Just be patient a second.' Karen addresses her friend. 'Tea?'

'Love one.'

'Then I want to hear all about tonight.'

'Let Molly open her present first.' Anna sits down next to Lou.

Molly doesn't need to be given permission twice. There is a frenzied tearing of Barbie paper and then – 'EEEEEEEEEEEEEEEEE!'

Karen laughs. 'That's a hit, whatever it is. What is it?' She stops filling the kettle and comes to see.

'Mummy, mummy, mummy! It's a Dora laptop!'

'Wow.' Luke peers over his sister's shoulder.

Karen ruffles Molly's curls. 'Now you can be a writer, like Godmother Anna.'

'Hardly,' says Anna. 'This computer looks a lot better than mine. I wish I had a 3D Dora who bounced up and down when I got my words right doing copy.'

'It's got lots of games,' says Lou, trying her best to see the box over Luke and Molly's heads. It's not easy when they are tugging it this way and that in a bid to undo it as fast as they can.

'I thought it would help with reading and counting,' says Anna.

She's so generous, thinks Lou. Beside it her own gift seems meagre.

'Thank you,' says Karen. 'What do you say, Molly?'

'Thank you.'

Anna bends down for Molly to kiss her cheek. 'I'm sorry I missed your party yesterday.'

'Don't be.' Karen raises her eyes to the skies. 'I've never heard so much shrieking.'

'It sounds fun.' Fleetingly, Lou wishes she'd been there.

'Here you two, pass that box over and I'll do it,' says Karen. Gently she prises the plastic toy from its protective polystyrene. 'Come on, I'm going to set this up for you on the end of the table. I'll just get the extension lead.' She turns to Anna. 'With any luck it'll keep them quiet for a bit and you can fill us in.'

As she leaves the room, Lou says, 'I hear you're Internet dating. Karen told me.'

'Yup.' Anna drops her voice. 'Actually, I'm trying to persuade her to do it too.' She jerks her head towards the door.

'Really?'

'It's been over a year.'

'I know, but   '

'It's quite fun, you know.'

'I know, I've done it. Not for a while, obviously . . . '

'Gosh, sorry, that was tactless. It's probably the last thing you want to hear at the moment. How are you doing? Sofia moved out yet?'

'She's collecting the last of her stuff today.'

Anna reaches across the kitchen table and squeezes Lou's hand. 'Aw. I am sorry.'

Lou gulps. To be shown sympathy only makes it worse. 'It's OK. I'm OK, honestly.'

Molly looks up from her toy. 'What's happened to Sofia?' Her face is anxious.

Lou hunts for the appropriate words for a small child. 'I'm afraid we're not going out together any more.'

'Oh,' says Molly. 'Is that why you're all sad?'

Dear me, thinks Lou. Is it that obvious? 'Yes, I suppose it is.'

'Does that mean you're going to go out with a boy now?' asks Molly.

Lou laughs. 'No.'

Molly resumes examining the buttons on her laptop.

Lou and Anna shake their heads.

'I feel terrible about that day, you know,' says Anna. 'I was thinking about it afterwards. I was awfully interfering.'

'No, you weren't. Don't worry. I couldn't have asked you

to drive me up to London one minute, let me offload on you all the way, then expect you to bugger off. Sofia knew that.'

'I should have kept my trap shut.'

'It wasn't your fault. The issues were far too big.'

Anna lowers her voice again. 'I think it's just that Sofia reminded me of Steve, going off and getting drunk, then being so unpleasant to you. It made me more impatient with her than she – and certainly you – deserved.'

'Maybe. Anyway, it's done. She's gone. Come on. I could do with cheering up. I want to hear about this online dating.'

'Got it.' Karen returns with the cable and slides past Molly and Luke to plug it in.

'What did you put in your ad?' asks Lou.

Karen turns on the laptop and locates a spelling game for the children. Luke, being older, takes over, and soon the 3D Dora is bouncing up and down in encouragement.

It's amazing how adept Karen is at sorting entertainment for her kids, thinks Lou. I wonder if I'll ever be like that.

Anna leans forward, eager to share. 'Even though I write ads for a living, I found it really hard to describe myself. Yet I seem to have had more interest than I know what to do with.'

'Seriously?'

'A hundred and ninety hits.' Lou can tell she's flattered. 'They haven't all emailed me, though lots have made me a favourite.'

Molly looks up. 'You're *my* favourite.'

'Molly, bless you,' Anna smiles.

Compared with some of the kids I see in my line of work,

Molly is such a sweet-natured child, thinks Lou. If only some of them could have this much love and attention, maybe they wouldn't have the issues they do.

'Perhaps I've had a big response because I said I liked children but didn't want them at this point in my life. I seem to have ended up with every single dad in the South East winking at me.'

'Nothing to do with you being attractive, then,' Karen teases.

'No. Lots of the women on there are gorgeous. Maybe I'm an easier prospect than a woman with kids.'

'Like me, you mean?' says Karen.

'Oh cripes. I'm sorry, I didn't mean it like that.'

Karen shrugs. 'It's fine. It's true, anyway.'

Lou is finding it hard to focus on the conversation, knowing that Sofia is at the flat packing up her stuff. She imagines Sofia loading her car with all her CDs and DVDs. Music they've listened to, films they've watched, together . . . Then she tunes back in. 'You *would* make a great stepmother.'

Molly stops playing, wriggles down from her seat, goes over to Anna and tugs at her sleeve.

Anna looks down. 'What is it?'

'If you're going to be a stepmother, does that mean you're not going to be our godmother any more?'

Anna hoots with laughter. 'Er, no, Molster, it doesn't.'

'Oh.' Molly frowns. 'It's just in Cinderella, the godmother's good and the stepmother's horrid.'

'You've been watching too much Disney,' says Karen to Molly. 'Not all stepmothers are horrid.'

As Molly goes back to her chair Luke scoffs, 'Anyway,

that's just a *story*, it's not real.' He gets a question right and 3D Dora bounces again.

'I want a go,' says Molly.

'Luke,' says Karen firmly. 'Let your sister have a turn. It's her present.'

Luke scowls. 'But she's rubbish at it.'

And Molly starts to cry.

Karen sighs and pulls her daughter to her side to comfort her.

Perhaps handling these two isn't plain sailing after all. Still, being a step- or godmother wouldn't be enough for me, thinks Lou. She pictures Sofia once more, and her heart twists.

'Lou . . . ' Now Karen is waving her hand in front of Lou's face. 'You've gone very quiet.'

'Sorry.'

'*We're* sorry,' says Karen. 'Everyone was getting a bit carried away. You OK?'

'Mm.' She blinks away tears.

'Any more news on the IVF?' asks Anna, more gently.

'I've got my first consultation at the clinic a week on Monday.'

'Good luck,' says Anna. 'You going on your own?'

'Yup. But don't worry. It's not like when I discovered that lump – this is something positive, hopefully. Though there is one thing I do want you both to know, but don't go round telling everyone.'

'What's that?' asks Karen.

Being online this morning, then seeing Karen with her

children this afternoon, has confirmed it for Lou. Never mind the squabbles.

'I'm going to share my eggs,' she says. 'So another woman can have a baby too.'

14

'What are you doing?' asks Rich.

His wife is sitting at the laptop, which is open on the kitchen table. He leans over her shoulder. 'Mm, you smell nice.'

Cath leans back against him for a moment. 'Look, I found this forum.'

He reads the chunk of type on screen:

. . . I really think it's God's will that two strangers can have such a magical relationship, and one day your child will understand how much you want to be a mum, and thank you for the journey you have been through. Rainbow Girl

'I'm not sure about God's will.' He continues to the next post. It appears to have been sent that afternoon.

Hi Rainbow Girl, Shadow and Annie33, Thanks for sharing your experience. Isn't this website brilliant? I discovered it today and I'm going through this on my own, so reading your stories has helped me feel less anxious, and I've decided to see if I can donate my eggs too. I'm not religious myself but I know what you mean, Rainbow Girl, about it being a very special thing to share with someone. You are an inspiration. Louloubelle

'What do you think about these women who opt to have a child on their own?' says Rich. That it seems so easy to cut men out of the loop continues to unnerve him.

'Up to them, I guess,' says Cath.

It's not the reply he was hoping for.

She clicks off the page.

'Hey, I was reading that!'

'Sorry, too slow. I want to register with this site.'

'Really?'

'Yup. Then I can join in the discussion.'

There's no point arguing.

*   *   *

Molly and Luke are in the living room watching a DVD; Anna has gone to meet her date. Once more it's just Karen and Lou in the kitchen.

'Are you in a hurry to get home?'

Lou has a vision of the flat, emptied of Sofia's possessions. 'Not specially.'

'Then stay for a bit, keep me company while I cook the kids' supper?'

'That'd be good. Can I do anything?'

'Peel these if you like.' She hands Lou a bag of potatoes. 'Do you mind if I ask you something?'

'Of course not.'

'You know the IVF and everything? I know I'm probably being a bit stupid, but who's going to father the child?'

'I thought I'd use an anonymous sperm donor.'

'Ah, I see.'

Can Lou detect judgement in Karen's voice? She is not naive; she knows her decision to try for a child will unsettle some people. 'Do you have a problem with that?' she asks, trying not to sound defensive.

Karen hesitates while she reaches up high to place a salad bowl on a shelf. 'Oh, no, not a problem, no. It's just, I was thinking, well, I really hope you don't mind my saying this . . . ' Her voice trails off. She seems flustered by the subject.

Oh dear, thinks Lou. Karen is so warm and compassionate, she'd assumed she would have her support. Lou girds herself for a confrontation but Karen says, 'It's very hard doing it all on your own, you know,' her voice cracked with emotion.

But of course: Karen is a single mum.

'It's pretty lonely.' Karen gulps. 'I miss Simon every single day. We all do . . . Luke more than Molly, I think. He's older, he can remember his father better . . . ' She stands motionless, plate in hand. Lou senses she's disappeared into the past. Then she's back. 'I don't want to speak out of turn.'

'You're not,' says Lou.

'It's just I was thinking – well, worrying – this all seems very fast. It's a massive decision you're taking.'

'I don't feel I have much choice,' says Lou. She explains that fibroids often recur, so she oughtn't to delay having a baby, and if she wants to share her eggs, she has only a year before she's too old to qualify.

'I didn't realize that. What horrible pressure. You poor thing.' Karen removes a box of fish fingers from the freezer. 'Life's a bugger, isn't it? Makes you wonder what you and I did to deserve everything it's thrown at us over the last year. Perhaps we were complete bitches in a past life.'

'How do you find it, bringing up Molly and Luke on your own?'

Karen tips some cooking oil into a tray and spreads it around with a wrapper she's saved from a pack of butter. How efficient, Lou thinks.

'Tough.' Karen looks directly at her. 'Bloody tough. And I'm lucky. They're good kids on the whole. But Luke's developed this habit of being rude to me – I think it's because he misses his dad, and he's angry – you'll probably know more about that than me. He finds social situations difficult and he seems to have problems with empathy. Only yesterday he said, "You look really old and fat in that, Mum," and I had to explain it wasn't the ideal way of getting me on side or the kind of comment I liked to hear – even if it is true.' Karen laughs, but Lou can sense she is smarting. 'So today he snuggles up to me and says, "You look really young and I like everything you wear." ' She smiles. 'I told him we might work on something in between.'

'Here you are, these are done.' Lou passes Karen the saucepan of potatoes. Karen puts them on the stove.

'I mean obviously it's different for me, because I did have a partner . . . ' Karen's voice fades again. 'So I – I mean we – are grieving as well. But still, it is a lot to undertake on your own, and I only work three days, down here in Brighton. My job's not that stressful, either, but you've more responsibility, and the commute. I don't think I could manage all that, personally.'

And Karen's very capable, thinks Lou. She gets to her feet, hunting for a bin to deposit the potato peelings. 'Would you like to meet someone else?'

'Here,' says Karen, opening a large ceramic pot on the countertop. 'I save it for compost at the allotment. But another man? Seriously, no. No way. Oh, I know Anna thinks I should do online dating or something—'

'I didn't know she'd spoken to you about it.'

'She hasn't directly, but I've known Anna since we were in our teens. I know when she's plugging something. She might be a copywriter and good at persuading people, but I can see through her "this is such *fun*, Karen" sales pitch – she's not very subtle. And I can tell you, I'm not about to do it.' She puts the tray of fish fingers into the oven and bangs the door with force. 'Sorry,' she says at once. 'That was a bit mean. I'm grateful to Anna, truly I am. It's just she and I are different – she's better at putting herself out there, she's more passionate, she moves faster than me.'

'She did seem to get over Steve quite quickly,' observes Lou.

'Probably because he treated her like shit. Excuse my language, but Christ I'm glad to see her shot of him! I liked him, don't get me wrong – sober, at any rate – but not as a partner for my friend. Did you hear he's back drinking again? No surprises there. It's such a shame . . . He had a lot going for him. Anyway, I can't forget Simon that fast, I really can't. I loved him. We were together twenty years.'

'I don't think she wants you to forget him.' Lou can see

both sides: Karen wanting to be allowed to grieve, Anna being keen to help her move on.

'I'm glad you understand. Anyway, I'm digressing. What I was trying to say is, naturally the children miss their dad, but it's more than that. I know I might sound awfully traditional, but I do think they suffer from not having a man about, too. Though I refuse to go out and get myself a partner just for the sake of it – that would be all wrong.'

Lou pauses for thought. Many of the kids she counsels have fathers who are either absent or inadequate or both, and whilst she wouldn't want to make sweeping judgements about their very diverse circumstances, all too often she sees the effects this has on the children. Truancy, drug-taking, self-harm, depression – Luke's tactlessness is a blip compared to the distress Lou sees on a daily basis. The last thing she wants is to create another unhappy child. Her relationship with her own mother is far from easy, so she knows what it feels like to be left wanting. How much worse it would have been without her dad. She wants to get it right.

'It's good to talk to you about it,' she says.

'It's one of the things I miss most about Simon – having him to talk to about the children,' says Karen. 'I don't know what I'd do without people like you – and Anna. But just simple things like this – sharing the cooking – I don't get to do with someone else any more.'

Again Lou thinks of Sofia, packing up her stuff, leaving her life. 'It's not how I'd have chosen to do any of this. But maybe there's a way I don't need to do it completely alone, even if I haven't got a partner.'

Hello there, I'm new to this forum too. A little over two years ago I went to the doctor because I couldn't get pregnant. I was desperate to have a child, but as at first I thought it was because of my age, it took a while for me to go. When I did I found out the real reason why: I had cancerous tumours on both ovaries. I had to have them removed, then chemotherapy and there was no possibility of freezing my eggs due to the progression of the cancer. As you can imagine, it was an extremely dark time. I was very scared, for months afterwards I was very down and anxious – I would never have got through it without my husband. He's so patient and kind, I'm very lucky. How he puts up with me sometimes I'll never know.

Finally, I've been told that I appear free of it, and now I only need to be checked every six months, so we are hoping to try for a baby again. I've had a scan of my uterus at my local hospital – they were able to save that, thank God – it seems in quite good shape considering. I live in Leeds but there aren't the same facilities here, so in the morning we're off to find out about the egg-sharing programme at a clinic in London. We've just got the money sorted, and though I know I shouldn't be too hopeful as there are so many hurdles, still I'm very excited. I'm 42 now so using a donor is my only hope. CathM

'You've been on that thing all evening,' observes Rich, coming back into the kitchen.

Cath yawns, stretches.

'Let's head to bed,' he says. 'Big day tomorrow.'

As if she needed reminding.

15

Cath glances at her watch. The consultant is running late and Rich is due at a meeting that afternoon; she doesn't want them to have to rush.

Over the last two years she has spent hours in waiting rooms; each has its own unique atmosphere. There's her GP's surgery in Headingley, with its scruffy plastic seating, dog-eared magazines and large collection of bashed and broken toys. There's the Oncology Institute at St James's Hospital, a multimillion-pound NHS showpiece with a vast glass atrium and waiting areas full of posters proudly declaring that everyone is 'aiming higher fighting cancer' which grated awfully when Cath was feeling at her lowest. And now there's this, with its careful fan of promotional brochures, well-tended potted plants and smart water cooler, it falls aesthetically somewhere between the two. Perhaps the people who run the clinic have decided that being too showy would only underline the exorbitant fees.

She looks around. Whereas her local surgery is packed with students and mothers with small children, here the age range is narrow (she'd hazard thirty to forty-five) and everyone appears pretty well heeled. But what unites them most strongly is that they all look as uncomfortable as she and Rich are. The woman opposite is studiously avoiding eye contact by picking at a loose thread on her jacket; a couple are holding hands so tightly it must hurt; beside them a man in uniform repeatedly checks his mobile.

It's as if none of us wants to admit we're actually here, she observes. But at least she isn't surrounded by huge pregnant-bellied women, as she was when she went for an ultrasound at Leeds General a week ago. She'd found that very hard.

Surely infertility is nothing to be ashamed of, she thinks. We're all in this together. Perhaps I should strike up a conversation. It only needs one of us and I'd feel much better if I could chat. But of course, this is London: strangers don't talk to one another. Maybe they all pour out their feelings anonymously online, as I have.

She checks the time again. Still the large white door remains resolutely closed.

Cath listens. Is that crying she can hear?

Is this fate, telling me to reconsider? she wonders. Maybe it's a sign that taking eggs from someone else and fertilizing them in a lab is an unnatural way of creating life. But I can't stop, not now. It's something I want so strongly, I don't care how unnatural it is. And anyway, isn't it *natural* to want to be a mum?

At last the door opens and a young woman emerges. She looks perfectly OK. Behind her is Dr Hassan. His hair is not as smooth and neat as when he gave his talk, and he is wearing a white coat over his shirt and trousers rather than a suit, but it's good to see a familiar face.

'Richard and Catherine Morris?' he says.

* * *

Lou is waiting in the Kemptown Bookshop cafe, preparing for another tricky conversation. Her friend soon arrives, panting up the stairs.

'Mm, that looks good.' Howie peers through his little round glasses at her bagel and latte. 'Can I get you anything else?'

'I'm fine.'

He takes off his jacket, removes his woolly hat to reveal the dome of his bald head, and goes to the counter to place his order. As he returns to the table, he looks round at the shelves. 'Ooh, remind me to get something for my hols while we're here.' He is a voracious reader, and talks fast too. 'I thought your day off was Friday, how come you can meet today? It's usually only us freelancers who get to do coffee in the week.'

'The rest of the staff have an INSET day – I didn't have to go in.'

'Ah, I see. Great to see you anyway, doll. I wanted to say how sorry I was to hear about Sofia.'

'Thanks.' Lou swiftly changes the subject. 'Though it's not that I wanted to talk to you about.'

'No? So what is it then?' He clasps his hands, clearly excited to hear. 'It sounded very intriguing, this being sworn to secrecy.'

Typical, thinks Lou. Howie loves to create drama. 'That's not what I said. It's just personal, that's all.'

'Oh, right.' He appears disappointed, and Lou hesitates. Howie is a dear friend and entertaining company, yet she's unsure he's cut out for what she's about to propose. But she doesn't want to prejudge: in the end, who is she to decide?

'I was wondering if you might . . . well, um . . . if anyone has ever asked you before, to . . . er . . . if you were interested in becoming a father.'

Howie's mouth falls open. And stays open.

Lou has known him many years, but has never known him at a loss for words. She looks at him, raises her eyebrows, smiles encouragingly.

Eventually, he lets out a guffaw. 'Are you serious?'

Lou is disappointed. It seems her instinct was right: the idea was a bad one. 'Mm, yes, sort of . . . '

'Me? A father? You want me to give you some special Howie sperm?'

Put like that, the idea is hardly appealing. 'Well . . . '

'Gosh.' Howie sits back, winded.

He already knows about her break-up with Sofia, but not why, so she explains. 'I was planning to use an anonymous donor, but changed my mind. Have you never considered it?'

Howie leans forward again. 'A straight chum of mine asked a few years back – she was in her mid thirties and had got her knickers in a right twist, convinced she was going to be left on the shelf for eternity. Luckily for her she met someone in the end, so luckily for me, I didn't get to "read" ' – he indicates quote marks in mid air – 'for twenty minutes in a room looking at the underwear section of a Freeman's catalogue.'

Lou laughs. 'To be clear – it's not just sperm I'm thinking of. Otherwise the anonymous route would be far less fraught. It's quicker and there are fewer hurdles, and I don't have the luxury of time on my side. But I suppose . . .' She hesitates, trying to work out how best to express the essence of what's she's been mulling all night. 'I think it's important my child has a dad.' She frowns, unsure if Howie needs much detail, but she is springing this on him – she's still acclimatizing herself – and she wants to make sure they understand one another as best they can. 'Perhaps because I was so close to my own father, and also, well, I see how important male role models are to the kids I work with. Ideally, I want someone to co-parent.'

'Ah.' He pauses. 'It would be a pretty massive test of a friendship.'

'I appreciate that. It's because I value our friendship I'm asking.'

Howie rubs his beard. 'Seriously, doll, I'm flattered, but in all honesty, I think I'll have to decline the invitation. It could have too many ramifications, don't you think? I do believe you'd be a great mum, but I'd be a lousy dad. It's enough responsibility for me borrowing a book off someone, never mind "loaning" some sperm. The fact you want the guy to play an active role seals it. I'm a funny old sod, and I'm pretty selfish, as you know.'

It's a shame, but on reflection Lou already knew this was how he'd respond. As a freelance journalist, Howie works the hours he chooses and holidays when he likes. His peripatetic life would be hard to let go, never mind integrate into any formal childcare agreement. And at least he can't now get huffy that he *wasn't* asked. Though she's at a loss as to where else to turn. She sips her coffee, perplexed.

'Perhaps you can find someone online? There must be some sort of would-be-gay-dads' group somewhere. You can hook up with just about anyone these days. I should know.'

That's another reason for reservations, thinks Lou: Howie's predilection for no-strings sex. But bringing up a child with a total stranger? She looks round at the men in the book-shop. The middle-aged guy behind the counter of the cafe can make a decent latte, but he's wearing a wedding ring. The elderly hippie peering at the shelves looks as if he still has a problem engaging with the real world – he's in sandals way before it's warm enough to justify it. And the young lad next to them is reading *Nausea*; that says it all.

She shakes her head. Getting together with a sperm donor via the Internet would be too random. 'I've no problem with dating online, believe me. I've been chatting to women going through IVF on a forum too, and it's been very helpful. The way everyone supports one another is fantastic. But it takes a long time to get to know someone that way, and my bio-logical clock seems to be ticking so fast. The fibroid might return if I leave it.'

'I see what you mean.' Howie peers into his empty cup as if the dregs might give him inspiration.

Then he looks up. 'I've had a brainwave,' he says.

16

Adam feels his mobile buzz in his pocket. Whoever it is can wait, he thinks. This patient is his priority.

He approaches the bed, his tread soft. 'How are you doing today, Mr Malhotra?'

The old man is sleeping. Adam has visited this house several times over the last few weeks; it's often the way.

'He's not been so good, doctor,' says his wife. She hugs her sari to her chest, as if to protect herself from her own observation.

'So what's changed, would you say?' Adam asks her. A glance at his patient reveals she is right: Mr Malhotra's breathing is shallower, his lips are cracked and dry.

'He's not eating,' says Mrs Malhotra quietly.

'What, nothing at all?'

She bites her lip. 'No.'

'Oh dear,' says Adam. 'I'm sorry to hear that. You were giving him soft foods, like I suggested?'

'Yes, I made him khichdi. But' – she gestures to a bowl on the dressing table containing a pale yellow substance – 'he has not touched it, you can see.'

'May I ask, what is khichdi?'

'Just rice and lentils and vegetables, doctor. Very mild. He likes it very much – especially when he is not too good. He says it takes him back to his childhood.'

She sighs heavily, and Adam's heart goes out to her. He has faced similar situations before – there are a lot of elderly people in the catchment area of his Saltdean practice. Mrs Malhotra's husband has not long left, he can tell, and he knows she knows it too. The most he can do is to help make these moments as physically comfortable as possible for his patient, and offer words of kindness to his wife.

'A package arrived an hour ago,' she says. 'It looks like something from the hospital. It's in the living room.'

'I'll go and see. You wait here.'

When he's heading downstairs, his mobile vibrates again: whoever it is must have left a message. He returns to the room a couple of minutes later. Mrs Malhotra is still standing where he left her, arms folded, in the bedroom. It's the waiting that's so tough, he thinks. He touches her elbow to bring her back to the present. She jumps, as if she'd forgotten about him entirely.

'It's the drip I requested,' says Adam. 'I can set it up, but we'll need some more light. Shall we open the curtains a little – do you mind?'

'Of course, of course.' She does as she's bid, revealing a pink and orange colour scheme that sing-songs defiantly in spite of the dullness of the day.

He senses she'll feel better lending a hand than watching powerless, so asks her to undo the smaller boxes. Removing the tape makes a ripping sound. Mr Malhotra's eyelids flicker.

'Ah, you're with us,' says Adam, leaning close to his ear. 'Good afternoon.'

Mr Malhotra gives a nod, barely discernible.

Adam assembles the equipment with practised speed. Mrs Malhotra tidies up behind him.

'There's very much packaging,' she says.

'It's a terrible waste. I'm sure they could use less.'

'I suppose they have to keep it . . . What is the word? Ah, yes, sterile?'

'But still, can't be saving the planet. Now, Mr Malhotra, I'm just going to insert a needle in the back of your hand.' Adam raises his voice a touch, to counteract the morphine. 'Because we're going to put you on this drip, here, see this?' He wheels the apparatus to the side of the bed.

Mr Malhotra is so doped up he probably won't feel anything, but Adam is aware his wife is flinching, so acts as fast as he can. Presently the tube is in place; he examines the bag to ensure the liquid is getting through, checks there is adequate pain relief in the machine and turns to her. 'There. Done. That should help.'

They pull the curtains closed again and go to the door, turning in unison to check before they head downstairs. Sure enough, Mr Malhotra is asleep again.

I hope he is dreaming of khichdi, thinks Adam.

* * *

Cath fixes her gaze on a crack in the wall. She feels a prick in the crook of her arm, hears the rustle of starched fabric as the doctor reaches past her.

'There, done. Just press for a moment, if you wouldn't mind.'

She wedges the pad of cotton wool firmly against her skin, looks round. Dr Hassan is focused on labelling several little vials of dark-maroon liquid.

'I didn't realize you were taking so much.' In spite of everything she's been through, seeing her own blood still spooks her.

Rich is sitting close by, looking apprehensive. 'What are you going to do with it all?'

'Given we're going to use donor eggs in your wife's case, we do standard tests for the blood group, hepatitis, HIV, rubella and chlamydia. We'll check your blood for the same things. We'll also check you for cystic fibrosis.'

'So do you test the donor for exactly the same things too?' asks Cath, at once captured by the thought of another woman going through a parallel experience. Will she see the same doctor, sit in the same chair?

'Yes, but we also look at their hormone levels, as they can tell us about the fertility of their eggs.'

'She'll be younger than me though, won't she?'

Dr Hassan nods. 'We don't accept donors over the age of thirty-five because there is an increased risk of Down's syndrome.'

'How long will it take to find someone?' asks Rich.

'Well, we have to make sure they are a good physical match. I aim to oversee each patient personally.'

That could take ages, thinks Cath. She's eager to get going.

The doctor seems to pick up her mood. 'Hopefully it won't

be too long, but two or three months is the minimum, really. I should warn you that it can be as much as a year.'

'A *year*?' How on earth can they wait as long as that? She's forty-two!

'Hopefully it will be much sooner.'

'So how like me will my donor be?' Again Cath feels the presence of this other woman, almost as if she were in the room. She wonders where she is at this moment, whether she's been to visit the clinic already.

'We'll take into account your height, skin tone, build and hair and eye colour.'

How eerie, thinks Cath. There's a mirror woman, then, somewhere out there, with mousy hair and blue eyes. 'You can match me with someone thinner if you like.'

The doctor laughs and turns to Rich. 'We'll take you into account as well. You both have blue eyes, so we'll avoid pairing you with a brown-eyed donor, if we can.'

'Makes sense,' says Rich.

Cath is still thinking of the mirror woman. It's all very well pairing us physically, but what if she's nothing like me otherwise? What if she is stupid, or bigoted, or bad at everything I'm good at? If she hasn't an artistic bone in her body, or is silent and aloof? Though surely Rich and I would influence a child by spending time with them anyway. If he or she is brought up in Leeds, they'll have a Yorkshire accent no matter where the donor lives.

The doctor interrupts her thoughts. 'You do need to understand that we'll have to harvest ten eggs from the donor to allow her to share them with you.'

'How can you guarantee that?' asks Rich.

'We can't, obviously. But that's why we check every donor, to make sure there's no imbalance or anything that might prevent them producing eggs. Then we stimulate their hormones to make them produce more.'

Cath frowns. 'So what's the usual number of eggs harvested after that, then?'

'We aim to get at least ten; it's often more.'

'What if there's an odd number?'

'We usually give the extra one to the donor, for obvious reasons. This is something you should talk through with our counsellor, so you can think about it seriously before you go ahead.'

You're telling me, thinks Cath.

'We'd also recommend that you consider the option of ICSI, to maximize the chances of success.' He pronounces the word 'ick-see'.

'What's that?' asks Rich.

'It stands for Intracytoplasmic Sperm Injection.'

'I've seen that on the telly,' says Cath.

'Quite likely,' says the doctor. 'In traditional IVF, many sperm are placed together with an egg, with the aim that one of the sperm will enter and fertilize it. With ICSI, the embryologist takes a single sperm and injects it into an egg with a sort of needle.'

'And the needle doesn't harm the egg?' asks Cath. She seems to recall reading something about increased risk of birth defects with ICSI.

'There's been some research into it, but the studies are inconclusive,' says Dr Hassan. 'It's often used for men with a low sperm count, for instance, or poor sperm movement.'

'But there's nothing wrong with my sperm,' says Rich, indignant. Cath is momentarily stung that he should seem so defensive about it. Then he adds, 'Or not as far as we know.'

'No, no, I appreciate that,' says the doctor. 'But here we use ICSI in other circumstances, such as egg sharing, too.'

'Is it more expensive?' asks Rich.

'Slightly,' nods the doctor.

'How much more is it?'

'About £800.'

Cath's heart sinks. The bank was unwilling to lend to them as it is.

Dr Hassan reads her expression. 'In the long run it's often more cost-effective for egg-sharing couples, because of the excellent success rates.'

'So we're less likely to have to come back?'

'Exactly.'

We'll do the sums later, thinks Cath. She pushes on. 'Is there any difference in terms of the treatment?'

'Not really, since ICSI is done in the lab. We wouldn't recommend it if we didn't think it's likely to produce a better outcome, but by all means look into it yourselves and discuss it with your counsellor in due course.' He turns to Rich. 'So, as we're on the subject, perhaps this might be a good moment for you to produce a sperm sample? You can do it while I give your wife an ultrasound.'

And before Cath has a chance to say she'd like her husband to stay, the doctor has handed Rich a jar and sent him off down the corridor.

17

As Adam gets back in his car, he remembers that his mobile rang earlier and whoever it was left a message. He's been longer with Mr Malhotra than he had intended, so clips in the earphone to listen whilst driving.

'Wotcha doc,' says a familiar voice. 'It's me. I'm sitting in our favourite haunt – the Kemptown Bookshop cafe – with my friend Lou. Remember her? You've met a few times. Anyway, we've just been talking about something that I think might interest you. She'd prefer for me not to go into it on your voicemail, so call me back, as I think it might interest you . . . *very* . . . *much* . . . *indeed.*'

Get on with it, mate, thinks Adam. Some of us have jobs to do. Nonetheless, his curiosity is piqued. He cuts the voice-mail short and presses ringback.

* * *

'I'll pass you over,' says Howie.

Lou takes his phone. 'Is that Adam?'

'Yes, it is. Lou, hello, how are you?'

Lou feels stupidly nervous. 'I'm good, thanks.' She's often sought out Adam at Howie's parties, finding him refreshingly open and easy to talk to. She says to Howie, 'I'm sorry, but I'm just going to take this outside.' It might seem mean excluding him, but she's justified, surely. She heads out of the bookshop and onto the pavement. It's very blowy – St George's Road runs parallel to the seafront – and there's the noise of traffic, but at least it's just the two of them. 'Is this a good moment?'

'I've a few minutes, yes. I'm in the car on my way to see a patient.'

She'd much rather meet Adam in person, and she's barely had time to prepare herself for the call, but unless he's interested there's no point going further. He sounds busy, so she tries to be swift. She explains that she's poised to undergo IVF and wraps up by saying, 'I understand you've been asked to father a child before but said no, is that right?'

'Kind of . . . Initially I said yes, actually. One of my closest friends, Evie, and her wife, Nikita, asked me. I think you might have met them at Howie's last bash, too. They live in Hove. Anyway, now they have a little boy, and Nikita is expecting another baby soon, but before that, when they were seriously discussing having children, they approached me about being a donor to both of them; the idea was each would get pregnant and have one child. Hold on a moment . . . ' There's a pause. 'Sorry, that was a roundabout.'

'So why didn't you go through with it?' Howie has already outlined some of this, but she'd like to hear it from Adam.

'Well . . . at first it seemed like a great prospect, so I went

143

and donated sperm, had all the tests and got it frozen and everything, you know?'

Lou has done her research and is aware of the protocol. Any *'known donor sperm'*, as it's called, has to be quarantined for six months before it can be used. The same is not true for spouses or partners, but it would be a legal requirement for someone like Adam.

'Anyway,' Adam continues, 'so I was very into the idea, but the more we talked, the more I came to understand the implications. Really what they wanted was that they would be the parents and I would have some kind of loose uncle status, no more.' He sighs. 'Why are you asking?'

She answers with another question – she doesn't want to give too much away until she's more sure he's onside. 'So let me get this straight: you *might* be interested in becoming a father . . . in the right circumstances?'

'Yeah, I suppose . . . I've sort of always seen myself as having kids.' Lou gets why: his warmth and openness is why she gravitated to him at social gatherings herself. 'But with my friends, I decided I couldn't see a child all the time knowing I was the father, so I pulled out. Frankly, I'd rather donate anonymously to a couple on the other side of the world. Though actually . . . hang on, another roundabout . . . ' Lou is on tenterhooks. 'I wouldn't do that either. I couldn't be that detached. I find it hard enough with some of my patients, let alone my own offspring.'

Lou wants to applaud: he seems such a kindred spirit. Clever old Howie, she thinks.

He continues, 'I don't really see myself being just a mere

sperm donor – though I know there's a shortage – that's too clinical. I'm not that altruistic, I'm afraid.'

Lou knows she mustn't seem too eager. If he's not into the idea with her it could be embarrassing. She ventures, 'How about if you *could* have a more active role in a child's life?'

'Depends on the situation, who with, where, when . . . '

'I understand – it's a massive decision.'

'I have googled several times, to see what else is out there.'

'Really?'

'Not that I got anywhere much. It seemed too haphazard, doing it that way. Mind you, this is a pretty weird conversation to be having in a car . . . ' There's another long pause. This is when he says no, thinks Lou. 'I take it you're asking if I'd like to be a father?'

'Um, er . . . Yes.' No sooner has she said it, than she wishes she could back-pedal. 'Or at least discuss it, if you'd be willing, as a possibility. I'm like you, in some ways; using the Internet seems a bit clinical, such an unknown quantity. Like dating but worse . . . ' Shut up, Lou, she thinks. Adam may be online in that capacity himself; as far as she can remember he's been single a while. 'Don't get me wrong, I've nothing against meeting people that way; I've done it – I just mean imagine if it went wrong and you ended up tethered to someone dreadful for the rest of your life. That wouldn't be great for the child either.'

'Happens to a lot of people.'

'Yes, I know.'

Lou can hear the engine has stopped.

'Listen, I could talk to you about this for ages, but I really must go,' says Adam. Lou's heart sinks; he is going to turn her down. Of course he is. He barely knows her, and he may not have liked her that much when they did meet. Maybe she imagined they got on. 'I've been running late all afternoon. I'm so sorry. Though yes, to answer your question, I would be interested in at least discussing it, though of course I can't say this quickly if I definitely would go through with it. Why don't we hook up?'

Inside, Lou dances a jig. 'That'd be great.'

'Tell you what. You live in Kemptown, don't you?'

'Yes, on Magdalen Street.'

'I come past your road on my way home from Saltdean. How about we meet for a drink at the Crown tonight, if you're free?'

18

'Ah, *there* you are,' says Sukey, opening the door. 'I wondered where on earth you'd got to.'

'Sorry.' I said half five, Cath thinks. It's only ten to six, and when you have to get across London, I call that on time. And a 'hello' would be nice. But she refrains from saying anything.

As Cath follows Sukey down the hall, she recalls Rich's first impression of her sister-in-law. 'Blimey, she looks high maintenance,' he'd said. Given that Rich had merely glimpsed her going up the stairs, Cath had been impressed. 'How do you know?' 'High-maintenance arse,' he'd nodded. It's true: Sukey is always immaculately made-up and turned out; even after giving birth to twins, she plunged back to a size 10 within weeks as if she were an elastic band. 'You wait,' she'd said. 'Her real talent is for making you feel you're always wrong.' Here they are, barely two sentences exchanged, and Cath is seemingly at fault again.

She enters the kitchen and gasps. Since she was last in Twickenham, Mike and Sukey have had an extension built.

It all looks so expensive, so pristine, so well organized that she's first impressed, then jealous, then self-critical. While her and Rich's kitchen is neither small nor Spartan, it is ill planned. Recipe books, spice jars, mismatched crockery, postcards from friends, houseplants in need of re-potting, olive oil bottles that are too tall for any of the cupboards – their kitchen has evolved, whereas this vast arena has clearly been conceived by an architect. It shines with polished chrome and white laminate; everything is neatly away, out of sight. If Cath found it hard to imagine children living in the house before (and she did), she now finds it impossible. She wonders if perhaps Sukey has put out the twins with the recycling by mistake.

'Have a seat.' A flick of the wrist conveys that Cath should sit at the breakfast bar, not the main table. 'I'll make us some tea. What kind would you like?' Sukey opens a cupboard, removes a large wicker basket.

Cath climbs onto a high stool and sees what's being proffered. There is every manner of fruit and herbal infusion – Sukey is as meticulous about her diet as her home. 'Just builders' is fine.'

'Ha! You're so like Mike,' laughs Sukey.

Cath is usually pleased to be compared with her younger brother, but suspects a backhanded compliment. Surely most people drink regular tea, she thinks, and after hours of being poked and prodded I've earned one? She wishes Rich were here to witness the nuances of the encounter, but he'll get here after his meeting; she'll have to cope as best she can.

While the kettle boils, Cath notices Sukey doesn't ask how her day has gone.

'Where are the children?' Cath is weary, but has been looking forward to seeing her nephews.

'Doing their homework. Perhaps it's best not to interrupt.' The boys go to a private school with exacting academic standards.

'And Mike?'

'Upstairs in his office.'

Before Sukey can prohibit that too, Cath says, 'I'll just go and say hello,' and gets down from her stool to hunt him out. On the way she can't resist sneaking a peek at the twins. They're in the dining room, heads down, focused on their notebooks. Alfie glances up and sees her.

'Auntie Cath!' he exclaims.

'Shh,' she says, putting a finger to her lips. 'I'll talk to you later.' And she blows him a kiss, even though she knows it'll make him cringe.

Mike works in a converted loft at the top of the house. She taps on the door and he swivels around in his leather chair.

'Sis! Hello, sorry, I didn't hear you arrive – I'd have come down.'

'It's OK.' She plants a kiss atop his receding pate. 'You busy?'

'Boring figures; nothing that won't wait.' Mike runs his own business, importing wine. He leans back in his chair, folds his arms behind his head. He looks older, thinks Cath, even though it's only a few months since she's seen him. Maybe he's put on weight. It's hard to tell: no matter how healthy the menu Sukey urges him to adopt, he remains big and bear-like. 'So, how was the hospital?'

'Clinic.' Cath wrinkles her nose. 'Bit of an ordeal, to be honest. I mean, they were perfectly nice, really understanding in fact, but there's an awful lot for us both to get our heads round. So many tests. Plus it's so expensive. It's nine and a half grand a pop. If you'll forgive the pun.'

'Bloody hell.' Mike lets out a long breath. 'Isn't it cheaper up north?'

'Actually, no. The nearest clinic that offers egg sharing is Newcastle – still a schlep. There's little between them all cost-wise, but more choice of donors here. The best alternative would probably be to go abroad, though that's got drawbacks too. Still, I hadn't quite realized how much we'll have to be up and down to London – it's a big commitment. We might need to stay again soon, if that's OK.'

'Um, I'd need to check with Sukey but—'

'It'd be a real help. There's no way we can afford to stay at a hotel each time. Though' – Cath grins, feeling a swell of optimism – 'it'll be worth it. I know it's dear, but, well, you'd have paid nine and a half grand for the boys, wouldn't you?'

'Of course.'

Cath and Rich think the twins are somewhat spoilt, but there's no denying Mike and Sukey adore their kids. 'And at least this way we're not relying on my crappy old body.' Cath gestures at her middle. She can say this to Mike; he's similarly derisive about his own physique: Rich would protest she's being hard on herself. 'We'll get nice new eggs from a woman in her twenties or early thirties.'

'So what happens next?'

'We have to be synched with our donor.'

'We . . . ?'

'Yes, Rich too. We need his sperm, don't forget. They've taken a sample to test it.'

'Oh yes.' Mike looks embarrassed. 'It sounds very complicated.'

'It's far more complicated for the woman who's donating. She has to take these drugs to make her produce lots of eggs, whereas I've three weeks of taking pills and one injection. That's it.'

'Long as it works. What are the odds of it not?'

Cath can feel him studying her reaction. She doesn't want to think about that. 'I believe it will.'

'I know other people who've been through IVF and they've had to have several goes.'

'But it's been successful in the end.'

'Mm, but at nearly ten grand a throw, can you afford to do it more than once?'

'Nine and a half.' Cath wishes Mike wouldn't bring her down. It was one of the reasons that attracted her to Rich initially – he reminded her of her little brother. Not physically, but when she met Rich she could imagine him being friends with Mike, and that seemed to bode well. Time has proved her right, but she wishes Mike would adopt a different tone. She's had her enthusiasm tempered by Rich already; only yesterday her mother was the same. Don't they understand how much this means to her?

Mike coughs. 'There is one thing I wanted to, um, say . . . ' He looks down at the floor, swivels his chair to and fro. The action reminds her of the way he used to scuff his shoes when he'd been caught doing something he shouldn't as a child.

'What?'

'I'm glad we got the chance to talk just you and me, as, well, er . . . I know this is a bit awkward, but . . . '

'Yes?'

He coughs again. 'It might be easier if you didn't mention it in front of Sukey.'

'Oh.' Cath frowns, immediately wary. 'Why?'

Mike scratches his head, appearing to hunt for the right words. 'It's only she seems to have a bit of a thing about it.' His mouth contorts.

'About what – my having a baby?' Cath is shocked, has to lean back against the door frame. She and Sukey don't get on that well, she knows, though she and Mike have never admitted this to one another. But Sukey not wanting her to have a child?

'It's not your having a baby as such . . . '

'So what is it, then?' Anger mounting, Cath has an urge to go back downstairs and have it out with Sukey there and then. How dare she? When Cath has always been so atten-tive towards her children!

'Hold on a minute—' Sensing her reaction, Mike gets to his feet. 'It's not that simple. It's the whole egg-sharing issue, you see. She doesn't agree with it, um . . . morally. Doesn't think it's natural. Or right.'

'Then I want to talk to her about it.'

Mike shakes his head. 'I wouldn't. You don't know how much I've tried, honestly.'

Maybe that's what's ageing him – he's bottling up so much tension. He spends a lot of time smoothing things in the wake of Sukey's rigidity, Cath has seen it countless times.

'Let me chat it through with her, Mike. I can explain the ins and outs so much better than you.'

She turns to go and find her, but he follows, grabs her arm. 'Really, Cath, it's best left alone.' His voice is firm.

'I don't want to leave it alone, it matters too much to me.'

'Do you think I don't know that?'

'So all the more reason. You understand, she should too.'

'Sukey doesn't work that way – I often have to let things go that I get and she doesn't.'

How awful, thinks Cath. The desire to defend her brother only makes her more determined. 'Honestly, I'll talk her round.'

But Mike steps in front of her, barring the way. 'Cath, I don't think you get it: this is a no-go area. Seriously. She's like a dog with a bone about it.'

'In what way?'

Finally, he comes out with it. 'I had to push to make her let you stay.'

Momentarily Cath is speechless. Then she says, 'But I'm your sister!'

Again he looks at the floor, his shoes; his lips twist. Finally, he admits, 'She says any baby of yours will be no relative of ours – or the boys' – and no matter how hard I try to make her see otherwise, that's her view.'

'You're kidding!'

'I'm not. You *can* stay here with us – I managed to persuade her that was only reasonable, though I'm not sure it would be next time. I'm really sorry, truly I am. I didn't want to tell you, but I guess I had to.'

It seems there's nothing she can say or do just then, so Cath heads downstairs after her brother, seething.

Forget tea, she thinks. What I need is a stiff drink.

19

It's early evening; the Crown is almost empty. Adam is propping up the bar. He waves her over.

'Lou, how lovely to see you.' He pecks her on each cheek. He smells of aftershave. It's not to Lou's taste, but she can't have everything.

Discreetly, she takes in his appearance. His face is very round, she thinks, a bit Munchkinish . . . In fact, he's pretty round all over – he's got a definite belly on him – and hmm . . . he's not that tall. He's probably only the same height as she is: about five foot six. He may be five foot seven, but no more than that. That really is a bit short. Though his hair is good. It's rich auburn, thick and fluffy, not bad for a man of – what? She'd guess he's forty. And he's got nice skin too. He's unlined, has a healthy glow to him. So he should – he's a doctor. Not that it always follows.

'Great to see you, Adam.' She wonders if he's assessing her in the same vein.

He steps back and smiles. She can see laughter creasing up his eyes; they're deep brown, like berries. His expression seems to say *we're in this together*. He is wearing an olive-green jacket and cords, his shirt is unbuttoned at the neck. His style reminds her of a geography teacher; she can almost picture him with children already.

'So, can I get you a drink?' she asks. His glass is nearly empty. Perhaps he's not entirely clean-living.

'I could murder another bitter. I've had a heck of a day. But better not, I'm driving. Packet of salt and vinegar crisps would be good, though.'

She signals to the barman and orders herself a lime and soda. She could swear she can feel him checking out her profile as she does so.

'Cheers then,' he says. 'Bit odd this, eh? Like a date, but not.'

'My mother would love it,' says Lou. Here they are in a good old-fashioned pub with all the trimmings – brown leather chairs and worn oak tables, deep red carpet, beer on tap, locals playing darts – a man and a woman enjoying a drink before dinner, just as Irene and Lou's father occasionally used to. All too easily Lou can imagine her mother convincing herself that she and Adam are a 'proper' couple.

Adam laughs. 'Oh dear, one of those.'

Lou nods. 'Exactly. Sofia used to say it's like she's still living in the 1950s.' Lou gulps. The mention of Sofia still hurts – she mustn't go there.

'Sofia, oh yes . . . I hope you don't mind my asking, but before we go any further, I would like to know: where does she stand in all this?'

'Actually . . . We broke up a few weeks ago.'

'Oh, I'm sorry . . . ' Adam reaches for Lou's hand. Anna

did just the same, thinks Lou, and I don't even know Adam that well. I must prompt concern. She's not entirely comfortable being the object of pity. Or maybe she's more aware of the gesture because she's been so missing physical contact.

She may as well be honest – she doesn't want to start off avoiding the truth. 'It was partly the issue of kids that led to our break-up.'

'She wasn't keen?'

'Frankly, no.'

'That's a shame. You were a great couple.'

'Mm . . . ' Again Lou swallows.

'Sorry, tactless of me. Let's change the subject. You can fill me in on Sofia another time. Your mum – you were saying she'd love to see this – you and me . . . ?'

'God, I hate to think what she'd say if she knew the actual reason we're getting together.' Oops, that might sound rude. Lou explains, 'It didn't seem worth the aggravation of telling her about the baby thing till I'd worked it out properly for myself.'

'She'd have a problem with it?'

'I think so. I only came out to her a year ago. She's getting there . . . But my having kids: I might be wrong, but I can't see her approving.'

'Oh dear.' Adam takes a sip of beer. 'It sounds as if you're having to deal with a lot of opposition.'

'You could say that.' His observation makes Lou appreciate just how much she's had to face over the last few months. 'Though I guess many gays have a tough time becoming parents for one reason or another.'

'Perhaps one thing we gain from being gay is we have to

jump through so many hoops to make it happen, we think everything through more carefully.' Adam takes a large mouthful of crisps; healthy appetite, she notes. Good. Picky eating riles her; she wouldn't want it in her children. He continues, 'I know lots of straight – and gay – people who disagree, but personally, I think parenting has so much more to do with character traits than orientation.'

'Me too.' Lou considers her mother and father: both straight, yet when he was alive, her relationship with her father was much easier. Perhaps he could have helped her broach the subject with her mum. She says, 'Sofia was convinced my mum would freak if I have a baby.'

Suddenly Adam thumps the top of the bar so hard the liquid in their glasses sways from side to side. 'No disrespect to your mum . . . but it drives me nuts when people think they can judge who should and who should not be parents!' he exclaims. Lou is surprised – and pleased – by the force of his reaction. 'God knows how many patients I see – I presume your work's even worse – where straight folk don't give a second thought to major life decisions and go around making every bad choice possible – especially about having kids. Yet no one makes sweeping statements about how their sexuality affects their parenting skills.'

'Tell me about it,' says Lou, leading the way to one of the round oak tables. Even so many weeks after her operation, she's not comfortable standing for long. 'You should see some of the parents of the kids I work with. At school we've got this boy whose mother's had six children by five different men.'

Adam pulls up a stool. 'Crikey. Are the children all still living with her?'

'No, four are in care.'

'Four!'

Lou nods. 'And Aar—' – she stops herself revealing his name in the nick of time –'he's a lovely lad underneath, but no wonder he's got anger issues.'

Adam holds out his crisp bag and Lou delves for a handful. Already she's finding it a relief to talk to him. Sharing with Karen and Anna has been a great help; given she's known them both a relatively short while, it's remarkable how comfortable she feels with them – probably because of everything they've been through. Nevertheless, neither is exactly on her wavelength when it comes to having kids. Sofia and Howie are even further from her; neither has reached that point in life, maybe they never will. But with Adam, at last she feels able to air some of her most fervent beliefs. 'You know, I hope some of what I've experienced would actually make me a *better* parent. Because my own mother's not that tolerant – she's rather uptight, generally – I'm aware of how I might do things differently – hopefully better – if I were to become a mum myself.'

Adam picks up the baton. 'I was bullied at school – it's that common story; I didn't quite fit in. I was never part of a group. So I gravitated to the teachers: they protected me, I suppose, I always seemed to get on better with adults. Then the other kids resented that, decided I was a teacher's pet. I guess they sensed I was different; you know how quick some can be to pick up any weakness and home in . . . ' It's hard to imagine this now: Adam seems so at ease with himself. 'But like you, I believe these experiences can give us a more acute awareness of children's feelings and the effect these things have on them.' He tips the remainder of the crisps directly into his mouth from the packet. 'I recall you saying something about your own childhood giving you compassion for the kids you work with.'

Lou is flattered he's remembered their conversation; it was a while back. 'It's true, they are linked.' She assimilates a moment then says, 'I think you've hit on one of the main reasons I want to have a child.'

'Oh?'

'Mm. It's simple really: I just want to create a happy person.'

Adam smiles. 'That's a lovely reason. And a much better explanation than many people might give.'

'I hope they wouldn't suffer because of my orientation, though we have become much more accepted, don't you agree?'

'I guess so. Anyway, who'd ever want to be *totally* normal? Imagine having no quirks or idiosyncrasies. It's what makes us us.'

At that moment the door of the pub opens. An old man enters; makes his way, unsteady, slow, to the bar. Lou recognizes him: he lives in the attic flat directly opposite; the street is so narrow his window is no more than twenty feet from hers. She's chatted to him occasionally in the newsagent, he's been a resident of Magdalene Street for decades, but this is the first time she's seen him in here. He is fragile and solitary; she's always assumed he doesn't get out much, but there's a touch of the dandy in his dress tonight and his long, cobwebby hair looks recently combed. He orders a whisky mac, carries it shakily to a nearby table, sits, gets out a broadsheet paper and pen, folds the pages back, and begins the crossword as if this were his second home. He reminds her of a character from a fairytale, and she feels honoured to add to her picture of his routine. She and Adam pause a moment, watching him transfixed, silent save for the sound of Adam crunching. Then Adam swallows, and they come back to earth.

20

There's a knock on the bay window. Rich gurns at them through the pane. Thank goodness he's here; Cath is bursting to tell him about Sukey. But Mike beats her to answering the door.

Rich steps into the living room, the cool of outdoors clings to him. 'Phew, that was a long one. Bloody planning.' He throws down his jacket over the back of the vast leather sofa. 'Got to go back tomorrow first thing. That meeting ran over, which meant I didn't get to see the designers.'

'Can I get you a drink?' says Mike. He's waiting until Alfie and Dom are in bed before having one himself. Apparently it's his turn to bath them.

Cath and Sukey each have a gin and tonic. Sukey is sipping delicately. Cath's nearly finished hers already.

Cath seizes the opportunity. 'I'll get you one.' She's keen to talk to Rich alone.

But Rich sits down with a heavy sigh. Cath chivvies, 'Don't you want to choose what you want?'

'You do it, love.' Rich loosens his tie. 'You know what I like.'

Alone in the kitchen, she locates a cold beer for Rich, then uses the excuse to make herself a fresh G&T. She gloops in a generous measure of spirit and returns to the living room, ice clinking.

The twins are sprawled on the cream carpet close to the TV screen, playing on their PS3. The volume is low, but Cath can still detect the staccato of gunfire nonetheless.

Sukey's a mass of contradictions, she thinks, forbidding the boys to talk to their aunt while they do their homework, yet allowing this.

Rich smiles at her. 'All right, love?'

'Mm.' She gulps, and as she does so, bubbles go up her nose. The alcohol appears to be going to her head. She hopes they're going to eat soon.

'Went well today though, don't you think?' he says.

Oh dear, thinks Cath. She can't tell him to steer clear of the subject with Mike and Sukey present.

'How was the rest of the afternoon? The consultant say anything else?'

'Not really,' mutters Cath.

'Everything is OK, isn't it?'

'Yes, yes. I'll tell you later.' She flashes him a look to warn him he's on dangerous ground.

Mike stands up. 'Right, boys. Bed.'

'Aw . . .'

'Nope, that's it. I warned you five minutes ago. It's half seven, bath time. I've already run it ready.'

'Can't we finish this game?' The gunfire is getting faster; bombs explode in a blaze of yellow and noise. At the bottom of the screen the scores are mounting; they're almost neck and neck.

Sukey gets to her feet too. 'Alfie. Dom. Do as your father says.' She turns off the television.

Squirming in protest, they traipse upstairs in Mike's wake.

Perhaps she doesn't spoil them quite as much as their father does, thinks Cath. Although she's not averse to spoiling them herself, she's sure she'd never permit them to play such violent games if they were her children.

'I'd have loved a PS3 when I was that age,' says Rich.

'You'd love one now,' says Cath.

'True.'

'But we're not getting one.'

'Even if we have a little boy?'

'I'd rather avoid those stereotypes of boys' and girls' toys myself.' Because she can't express what's really bugging her, Cath redirects her irritation towards her husband.

Rich looks deflated. Then he brightens. 'Well, we'll have to come here and he can play with his cousins'.'

Cath glances at Sukey. Her face is implacable.

'You're rapidly making me want a girl,' says Cath.

Sukey gives a little cough, then says, 'Are you going to choose the sex of your child?'

Uh-oh, thinks Cath. But Rich walks straight in. 'They won't allow us to, actually.'

'Really? I thought you could determine just about everything.' The first mine goes off, but Rich doesn't notice.

'You'd be surprised,' he continues. 'It's all very tightly regulated. For instance, we found out today – didn't we, love? –

that you're only allowed to implant two embryos at a time. That wasn't the case a few years ago. But there was concern about the number of women having multiple births as a result of IVF, so they've changed the rules.'

'But they won't be your embryos, will they, Cath?' says Sukey. This time there is no mistaking the hostility.

Cath flinches as if she's been hit. 'No, they won't be mine.' She can hear her voice quiver.

Rich looks across at her; she can feel her face burning. His lips set in a thin line. She might be more stubborn than her husband, but he has his limits, and if there's one thing sure to rile him, it's an attack on his wife. 'I think that was a bit uncalled for.'

'But it's true, isn't it?'

'Yes, strictly speaking. But Cath is the one who'll carry the baby to term.'

'Still, when you have a baby, it won't exactly be Alfie and Dom's cousin, will it?'

This is more than Cath can stomach. At least when her mother questions her actions, she knows there's a deep vein of love running through it. She fires back, 'What gives you the right to be so judgemental?'

Sukey starts in surprise. 'I'm not being judgemental.'

'Feels like it to me.'

Sukey gulps.

'Er . . . It's purely I wouldn't feel comfortable doing what you're doing, if it were me. Carrying another woman's child.'

'I don't think you realize, I don't have a choice. I – we – really want a baby.'

Sukey frowns, but carries on. 'You see, when I was pregnant with the twins, it was such a personal thing, that natural bond to my babies . . . '

'I'm sure I'll develop a bond. I'll be carrying it inside me for nine months.'

'Do you think it will be the same?'

'But I don't have any other way of having children.'

'It's just not what I would do, that's all,' says Sukey.

'Are you saying everything people do that's different to you is wrong?'

'Oh, I'm not saying it's wrong . . . for you.'

'Good. Because if Rich and I want a family, this is one of the very few ways we can do it.'

Sukey picks her tumbler off the glass coffee table, takes a sip. 'I appreciate that.' She turns to Rich, as if to woo him to her side. 'Though actually, if I did have limited options, I still wouldn't have IVF.'

I gave her an escape route and she ignored it, thinks Cath. 'Why not?'

'It's not natural,' says Sukey.

'Nor's a PS3,' says Cath.

'It's hardly the same.' Sukey's voice rises. 'You understand what I mean.'

'No, I don't. Illuminate me.'

'I don't really believe we should mess with our bodies like that. Cath, you know me, I prefer to pursue the alternative route.'

'That's because you've never been ill.'

'I have! I had a cold only last month.'

'A cold is hardly cancer.'

Sukey hesitates while she lines up her argument. 'Maybe that's why I've not been seriously ill.'

'I'm sorry?'

'Because I take good care of my body. Vitamins, herbal remedies . . . '

'Hang on a minute.' Rich is with them now. 'Are you saying what I think you are? Not just that IVF is unnatural – which is fair enough I guess, if that's your opinion, though I'm not sure you'd be so confident of your view if you had been through what Cath has – but are you implying people who get ill bring it on themselves?'

Sukey flushes. But it's impossible to unwind what's been said: instead she strengthens her stance. 'I think if we honour ourselves with the right foods and thoughts, then we are much less likely to get ill.'

'Cath did absolutely nothing wrong to bring about her cancer,' says Rich. His voice is a growl.

Sukey glances from one to the other and back again. 'I can't apologize for what I believe.'

Just then, Mike walks back into the room clutching a bottle of beer. 'They're tucked up, at any rate. Though I can't guarantee they'll stay there.'

He looks around at their faces, but before he can appraise the situation fully, Sukey says, '*You* believe in alternative medicine, don't you, darling? It's worked so well for you too, hasn't it?'

Cath sees the panic in Mike's eyes. She feels for him. For the sake of her brother, she tries to be conciliatory – it will be better for her rather than Mike to broker peace. 'I've nothing against complementary medicine at all. I found a number of holistic therapies really helpful when I was ill.'

'You had those lovely aromatherapy massages when you were having chemo,' adds Rich.

'Ooh yes . . . They were fantastic. And acupuncture, when I got anxious. But it's important to remember there's a difference between complementary and alternative.' Cath is willing to retreat a little, not completely.

Sukey has another sip of G&T. 'But putting all that poison into your body . . . The side effects are so dreadful.'

'You can't treat cancer with bloody arnica.'

'Arnica's for *bruises*. It's marvellous stuff,' says Sukey.

'I know. We use it, don't we?' says Rich. 'But we don't have limitless resources – we're pushed to have IVF as it is. We could squander everything on complementary therapies and get no closer to having a child.'

'Exactly,' says Cath. She sighs. She spells it out in black and white. 'Sukey, you do realize, don't you, that if all I'd had until now was natural healing, I'd be dead?'

But Sukey merely dodges the bullet. 'I wasn't really talking about your cancer treatment anyway. I was talking about IVF.'

'Right. Of course you were.'

There's a long silence. This is where Mike could intercept, thinks Cath, but he doesn't seem to know how.

'I'm not quite sure you've heard what Cath has been saying,' says Rich eventually. 'Cath doesn't have any viable eggs. End of. I can't see what alternative therapy would do for that.'

'Make my ovaries grow back, perhaps,' Cath mutters.

'Have you ever practised acceptance?' says Sukey.

Rich's jaw falls open.

'Like the Buddhists,' Sukey explains.

Mike clears his throat. 'I'm not sure that's very appropriate in this case, sweetheart.'

Cath can't stand to be patronized a second longer. 'Sukey. I find it absolutely astonishing how you manage to make people feel so awful. You always make me feel guilty no matter what I do. Often it seems you positively relish making me feel bad.'

'Do I?' says Sukey. 'I'm sorry, I don't mean to.'

Mike says, 'I hardly think that's fair—'

'Don't you dare defend her!' That she's seen his attempt at mediation coming only makes Cath more enraged. 'You always back her up, even when she's absolutely out of order. Christ Almighty, Mike, don't be such a drip! Telling me not to broach the subject in case it offended your wife. Making *me* pussyfoot round *her*, when I'm the one with no fucking ovaries!'

BANG! She slams her tumbler down on the table, glass on glass. Then she gets up and storms out of the room.

21

'So this egg sharing,' says Adam, tearing open a second packet of crisps. 'I'm wondering, how would you feel if you didn't get pregnant and the other woman did?'

Lou shrugs. 'Hard to say till it happens. My feeling at the moment is that I'd like to know that even if I didn't carry a child myself, I'd enabled someone else to, so to speak.' She looks down at the floor, as if the beer-stained carpet might help her find the right words. Instead she finds herself distracted by Adam's towelling socks, peeking out from the gap between his cords and his lace-ups. They are greying, have seen better days. So he might be able to deal with life and death, but he hasn't mastered separating his whites, she thinks. She finds it rather endearing. She refocuses. 'I suppose I see it like this. If I couldn't produce my own eggs, I hope someone would donate eggs to me. If I want it one way, it has to work the other too. I know some people won't believe me' – privately she accuses Sofia – 'but the finance is a minor issue. I genuinely want to take part.'

'You know the chances of IVF success aren't always great? They may be even less for your recipient than for you.'

Adam holds out the bag and again Lou reaches in. 'I do. From what I understand, my odds at the age I am are better than if I leave it. The crucial thing is I gather those odds aren't lessened if I keep all my eggs or share a few.' She is conscious he will know more about the medical implications than she does.

'I still think it's generous, though.'

'I like helping people, but don't be fooled, I'm not that selfless. I get a lot back from knowing I've helped someone. I don't see this as any different.' Lou hunts for the right words; this is important. 'I've been thinking about this a great deal lately, because of what's happened, and deep down I've realized that I have an intrinsic belief I'm meant to create life. It's part of what makes me a woman.' It's good to say this aloud; she hasn't confided it to anyone. 'Sofia couldn't get her head round this whole egg-sharing thing, but I felt she was missing this point: I would be far more distressed at being unable to do what a woman is meant to do, than knowing that my egg donation worked for someone else and not for me.'

'You don't think you might be bitter?'

'No, not really . . . Why would I feel resentful because my egg helped another woman become a mother? Compared to what some women go through, my operation was a minor hiccup, but it did make me appreciate how much having a child mattered to me.' She frowns, suddenly sensing her mirror woman. 'For someone who can't use her own eggs at all, I can only begin to imagine how upsetting it must be.'

Quietly, Rich tiptoes into the spare room. Cath is sitting on the edge of the bed, staring at her hands. He checks if she's crying; she isn't.

The mattress dips as he sits down beside her. 'You OK?'

'No, I'm bloody well not OK.'

Stupid question, Rich berates himself. 'I agree it was completely uncalled for.'

'It was more than that. It was cruel. Sukey's poisonous. I don't know how Mike can have married her. If she wasn't so damn pretty, he wouldn't give her the time of day, I swear. Did you know she doesn't want us to stay, while we're down here at the clinic?'

'Really?'

'Yes. Apparently Mike had to talk her round so she'd allow us to come today. I tried to get you alone to warn you but you didn't take the hint.'

'Oh.' Once again he's been too slow. Is all this his fault? 'Sorry.'

'It's OK, you weren't to know.' She reaches for his hand.

Phew, thinks Rich. If Cath had ended up attacking him too he wouldn't have been surprised. When she's very upset she often can't contain her emotions, and in this instance he wouldn't blame her.

'She talks such claptrap,' says Cath. 'You know she's reading that stupid book?'

'What's that?'

'Oh, I can't remember its bloody name. But it's on the living-room table – some Australian woman going on about how you can have whatever you want in life if you wish hard enough.'

'If only that were true,' says Rich. No one could have wished Cath's cancer was a misdiagnosis more fervently than he had.

'Quite how you tie that in with a philosophy of acceptance only she could fathom. Then again, we both know how evangelical Sukey can be.'

Rich nods. 'I'd have expected that attitude to conventional medicine if she was some born-again religious nut. But she's not.'

'Sukey wouldn't know God if he came along and thrust a burning bush in her face.'

Rich laughs. 'And now Buddhism!'

'I tell you, it's because she doesn't like me.'

'It can't be that.'

'It is, I swear. Well, I don't like her either. I never have. If she wasn't married to my brother, I'd be more than happy never to see the sanctimonious cow again in my life.' Cath lurches from one grievance to another. 'Suppose Sukey'd had to fill in a whole load of forms like we're going to have to before she was allowed to become a mother? It makes me so cross that we have to be tested at every bloody stage. No one had to check their parenting skills before they had Alfie and Dom, did they?' Before Rich can respond, her mood has changed again. 'I want to go home.' She gets to her feet, retrieves their still-packed suitcase from the chaise longue at the bottom of the bed, snaps shut the fasteners and starts lugging it to the door.

'Wait.' Rich hurries to block her path. 'Stop a moment.

Think. Do you really want to drive a wedge between you and Mike like this?'

'He should have stood up for me.'

'He didn't witness the whole thing, he doesn't know what happened.'

'He's always so quick to defend her. It's as if she can do no wrong.'

'Can you imagine how awful it would be if he did take issue with everything she says? I wouldn't like to take her on, that's for sure.' Rich persists, 'And what about the boys? You don't want to make it difficult to see them.'

Cath bursts into tears. 'I'd see more of them if weren't for Sukey . . . She has no idea what it's like, has she? There she is with her pert behind and weeny hips *and* the twins and a devoted rich husband. And here am I, all fat and horrible, having gone through an early menopause.' Rich wants to contradict her – but she's going way too fast. 'Does she know what *that's* like? How unfeminine I feel? I don't even have a job I particularly enjoy!' She's like a skier hurtling out of control; he is on the sidelines, powerless to stop her. 'You know what? I wish *she* could have cancer, and then she'd know. It would serve her bloody well right.'

'Now, love . . . '

'Don't "now love" me! If I was a witch, it's the first thing I'd do. Ta-dah!' She waves an imaginary wand.

Rich chuckles.

'I hate her,' Cath sniffs.

'I know you do.'

He pulls her to him, cuddles her in tight. She's gone all floppy, worn out by the argument. She rests her chin on his shoulder. Even like this – especially like this – he loves the feel of her. The softness of her hair, the scent of her skin, the way she moves when she relaxes her muscles. It's the Cath only he experiences.

He mutters into her ear. 'Do you think we could just get through tonight, though, my love? You're so tired after the clinic – they took all that blood. And now you're upset – we both are . . . I think we could do with a decent night's sleep.' He brushes her fringe away from her face, looks into her eyes. Her lashes are wet with tears, her make-up blotched down her cheeks. 'I don't really know where we could go, not at this hour. I'm not sure we'd be able to get a train back up north and it's awfully late to find a hotel.'

Cath hesitates, then says, 'OK . . . I don't want to eat dinner with them, though.'

'Fine.' How can he get round that one? He has an idea. 'What if I say you're not feeling well and are having a lie-down?'

'But I'm hungry.' She sits back down on the bed.

Typical. 'I could bring you some cheese on toast or some-thing.'

'And a glass of wine.'

'They won't think you're very ill then.'

'Just sneak one. They don't need to know.'

'OK.'

'There's usually a bottle in the fridge.'

'I'll do my best. Now you put your feet up, try to relax. Sukey's not worth it, truly she's not.'

* * *

174

'I have to confess I'm starving,' says Adam.

Even after all those crisps? Lou suppresses a smile. She's sorry to see him leave; she's getting so much from their conversation and yet it feels they've only just touched the surface. 'How about you come back to mine and I make us some dinner?'

Adam shakes his head. 'I really must get home.'

'Oh.' Lou is disheartened. Perhaps he's not interested in pursuing the idea of co-parenting any more deeply after all. Maybe the complications of egg sharing have put him off . . .

He appears to pick up on her dejection. 'Believe me, I'd much rather carry on chatting. It's only boring paperwork that needs sorting, but I've already procrastinated the whole weekend. Can we do another night?'

'Sure.'

'Wednesday? I'd love to talk more.'

'Perfect.' Lou grins.

They say goodbye outside the pub and Lou strolls along the high street back to her flat. It's April but surprisingly warm and sunny; it's still light, spring is in the air. A woman struggles to manoeuvre her bags of groceries past a cluster of people smoking outside a bar and a jogger flashes by, dressed in a tiny vest and even tinier shorts, showing off well-oiled muscles. The old man who runs the corner shop is pulling down the blinds, locking up.

From what I've seen so far, I really like Adam, Lou concludes. Nevertheless, this is one of the most important decisions she'll ever make and she'd like more insight into his character. Given how keen he is, doubtless he's been trying hard to make a good impression.

She turns into Magdalene Street; there's litter everywhere, the seagulls have been busy again. The rubbish is worse than ever since the council cuts, and mounting the steps to the front door Lou sees someone's tagged the whitewashed frontage of the house with black paint. Brighton is such a tapestry of light and dark.

It's possible Adam's got a dark side too, she reminds herself. I'd hate to discover that when we're too far down the road to turn back. But how on earth can I get to know him properly, when my time to have a baby is fast running out?

22

'I'm sorry about last night, mate,' says Mike, backing the 4x4 out of the drive.

That's why he offered to give me a lift, thinks Rich. He suspected an ulterior motive – it's sunny and the station is not far on foot.

'Is she all right?'

'I think so. Seems a bit better this morning.' This is a lie; Rich has left Cath seething in the bedroom. 'Still, might be best if you can avoid leaving them alone together before she heads off.'

'It's more than my life is worth. But anyway, I wanted to ask, how do *you* feel about all this?'

Rich contemplates, half watching a lollipop lady safeguard a chain of schoolchildren, dressed in green pullovers, crossing the road. 'I can see both points of view, actually. Between you and me, I worry about the drugs regime myself. But apparently it's the other woman we should be thinking of rather than Cath. And at least she'd be taking the drugs anyway.'

'I didn't mean that,' says Mike. 'If you ask me, Sukey was very insensitive. She can be so stubborn sometimes.'

Rich raises his eyes skyward. 'She's not the only one.'

'I was referring to the IVF thing in general,' says Mike. 'It often doesn't work first time. I gather it's a numbers game. You hear about these couples who keep going and going, end up spending sixty, seventy thousand pounds. It must be hard to know when to call a halt.'

'I can imagine.'

'My guess is that with her history, it might be hard for Cath to get pregnant, though obviously I'm not a doctor.'

'Hopefully it will be easier using donor eggs.'

'Yes, but still. And aside from the money – I was concerned about your . . . um . . . Well, I suppose one thing I wanted to ask is what you'd do if Cath were to get ill again, for instance – it's a lot to take on, a baby, you know.' Mike glances across at Rich. 'Feel free to tell me to mind my own business, but Cath's my sister and I'm concerned for both of you. What if, er . . . you know, you ended up having to bring up a kid on your own?'

'They caught the cancer before it spread. So the odds are she'll be fine.' Nonetheless Mike is voicing Rich's own fears.

'I know, and she seems really well now, which is great. It's just a huge commitment, isn't it, all this?'

'Mm.'

'And my sister can get so carried away. You are on board with it all too, aren't you?'

'Frankly? Yes. I know what you're saying, but Cath's illness changed my view of life, a lot. I used to think I had every-thing planned – insofar as I ever plan anything – and now

I realize I can't do that: you never know what's coming. I can't refuse to do this with Cath because there's the possibility she *might* be ill again. I couldn't live with myself and do that. I have thought about it, but I've made my decision: I want her to be happy more than anything, and she's got her heart set on trying for a baby. And should anything happen to her, I'd rather we'd done this and had a child than that we hadn't.'

'Even though it wouldn't be hers?'

'It wouldn't be her eggs,' corrects Rich. 'But it would be hers in every other way, and genetically it would be mine.'

'And have you and Cath talked about what you might do if it *doesn't* work?'

'We saw a counsellor together yesterday – the clinic insists all patients do – and it did come up.'

'It's only, forgive me, but you both seem to be setting such store by it.' They are at the station forecourt. Mike pulls the car parallel to the taxi rank and turns to face him. 'When I was chatting to her yesterday before you got to us, I was worried that she didn't really seem to be considering that possibility.'

'You know Cath is good at talking the talk when she has to, and an hour of counselling isn't very long to cover so many issues. Perhaps we skated over it a bit.'

'Hmm . . . I'd just hate for her to be so dreadfully disappointed, when she's finally back on an even keel.'

A driver toots behind them; Rich had better get going. He pauses briefly, hand poised to open the door. 'I know, Mike. It worries me too.'

* * *

Hi there, I've gathered when I have IVF I'll have to go through a period of shutting down my hormones, and I'm worried about the side effects of the drugs. I'm quite into alternative things and switching off my hormones chemically sounds so extreme. Louloubelle

Louloubelle, Hello again! I went through similar fears when I was starting out – taking eggs from my body and fertilizing them in a lab seemed such an unnatural way of creating life. I'd heard of women experiencing hot flushes, night sweats, mood swings, blinding headaches – all symptoms associated with the menopause because we're basically closing down our hormones so the doctors have greater control over our ovaries. But it's important to remember that during IVF you're simply creating the right circumstances for fertilization. The real miracle of why some eggs fertilize, implant in the womb and grow is still all down to God. Rainbow Girl

See? thinks Cath indignantly, at least *these* women understand one another. She's poised to comment when the purr of an engine in the drive reveals Mike is back from the station. In the light of a new day, she appreciates his arbitration skills; she needs his presence if she's to face Sukey over breakfast.

* * *

Thank goodness I don't have to deal with a commute like this every morning, thinks Rich. His regular drive down the

M1 to Leicester bores him stupid and he doesn't enjoy travelling by train to London either, but at least he gets a seat, and two days he can work from home. Here his face is unpleasantly close to a guy with halitosis, and he's having to hang on, arm raised so he doesn't fall over, with a young woman wedged into his armpit. He's hardly past Richmond and this is a stopping train; Waterloo is miles yet. If he turns his head, he can just see out of the window, get a sense of space.

The station at North Sheen overlooks allotments surrounded by blocks of flats. How sought-after this land must be in the depths of affluent suburbia, he muses. Each plot seems so well tended, all set for the summer. There are smart wigwams ready and waiting to support the ebullient twirls of runner beans, giant bathtubs bursting with spring greens, beds edged neatly with floorboards, and carefully aligned trenches with mounds of earth for planting new potatoes, like the hills of ancient forts.

I bet the allotment police are ferocious, booting people off who don't plant properly, he thinks. I can't ever see myself putting that much effort into gardening.

But Rich has surprised himself before now; he might do so again. He never would have guessed he'd be able to put anyone before himself, yet when circumstances forced him to, it transpired he could do it without a second thought. Like the time Cath came running in from the bathroom, for instance, clutching handfuls of her hair and weeping. He didn't have a chance to say he found it devastating too; he simply got his beard trimmer and shaved it off for her properly, carefully holding her scalp as he did so, kissing her forehead when he'd finished. He can remember it as vividly as yesterday. And so it might be with a baby; he's much more confident as a result of what they've been through that it will. He's no longer scared at the prospect of being a father – he's only scared it might not happen.

Nonetheless, in spite of these reservations, he's increasingly excited. Everyone at the clinic was so supportive, so understanding of their circumstances, so encouraging. If it does work, imagine. He – Rich – will be a father, a dad. What a world of possibilities that would open up.

23

Ouch, thinks Lou. The supermarket carrier bags are cutting into her palms. She pauses for a rest before lugging them down the final stretch of St James's Street back to her studio.

Hmm, she thinks, looking up: I'm right by Howie's flat, why don't I pop in and say hello? He lives above a dog-grooming parlour and his living room window is cast wide open; it seems he's home. She rings the bell and shortly sees his blurred outline through the frosted glass of the front door, heading down the stairs.

'Lou, hi! Good to see you. Fancy a cuppa?'

'Is it a good moment?'

'Sure . . . Come on up.' He eyes her Co-op bags. 'Blimey, doll, what a lot of shopping.'

'I'm cooking for Adam later.'

'Leave them there if you like,' says Howie, and Lou follows him up. His living room doubles as an office; there are papers and open books everywhere, fluttering in the breeze. His computer is on and there's a half-eaten sandwich on his desk.

'I won't stay long,' she says.

'Nah, it's fine, I was going to call you anyway. I was dying to hear – so tell me, how did it go with Adam? Can't have been a total disaster if you're seeing him tonight.'

'It was good, thanks.'

'You two going ahead, then?'

'Yes, maybe . . . I hope so . . . '

Howie whoops, delighted. 'Just call me Cilla.' He sits on his work chair and swivels to face her.

Blind Date hasn't been on TV in years. 'You're showing your age there,' she teases, lifting some files to make room on the cerise velvet sofa. It's typical of Howie to want to claim credit: doubtless if she and Adam do have a baby, he'll tell all of Brighton it was down to him. But she can't begrudge him. 'It was a brilliant idea getting us together,' she says.

'Well, I knew he'd got a long way down the road with Evie and Nikita. He was pretty gutted when it didn't work out.'

'Oh really?'

'Mm.'

She'd like to know more, but Howie is clearly busy and she has a meal to make; she cuts to the chase. 'It's only, I was wondering, actually, if I might ask your advice? You're always so insightful.' Flattery is likely to make Howie open up and she wants an honest appraisal. 'So . . . is there anything I should know? Like skeletons in Adam's closet?'

Howie hesitates, scratches his goatee. Either there's something truly heinous, or he can't think of much.

'What's his relationship history? Go on, spill the beans.' Normally Lou is discreet; she winces at manipulating Howie by gossiping like this, but needs must.

'Ooh, well . . . He was with this guy for years. Best part of a decade, I'd say. Norman. He's Mexican.'

'A Mexican called Norman? That can't be for real.'

'He may have made it up, you never know. He was terribly theatrical, very different from Adam, he was: more camp, flamboyant, younger, bit of a flirt.'

'So why did they split?' says Lou, already concluding that Adam sounds too good for him.

'Ah. Norman was unfaithful a handful of times. No more than that.'

That's quite a lot, thinks Lou. Therein lies the difference between me and Howie. I'm with Adam on that score.

'Though really, they just grew apart. After all, what appeals when you're twenty-five isn't necessarily the same in your thirties.'

Lou sighs: there's a mirror of her own life there too. 'So, Adam outgrew Norman, you reckon?'

'Er, yes, if you like to put it that way.'

'How would you put it?'

'C'mon, let's be honest here. Adam's a smashing guy. I love him to bits. But you can't blame Norman for wandering.'

'Eh?'

'Adam's successful, kind, solvent, bright . . . '

Oh dear, thinks Lou. I've obviously failed to pick up something.

'He's got his own pad, he's tidy, drives a decent car . . . But, you know . . . ?'

'No.' By now she is sitting on the edge of the sofa. 'You've got me worried. Tell me!' She could swear Howie is enjoying the suspense. Has Adam got the clap? He can't have, he's had all the tests. A criminal record, then, a drug habit? It's my job not to be blind to these things, Lou thinks. What on earth have I missed?

'If you ask me . . . ' Howie coughs and looks away. He seems reluctant to say it. Finally he bursts out, 'He's just not very fanciable, doll. Norman was hot, but Adam, erm . . . He's no oil painting, is he?'

*   *   *

Adam checks his face in the mirror in the surgery washroom. He looks tired; it's been non-stop all day.

What sort of a dad do you think I'd make? he asks his reflection.

The prospect certainly excites him; it was a smart move of Howie's to put him in touch with Lou. The idea of adoption hasn't the same appeal as fathering his own child; the biological aspect matters to him, maybe all the more because of his profession. He can't kid himself genes aren't important when almost every day he sees evidence of hereditary disease. Still, he's wary of rushing in headlong.

I don't want to muck Lou about, he thinks. I know what that feels like.

He gets in the car, checks the clock. It's not worth going home – perhaps he can kill a few minutes at his friend's. Presently he rings the doorbell.

'Adam!' A voice answers from above his head; a window is open, Howie is leaning out.

'Hi.' Adam grins up at him.

'Gosh, that's a coincidence,' says Howie.

'Really, how come?'

'I, er . . . was . . . um . . . just thinking about you, actually.'

I wonder why, thinks Adam.

'Wanna come up? I'll chuck you the keys.'

Adam ducks, and with a clatter they land on the pavement. He lets himself in and climbs the stairs to Howie's flat. It's a right tip in here, he thinks, stepping over the piles of books and magazines scattered between him and the pink sofa. 'I hope it's not a bad moment?'

'No, no. You've timed it perfectly, before I got back down to this article. So, tell me, how did it go with Lou?'

'Great. We got on really well. I'm due there for supper in a few minutes, as a matter of fact.'

'That's wonderful!'

'She seems very nice,' says Adam.

'She is,' Howie nods.

'But I was thinking, it's a huge decision . . .'

'Of course.'

'So I guess I should do my homework.'

'Very wise.'

'And you know what happened to me before. I've heard other stories too, lesbian mothers cutting the man out once they get a partner, you can imagine . . .' Adam frowns, trying to work out how to phrase this. 'So, before we go any further, I thought . . . um, perhaps you could tell me . . . Is there anything more about Lou I should know?'

'Lou? Goodness!' Howie hesitates, then says, 'Seriously, I'm very fond of her.' Then he sighs. 'It's a shame she's had such a tough time lately.'

'Yes, so I gather.' Suddenly Adam worries: I hope she's not having a baby to try and buoy her spirits, fill a hole in her life. That would be a mistake . . .

'And she's dealt with it all pretty well. She's surprisingly tough underneath, I reckon.'

Ah, thinks Adam. Is Howie implying that deep down, Lou is hard? That's exactly what worries me. If so, she'd have few qualms about using then dropping me.

'I love her to bits, you understand.'

'Sure, sure.' Oh no, thinks Adam. Here it comes . . .

'So, if you're asking me whether I think this is a good idea . . . '

Of course I'm asking you! thinks Adam. He wishes Howie would spit it out.

Howie's face breaks into a smile. 'Then, yes, my friend, I do. Lou's one of life's good people, I reckon. Obviously I can't read the future, but if you really want my opinion, you could do a lot worse.'

Phew, thinks Adam. I hope to God he's right.

* * *

'Ooh, this is lovely,' says Adam, stepping into Lou's studio.

He's breathless from climbing the stairs, Lou notices. He can't be very fit.

Adam looks round, appraising, pauses at the collection of framed photos on the windowsill, peers closer. Funny he's homed in on those, I'd do the same, thinks Lou. He points at a black-and-white shot. 'This your mum and dad?'

'Yup.' Lou crouches to rummage in the fridge.

'Fantastic wedding dress your mum's got on,' he observes. His tone seems ironic.

'Isn't it?' says Lou. She bristles slightly, however: it's one thing for me to criticize my mother, she thinks, another for someone else to. I don't know him that well yet and Howie was right – Adam is hardly the king of style.

Then he says, 'Your dad looks great, though. Very dapper,' and Lou forgives him. 'Were you close? From what you said the other day, I got that impression.'

'Yes,' she says. She tries to sneak another look at Adam's appearance. He could really do with a shave, and his clothes are ever so crumpled. She pictures him through Howie's eyes. I can see that he's not that fanciable, she concludes. What if my baby ends up looking like him? Immediately she feels guilty. That's not what we're about anyway, she reminds herself. She softens. Adam's got a *nice* face; maybe he's just tired. He seems to work very hard. No, she decides, the conversation with Howie has left a bad taste in my mouth. It felt uncomfortably close to bitching, even at the time, and now Adam is here in person, I'd rather be honest. 'I suppose it's because my Dad and I were close I'd prefer not to go into this alone. I loved him.' She shrugs. It's hard to put how much she misses him into words.

Adam nods.

'If we had a kid, I hope you'd have as much fun with him or her as my dad and I did,' she says impulsively.

'That's a sweet thing to say,' Adam smiles. She can feel him looking at her, evaluating. Suddenly he says, 'Can I do anything?'

Maybe he's uncomfortable that she's preparing the meal

single-handed, but Lou truly doesn't mind, keen to show off her culinary skills. She used to enjoy cooking for Sofia; she misses it, and if this works out with Adam they'll both end up cooking for their child. 'No, just chill, I'm fine.' She tips sliced vegetables into a frying pan. 'You OK with frittata?'

'Yum.' Adam takes a seat on her sofa, leans round so he can chat while she is in the kitchen area. 'By the way, I've checked it out at the sperm bank, my samples are all still fine to use.'

'That's great!'

'Isn't it?' Adam beams. 'My guess is it'll take a few weeks, but all the same, that's got to be better than waiting over six months.'

'Quite.' Adam seems a proper grown-up, Lou concludes. Responsible, forward-thinking. I mean, honestly, Howie, she argues with her friend in his absence. So what if he's no oil painting? It's not as if you're exactly Adonis. And if our baby's a bit plain, does it matter? Do I mind *that* much? Not really. As long as it's happy and healthy, that's the main thing.

* * *

Well I never, thinks Adam, clicking up his seatbelt and turning on the car headlights. What a strange forty-eight hours it's turned out to be.

Normally he'd listen to the radio, but after chatting much of the evening he needs silence to gather his thoughts. Adam is not religious and personally has little time for talk of God, or higher powers, or reincarnation, though he strives to respect those who do. Even the notion of karma seems to him an over-optimistic way of looking at the world. Nevertheless, tonight he feels almost blessed by fate, if not quite.

So much of what Lou has been saying makes sense to Adam that he finds himself smiling again as he drives down Marine Parade. 'We mustn't change childcare arrangements too often once a baby is born,' she'd said, so they'd agreed to have a proper legal and binding agreement going into this from the start. And when he'd asked what might happen if she had a relationship in the future, she'd said, 'If either one of us does, we're the child's parents, and we'll always be the primary carers,' and inside he'd clapped for joy. Insofar as he can tell, she sounds genuinely keen for him to be involved. That they live so close, and that neither has plans to move, will help.

I'll have to give up a lot, he thinks, sparked by the sight of the Pavilion. The oriental turrets and domes glow orange and extraordinary in the floodlights, homage to pleasure and decadence. Supper at a friend's like I've just had may be out of the question, never mind a full blow-out.

Still, he's already realized that if he has a child, a vast canyon will yawn between himself and a significant number of his playful, fun-loving friends. And he's not the party animal he used to be; he was never as much of a tart as, say, Howie, and his experience with Norman left him scarred and hurt, so casual sex has less appeal than it did.

And won't Lou and a baby take up my time anyway? he thinks. He wonders about his work, who will look after a child during the day. They need to talk much more about that. Currently Adam is committed to very long hours; he can't see that changing immediately.

191

Although I could cut down, he muses. He has had a vexing sense that his crazy timetable is to safeguard himself from admitting he's lonely. But reduced hours would mean less money, which might be hard. He had been hoping to buy a new car – the one he's got is perfectly respectable, but he'd been investigating getting a soft top, something swish and eye-catching, as a reward to himself. That would hardly be appropriate for a man ferrying around a toddler . . .

Then he remembers Mrs Malhotra watching, powerless, as her husband faded away. Earlier that afternoon he was back with them to increase Mr Malhotra's morphine dose. The old man has declined, may not live to see another day.

These hurdles are mere practicalities, they must be resolvable, surely, thinks Adam. Yes, I could carry on going out, sometimes have a few too many. Yes, I could slave eight till eight till I drop. Yes, I could buy a convertible. But ultimately, life is about people, lived experiences, not hedonism or money or possessions – and nothing is as fundamental as the desire to procreate. Something, call it serendipity if not fate, has put Lou my way. And whilst there will be another chance to buy a fancy car, there will not be another chance like this to have a baby.

24

A July morning and Cath is at work, sitting on a metal chair by the staircase. There are spots allocated to attendants around the museum, but this, to Cath's mind, is the most stimulating, and she looks forward to being assigned it on her rota. Much of her job she finds dull, but here she can watch people coming and going round the Victorian collection to her right – she tries to guess which paintings they'll home in on as they pass her, and see if she is correct when they get there. She can admire a couple of her favourite pieces: a few feet away a life-size bronze woman arches and stretches as she wakes; down the hall is an imposing man made of bricks. But mainly she enjoys being in the path of visitors coming in the entrance to her left; it's where she has most interaction with the public. Some of her more antisocial colleagues prefer to be tucked away: she likes to answer questions, share her enthusiasm about the works of art, and chat. She can direct people to the first floor to see some of the most popular pieces – the Henry Moore, Francis Bacon and Paul Nash. And the Stanley Spencer oils are on the staircase itself, so she can debate them with passers-by.

The gallery is busy today: there's a group of A-level students from Leeds Grammar – their teacher has brought them to mark the end of their exams – and despite being high summer, it's raining, which invariably means more shoppers in town. The museum is not far from either the lumpen Sixties-built Merrion Centre or the sheer glass-walled retail space of the Light, so on damp days it attracts a more diverse cross section of the population than usual, seeking tea and the chance to dry off in the Tiled Hall cafe. Academics discussing university politics and pensioners wheeling tartan trolleys of Morrisons' groceries stand in line behind ladies dripping with ribbon-handled carrier bags from designer boutiques, all keenly awaiting a pot of Yorkshire's finest.

Cath's jacket is draped over the back of her chair; presently she feels her phone vibrating in the pocket. She's not supposed to have it turned on, let alone answer it, but she's been awaiting a certain call for three months – three *months*! – and with her mounting impatience has come an unwillingness to comply with the rules.

She sneaks a look. Oh my God! At last! It's them!

Unfortunately: 'Excuse me.' A beanpole of a man bends to speak to her. 'I was wondering if you might tell me where I can find *The Lady of Shallot*?'

The mobile is still buzzing, but she'll have to leave it.

'Upstairs and left,' she states, then feels bad for being curt. 'In Modern and Contemporary Art.'

'It's hardly modern,' frowns the man.

'I know.' Normally Cath would love to exchange thoughts

on the painting with him, but right now she has more pressing concerns. She smiles in a way she hopes communicates *I agree, but please don't engage me in conversation*. The man heads up the stairs two at a time, long-limbed and eager.

Seconds later a lone vibration indicates the caller has left a message. Cath tries to stay calm but she can't hold off, she just can't. She slips the phone surreptitiously from her pocket, curses her hair for being so fine – she could do with a pre-Raphaelite curtain right now – and turns her head to the wall so she can listen unobtrusively.

'Mrs Morris, I'm calling from the Marylebone Fertility Clinic,' says a woman. Cath doesn't recognize her voice, but she and Rich saw several members of staff when they visited; they all sounded alike: southern. 'If you could give us a call back when you have a moment, and ask for Mrs Donoghue in Embryology, I would appreciate it.'

Argh! Why couldn't she be more specific? It's nearly an hour until lunch – Cath is on a late shift, and she's been living in limbo long enough. She glances left, right; grabs her jacket. If anyone sees, she'll say it was an emergency.

She hurries down the stone steps – slips in the wet and has to grab the handrail – and around the side of the building. She leans against the wall in the hopes of gaining some shelter but giant raindrops plop directly on her from the roof. She hasn't time to move; she holds her jacket over her head as a makeshift umbrella, and presses the button to return the call.

* * *

Lou is midway through a session with a student when her phone rings.

Damn, she thinks, I forgot to turn it off after talking to Adam.

'Sorry,' she tells her student. He's slouching before her in an armchair, legs folded, nonchalant. She reaches for the off button without even checking the number. Whoever it is will have to leave a message.

* * *

It feels as if she has been on hold for aeons. At last there's a click and Cath is connected.

'Thanks for waiting, Mrs Morris. I'm sorry, I was on another call. You got my voicemail?'

'Yes.' Cath's fingers are trembling so much she almost drops her mobile.

'I was ringing with good news.'

Her heart is racing.

'We had to wait to find the right person . . . ' – Cath wishes Mrs Donoghue would speed up; she sounds like a faulty cassette tape – 'so I'm sorry it's taken several weeks to get back to you . . . '

Three months, Cath wants to yell. *Three months!*

'I gather you've rung to chase us a few times. Anyhow, I'm happy to let you know that now we have found a potential match for you. An egg donor, I mean.'

Cath hears herself gasp.

'We've received the lady in question's Welfare of the Child

196

form, she has had all tests, and she's CMV negative, like your husband.'

Cath can't recall what that means, but it's not her prime concern. 'Who is she?'

'You appreciate donors are anonymous.'

'I know.' But surely they can tell her something? Without any detail it doesn't seem real. Again she feels the presence of this mirror woman, somewhere far away, maybe . . . Or maybe not. She could be over there, crossing the Headrow, with a briefcase and umbrella . . . There, ponytail flying, running for the bus in her stilettos . . . There, walking with her other half towards Cath and the museum . . .

'I can give you her basic physical characteristics,' says Mrs Donoghue.

'Please, that would be great.'

'Obviously we've tried to match her to you and your husband as best we can. Dr Hassan has overseen it personally.' There's a rustle of paper. 'So . . . she is in her thirties, and we have her down as five foot six.'

That's an inch taller than me, thinks Cath.

'She's Caucasian. With brown hair and blue eyes.'

Exactly like me.

'And we've described her build here as athletic.'

No one could ever describe me as that, thinks Cath. She tries to picture her. 'You mean she's muscly?'

'She's lean; that's what we're meaning.'

They've met, concludes Cath, playing detective. 'I'm not lean at all.'

'Nonetheless we believe, given your husband has an athletic physique himself, she is an appropriate match.'

Cath feels a pang of jealousy. It's hard not to resent this woman who is giving her husband something she is incapable of. Immediately she chides herself. Their donor is being so generous; that it's a symbiotic relationship was one of the reasons egg sharing appealed to Cath from the start. She pushes, 'Can't you tell me *anything* about her circumstances? I'd like to know how we're helping her too.'

'I'm afraid I can't – I honestly don't even know myself. There is a different embryologist in charge of her.'

Oh, so they won't have encountered one another after all. 'Can you let me know how her treatment goes?'

'Yes, we'll do that. You'll need to be kept abreast anyway – the number of eggs we collect will impact on you both.'

'Of course.' If they don't collect enough, both IVF treatments could fail before they've even begun. 'So what happens next?'

'We'll need to synchronize the two of you, cycle-wise.'

Cath is confused. 'But I don't have a cycle.'

'No, so in your case we'll prepare your uterus to ensure it is in the best possible condition for when the embryos are transferred.'

Sounds like lining a baking tray, thinks Cath.

'You will simply take oestrogen tablets without any preliminary treatment.'

'Right.' Although she's keen to wrest as much information as she can, Cath is increasingly conscious she's been away from the gallery a while. 'I'm sorry, but I am going to have to go. I just want to be sure – is there anything I need to do right now?'

'Not yet. We'll have you come down to the clinic in the next few weeks. We'll be in touch to confirm.'

Once again Cath is left waiting, powerless; it's all down to her donor. What a strange set of circumstances, she thinks, to have someone, somewhere, going through this in tandem, having such a profound effect on my life, yet not knowing who I am.

*   *   *

Half an hour later Lou returns the call.

'It's Ian, the embryologist from the clinic.'

'Oh yes?'

'We've found an egg recipient.'

'That's fantastic! Oh, I'm so pleased. So what's she like?'

'You know I'm not permitted to tell you very much.'

'Of course – just let me know what you can.'

'Physically, you're remarkably similar. She's a bit heavier than you, otherwise a perfect match.'

'Can I ask why she needs my eggs?'

'I can only let you know that hers aren't viable.'

'Can you tell me how old she is?'

'Older than you, that's all I can say.'

'OK,' says Lou. As a counsellor she bumps up against the issue of confidentiality every day. Nonetheless she is intrigued; fleetingly she pictures this other woman, then she pushes the thought away. Time is pressing. 'So what's next?'

Ian explains, 'You'll receive two types of drug: first, an injection to prevent you from ovulating, on day twenty-one of your upcoming cycle. After approximately two more weeks, you'll be given a stimulant.'

'Will I need to come into the clinic?'

'You can do the injections remotely, though you will need to come in for a scan every few days. Are you going to be injecting yourself?'

'I think my, um—' – she chooses her words carefully – 'the father of the child is going to.'

'Great, a lot of women do it that way, it's often easier.'

'My, um, friend – well, actually, he's a doctor.'

'That's perfect. Sounds like you'll be in excellent hands.'

*   *   *

Call me between two and three, says the text. At 2.03, Rich does as requested. He knows that although she's given him an hour's window, Cath is really asking him to phone as soon as possible.

'Guess what?'

Through the microphone of his Bluetooth, he can hear the sound of traffic. Presumably she's on her lunch break. He'll be way too slow for her if he speculates. 'What?'

'They've found us a donor!'

'They haven't!' He can hardly believe it. Finally! Keeping Cath from going crazy these last three months has been hard work – and they'd been warned it could be up to a year. He can't imagine how she would have dealt with that. Lord knows how couples who have to wait even longer for treatment on the NHS manage.

'Where are you?'

'Just got on the motorway.' Rich has been at the head office in Leicester. 'I'm coming back now.'

'You on your own?'

'Yes.' With so much background noise, it's hard to hear.

'So, do you want to know about her?'

'Of course.'

'She sounds exactly like me. It's so spooky.'

'Really?'

'Yeah, same height, almost, same colouring, everything. Just a bit thinner, that's all. Lucky cow.'

'You told Dr Hassan she could be slimmer,' Rich reminds her.

'So I did.' Cath laughs. 'I think it's just a coincidence, though.'

'I'm sure,' says Rich. From what he has been given to understand, there's no surfeit of egg donors; to a large extent, they have to take what's given. In a way, that is easier. He can imagine it would be confusing to be surrounded by options. And whilst he can see that choosing a donor has its appeal – Rich likes getting what he wants as much as anyone – the notion of selecting every aspect of a baby's genes as one might pick a car, down to its hubcaps and upholstery, makes him uneasy. We'll have blue eyes and brown hair is one thing; we want a Ph.D. and a perfect 10 smacks to him of engineering.

Rich loves Cath precisely because she's a one-off: an attractive, idiosyncratic, infuriating mix of impatience and enthusiasm, insecurity and creativity, passion and humour. She's irreplaceable; when confronted by the stark reality of losing her he became very clear about that. And just as Cath's cancer was a random act, so, Rich believes, is life generally. It seems fitting that their donor is someone who has by chance come their way through an act of kindness. There's only one Cath on the planet, and no amount of box-ticking could replicate her.

He stops musing, realizing he's missed Cath's question. 'Sorry?'

'I said, "Are you happy?" '

'Of course I am, love, it's fantastic news. Are you?'

'YEE-ESSS! I'm *so* happy,' she wails, and promptly bursts into tears.

25

Hi all . . . Well, today went RUBBISH . . . Now I know why they say the NHS is a lottery – everyone in my postcode who is not currently on down reg medication etc. will NOT get IVF till NEXT YEARapart from those who can afford to pay!!! I can't possibly drum up several thousand pounds. Honestly, I'm f****ing gutted!!! I cried all the way home and am still in tears. I've barely been clinging on and now have no idea when we'll actually get started . . . So so so so so so p'd off!!! Effing politicians. Since when was it fair to clamp down on infertility? Plus I was on bus and actually heard two people moaning about their youngest kid turning 12!!! Yes, 12 years old and the mum has to go to back to work full time . . . Argh!!!! How terrible!

Know it's not great but came in and hit the bottle. So a little tipsy writing this message.

Hope everyone ok? Cause I'm not!!!! Daisy x

The intercom goes just as Lou is wondering what she can write to help Daisy feel better.

She presses the buzzer to let Adam in. While he climbs the stairs she returns to her laptop and logs off.

He pushes open the door to her flat. 'Hi, how are you?'

'Bit nervous, though I've sorted the medication.' She leads him to her bathroom cabinet where she's lined up her supplies in date order.

'Wow, med central,' says Adam.

'There's more in the fridge. Bit OCD, isn't it?' Lou laughs at herself. 'I thought it would be easier if I lay on the bed. What do you reckon?'

'Probably.'

'OK, let's get it over with. Here.' She hands him some antiseptic wipes that came with the drugs. While Adam assembles the syringe, Lou watches. 'You make it look so easy.'

'I'm used to it. Right then, lie back.' She does as she's told. 'I'm going for your tummy, OK?'

'Sure.'

He eases up her T-shirt, disinfects her skin, there's a quick sting in her abdomen, a tiny pause while he removes the needle, and he cleans the area again. 'There.'

'That it?'

'Yup.'

She sits up. 'Gosh. That was nowhere near as bad as I expected. Thanks.'

'You know I'm happy to do this every night, if you like?'

'Coming each day might be a bit of a bore for you.'

'It's fine, I want to help. You're on my way home.'

'Mm. Though I don't always get back from work at the same time,' Lou prevaricates. She's thankful that Adam wants to play an active role and she doesn't want to exclude him when he's keen. It must be strange for him, as it is for her, that they're not a couple, yet are on this road. Administering the drugs on her own is bound to be tricky; were she still with Sofia, she could have helped. She should probably take Adam up on his offer. And yet . . .

Lou has experienced so many hands and gels and scanners and needles over the last few weeks, it's as if her body is fast becoming public property. There were also the scalpels and surgical instruments of her operation: that she was anaesthetized throughout only accentuates the sense she's been handing her fate over to others. Most significant of all, she'll be giving a part of herself away again when she donates her eggs. A warning bell is going off.

'Let's see how we go,' she says.

*　　*　　*

Daisy love, What a bummer. I hope the next few months pass swiftly. You know, the toughest thing for me about this whole malarkey is the uncertainty and waiting, so my heart goes out to you TOTALLY. It's bad enough having doctors and everyone else telling us what to do, let alone politicians. Right now I'm having to 'go with the flow' and wait for the clinic to phone me with news of my donor's down regging. It's driving me nuts. So I think I'll join you in a glass of wine in the hopes of making this particular evening go faster. Here's praying things turn around for you soon. CathM

Cath gets to her feet, goes to the fridge, reaches for a bottle of white. She's about to unscrew the top when a little voice inside her says *No*. She's supposed to be looking after herself; if she has one, she might have another.

'My body is a temple,' she tells the cat, and switches on the kettle.

She returns to the laptop, replaces the penultimate line of her message with *Have a glass of wine for me, I'm on the peppermint tea,* and sits watching the cursor flash at her.

There's nothing on telly, she's checked already; she's responded to posts on two fertility forums, and if she goes on Facebook she'll probably be drawn to look at her friends' pictures of their babies and children, again.

'Well?' she asks the cat. Bessie is half sitting, front legs neatly together like an ancient Egyptian hieroglyph, on the table. She shouldn't be on a surface that comes into contact with food, but both Cath and Rich are too soft on her. Bessie half opens her eyes, closes them again, slowly. Cath could do with some of her laissez-faire attitude.

She casts her gaze about the room. Taps her leg, restless.

This really won't do – she's weeks to get through yet. She has to find a way to kill time.

She can hear the kids next door playing. She looks out of the window – it's still light, and over the hedge she can see their pigtails flying as they bounce in turn on the trampoline. That must be fun, Cath thinks. She catches the eye of the eldest girl and waves. I need to do something physical too, burn off energy. Jogging or cycling doesn't appeal – rarely does. If Rich were here . . . but he's not due back for hours.

Her eye falls on their garden. All the houses in their terrace have a decent ribbon of space overlooking Meanwood Park, so they are surrounded by vegetation. Cath appreciates the greenery, but it's hard to keep pace, and they've not managed to claw back control since she was ill. It's been a wet July; the shrubs seem to have exploded like fireworks, and their patch of lawn needs mowing, though it's a bit late to start up a machine. She notices the ivy is working its way into the brickwork of the far wall; she could start by tackling that. She locates some gardening gloves and her wellington boots.

'Right then, Bessie,' she says.

She needs tools if she's to do this properly but the climber has also wound its way round the bolt to the shed.

Fiendish so and so, she says silently, pulling off the tiny suckers.

Finally she yanks open the door and a shaft of sunlight illuminates the interior. Folded chairs lie willy-nilly atop badminton rackets and old cans of paint; stacks of plant pots lean like precarious towers of Pisa against dog ends of carpet and the cardboard boxes from Rich's PC. The rusting fork, spade and secateurs have clearly been hurled in with no regard to safety; a bag of barbecue briquettes spills black dust over the floor. There's barely space to place her feet. She curses her husband – she'd no idea it was such a tip – and gets to work.

* * *

'I've been thinking,' says Adam. 'One thing we haven't really talked about.'

'What's that?'

'Childcare.' He hesitates. 'I don't mean to sound nosy, but

I have to ask, financially, how were you envisaging it working – I mean in terms of your job, having a baby and so on, given you're up in London and, er . . . '

Lou helps him. ' . . . Not that well paid?'

'Mm.'

'To be honest, I've been so taken aback by all that's happened over the last few months, I'd only got as far as thinking money wouldn't – and shouldn't – deter me. The timing is so crucial, I just thought, I'll bloody well make it work. I hope that doesn't sound irresponsible. I just find sometimes when people say, "I can't afford to have a child," what they may mean is, 'I'm too selfish." Not that having a child isn't selfish in some ways too. But my parents didn't have much money when my sister and I were young; they got by because they had to.'

'But you'd have to take some time off work, surely?'

'Of course. The last thing I want is to be like one of those high-flying executives, back at work forty-eight hours after labour. I am entitled to some maternity pay, and obviously I couldn't commute with a baby.' She looks at him. 'Why, what are your thoughts?'

'Oh, mixed, really. I want to be involved, obviously, too . . . But my job is pretty important to me, I guess – sorry, not that yours isn't, but it's a big shift to be making, and like you say, it's all so fast. Part of me thinks it'd be good for me to split the care with you fifty-fifty, part of me isn't so sure I'd be happy – or even able to. And then I think, oh honestly, Adam, don't be such a cliché, there's more that defines you as a person than your job, it's so typically macho to feel that way . . . And then I say to myself, well come on, Adam, Lou probably earns less than you, it makes sense for you to be the one still working if need be for a while, perhaps you could help support her . . . But then I worry about divvying up things in such a traditional way; I don't want to end up with you and me having stereotypical roles . . . One of my whole reasons for wanting a baby is to do it differently. See what I mean? To say I'm in two minds is an understatement.'

Lou smiles. We're both safeguarding our respective worlds, she thinks. There's me not wanting to give away too much physically, here's Adam not wanting to give away too much emotionally or financially. We are both testing, questioning. Which is not surprising: this is all so uncharted and we're still getting to know one another.

'You don't have to work it all out on your own, you know,' she says.

'Sorry?'

'We can work it out together.' Lou can sense this is not the way he is used to doing things. 'I think in the end, it's quite simple. We must remember this isn't about you, or me, ultimately. There's one person who is more important than either of us. Our baby. Let's remember what we said about producing a happy person. I don't want to be naive, but if we focus on that, hopefully we can find a way that makes both of us happy, too.'

*　　*　　*

'Hello?' Rich calls, stepping over the threshold.

The lights are blazing downstairs, but there's no sign of

Cath. He feels a draught coming down the hall – the back door is open. That's odd, he thinks, it's nearly midnight. Why would she be outside? Alarmed, he heads into the garden.

'Cath?'

'I'm in here.' She emerges from the shed onto the lawn. A triangle of light from inside illuminates her in the darkness: she appears covered in dirt, her hair is wild.

'Good Lord, what are you doing?'

'Tidying,' she says, as if he's a fool for asking.

'Love, it's very late.'

'I know, but I've been as quiet as quiet can be. I was going to cut back the creeper, then I came in here, and God, Rich, you left it in complete chaos. I could hardly get through the door.'

'Sorry.' Rich feels a twinge of guilt. Once he'd started piling things in, doing otherwise was impossible. 'Isn't it a little odd to be doing this, um, now . . . ?'

'I suppose . . . Though you know me. I'm crap at waiting. And once I got going . . . ' She drops her hands, exasperated. 'I had to do *something*. Anyway, I'll stop in a sec. But first, come and see.'

Rich is intrigued, but concerned. He's seen his wife like this once before.

A few months after she finished chemo, he watched her behaviour grow increasingly erratic: at first she was just a bit hyper, then she was unable to sleep; eventually she grew so manic she was ironing at 3 a.m., getting up and going for runs – runs? Cath? – at the crack of dawn. It was when she spent twenty-four hours straight stripping woodchip from the bathroom walls he became convinced something really serious was amiss. But no matter how vehemently he'd told her to slow down, she wouldn't, until one day she crashed, like a moth drawn to a fatal flame. After that she spent three weeks refusing to get out of bed and weeping, until he finally persuaded her to go back to their GP, who diagnosed post-traumatic stress. With hindsight, the timing should have been a giveaway; she'd used every ounce of her mental strength to get through the cancer diagnosis and treatment. When she was out the other side, it was as if her brain finally caught up with her body and folded in protest, and she succumbed to the depression she'd been suppressing so long. He prays they're not heading down the same path again.

She tugs his arm, pulling him back to the present. He knows she won't rest till he's admired her handiwork.

He'd forgotten how big the shed is; the space looks vast. But what startles him most is something else entirely: lined carefully along the shelves are dozens of pots. He realizes at once they are Cath's – her parents have quite a display. But he's seen nothing resembling this. These pieces are so striking he's sure he'd remember if he had. There are tall, thin porcelain vases, ghostly silhouettes of white against the dark of the shed walls. There are delicate cups etched with leaves and flowers, and plates so slender they're almost translucent, decorated by a simple contrasting texture. There are teapots and jugs in shapes so pleasing it seems hard to believe they've been fashioned by just one pair of hands, and giant fruit bowls in the palest of grey, woven like cobwebs. En masse, even in the dim light of a 40-watt bulb, they are breathtaking.

It takes Rich a moment to find his voice. Seeing this collection is like seeing a whole new side to his wife.

'Why did you never show me these?' he asks. 'They're amazing.'

Cath shakes her head as if she doesn't know herself. 'They're the last things I made,' she says. 'Before I stopped.'

Together they stand there, looking.

26

Lou is in the staffroom. Opposite her is Shirley, the Head, forking the contents of her plastic lunchbox into her mouth while she talks about the last day of term. But Lou's had a thumping headache all morning and is finding it difficult to concentrate. Presumably it's the medication – she woke repeatedly in the night pouring with sweat. She could miss vital information; she should say she is feeling unwell. It's just the two of them, an opportunity to bring her boss up to speed, yet Lou is worried she'll need time off in the future and doesn't want to try Shirley's patience. All the staff are under enough pressure as it is; the pupils are demanding and funding is tight. If she can just make it through to the holidays, by September she'll know if she's pregnant. Most women hold off on telling their employers at least that long, why should she be an exception?

The door opens. It's Brian, the maths teacher. 'Budge up.' He wants a space at the table. There's a waft of peanut butter – Brian's favourite – as he unwraps his sandwiches from their silver foil. The smell is a fast track to Lou's child-hood.

*

'*Pea-Mite,*' her father is saying. 'That's what I call it.'

'Goodness, Frank, how disgusting,' says her mother.

Lou's sister, Georgia, pulls apart the white bread and wrinkles her nose at the brown smears. 'Ew.' She discards the sandwich, reaching instead for the ham ones Irene has prepared.

'Mm . . . delicious,' says Frank, pointedly. 'Can I tempt you, Louloubelle?' He holds out a triangle, winks in camaraderie.

'OK.' Lou reaches across the picnic rug, takes a bite. She can appreciate why he likes it; the yeasty tang of Marmite combined with the sweetness of peanut butter is strangely appealing, and she's enjoying the fact that her father has made his own lunch in defiance of his wife. Her mother is a perfectly adequate cook, but never experimental.

Lou finishes the sandwich, takes a pack of Chipsticks and sits on the rug, legs crossed, the sound of crunching filling her ears, looking out over the tall grasses. Next to her Georgia is lying on her tummy, reading a photo love story in *My Guy* magazine, riveted. Not far away two boys close to Lou's age are playing football on a stretch of lawn; a man she supposes must be the father of one is in goal.

They're not bad, she thinks, watching them tackle one another, and wanders over to take a closer look, trying to appear nonchalant. She stands there, breeze against her bare legs, on the edge of the pitch, eyes scrunched up against the sun.

'Hey! You wanna join us?' shouts one of the lads.

Lou thinks they mean someone else: turns, looks behind her. No; it's her they're asking.

'Oh, yes,' she says. She likes football but rarely gets the chance to play. At school she is only ever offered netball and hockey in winter, tennis in summer, and there's no way Georgia would kick about with her.

'Great, we can play Wembley then,' says the boy. 'Dad, you stay in goal.'

'Er . . . I don't know the rules,' says Lou.

'You don't know Wembley?' says the boy.

Lou tries not to mind his scorn.

'It's easy,' says the dad. 'It's just a knockout game. Each of you tries to score while stopping the others.'

'That's it?'

'Pretty much. If you don't beat them to it, you wait on the side while the other two continue.'

Lou doesn't need more detail and before he has the chance to stop her, she's scooped the ball from between the feet of the scathing boy. She dribbles it down the field and *THWACK!* into the goal.

'You could wait for me to get back,' protests the dad, laughing, and pants to his place between two jumpers.

Three games and two wins later, Lou has proved her point: she might not know the right names, but she's no pushover.

After a while her father gets up and comes to watch.

'Want to join in too?' asks the other dad.

'Nah, you're all right.' Frank smokes heavily: running around isn't easy. Although he stays on the sidelines and doesn't say much, Lou can sense him cheering her on.

Eventually, they call time. While the two boys and the man gather up their things, Lou returns to the rug and flops down exhausted next to her sister to cool off.

'Not too near to me,' says Georgia, who remains immersed in her magazine. 'You're all sweaty.'

Lou is still lying on her back, face pink, T-shirt and shorts drying off, when the three of them walk past.

'He's good, your son,' says the man.

'Who, Lou?' says Lou's father.

'Yes. He play for anyone?'

'Um, no.'

'You should get him to trial for Hitchin Tigers. These two both play, don't you?'

The boys nod.

'He's just as good as them. Really fast, too.'

'Right,' says Lou's dad.

Lou catches her mother frowning.

After they've gone Frank turns to his daughter. 'I didn't know you could play footie like that.'

Lou is chuffed; she can tell he is proud. 'Do you think I could try for the Tigers then, Dad?'

'What do you want to play for the Tigers for?' asks Georgia.

'I daresay we could look into it,' says Lou's dad.

Irene tuts. 'Oh Frank, of course she can't.' She looks at her daughter. Lou can feel her appraisal, head to toe. 'He thought she was a *boy*.'

Georgia sniggers.

It's as if Lou has been smacked. No matter how hard she tries, it seems she can never impress her mother.

*

The staffroom isn't cold, but Lou shudders.

Never mind telling Shirley what she's embarking on; if she does conceive, she'll have to let her mother know she's going to have another grandchild.

Georgia's offspring are Irene's pride and joy: she sees them all the time. But her sister has chosen a conventional route to parenthood – she married her husband, Howard, a financial consultant, at twenty-four, and they live in one of the most sought-after properties in a smart village nearby. They drive a huge new VW, go to posh dinner parties, and these days Georgia, like her mother, reads a newspaper Lou wouldn't give houseroom to.

So how will Irene react to Lou's co-parenting plans? She'd like to give her mother the benefit of the doubt, and lately they have been striving to understand one another better. Irene will like the fact that Adam's a doctor, surely, yet the set-up is bound to throw her. She'll worry about money, Lou's work, what other people will say, what she will say to other people. In short, even if she tries to mask it, Irene will be critical; when it comes to Lou, it's her default position.

* * *

The phone rings in the hall; it's Peter, Cath's father.

'I'm afraid Cath's in the bath,' Rich tells him, knowing it's his wife Peter will want to chat to. 'Shall I get her to call you back?'

'Er, yes,' says Peter. 'Though actually, while you're on the line, how's she doing, do you reckon?'

'Oh. Good . . . ' Rich moves into the kitchen so he's out of earshot. 'She should be starting medication shortly—' He stops, remembering the conversation with Sukey and Mike. He's rapidly learning that Sukey isn't the only one who seems to feel entitled to express her opinions on egg donation – only the day before a colleague made his hackles rise. 'For her the drugs are relatively mild.' He casts a veil over the fact that Cath will have to have scans to monitor how the lining of her uterus is developing. Cath may be Peter's daughter, but he's an old-fashioned man.

'So how long does she do that for?'

'Depends on how the donor responds, but two weeks, roughly.' Rich looks out at the garden. Everything is trimmed and tied back and tidied away. The waiting is excruciating for Cath, so the house is unnervingly pristine too, but he doesn't want to alarm Judy and Peter. They've been through enough as it is. Rich is conscious he and Cath should be looking after them these days, not the other way around. Instead of voicing concern he says, 'After that we'll have to go back to the clinic.'

'You're staying with Mike and Sukey?'

'Er . . . Probably not, actually.'

'Oh dear, still a bit tricky there, then?'

'You could say that, yes.' He avoids being drawn. He'd like to repair the rift with Mike and Sukey but it's unfair to enlist his parents-in-law as peacemakers. Cath remains unwilling to bend, and this is her family, she could well accuse him of interfering. 'I'm hoping it'll blow over if we give it time,' he says.

'Probably wise.'

There's a silence while they both ponder what to say next. Put the two of us on such personal terrain and we're pretty awkward, thinks Rich.

'Is that Rich?' Judy must have come into the room.

'Yes,' says Peter.

'Have you told him about the money?' she says.

'Ooh, no,' says Peter.

'Silly old man,' says Judy, her tone one of affection. 'Let me have a word.' She comes onto the line. 'Hi, pet. We just wanted to let you know that we've cashed in a few savings to help you with that funny itsy thing.'

'Itsy?' Rich is puzzled.

'You know, the extra thing in the IVF. Cath said it was £800 and you were both having a bit of a problem raising the money.'

'Ah, you mean *ICSI*.' Rich smiles to himself. Then he frowns: he'd no idea Cath had asked her parents for assistance. He's at once perturbed, grateful and embarrassed. Again he has the sense they should be helping their elders, rather than being bailed out by them. He's annoyed with his wife for not consulting him. Though maybe she thought he'd say no. And the truth is they *could* really do with the cash. Now is not the moment to be macho.

'Wow, that's wonderful,' he says. 'Thank you so much.'

'No problem,' says Judy. 'We'll pop a cheque in the post.'

But it is a problem, thinks Rich, once he's rung off; now

there are even more people with an investment in the treatment. He's just considering giving Cath a piece of his mind when, again, he stops himself. Don't be a fool, he realizes. Judy and Peter would have an investment in this IVF whether they contribute financially or not. It's a possible grandchild they're all talking about.

27

It's Karen's birthday tonight, says the text, *and she's got a babysitter, so I've lured her out for bangers and mash at the Shakespeare's Head. Realize it's late notice but be great if you could join us. I'm bringing my new beau and I'd like you to meet him. Plus I worry it's a difficult day for Karen without Simon – perhaps we can take her mind off it. Ax*

Oh dear, thinks Lou. She's been up to London for a scan and is on the train home, but her head is still thudding. She's supposed to take her medication at the same time each day and her syringes are at the flat, so she'll have to go home first; she is very tempted to make her excuses. On the other hand, she wants to be there for Karen, and she's curious about this new man. Anna met him online and seems very taken with him. Karen's told Lou that from the photos he didn't appear as good-looking as Steve, Anna's ex, and they're both keen to check he seems likely to treat their friend well.

Lou shifts in her seat, trying to get comfortable. Her abdomen and breasts are tender; she's bloated. Whereas the initial drugs shut off the supply of oestrogen, now she's taking hormones to make her body produce more eggs. So in less than a fortnight she's gone from menopausal to premenstrual; neither has exactly made her feel genial.

Don't be so self-pitying, she scolds herself. Celebrating a birthday can't be easy in widowhood. I'm not even pregnant yet, and I don't have to get up early as it's the school holidays. I should snatch this chance to socialize.

An hour later, she arrives at the Shakespeare's Head. The wooden tables on the pavement out front are heaving with people; Lou guesses many are students who are staying in Brighton over the summer. There's a young man strumming a guitar, two Indie kids smooching, a group backslapping congratulations to a guy who sounds to have landed a new job, the usual crowd of smokers, and a few commuters in suits en route home. By the door is a couple with a bewitchingly beautiful Weimaraner dog who is wagging his tail, relishing the attention of customers going in and out.

Inside, it takes Lou a moment to locate her friends; they're not in the main room, with its rowdy board-game players and even louder music. Instead they're in a small candlelit room at the back.

'Ah, here you are,' says Lou. 'Happy birthday!' She hands Karen a bouquet.

'Hello!' Anna and Karen rise to greet her with a kiss.

'Was getting a bit cold outside,' explains Anna.

'Bit noisy next door,' says Karen.

'Another year older, another year more middle-aged,' says the man next to Anna, raising his glass. The three of them chink drinks, then he gets to his feet. 'Hi, I'm Rod.' He shakes Lou's hand. 'What can I get you?' In spite of his vertically striped shirt, he can't hide the fact he's overweight. Lou takes in a cloud of white hair, ruddy face and thick black eyebrows. Karen was right: he is not especially handsome, but he seems confident.

'Well?' says Anna, while he's at the bar. 'What do you think of him?'

Lou laughs. 'Goodness! I need a bit longer to make my assessment.'

'You didn't even introduce her,' chides Karen, admiring her flowers.

'Didn't I?' says Anna. Lou can tell she's flustered. It's strange to see her friend this way; normally she's guarded, inclined to play it cool. On first impression she can appear intimidating, icy. But there's a skittishness to her tonight and Lou can see she is blushing.

Lou turns to Karen. 'Anyway, have you had a nice day?'

'I have. The childminder helped Molly and Luke make me this.' She puts down the bouquet, reaches into her bag and pulls out a large card. There is Karen, dressed in a triangle skirt and giant earrings and shoes, with an even bigger smile. Lou guesses Molly drew this. Alongside is a more painstaking rendition of a cake laden with candles. 'Forty-three exactly. I counted. So now the world knows.' They must be Luke's contribution.

'That's gorgeous.'

'And this afternoon Anna – bless her – paid for me to have some beauty treatments in town.'

'Sounds great,' says Lou. There's a beat's silence, while they all think that it should be Simon pampering her. But will it help to say so? It's a fine balance, giving Karen the

223

space to express her grief when she needs to, taking her mind off her loss when she'd rather not focus on it.

As if she reads Lou's mind and wants to steer her, Karen says, 'Look, I had my nails done,' and proudly brandishes a set of startlingly bright red talons.

'Wow,' says Lou. They don't seem Karen's style at all.

'They're not real,' confesses Karen, leaning in close. 'They're extensions,' she whispers.

'Oh,' says Lou. Well, if they make Karen happy.

As Rod returns with Lou's lime and soda, Anna looks up, then suddenly pales.

'Shit.'

'What?'

She shrinks down in her seat. 'Steve.'

'Oh no,' says Karen. 'Where?'

'The bar,' mutters Anna, sliding lower. 'You can see him through the hatch, straight across, there.'

'Has he seen you?' Karen edges forward and lets her curtain of chestnut hair fall to one side so as to shield her friend from view.

This is all we need, thinks Lou. She's never met Anna's ex in person but they've spoken on the phone – Lou tried to persuade him to get help with his drinking. She wonders which of the men at the bar he is. She suspects he's the one with straw-coloured hair and a tan – because yes, he's handsome.

'I'm not sure,' says Anna.

'Well, if he causes any trouble I'll sort him out,' says Rod, immediately puffing up like a threatened tomcat.

'I wouldn't,' says Karen.

But it's as if Rod has given off some pheromone alerting Steve to the presence of a sexual rival – at that moment he clocks them.

In a flash he has made his way over to them, swaying. 'Who's this?' he leers.

Doubtless body language has betrayed that Anna is with Rod: if Lou could read it, Steve certainly will.

'I'm Rod,' says Rod, and holds out a hand. Steve doesn't take it; Rod lets it fall.

'You're ancient,' Steve says.

'It's Karen's birthday,' says Anna quietly. 'Don't ruin it, Steve.'

Steve leans down to Anna's level. Lou can smell the booze on him. Perhaps he isn't so good-looking after all; his grimace is not attractive.

'Leave us alone, mate,' growls Rod. 'Can't you tell she doesn't want you bothering her?'

'Oh, it's your birthday, is it?' Steve says to Karen. 'Well, *happy birthday.*'

'Thanks,' she mutters. Lou can see she is flushed with embarrassment and nerves.

'This all looks very cosy. So this is your new boyfriend, then? Nice to see you've gone for someone your own age this time. And who's this? I don't think I know you . . . You a boy or girl or what?'

'Oi, that's enough.' Rod pushes back his chair. The atmosphere sparks with aggression; those sitting nearby sense it and bristle. Lou can see this escalating into a full-blown fight, chairs flying, any moment. But she's not scared; she's used to dealing with threatening behaviour. She's more worried about Anna and Karen. It's a significant night for them both.

'I'm Lou.' She is pointedly friendly. 'It's nice to meet you, Steve. We've spoken, actually, on the phone.'

He looks confused.

'You've had a bit too much to drink,' she says gently, and stands up to face him.

'So?'

'Come outside. I'd like to talk to you.'

'Why?'

'Just follow me. I can't chat to you about it here.'

'Lou—' Karen catches her arm.

'I'll be OK.'

Out front, she takes a seat next to the couple with the Weimaraner. With such a big-jawed dog on hand, she calculates Steve is hardly likely to lash out. She pats the wooden bench alongside her to indicate he should sit.

'Is she with him?' He jerks his head back inside.

Oh dear, thinks Lou. She can sense his pain. But she can't lie to him. 'Yes.'

'Who is he?'

'His name is Rod. Anna's not been with him long, though really, this isn't about him: this is about you.'

'He looks like a cunt,' says Steve.

Lou refrains from wincing. 'I don't think he does . . . But I don't think it will really help you to focus on Rod right now.'

Steve looks at her. Behind his anger and bewilderment she can see a glimmer of interest. 'What you want to talk to me about, anyway?'

She reminds him that she was the one who recommended he try AA. 'It was a long while back, on the phone. I just wanted to ask you, why did you stop going to meetings?'

'How d'you know I stopped?'

'"Cos you're drunk, my friend.' She shakes her head. She's seen this often in addicts – the denial, the rage, the hatred. She wants to get past these defences. 'It's OK, I'm not going to judge you or anything; what's done is done. Though it might be an idea not to have any more booze tonight.'

'Don't you go telling me what I can and can't do!' he says. His voice is loud; too loud. People close by turn and stare, wary.

It's as if he senses general condemnation; something in him seems to shift. He mutters, 'I can't manage it . . . I was doing all right, and then . . . it all went wrong.'

'What went wrong?'

'I dunno . . . ' He looks at his feet. Lou notices the dog's lead, wound around the leg of the table. It's thick black leather, with a chain. 'It's so boring, not drinking.'

No point in saying that intoxication hardly makes him riveting company. 'Do you have a sponsor – someone to support you?'

'Yes, but I've not seen him in ages.'

'Why not?'

'Oh, he got fed up with me.' At once, it seems as if he's about to cry. Still, it's better than having him all fired up. This lurching of emotions is also familiar.

She lowers her voice. 'Look at his colour,' she says, admiring the dog's silver-beige coat. 'Here,' – then she strokes his long floppy ears – 'feel. They're so soft.' Soon they're petting the

Weimaraner together. His owners keep a close eye, but the dog, unaware of the role it is fulfilling, obliges without fuss.

After a while Steve seems to forget about drinking, his maudlin mood, Anna and Rod, completely. Finally he gets up, announces he is leaving.

'Bye,' he says.

Lou has no idea where he is going, but doesn't try to change his mind. He veers off down the road.

Back inside, Anna and Rod and Karen are relieved to see Lou return alone.

'Gosh, thanks for that,' says Anna. 'How did you do it?'

Lou shrugs. 'Used to it, I guess.' She's like Adam with the injections, unfazed.

'I thought he was set to ruin another evening,' says Karen. Lou suspects she's remembering her husband's funeral where Steve caused a dreadful scene.

'Me too,' says Anna.

'Well,' laughs Karen, slightly hysterical, 'I don't know about you, but I could do with another drink.'

'I'll get them,' says Rod.

The rest of the evening passes in a blur of laughter and conviviality. They're joined by a few other local friends of Karen's, and Rod pulls out the stops to charm them all. It's only on her way home that Lou is free to consider what has happened.

Steve is a hazard to himself, she thinks, picturing him staggering from the pub, and not just because he might get knocked over. Odds are he will carry on drinking – Lou doubts he'll go back to ΛΛ in the near future. She can tell. What has made him susceptible to the allure of alcohol, why can he not stop when others, like Karen and Anna and Rod, can? She wonders if his parents got it wrong somehow, if he was abused in some way, or if they were alcoholics and he had a genetic predisposition. Who knows? Even after all the counselling Lou has been through and practised, she doesn't have any neat answers.

What a muddled up – and muddling – world I'm bringing a child into, she thinks, rubbing her tummy as she walks. She recalls the images she saw that afternoon on the scanner; the honeycomb of follicles developing around her ovaries. Apparently when they get to 18mm they'll be 'ripe for harvesting', as the sonographer put it, as if she's a fruit tree. Each follicle has the potential to become an egg; each egg could then become a baby. So which, if any, of the blurry dark shapes she saw on the sonogram is destined to become her child? If she is that lucky, and does get pregnant, will she and Adam be able to care for a child adequately, nurture it so it doesn't end up on a self-destructive path like Steve? Or can no amount of loving insure against that? And what about the other baby, the one she won't see? Which of the blurry shapes she saw is destined to become *that* baby, and what sort of parents will that child be born to?

28

'The clinic rang,' says Cath, as Rich walks into the kitchen. She is cooking supper. 'They should be ready for us the day after tomorrow.'

Rich slings his jacket on the back of a chair. 'So it's really happening at last. Wow. How exciting.'

'I know.' Cath grins and jumps up and down waving a wooden spoon, excited as a little girl. 'I can't believe it!'

'So, what's the plan?' The smell of garlic and herbs prompts him to open the fridge and pull out a beer, but just as he reaches for the bottle opener, Cath bars his way.

'Whoa. We need you as healthy as possible.'

Rich pouts, deflated.

'Bloody hell, darling, I've had to go without for ages, and if I get pregnant I won't be drinking for months. You can manage a couple of days.'

'Of course.' He adjusts his expression to show he is amenable. Perhaps he'll sneak one later, when she's else-where.

'So apparently her follicles are ready. She just has one

more injection tonight, then on Wednesday morning her eggs are collected.'

'Oh no,' he says.

'What?'

'I've got a meeting on Wednesday.'

'Well, cancel it,' says Cath. 'Or reschedule it, rather. We've got to keep Wednesday free.'

* * *

Adam examines the paperwork. 'So, tonight it's this Otrivelle injection to do?'

Lou nods. 'Later, though. It has to be thirty-six hours before egg collection.'

'Which is . . . ?'

'Ten a.m. Wednesday. Though we have to be at the clinic earlier.'

Adam checks his watch. 'Would you like me to stay, to do it for you?'

'Don't feel you have to.' But Lou can tell he wants to and she'll only sit around getting anxious, otherwise. She's softening to his offers of help. 'Actually, yes, that'd be good. Thanks.'

'Do you want to get a DVD or something?'

She might not be able to concentrate on a whole film, and they are sitting out on her small roof terrace enjoying the evening sun. 'Seems a shame to move.'

They look around. It's a view she never tires of. To the west she can just make out a car wending its way along the spaghetti tracks of the roller coaster, small as an ant at the far end of the pier. To the east is the concrete crescent of the Marina breakwater, hardly Brighton's greatest architectural achievement. Between is the sea, calm, flat, green; in the distance is a ship, Monopoly-sized, maybe a ferry on its way from Newhaven to Dieppe. But tonight it's the sky that surpasses everything. It's what Lou thinks of as a Higher Power moment, when the sun's rays spread in a giant fan from the clouds to the sea. She half expects to see cherubs tumbling to earth through the billowing vapour.

Adam sighs contentedly.

She has an idea. 'You know what I really fancy?'

'What?'

'A game of Scrabble. We can play here.'

'You like Scrabble?'

'I do.' Maybe he doesn't think of her as a wordsmith, but she used to play with her father. It only underlines how little she and Adam really know one another. Are we mad, she worries, embarking on such a major commitment when the main thing we share is a desire to procreate? And what if one of them meets someone else? Whatever they've agreed in principle, it's sure to change the dynamic between the two of them. She pushes the thought away – there are people depending on them. 'I'm not *that* good a player though, never fear. You up for it?'

Adam is already clearing their drinks off the small metal table before them, making room for the board. 'You bet.'

*   *   *

'Oops, nearly forgot,' says Cath, throwing back the sheets and sitting up. Her medication is in the bathroom.

'Ah . . . before you do that—' Rich grabs her arm. 'Come here . . . '

Cath leans back into him. He smells clean and tooth-pasty. She knows at once what he is after.

'Let's not allow the treatment to get in the way the whole time.' He slips a finger under the shoulder strap of her night-dress and it falls aside.

'You're supposed to abstain from any form of sexual activity,' she reminds him.

'*I* am,' he says. 'Not you . . . '

'Mm,' she sighs as he kisses her breast. He's right: it is easy to forget, with all the external pressures, to make love.

He sucks a little harder; she can sense his desire, which arouses her more, in turn. He turns his attention to her other nipple, then tracks his tongue down her abdomen, teasing.

'You really mustn't come,' she says, and almost resists. But it feels particularly special to be intimate tonight. As if in spite of it all they are making their baby together.

* * *

Adam puts down the word with a flourish.

'No way.' Lou shakes her head. He chuckles and she sees he still has two tiles in his hand. 'Oh no . . . !'

'Oh yes . . . ' He adds them. He's got rid of all seven letters, an additional score of fifty.

'No wonder you were happy to play. I might as well give up.'

'Probably best – it's time for your injection.'

'Really?' The evening has gone so fast. It's dark; the lights of the pier shine bright against a purple sky, the air is growing chilly.

Inside, Lou lies back on the bed, lifts her T-shirt and braces herself.

'Ready?' says Adam.

'Yup.' She looks away, a tiny jab, and he is done. 'Funny to think that might be my last one.' The procedure seems almost ceremonial as a result.

'I think I'll get off home.' Adam wraps the needle and disposes it safely in the sharps tin supplied with the drugs. 'If you don't mind.'

'Of course not,' she says, though she feels a pang of sadness at being left alone. They have been so at ease with one another – as comfortable with periods of silence as they are with banter or intimate chat – that it's highlighted how she lacks day-to-day intimacy without Sophia here. She says goodbye and flips up the lock. It's just her and her studio. Still, Lou is determined not to be maudlin.

*   *   *

'Right, that's it, all done,' says Cath, returning from the bathroom and climbing back into bed alongside her husband.

But Rich is already asleep. She strokes the back of his neck, thinking how much she cares for him, how blessed she is to have a husband she still fancies so much. Then she leans to turn off the light, reverses her body until it's wedged tight alongside his, closes her eyes.

She can't feel the pessary as such, but she can imagine it gradually dissolving, the progesterone doing its work, thickening the lining of her womb. It's very strange to think that somewhere a mirror woman is going through a similar process. She wonders if she is snuggling up to her partner after making love, too.

29

Adam is driving home from work – he's escaped earlier than usual. It's a glorious evening.

If everything goes to plan, the next day he will be on his way to becoming a father: what a strange – and powerful – thought. Not many people end up planning conception so specifically, to the day, the hour, almost the minute. Such exactitude appeals to the scientist in him. Yet there remains an element of mystery to it all; it's beyond the realms of his experience – and he's excited too. Just then he spies a parking space close to his favourite cafe on the prom; its cornflake-yellow awnings beckon. On impulse he stops the car, reverses in. He has an urge to pay tribute to this moment.

The counter would usually be closed at this time, but the opportunity provided by sunshine and school holidays is evidently too good to miss and the place is heaving. He purchases a latte, shoos a pigeon from a chair and sits at one of the green plastic tables by the beach. From here he can see right down the esplanade. On the nearby lawn two teams of middle-aged men are playing five-a-side football with more enthusiasm than skill, a couple of trim young women are doing star jumps with considerably greater flair, and a party of teenagers is having a picnic. Adam is perturbed: they appear to be scalding the grass with the heat from their foil barbecue, and their beatbox is turned up way too loud – he can hear it from where he is sitting. On the broad stretch of tarmac straight ahead an elderly couple dressed in very wintry clothes for such warm weather stroll slowly hand in hand. They're a marked contrast to a golden-skinned guy in nothing more than the shortest of shorts and rollerblades who swoops and swirls in great arcs around them, bottom protruding like a cat on heat. He smiles and catches Adam's eye; clearly he is showing off to lure suitors, but tonight there's no way Adam is remotely inclined.

All around, people are chatting and laughing; at the very next table, a father and his son are bantering amiably. The boy must be, what – eight, nine? He has a shiny chrome scooter propped up against the railings. His shoes, with their Day-Glo laces, look new and trendy, and his face has a healthy glow from a day in the sun, whereas his father's T-shirt is faded and the back of his neck is burnt, peeling.

The dad has obviously looked after his son better than he has himself, thinks Adam. I wonder if I'll be like that, too.

*   *   *

This has to be one of the least appealing roads in the entire country, thinks Rich. Considering it runs close to some magnificent countryside, the view is dull as ditchwater. Still, perhaps it's good that he's driven up and down it so often he could virtually navigate with his eyes shut: he's tired. As usual he was caught late with work; at this rate he and Cath won't get to London till almost midnight.

Cath is leaning against the car window, hypnotized by the white lines flashing past to her left. She appears not in the mood to talk, so he reaches for the button of the radio. But before he has a chance to select a station, she says, 'Do you have to? I was hoping to snooze.'

He knows better than to argue. She's pretty wound up about the next few days, though at least they have a place to stay. Cath's brother and his family have gone abroad for a fortnight and Mike has managed to broker a deal with Sukey: while they are away Cath and Rich can use the house. This is a relief. They cannot afford hotel bills too.

Presently Rich sees Cath's head loll forward then jerk up; he glances across – she is sleeping. Good, he wants her well rested. He feels a surge of love for her. Cath is undertaking so much, yet in many ways is more sensitive mentally – and certainly physically – than he is. She will need to draw on such emotional strength in the journey that they are about to embark upon. She is the one whose commitment will be tested, who – should they conceive – will have to look after herself for the duration of a pregnancy. His role is comparatively simple: providing sperm will only take minutes. Then his life can resume, pretty much as it is now, until – touch wood – the baby comes. He can have a beer, eat badly, relinquish exercise – it will make no odds.

He checks her again. She looks so vulnerable there in the passenger seat: wisps of hair splayed out against the glass, cheek resting on the makeshift pillow of her cardigan, trusting him utterly to focus on the road ahead and get her safely to their destination.

* * *

It's approaching 7 a.m., and Lou, too keyed up to sleep, is showered and dressed and gazing out of her attic window. She looks across the rooftops, trying to imprint today's seascape on her memory; maybe, if the IVF works, in the future she'll want to tell her child about this particular morning. It's hazy, but lately it's been hot; the mist should clear. The sky is a watercolour wash: pale blue up high, lilac close to the horizon. The boundary between cloud and sea is scarcely visible and gives the day an uncertain feel, as if it's hard to pin down, floating.

Her eye falls on her windowsill, where she keeps some of her most treasured possessions. There, next to the battered Russian dolls she was given as a child and a trophy she won playing tennis as a teenager, is the photograph Adam commented on of her parents on their wedding day. '1971. Same year Bianca married Mick,' Lou recalls her dad telling her, but it's hard to imagine the dates coinciding. She has seen pictures of the Jaggers – Mick, louche in his pale linen suit and trainers, with his long hair and cigarette; Bianca in head-to-toe Yves St Laurent, audaciously bra-less. St Tropez and St Albans might as well be light years apart: a duo further from her parents is hard to imagine. In this shot, on the steps of the parish church not far from where her mother lives now, Irene is standing with her court shoes neatly together as if she's a Girl Guide waiting to have her uniform inspected. Her long dress is elaborately ruched and frilled, but she couldn't look more strait-laced if she tried. Her hair is piled up in a bun, hardly the height of fashion then, and there isn't an inch of décolletage on display – her collar buttons to her chin and finishes with a ruffle. Beside her, Lou's father looks scarcely more comfortable. He is three-piece-suited and polished-booted in accordance with tradition, right down to the white carnation pinned in his buttonhole. He's holding Irene's hand, but they're a pace or two apart, rigid. Not even their heads are inclined towards one another; their smiles are unsure.

Lou thinks of the decades they spent together, a marriage typified by that same tension. She examines the photo again: they're like a pair of sunflowers in separate pots; they each have their own root system, self-sufficient. But, also like sunflowers, they appear fragile in solitude, as if their stems are not quite strong enough to sustain them in isolation.

*　*　*

Adam can see Lou waiting at her window, toots the horn to get her attention. A couple of minutes later he leans over to open the passenger door and she edges awkwardly into the seat.

'You OK?'

'I'm about to pop,' she says, putting her rucksack between her feet. 'The eggs must be the size of tennis balls. I swear I can feel them knocking against one another. Couldn't get my jeans done up this morning, had to opt for trackie bottoms.'

'Probably wise to wear something comfortable,' he says. 'I

made us a thermos of tea if you can fit a cup in.' He gestures towards the flask slotted into the drinks holder behind the gearstick. 'Help yourself.'

'I'm not allowed anything to eat or drink prior to the procedure,' Lou reminds him.

'Oh no, nor you are. Dumb of me, sorry.' Concentrate, Adam tells himself. *The last thing we want is an accident on our way to London, and the junction onto Marine Drive is tricky.* Once they're on the main road, he says, 'So how are you doing otherwise?'

'Nervous.' Lou turns to him. 'And excited, I guess . . . ' She bites her lip. 'I'm crossing my fingers today is successful. How about you?'

'Same,' he nods. They stop at the lights by the Pavilion; the turrets and domes glow powder-pink in the morning light. *Being here brings back their initial conversations about having a baby: he drove home this way after dinner. The fears that he had then have largely abated. He's not gone around shouting about it, but lately he's been feeling increasingly elated at the prospect of becoming a father.*

Lou turns to him. 'You are sure we're doing the right thing, aren't you?'

He can feel her check his expression. She does sound really anxious, he thinks. Perhaps she's concerned he won't pull his weight, yet helping her with the injections and spending time with her has deepened his commitment. 'Don't worry, of course we are.' He smiles at her.

'It's just . . . ' She coughs, awkwardly. 'We still don't know each other that well, do we?'

'I suppose . . . ' They've spoken of this over the last few

weeks already, but it's understandable she might want more reassurance. Or perhaps she is so hormonal she has forgotten their previous conversations. 'But there are hundreds of people who know each other less than we do when they get pregnant, and they manage,' he points out. 'Often they make a surprisingly good job of parenting.'

'I'm not sure I want to set my standards against some irresponsible teenager,' she says. Her vehemence takes him aback. Although maybe she's referring to the kids she works with, or their parents. She's bound to be passionate about ill-planned pregnancies when she is witness to long-term distress in their wake.

'I hardly think you need worry that I'm an irresponsible teenager.'

She shrugs. 'I suppose.' He notes a strange tone to her voice.

She is quiet for several moments, frowning. The atmosphere inside the vehicle grows uneasy.

Then Adam realizes what Lou might be trying to say; it hits him in the solar plexus, and it's all he can do not to swerve the car. Is it possible she's considering cutting him out? He panics, struggling to stay focused on the road.

It would be as I feared, he thinks. I couldn't bear that. Not now, at this stage.

Don't be silly, Adam, he argues with himself. Lou's not like that – it's not in keeping with the woman you've got to know. And Howie's assured you she's one of life's good people, too.

Then again, she has just been saying they're comparative strangers . . .

Adam's thoughts tumble as he tries to assess the implications. If she has decided she doesn't want to go through this with him, she might still have other options. In spite of everything she has said about needing – and wanting – to do this fast, she could probably find another donor quite easily. She may even be able to switch to using an anonymous donor at the clinic, if she wants, almost straight away. They might encourage her to do that – they'd make more money, it's often less complicated medically, and it's certainly less of a legal minefield.

Good grief. I really am expendable, thinks Adam. I hadn't reckoned on anything changing, let alone at this eleventh hour. But Howie also said she was tough underneath; perhaps I'm seeing evidence of it.

He veers off the roundabout onto the A23, panic rising.

There are no such ready alternatives for me, he thinks. Who else am I going to find to co-parent with? A proposal like Lou's comes along once in a lifetime, if ever. I'll be back where I was: with offers of playing a loose uncle to a child I father for a lesbian couple, or using a surrogate to go it alone . . .

He's put so much time and energy into this already – not just helping Lou, but getting himself in the right headspace again. After all these weeks of building up his hopes, the possibility of not being a dad is devastating.

He swallows, considering what to say, how best to handle the situation. He doesn't want to pressurize Lou, but it's almost impossible to keep the desperation from his voice.

'Are you having doubts . . . ?' he ventures. He can hardly bear to hear her answer.

She nods. 'I guess, a few.'

He tries to sound less mortified than he feels. 'I think I understand . . . We wouldn't be human if we didn't have concerns, would we?'

'Wouldn't we?'

He can sense her looking at his profile again. He feels his face flush with worry. 'If you want to look for another donor or something, I suppose that's OK . . . '

'Oh.' She seems taken aback. 'Really?'

She must be pleased I'm making it easy for her, he thinks. But why be difficult? It's not in his nature to force people into doing things they don't want to, let alone something as major as this. 'Mm,' he nods, disappointed beyond words.

Again they say nothing. The stretch of motorway yawns in front of them. Again he glances across at her. She is continuing to frown.

'Er . . . don't *you* want to do this, then?' she says.

This conversation is increasingly bizarre. Unless he's misreading her – and it is hard when he can't see her face for more than a split second at a time – she sounds perturbed at the prospect he might not be keen.

They are approaching a service station; the junction is a few hundred yards ahead.

This is ridiculous, he thinks, suddenly enraged. If she doesn't want me to be involved after all, then really, I am not prepared to drive her into London. I'm not a bloody chauffeur.

He indicates, pulls onto the slip road, turns into the garage forecourt, stops the car and swivels to face her.

'What's the problem?' he says, unable to conceal his anger and upset. 'Don't you want me to father the child?'

*　*　*

Cath is standing in the porch, keys in hand.

'Come on,' she shrieks.

'Keep your hair on,' says Rich, coming down the stairs. 'My appointment isn't till eleven.'

'It's ten to nine!'

'Love' – he pulls on his jacket – 'it takes just over an hour into town. I'll be ever so early.'

'I don't want you to be late to give a sperm sample,' says Cath.

Hmm, thinks Rich. Waiting has never been his wife's strong point, but now is probably not the time to say this. She's so pent-up with apprehension about the morning ahead, if he's not careful she'll explode at him, and he's finding it hard not to feel pretty tense himself.

*　*　*

Lou stares at Adam, aghast. 'Of course I do.'

'So what is it, then?' He appears furious.

'It's me,' she says. 'It's me.'

'*You?*'

'Yes.' She finds herself crying. How can she begin to explain? He still hardly knows her.

'Here.' Adam passes her a tissue.

Lou is not one to weep easily, but she seems to have

245

mislaid the lid to her emotions. She blows her nose and looks around, struck by the ludicrousness of their situation. They're in a Texaco garage; beside them cars whizz past on the dual carriageway, hurtling northwards. Before them is a shop; by the automatic doors are a couple of buckets of bedraggled flowers, a stand of newspapers flapping in the breeze, several bags of barbecue fuel. At a pump nearby a man in a lilac shirt and suit trousers is refuelling his Jaguar for the commute to work. He sees Lou's tears and turns away, embarrassed.

She sniffs and tries to work out what to say. Adam seems to have misconstrued her: she'd best come out with it. 'I'm worried about being a mum.' She thinks of the photo on her windowsill, her parents with their separate root systems. 'What if I'm crap at it?'

'Oh,' he says.

'My mother is a nightmare,' she admits, then feels bad for being so harsh. 'Or at least, she wasn't a very easy mother for, well . . . someone like me.'

'That doesn't mean you won't be any good at it,' says Adam. Lou can sense his anger dissipating. His cheeks return to their usual colour. 'Quite the opposite, perhaps.'

She gives him a half smile. He's got such a kind face, she thinks, not for the first time. But we are a very odd couple. Far odder, in terms of convention, than my parents, and look what a mess they made of things. She can picture them now; her mother's lips a thin line of silent disapproval, her father umming and erring, often understanding Lou better, yet unwilling to risk a scene by arguing on her behalf. In many ways it's what they *didn't* say that hurt: her mother's raised eyebrows at what Lou chose to wear, the glares directed at her father if he was too soft on her, the dismissive shrugs when Lou would try and explain something she felt passionate about.

Adam pours himself a beaker of tea, takes a sip. 'Don't you remember saying you wanted to rectify some of your parents' mistakes?'

'Did I?'

'Well, maybe you didn't say that exactly, but it was along those lines. The first time we chatted in the pub. Anyway, if it's any consolation, I worry too. I guess everyone does. I remember my sister saying worry is the default position of every parent.'

'We haven't even got that far,' says Lou. Nonetheless, he is helping her feel better.

'From what you've told me, your mum does sound a rather difficult woman, but that doesn't mean you'll get the same things wrong she did. And she can't have got everything wrong. You're pretty OK, if you ask me.'

'Aw, thanks. They didn't get it *all* wrong,' she admits. 'My mum's trying, these days, and my dad . . . ' She gulps, feeling an ache of longing for him still to be alive. 'He got lots of stuff right.' She's struck by how hard it is going through this without either of her parents' support.

'There you are then. Plus there's another thing,' Adam grins. '*My* mum is ace. So here goes: we can just reverse our role models, how very appropriate. I can follow my mum's example, you can follow your dad's. We're trying to avoid stereotypes after all.'

Lou watches the man in the lilac shirt as he walks past

247

them to his car, still avoiding eye contact. She thinks of Irene again, of the gulf between them. 'Do you really think I'll be a good mum?'

'I think you'll be bloody brilliant.'

'How can you be sure?'

'I can't be *sure*,' says Adam. 'But I hope I'm a reasonable judge of people, and I wouldn't be doing this with you if I didn't think so.'

Lou wipes her eyes. It's good to hear him voice this.

'For starters, if you weren't a nice person you wouldn't be donating your eggs.'

'Thanks,' she smiles.

'And you . . . ' Adam looks at her. 'Are *you* OK with the idea of my being the father?'

'Of course I am.'

'Phew.' He pats her knee and hands over the beaker. 'So, pop this back. And now, Lady Penelope, if you don't mind, Parker had better get back on the road, before we're late for our appointment.'

30

'I'll let the consultant know you're here,' says the receptionist.

Lou looks around the lobby. The couple sitting on the sofa are Chinese. Well, we'll certainly know if they get all our samples muddled, Lou thinks. Then she scolds herself; she is being paranoid.

Presently Dr Hassan joins them. 'So, today's the big day.' His mauve-checked shirt looks crisp and pressed and his white hair just combed.

'Yes.' She and Adam speak in unison.

'We need to prepare you for theatre,' says Dr Hassan to Lou. He addresses Adam. 'I take it you're not coming in?'

'I'm happy to if you want,' Adam says to Lou. 'But you said no.'

'I'd really rather do it on my own, if you don't mind,' she says. He might have put needles in her tummy, but the operation is more intimate.

'She'll be in with us for a while,' Dr Hassan continues. 'And as we're using your frozen sperm, I suggest you come back later.'

249

Once Adam has gone, Dr Hassan leads Lou into a private room with a single bed and closes the door. 'After you,' he says, gesturing to an armchair. He pulls up another opposite.

Lou says, 'Adam is not my partner, you see.'

'No, I remember,' says Dr Hassan. 'But each woman likes to play it differently with their donor, I've found.' She can tell from his expression that an arrangement like theirs is nothing unusual as far as he is concerned. 'I'll just run through the procedure with you. OK?'

Lou nods.

'So, we'll be giving you an intravenous anaesthetic in just over half an hour.'

'Will I be able to feel anything?'

'Not at all. Although it isn't as strong as a general anaesthetic, so you'll be awake for the procedure. We'll be inserting an ultrasound probe into your vagina. We pass a little needle through this directly into the ovarian follicles – these are the structures in the ovary which contain the eggs – ' – Lou nods, she's well versed in these terms by now – 'and the eggs will be gently sucked out.'

'I seemed to have loads of follicles in the last scan – do you take eggs from them all?'

'It's usually possible to collect them from most of the larger ones. We'll inspect them in the lab to get a preliminary idea of their maturity and let you know later today.'

'I see.'

As the doctor scrubs up, Lou makes a silent wish. *Please get lots. I want to make sure there are enough to give my recipient at least five.*

'What if she doesn't produce enough eggs to share with us?' says Cath, as they cross over the junction of Wigmore Street.

'She will,' says Rich. 'They must have had a pretty good idea when they did her scans.'

They're approaching the clinic; elegant Georgian frontages flank them on either side. On the threshold, Cath stops and looks up. Everything about the building is symmetrical: the wrought-iron railings that line the black-and-white-tiled steps, the pillars on either side of the glossy red front door, the classical windows rising four floors above. Even the scarlet geraniums and trailing ivy in the smart pewter window boxes are perfect echoes of one another. Apparently her donor will be having her eggs collected at some point today. Cath wonders if she is inside at this very minute, behind one of the net curtains.

'How can you be so calm?' she asks her husband.

'I don't know, love. But look, you really don't have to come in. Why don't you let me get it over with – go and have a look round the shops or something – and I'll meet you after?'

He has a point. They probably won't welcome her being there – the receptionist may even have to send her away, given that anonymity is part of the protocol and she and her donor are not supposed to meet one another. Anyway, Cath is far too twitchy to sit still. She is keen to distract herself. 'OK . . . I'll meet you in . . . what? An hour?'

'Sounds about right. Where?'

She plucks the first place she can think of from the air. 'Topshop?' There's a giant one on Oxford Circus. But Rich looks distinctly underwhelmed, and on second thoughts she's not in remotely the right mindset to look at clothes. 'All right, in the cafe in John Lewis,' she relents. 'At midday.'

Presently she crosses the gardens of Cavendish Square, the grey facade of the department store rising ahead of her.

If I go in the rear entrance I can avoid the worst of the crowds, she thinks.

The gold-engraved signage beckons her in as if with a stately bow, and before she knows it Cath is surrounded by cosmetics and beauty serums. An assistant tries to assail her to test a new perfume, but she keeps walking. Nor can she face the over-made-up women behind any of the counters. She's all too conscious of what her husband is doing at the clinic a couple of blocks away, and that's not the only thing preying on her mind. It's as if there's an invisible thread connecting her to her donor; she could swear she can feel twinges in her abdomen, as if a phantom surgeon is operating on her too.

Eventually she locates a guide to the layout of the store, and soon she is riding the up escalators. She glides past ladieswear and lingerie, up through bed linen and garden furniture to the fourth floor.

Aah . . . *Haberdashery.*

For Cath, even the word is reassuring. Here, surely, she can treat herself to something that won't cost the earth.

She steps from metal onto carpet and tries to take it all in. There are countless rolls of ribbon: spotted, striped, tartan, satin, grosgrain and velvet. There are endless trimmings: lace, sequins and appliqué; feathers, buttons and bows . . . There are neatly stacked shelves of yarn, sorted by hue and texture

. . . And there are beads in every colour of the rainbow and almost every shape under the sun.

Reels of cotton, strings for necklaces, glue, scissors and stencils – everything, everywhere is calling out to her: make me, assemble me, sew me. The sheer potential is over-whelming.

She picks up a basket and starts to move around the displays, impulsively plucking items that please her, like a magpie lining her nest.

* * *

Rich shuts his eyes, tries to imagine himself somewhere else entirely. It's all very well asking him to 'produce a sperm sample' as the assistant put it, but this small, stark room is hardly conducive. There's a TV with a DVD player in the corner of the room; he knows from his previous trip to the clinic he's expected to use it. But whilst Rich doesn't think of himself as overly romantic, conceiving a child with the help of another woman feels pretty unsavoury; a kind of vicarious infidelity. He thinks of other couples who can fondly remember the special time or place where their offspring were conceived. Didn't his own mother let slip he himself was the result of a particularly cold New Year's Eve, which she and his father welcomed in with a 'cosy' early night?

When he's done, he seals his donation in a plastic cup, places it on a shelf and presses a bell. Presumably they wait a few minutes before collecting it so as to avoid an embar-rassing handover in the corridor.

Why don't they let partners in there to help? he wonders

as he makes his way back down Harley Street. If he were braver and were not in a hurry to be with Cath, he'd have suggested it.

The one bit he'd have found interesting – seeing what the technicians did in the lab – he's not permitted to be party to. Apparently the sperm are washed and spun at high speed to help select the healthiest – he'd have liked to have seen how they did it. But the technician who'd briefed him was firm. 'The eggs need a few hours to incubate and mature,' he'd said. 'There really is no point hanging around.'

Presently, he pushes open the doors of the department store, where a heady smell of perfume greets him.

*　*　*

There's a tap on the door.

'Come in,' says Lou.

It's a nurse. 'I've got you a cup of camomile tea and a biscuit, when you're ready.'

Lou props herself up on her elbows. 'Is, um . . . Adam here?'

'Your friend?'

'Yes.'

'I'll just fetch him.'

Shortly his auburn-topped head pops round the door. She is happy to see a friendly face. 'Everything OK, Lady P.?'

He's followed by Dr Hassan. 'Well, that went very well,' he beams.

'How many eggs did you get?' asks Adam.

'We need to check them thoroughly first, but we'll give

you a ring this afternoon, Lou. It all looked pretty good in there to me, though – I'm sure we got enough. Ah.' His eyes crinkle with pleasure. 'I see you're eating your biscuit. Good.'

Funny how he can segue straight from my uterus to my diet, thinks Lou. Bodies must be bodies to doctors.

'Now, you're not doing anything silly like going back to the office, are you?'

'I work in a school. We're on holiday.'

'I'm driving her back to Brighton,' explains Adam.

'Excellent. You should take it easy for the rest of the day.'

'Will I have any side effects?' asks Lou. She has a vague sense of something having happened inside her, no more than that.

'It varies from woman to woman. Some get cramps; others very little pain at all. You'll probably have a small amount of bleeding so we've put a pad on for you. If you're worried later, you can always give us a call.'

*   *   *

Rich is not surprised to see Cath with a huge plastic carrier bag before her on the coffee table – some kind of retail therapy was inevitable.

'What did you buy?'

'Things. I'll show you in a sec.' She leans forward, eager. 'How did it go?'

'Not much to report really. No different from the first time – a bit grim.'

Cath wrinkles her nose – he can tell she finds the whole

255

idea distasteful. 'Well, let's hope you get as many little goers as before.'

Rich nods. He's been too diplomatic to say so, given the circumstances, but he's rather chuffed about his sperm's motility. Apparently when they tested his initial sample all those weeks previously, it was well above average. He pictured millions of microscopic tadpoles swimming eagerly to their destination, and felt a surge of masculine pride.

'Did they say anything about our donor's egg collection?'

'Not yet, no. They'll ring us this afternoon, apparently. So, c'mon, show me your wares.' He is keen to distract her.

She tips the contents of the bag onto the table: it contains several smaller paper bags and he tries not to flinch at what she might have spent. He opens them one by one. Inside are several different pieces of fabric, a packet of needles, a box of pins, a reel of thread, some weird white padding and a pair of pinking shears. He is flummoxed. Perhaps she is planning a spate of mending? Given the state of their finances, that might not be such a bad idea.

'I'm going to do some patchwork.'

'Eh?'

'I thought I'd make a little bedcover – you know, a quilt.'

'Ri-ight . . . ' Their home is full to bursting already, and he's never known Cath be into sewing. She has an old machine in the loft but he's never seen her use it.

She clasps her hands together. 'Something we might use for the baby.'

He looks at her, eyes wide.

'Or maybe not,' she adds hurriedly. 'If you think that's tempting fate?'

But it's too late. Once again Rich fears Cath is getting way ahead of herself.

* * *

Back in the passenger seat of Adam's car, Lou turns on her mobile.

Someone's left a voicemail. Maybe it's Ian, the embryologist from the clinic? Though that would be awfully quick . . . But not if something has gone wrong – he'd ring at once to report . . . Her heart starts to race.

However, it's just Anna, wanting to know how the procedure has gone. Lou is still feeling too fragile to chat, so texts a reply. She copies in Karen – she may as well bring them both up to speed. She presses send, and her message goes off with a satisfying *swoosh*, as if carried up and away by a winged messenger. Suddenly she thinks of her sister, Georgia; she's nearer, as the bird flies to London, than either of them. This isn't right, she thinks, not telling her. Other than Karen, Georgia is the person I'm closest to who might understand what I'm going through. She is my sister, and although we are very different, she's had children, too. Maybe it would bring us together.

But if she tells Georgia, she'll have to tell her mother. Georgia tells Irene everything. Don't they both deserve to know she is donating her eggs? They are genetically linked, after all . . . Yet Lou can't cope with explaining the entire set-up, let alone having their feedback, now. She can imagine all too well what her mother might say . . .

257

If the egg harvesting then implantation is successful, in two weeks she'll know if she's pregnant; excitement about her having a baby may temper their reactions. Surely it makes sense to hold off at least until then?

31

'Oh my goodness, it's the clinic.' Lou grabs the phone. She's stretched out on the sofa in her flat, supposedly relaxing.

'Hello, Lou. This is Ian, your embryologist.'

'Hang on. I'm going to put you on speaker. I want my friend to hear you too.' Adam is in the armchair opposite. She puts the mobile on the coffee table between them. 'Yes?'

'Congratulations: we got twelve eggs.'

'Twelve!'

'Yup.'

Adam high fives her.

'That's fantastic!' Lou is so relieved she can barely get the words out.

'We're all delighted.'

'Me too.' She feels proud, vindicated and happy in one great big rush. Her body has come up trumps for them all. 'That's so brilliant!' she repeats.

'Yes, and you've an even number, which makes it simple regarding your recipient: we'll just split them in two, six each, if you're happy? It's your legal right to withdraw your consent at any time, so you have to be sure. Would you like a while to talk it over and call me back?'

'No.' Lou is adamant. Six is plenty – they can't implant more than two anyway. 'I'm fine. Please go ahead and let her know.'

'If you're sure? We'll do our best to ensure the quality of the eggs is evenly divided too.'

Although the decision is hers, Lou raises her eyebrows at Adam to check he's also happy. He nods, then coughs. 'Er . . . ' He leans towards the speaker. 'It's Adam here, yes, we're fine with that. Though can I ask – what about the sperm?' Naturally he wants to know – and how could Lou not have asked? It's equally important.

'Your sample was fine,' says Ian. 'It has a slightly lower count than when it was initially frozen, but we'd expect that, and it's still well within the viable range. There is a good chance of success.'

Once he's rung off, they sit back in their respective seats, shoulders drooping with depleted energy, like balloons after a party.

'Phew,' they say in unison.

After a while, Lou says, 'What's the time?'

'Half five.'

'It's a bit early, but . . . do you know what I fancy?'

'Not Scrabble again, please.'

'A takeaway curry,' says Lou. 'I'm famished.'

*　*　*

Cath is on all fours on the carpet in Mike and Sukey's living room, attempting to arrange forty-two squares of fabric into a pleasing patchwork design. She purchased a selection of cotton lawns – floral, striped, spotted, checked, plain and paisley – in a similar pale colour palette. She has already cut them up using her new pinking shears while Rich looked on, agog at her speed and dexterity, and is laying them out six squares one way, seven the other when—

Didlingding!

'That'll be them!' she says before her mobile has finished the sequence of its ringtone. 'Can you reach it?'

Rich stretches out for the phone. 'Hello?'

'Pass it over,' she orders. Perhaps she is being a bit OTT, but honestly, sometimes he can be so slow! 'Hello. It's Cath Morris here. Is that the clinic?'

'Yes,' says a woman. 'It's Mrs Donoghue. We've spoken before, if you recall, and I met your husband earlier.'

'Of course,' says Cath.

'I'm calling to let you know the results of the procedures we undertook this morning.'

'Yes?' She tries not to snap. Trusting everyone else to manage a process that affects her so profoundly is hard.

'It's good news all round. We collected twelve eggs from your donor.'

'Twelve!'

Rich beams in delight and gives her a nudge. 'Can you put them on speaker?'

Oops, she's not been thinking of him. 'I'm just putting you on speaker so my husband can hear.'

'Sure,' says Mrs Donoghue. 'Ready?'

261

'Yes.'

'So your donor has given her consent to proceed with the transfer.'

'Yippee!' Cath jumps up and gives Rich a hug.

'That's wonderful,' says Rich, when he can speak again.

'We'll divide the eggs evenly between you. And we'll do that in terms of quality too.'

'Thank you.'

'Though I do have to remind you, your donor does reserve the right to pull out at any point right up to embryo transfer.'

'Yes, we know.'

'In terms of your sample, Mr Morris—'

'Call me Rich,' says Rich. It does seem daft to address him so formally, given the intimacy of the subject.

'OK, Rich. Yes, well, in terms of your motility, it appears very good indeed. Even higher than previously. This time you had 120 million. That's right at the top end of the range.'

'Told you to stop drinking,' says Cath smugly.

Rich looks proud of himself.

Mrs Donoghue continues, 'So, we're going to be using ICSI, as you know.'

'Mm.'

'But I do have to remind you both that although ICSI has a good success rate, it doesn't guarantee the formation of an embryo. There's still a long way to go.'

'We appreciate that,' says Rich. He nods at Cath, as if to say these words of caution are aimed at her.

Caution be damned, thinks Cath. We're over the first big hurdle!

'Goodness!' says Lou as Adam plonks several bags from the curry house on the table. 'Sure you got enough?'

'In for a penny,' he grins. 'Anyway, I imagine you'll have all sorts of weird cravings if this works. We may as well get used to it. And, given that you're not supposed to drink for twenty-four hours, I got us some alcohol-free beer too.'

'I wouldn't mind you having the normal stuff.'

'Nah.' He cracks open a can and passes it to her. 'You're the one who deserves a reward. What you've done today is amazing.'

'Do you think?'

'I do. You're bringing hope to a childless couple – that's wonderful.'

'She could be single,' Lou points out. 'They treat women who aren't in relationships at the clinic, too.'

'I don't reckon she is,' says Adam.

Nor does Lou, but she's no idea why.

'She could be gay . . . ' he muses.

'I don't think that either. If she was in a relationship and had a problem with her eggs, it stands to reason her partner would use hers, don't you think?'

'See what you mean. Anyway, whoever she is, you've been beyond generous. Plus you're giving me the chance to be a dad, which, frankly, I didn't think I would ever get. And – touch wood – I can't wait to see the little bugger! So . . . ' He raises his lager. 'Here's to you.'

'Gosh, thanks.' Lou blushes. She doesn't feel she deserves

this accolade: not yet. 'I think we should take this a day at a time,' she advises.

'I know, I know, but I can feel it in my water; it's going to be OK.'

'Really?' This is a new, more reckless, Adam speaking. Usually he's pretty circumspect. The thrill seems to be getting to him.

'Aw, come on, Lou, let's look on the bright side, just for this evening. I know, I know, we shouldn't get too hopeful, but fuck it! I want to! I was walking to the offie, you know, past all the usual folk – the saddos outside the bars – and yes, yes, I know we're drinking and it's not yet six, but ours isn't real booze – and some guy wolf-whistled at me, bless him, and I thought, hey man, yes, yes, I know it's great being in Kemptown and stuff, and yes, I know I'm cute, if you like middle-aged ginger gnomes, but what you don't know is this is a BIG day for me, so thanks for the compliment, but I've got more important things going on right now – I might well be on the way to being a daddy!' He stops, realizes she is not quite with him and adopts a more serious tone. 'It's just sometimes, with all the drugs and the clinic and the fact we're not a couple and so on, it's easy not to remember the bigger part of this, which is you' – he points at her – 'and me.' He thumps his chest. 'We're having a baby. Or trying to. It's absolutely unbelievable. I mean, I like men, you like women; for thousands of years, forever in fact, there was no *way* such a thing would have been possible. Not without . . . ' He shudders at the thought. 'And now, thanks to science – and you – it is. I mean, just imagine, far up there' – he waves in a vaguely northerly direction – 'sixty miles away, or however far it is, in Harley Street, our little friend Ian – who I'm convinced is gay too, as a matter of interest – is busy with his miraculous Petri dish, making my half-witted sperm meet with your fabulous eggs and produce a new life. It is nothing short of incredible!' He takes a big swig from his can.

'I suppose when you put it like that . . . '

'Let's have a look online, see what it is they're doing,' Adam urges. 'Where's your laptop?'

'On the coffee table.'

'Go on, plug it in.' It's impossible not to be affected by his enthusiasm. A few moments later they're peering at the screen. 'YouTube,' directs Adam.

At least he's allowing me to operate the keyboard, thinks Lou. *ICSI,* she types into search, and there, almost within an instant, is a video of the procedure. Below it a comment has been posted:

It's messing with nature. I'm not religious but God intended for the sperm and egg to join INSIDE the body not be taken out and grown in a glass dish!!

'Stupid cow,' says Adam, and presses play.

A long needle, magnified to hundreds of times its actual size, rests in a liquid. Slowly, it approaches the almost perfect sphere of a human egg. There is a moment of resistance as it pushes through the wall – *ouch,* Lou thinks, feeling for the egg: it looks so brutal – then the spike is inside. When it is right in the centre, a clear drop of liquid, presumably the sperm, is ejected from the needle so that it enters the egg. Then the spike is gradually withdrawn and the video ends. It takes less than a minute.

'That's it, you and me having sex,' says Adam. 'So, how was penetration?'

'Ooh, you, honestly! What are you like?' Lou reaches for a cushion and thwacks him. 'It's the creation of a human life we're witnessing,' she reproaches him. 'I find it rather moving, myself.'

*   *   *

'God, I'm bushed,' says Rich.

Cath looks over at him. His eyes are bloodshot, his face drawn. It's early but, poor man, he is worn out. Driving yesterday after work, the stress of today; it's not surprising. And, no longer driven by adrenaline, she is yawning too. 'Let's go to bed.'

Rich heaves himself from the sofa.

'You head on up,' she says.

He mounts the stairs while she locks the front door and turns off the lights. On the landing outside her nephews' room she stops and, on a whim, pushes the door ajar. The curtains are open wide, a full moon provides a splash of illumination.

On the floor is a rug covered in bright-coloured circles; on the bunk beds are matching duvets: there's Superman on one, Spiderman on the other, comic-book style. The walls are yellow, the fitted furniture red. It's all very jolly – maybe Mike cajoled Sukey into such brazen primary hues; she's usually one for white and cream, purity. Certainly Alfie and

Dom don't appear to want for much: two gleaming scooters rest against the radiator, the shelves are covered in toys. There are larger boxes: Junior Scrabble, a Meccano aeroplane set – now there's a blast from Cath's past – a Horrible Practical Jokes kit, and a Super Stomp Rocket. She can imagine her brother having great fun with them all. There's a neat line of Wii games, a decent display of books – it's good to see that her nephews read – and a long row of stuffed animals. So they're still small enough to want that comfort, she thinks, touched.

Given that they're only eight and there are two of them, it's ever so tidy, Cath observes. She'd not expect otherwise – her sister-in-law would never go away leaving any kind of mess, even in here. But she suspects it's like this all the time.

I wonder if having such a buttoned-up mother spoils their fun a little, she thinks. Most boys would be allowed to keep their scooters in the hall, and it must be hard to play with someone clearing up after you the whole time. If I were their mum, I'd relax the rules. Or maybe it's just envy, making me critical.

* * *

Eleven p.m., and Adam has fallen asleep on the sofa. The doctor has said that Lou mustn't be on her own tonight after the sedative, so he's staying over, but after all the excitement of the day, the dear man was ready for bed before she was.

The laptop is still humming on the coffee table, a reminder

she needs to shut it down. As she opens the lid to locate the off button, it flickers to life: the YouTube clip is still on screen, paused at the final moment, along with the stranger's irate post. Provoked, she clicks for more feedback.

Weird how the egg doesn't become damaged or leak after the needle punctures it. Anyone know how they choose which sperm to use?

Operators select by looking under the microscope. Defective spermatozoa are discarded and, to put it simply, the person behind the microscope chooses a good-looking one – that means no malformations, good motility, etc. He then breaks the tail and suctions the head into the needle.

Gosh, Lou thinks. More microscopic brutality. I do hope it won't affect our baby. She continues reading:

IVF is God's gift to an unfortunate couple – what an amazing video.

God has nothing to do with this. Please stop saying He does!

Definitely it's God's gift. There are so many unsuccessful procedures of IVF and ICSI, if he wishes he will bless you with success, if not, even these modern-day treatments will fail.

I wonder what these people would say if they knew my set-up, thinks Lou. She suspects when they refer to an 'unfortunate couple', she and Adam are not what these viewers have in mind.

She switches off the computer, rises to close the curtains. Out of the window, she can see a glittering path across the sea, formed by the light of the moon. It's a bright circle in a cloudless sky, an echo of the shape of the egg on the screen: pitted and cratered, not quite perfect. Eerie it should be full today, when the lunar cycle is an echo of a woman's twenty-eight-day waxing and waning. And by the time the moon is a half crescent, she will know whether or not what they have been through today has been successful – whether she is pregnant.

She recalls the biology lessons she had as a girl, pictures the cells multiplying: two, four, eight, sixteen, in the Petri dish miles away. In a few days one embryo will have grown enough, with luck, to put inside her.

Until then, all she can do is wait.

32

Lou is running along the prom. Adam has gone to work, and there was no way she could remain still this morning. It's like when she was expecting her A level results. She recalls sitting on the stairs, waiting for the postman, legs jiggling with anxiety. Eventually there was a *kerflup* through the letter box, a pile of envelopes; she'd grabbed the one marked *Board of Cambridge*, ripped it open. And just as her sister had come to peer over her shoulder, wanting to know what the letter said before she'd even absorbed the results herself, Adam has already texted her from the surgery to find out if she's heard. She knows he means well, but it only made her jitters worse. The confines of her studio seemed horribly claustrophobic, the walls hemming her in.

In comparison, pounding along the seafront in the open air, feeling the paving stones beneath her feet, is better. Once more, it's warm and sunny. On the shingle, a young man is setting up rows of green-and-white-striped deckchairs in preparation for another busy day. *Trip trip trip* go her trainers up the steps to the pier – she darts round a party of elderly sightseers disembarking from a coach – and *trip trip trip* back down the other side.

She senses it before she hears it, vibrating against her tummy. She stops. Sure enough: her phone is ringing in her bumbag. She can hardly get the zip open fast enough. 'Hello?'

'Lou, it's Ian again.'

She is panting. 'Hi, hi, sorry, I was running.'

'I'm impressed.'

She wipes sweat from her brow with the bottom of her T-shirt, walks with a crunch of pebbles towards the sea, away from the noise of traffic and the listening ears of strangers. 'Well, I'll have to take a break from jogging if this works,' she says. 'So . . . ?'

'Four of your eggs have fertilized,' he says.

'Oh.' A stab of disappointment. That's two gone already. Is that down to Adam, or her? Was it a mistake to give so many away? 'Then we've lost some.'

'You have, but we'd usually expect about a 70 per cent fertilization rate.'

Then perhaps four is not bad. At the fairground at the end of the pier, a swing as high as a crane is swooping out over the water and back again. She can just discern the people aboard the ride – their stomachs must be churning. This is how she feels too: up one second, down the next, lurching from fear to relief.

Four little embryos *is* astonishing . . . Four microscopic beginnings of life, each with its cells multiplying: thirty-two, sixty-four . . .

Meanwhile Ian is still talking. 'So, we'll take all of them to blastocyst stage.'

'Right.' For a woman with a history of fibroids and internal scarring like Lou, the odds of successful implantation are greater if the cells are allowed to multiply further, and this is the next stage of development. Yet it means waiting several more days before any of the embryos can be replaced in her womb, and – Lou's heart plummets again – more might die before they get there . . .

But all we need is one, she says to herself. Just one.

* * *

'Mum?'

'Hello, darling.'

'I've got some news. I can't get hold of Rich – he's gone into town for an emergency work meeting, but I had to tell someone.'

'Oh?'

'All six of our eggs have fertilized! Isn't that amazing? The clinic just rang to let me know.'

'That's wonderful. I'll just tell your father.' Judy repeats the information: Peter must be close by. 'So now what happens?'

'We've got this awful bloody waiting.'

'More? Dear me, there seems such a lot.'

'It's agony. But basically they leave them to develop before putting them inside me.'

'Well I never. I would have thought the best environment for a baby to develop in was a womb.'

'Of course it is, eventually.'

'They're not putting all six in, are they?'

Cath laughs. 'God, no. Two is the maximum, but they're not keen on even doing that. The risk of complication in pregnancy is greater with multiple embryos.'

'That makes sense. We humans simply aren't designed to nurture so many.'

'Anyway, who'd want six children at once?' She'd be like Bessie the cat, having a litter.

'No, exactly. Take it from me, two kids is plenty.'

Hmph, thinks Cath. That sounds like a dig. Were Mike and I that bad? She refrains from rising to it, and says, 'I reckon it's Rich's sperm. To have all of them fertilize is amazing. Then again, he always was good at performing under pressure.' She is proud of him.

'True,' her mother laughs. 'It's likely not all the embryos will survive though, isn't it? I thought that was why they try to collect so many eggs in the first place.'

'That's right.'

'So what do they do if more than two make it? I hate to think of those poor little embryos just being thrown away.'

As if the staff at the clinic just sling them in a bin bag, honestly. 'They don't do that, Mum, or they won't with us, anyway.'

'Really? They give them to someone else?'

'God, no,' says Cath. Does Judy really consider this an option? If only her mother was more au fait with the Internet, she could have researched this. Cath sighs. 'We can freeze them.'

'Ah.' A pause. 'Really?'

'Yes. They'll transfer the healthiest, but we might have more than one or two good ones, so depending on the quality, we can have them put by in case we want to try again.'

'Is it really OK to freeze an embryo?'

'They've been doing it for years. They look at them under a microscope and choose the ones most likely to survive the procedure.'

'I can't imagine it does them much good being frozen and then thawed.'

Sometimes her mum can be so old-fashioned. 'You freeze fish and eat it,' reasons Cath.

'It's hardly the same. I find it extraordinary you can bring something back to life like that.'

'It's mind-blowing – these days, you know, they can even fly frozen embryos across the world and then use them.'

'Good Lord.'

'Though the chance of pregnancy with frozen ones isn't quite as good, still it gives us more options.'

'Next thing we know, we'll be freezing people and bringing them back to life . . . ' Judy laughs again. 'Maybe I should freeze your father. How long can you keep these embryos frozen for?'

'In some places it's up to ten years, though our clinic keeps them for five.'

Cath can almost hear her mother's mind whirring. 'And the lady who gave you her eggs, is she happy with all this?'

Cath mutters, 'She's fine.' She has a nagging concern that their donor could withdraw consent to use her embryos at any time, even once they're frozen, right up until they're transferred into Cath's womb. But she's not going to give her mum any more reason for pessimism. Of course implantation may not work; she and Rich may need a subsequent cycle, even cycles – though how they'd afford that

Lord knows. Cath pushes her worries away. Imagine if it *does* work, she thinks, we could even have another child – a sibling, in a year or two, using a frozen embryo from their donor . . .

Now wouldn't that be the most amazing thing ever?

33

'Mum?'

'Darling, is there something the matter?'

'We've lost three of the embryos,' Cath sniffs.

'Oh love, I'm so sorry.'

'The woman from the clinic rang earlier to tell us.'

Cath is sure she must be thinking, *I did warn you*, but that she's too kind to say it. She pictures Judy at home in her kitchen, biting her lip. She wishes her mum was nearer.

'You're due to go in tomorrow, aren't you?' says Judy.

'Yes.'

'So what happened?'

Cath fights back tears. 'Apparently Mrs Donoghue – she's our embryologist – came in this morning and checked under the microscope and they'd' – she gulps – 'died.'

'Oh love, I wish I was there to give you a hug. Where's Rich?'

'He's here. He's on the other line. But he's got to go into work in a bit. There are all sorts of nightmares going on there, too.'

'Really?'

'Yeah, more redundancies. He's OK, but he's had to lay off two of his staff, it's horrid.'

'That's a shame . . . It sounds like you could do with company, and poor Rich. Though you've still three embryos left, haven't you?'

'Yes.' Cath wails, 'But what if they die too?'

'Is that likely?'

'They thought all six looked all right in the beginning and now these have gone. So the others could easily not make it.'

Judy hesitates, then says, 'Wouldn't it be better for them to put them into your womb now, then? I still can't believe the best environment for nurturing an embryo is a test tube.'

'It's not a test tube. It's a Petri dish.'

'Whatever. It's hardly the same as inside you. What does Rich think?'

'He's speaking to the clinic now. Hold on – he's just finishing sorry, Mum, can I call you back?' And before Judy can protest, Cath rings off.

'Mrs Donoghue says the three left are very good quality,' Rich tells her.

'They said that before.'

'It seems that now she can see them even more clearly under the microscope. We've got two As and one A/B.'

'Great! So – they want us to go in now?'

'No, they still want us to wait until tomorrow.'

This is the opposite of her cancer diagnosis. Then, when the consultant discovered her tumours, it seemed he couldn't get her into surgery fast enough. The experience was dreadful, but at least she didn't have to hang around. 'My mum thinks it's a good idea to go in straight away too. I'd much rather – the odds must be better, surely?'

Rich lets out a long breath. She knows she's trying his patience. 'I think the clinic know what they're doing.'

But my mum's so often right, thinks Cath. Doesn't Rich realize?

*　*　*

'I'm just calling to ask how our blastocysts are doing,' says Adam. He's at his desk at work and has a rare few minutes spare – two patients in a row have failed to show.

'You just beat me to it,' says Ian. 'Giving Lou a ring was next on my list.'

'Oh?' Adam's stomach lurches. But Ian doesn't sound concerned, and Adam decides he wouldn't be so casual if there were a problem.

'Yes indeed, but as you've called, I'll tell you and you can let her know: they're still going.'

'All four?'

'Yup, growing away, which is excellent. We'd usually expect to lose some between fertilization and implantation.'

'And they're all good quality?'

'I graded them this morning and' – there is a rustle of paper followed by click on a keyboard – 'yes, you've got one A, two Bs and one B/C.'

'Oh.' Adam is disheartened. He's a high-achiever; anything less than a straight A falls short.

'Well, if push comes to shove – if you excuse my phrasing'

278

– he's *definitely* gay, notes Adam – 'and they all make it through to blasto stage, then we could use any of them. But as we've got one A-grade, I'm pretty convinced that's our boy.' Surely it would be unprofessional of Ian to express such optimism without being almost certain? Cruel, even. Yet then he says, 'So we'll see you in the morning, 9 a.m. sharp. Though as I say to each of our clients, don't count your chickens just yet.' And Adam is left hanging on the edge of uncertainty yet again.

34

Lou and Adam are sitting in the clinic reception. They're early, and Dr Hassan, they are told, is running late.

'Might be a good idea to have another couple of glasses of water while you wait,' suggests the receptionist.

Lou has been diligently drinking herbal tea all the way up the motorway; by the time she's finished a plastic cup of water from the cooler she is convinced she might burst. 'I hope Dr Hassan gets a bloody move on,' she mutters.

Eventually the large white door to his consulting room opens and two women leave.

'Sisters.' Adam winks at Lou.

It seems ages until the doctor invites them through. He takes a seat, waves expansively at the chairs opposite and they sit down. 'So, we now have three embryos,' he says gently.

'Three? But we had four yesterday,' says Adam.

'I'm afraid we lost the weakest overnight.' His expression is sympathetic; he folds his fingers together, rests his chin on his hands. 'But three is good, really. And you've got one very strong embryo there.'

'We only need one,' says Lou, more to herself than Adam.

'So now you need to decide if you're going to use one or two.'

'What do you think?' Lou asks Adam.

Adam frowns. 'Two, to give us more of a chance?'

'But what if they both work? We'd end up with twins.'

Adam shrugs. 'One each?'

But this is not what Lou would wish for. It is so much to take in, and after months of being able to take each step as it comes and mull things over together, they are being thrust into making a crucial decision. She tries to assess the implications: carrying twins, a dual birth, the stress of two newborns, the demands of two toddlers, the expense of two schoolchildren, the mood swings of two teenagers. She's reminded of a film she watched with her father when she was small, *The Time Machine*. At one point a horrible humanoid monster aged from life to death at such speed she could barely catch her breath. The scene terrified her – but then she could hide behind the sofa. Now she can't run away.

'What do other people do?' she asks the doctor, hoping for guidance.

'It varies depending on their age and circumstance,' says Dr Hassan. 'No two cases are exactly alike.'

No two embryos either, thinks Lou. But she doesn't want choice and uncertainty. 'What would you advise?' she pushes.

'I'd recommend just using the one,' says Dr Hassan.

'Why's that?' Adam's tone is gruff, combative.

'You've got one exceptionally high-quality embryo here, and there is the best chance with that. The other two are not such good grade.'

'But I can't go through this whole process again if it fails,' says Lou. 'Haven't we a better chance using two?'

'We can always freeze the two others,' says Dr Hassan.

'Though we'd still have to pay for another cycle,' she panics. 'I couldn't afford it.'

'Maybe I can help if we have to do that,' says Adam, with barely a pause. 'I've got some savings,' he whispers to her, though naturally Dr Hassan can hear.

Lou feels colour rising to her cheeks: she's touched and embarrassed.

They look at each other, then at Dr Hassan.

'So it's one, then?' the doctor confirms.

'One,' they say in unison.

Lou lets out a long breath, relieved at their decision.

'Lovely.' The doctor unfolds his fingers and relaxes a little also. 'So, next . . . I wondered if you'd like to come in this time?' he asks Adam. Lou is taken aback, but before she can gather her thoughts, Dr Hassan says to her, 'You'll be awake the whole time, and we can cover you up no problem. It's purely that this an event we find prospective parents really like to share.'

Adam checks her reaction.

She nods. 'OK.'

'If you follow me then, Lou, someone will come back and get you, Adam, when she's ready.'

The doctor takes Lou to the same theatre she was in before, where a nurse greets them. 'Now, if you just slip on this gown' – Lou doesn't need telling, she is already removing her tracksuit trousers – 'and lie down here' – she gets up on the bed and they help hoist her legs into the stirrups – 'we've a few minutes of preparation.'

Minutes?! Never mind enjoying the experience with Adam, Lou is extremely uncomfortable. Forget your bladder and concentrate on what they're doing, she tells herself. You'll want to remember. She peers over her breasts and down her body. The nurse is wielding a long cotton bud.

'I'm just going to clean your cervix,' the nurse explains.

The sensation is similar to a smear test. As she's re-arranging Lou's gown, there's a tap on the door.

It's Ian, brandishing a clipboard. 'I need to check a few details.' He confirms her blood group, then holds up a form. 'This is for you to read afterwards. Shall I slip it in your rucksack?'

'Please.'

'There's just one other thing, Lou,' says Dr Hassan. 'Would you like Adam to help me with the transfer or would you prefer me to do it?'

Lou agonizes for a moment, appreciative that Dr Hassan has asked her this while Adam is absent. He's clearly a sensitive man. Again she has the feeling her body is public property; she needs to safeguard something of herself. 'Actually . . . if you don't mind . . . I think I'd prefer you to do it. Is that OK?'

'Sure,' he nods.

Instantly she feels guilty, but there's no opportunity to talk it over, for just then there's another knock and Adam joins them. This is hardly intimate, Lou thinks. She closes her eyes for a second, and an image of Sofia flashes before her.

We could have done this in the privacy of our home, she thinks; plenty of women do, with a needle-less syringe. We could have made it romantic, possibly even erotic. At the very least we could have had a giggle.

Then Ian says, 'I'm just going to bring through your embryo,' and as he edges through the door at once she is back in the here and now, appreciating how phenomenal it is.

An embryo: their embryo; the first few cells of their baby are here!

'We'll scan your uterus while the embryo is going in,' explains Dr Hassan. 'That's why we ask for you to have a full bladder – it acts like a lens so we can see. You can watch too. Look.'

There is a monitor above Lou's head. The picture might be black-and-white and fuzzy; the scanner pressing her belly might be making her need to pee even more, but it is astonishing. She glances at Adam: he is stock-still, transfixed by the screen. She can see tears glistening in his eyes.

'So . . . ' says Ian, bending down, ' . . . he's in a tiny air bubble, going in now . . . '

He might be a *she*, protests Lou silently on behalf of the child. Then she's caught up again in how moving this is. What an honour to be able to witness these precious moments. She can feel herself welling up, too.

Presently, Ian stands up. 'I'll triple-check it's gone from the catheter under the microscope. Only a couple of minutes more . . . ' He leaves the theatre.

Lou lies legs apart, trying not to move.

Adam comes to her side. 'That was amazing.' His voice is hoarse.

'Wasn't it?' She blinks tears away and smiles. 'Though I've never needed the loo so badly in my life.'

'Let's count to a hundred,' says Adam, and begins.

At seventy-four, Ian returns and gives a thumbs-up.

'Right, you can go to the loo,' says Dr Hassan.

'I won't wee it out?' says Lou.

'No, you won't. The embryo is up way beyond your cervix,' says Dr Hassan.

The nurse moves a wheelchair to the side of the bed. 'Pop yourself on here and I'll take you.' She wheels Lou to the cubicle and says, 'Almost all women go to the toilet straight afterwards.'

I'd like to meet the woman who doesn't, thinks Lou.

* * *

'Will it hurt?' says Cath, lying back on the bed. She's taken off her skirt and shoes as instructed.

'It's completely painless,' says Dr Hassan. 'Like a smear test.'

Well, you've clearly never had one of *those*, thinks Cath.

'How long will it take?' asks Rich. He seems nervous, edgy. For once, Cath is surprisingly calm. At least she is *doing* something, not in limbo.

'About fifteen minutes, that's all.'

Such a critical part of our treatment and yet so swift, thinks Cath.

'I wondered if you would like to help insert the embryos?' says the doctor to Rich.

'Oh, er . . . yes,' he says. Dr Hassan shows him how to

hold the catheter, and Cath sees Rich's hands are shaking. It brings the significance of what they are doing home to her; in these few moments her husband is helping to impregnate her with potential new life. She watches his face so as to focus not on the clinical surroundings, but on the two of them: their relationship, their love for one another, their unborn child. She sends a silent wish up into the heavens, to a Higher Power she doesn't wholly believe in but doesn't reject either. *Please God, please, may one of these little embryos implant in my womb. Just one is fine, please . . .*

She turns her head so she can watch the screen, then the embryologist takes a photo of her uterus and it's over; the deed is done. She lets out a long breath as the catheter is extracted, smiles at Rich, who moves to stand close by her, and reaches for his hand. He squeezes her palm so tight in return it hurts.

Wow. What an experience that was. It takes her a few minutes to gather herself and come back to earth. Eventually she becomes vaguely aware she needs the loo. But she is also conscious of something else, some*one* else.

On impulse she asks, 'Did you do our donor's transfer today as well?' although she knows perhaps she shouldn't. She glances at Dr Hassan to see if she's disarmed him. It seems not; he doesn't appear to be a man who is easily fazed.

'I did,' he says. 'It went very well.' His manner communicates that he won't be drawn further.

I wonder how many embryos she had transferred? thinks Cath. Was someone by her side, and did she find the experience this affecting, too?

* * *

'How was it?' says Anna.

'Incredible,' says Lou, tucking her mobile under her chin so she can continue dusting.

'I can imagine.'

'Adam and the people at the clinic were brilliant.'

'Oh, I'm so pleased it went well. So where are you now?'

'At home.'

'Resting?'

'Mm.' Guilty, Lou pauses, cloth in hand. She is sick of taking it easy; lying around is not her forte. 'They said not to go mad or anything, but I don't have to stay in bed.'

'So no running, then.'

'No,' Lou laughs. For a comparatively new friend, Anna knows her very well. She refrains from confessing she went jogging early this morning, before the transfer. 'I had to stay horizontal for a while in the clinic, but now I can move about like normal.'

'And it won't dislodge if you stand up?'

'I'll just check it hasn't popped out onto the floor.' Lou examines the carpet, even though Anna can't see her. She's still high from the excitement of the experience, can't resist joking.

'I suppose that's a stupid question.'

'Not at all. I do have to take these pessaries to help the embryo embed.'

'It's not embedded already?'

Anna knows less about pregnancy than I do, thinks Lou. I guess that's inevitable. 'No. That'll be a few more days yet.

We've got what they call the "two week wait" to get through, that's the real key.'

'I'll keep everything crossed for you,' says Anna.

*   *   *

'I'll just bring the car round while you rest up for a few more minutes,' Rich says to Cath. They've driven to the clinic this time, so that Cath doesn't get bumped into or have to stand for too long on public transport. Even though they have been told that there's no way the embryos can drop out, neither Rich nor Cath is quite convinced.

On the way to the NCP on Weymouth Mews, he makes a call. 'All done, Judy,' he says.

'Thank the Lord. I've been thinking of you the whole day.'

It must be difficult being 200 miles away from your daughter at a time like this, he thinks. 'It went really well. We've even got a photo to show you.'

'Have you really? How exciting. This modern technology never ceases to astonish me.'

'You and me both.' He's half inclined to tell her he found the experience moving, but is too shy to admit it. Occasionally he finds Judy a little intimidating; it's not her specifically, rather her relationship with Cath. They are so close; revelation is part of the dynamic between the two of them. And whilst he is used to having intimate conversations with Cath, he isn't comfortable confiding emotionally in Judy.

'How many did you transfer, then?'

'Two, in the end, both good quality, apparently. And we froze the third, just in case.'

'The one that wasn't quite as high a grade?'

'That's right.'

There is a moment of silence. He knows what she's thinking: If neither of these two work, the odds of the frozen one taking are surely pretty slim. And what then?

35

The two week wait, Cath types into the search bar on the forum. Several threads come up. She clicks on the most recent.

I'm just back from the clinic so today is the first day of the 2WW – how easy should I take it, do you guys think? Louloubelle

Hi Louloubelle, Welcome to the most nail-biting, knicker-checking, twinge-and-pain-analysing time ever – the culmination of the roller coaster of IVF that everyone calls the Two Week Wait. Good luck! Rainbow Girl

Louloubelle, Some ladies take a fortnight off and do very little, others not. During this period a lot of women are on progesterone pessaries and some have additional injections. Both help to maintain the lining of the womb, so the embryos can get snuggled in and hopefully implant into the lining. Neither should prevent you from gentle activity, but don't go overboard. By the way, if you had a blastocyst embryo transferred you can do a test a little

sooner than day 14 – on day 10–12, as the embryo is more developed by the time it is put back inside. Shadow

Hi again, 24 hours have passed and I can now fully comprehend
the obsession of the Two Week Wait! I have been experiencing
slight period type cramps and presumably this is normal? Is the
bloated feeling normal too? Louloubelle

Hi Louloubelle, I'm a bit ahead of you and after egg transfer I also
had period type cramps and felt bloated, so yes, this IS normal.
Take care and try not to stress – easier said than done, I know.
Mia

Morning all, I am only at the start of the 2WW and the stress of
waiting and wondering is driving me insane! I wondered should I
be feeling symptoms of early pregnancy yet? Any insights greatly
appreciated. CathM

The cursor flashes back at Cath. Now what? If she sits an-
ticipating a reply she could be here for hours. She'd best
find something new to do; the house is cleaner than ever,
the lawn mown, the hedge neatly clipped. This time of hoping
and praying is agony, made worse because she knows that
worrying will only make the outcome she is so desperate for
even less likely.

* * *

Ouch. Lou flinches. I could swear that's a twinge.
    Immediately she feels a rush of hope – could that be the

291

embryo implanting? Or maybe she's about to start her period. Which on earth is it? She's online checking her emails; she could take a quick peek at the forums, see if someone can illuminate her. There appears to have been a further discussion about the two week wait that very morning. The most recent response is particularly resonant.

Hi CathM, I so know what you're going through! I'm a few months ahead of you so I'll pass on what I found out. During the 2WW you assume you'll feel something to say 'YES' you're definitely pregnant, but the trouble is you won't necessarily get lots of symptoms straight away. As the day of egg collection is classed as the day of ovulation, you then need to allow 6–10 days after this for the embryos to implant (this is down to God). Once implanted, your embryo is not suddenly going to produce mountains of hormones – these will build up over the coming weeks, during which time you can expect various symptoms. I think we are all so desperate for some sign that our imaginations run wild. So we analyse every cramp, moment of tiredness etc. What follows is a list of the signs of early pregnancy:

- Temperature drop on implantation day
- Implantation bleeding or spotting – a slight pink or brown staining on average 6–10 days after ovulation
- Lower abdominal cramps
- A positive urine pregnancy test as early as 10–14 days after ovulation. The more sensitive the test, the earlier it can read as positive (but don't bank on it!)
- A positive blood pregnancy test about 14 days after ovulation

But you're unlikely to have all these indicators, and everyone is different. Because most of the symptoms are directly related to the pregnancy hormone, things like nausea and breast tenderness don't usually appear until it has reached a sufficient level. This is about 1–2 weeks *after* you miss your period, so throughout the 2WW there's not much to look for. Infuriating I know! My advice to you would be to try not to think about it too much. Fill your days with activities that sustain you. I found my church a great source of strength at this time.

God's peace,
Rainbow Girl

Well, that's put paid to that, thinks Lou, rubbing her abdomen. It sounds as if nothing is certain yet. She could drive herself demented looking and imagining.

That's the problem with it being the summer holiday. She has too much time.

She closes the lid of her laptop. Enough is enough. She's arranged to meet Karen at the allotment: if she delays any longer, she'll miss the best of the day.

* * *

Fuff! Cath blows dust from the top of the wooden carry case, blinks, and eases off the lid. The inside smells damp and mildewy from the loft.

Goodness, she thinks, admiring the intricate gold patterns decorating the shiny black body, this is such a beautiful object. How could I have neglected it for so long? It must be ten, fifteen years since she's used it. She catches herself reflecting that they don't make them like this any more, so solid and weighty, crafted with such care, then laughs at herself for being fusty.

It's a hand-operated Singer sewing machine, a hand-me-down from her grandmother. The oak base is scratched, the chrome wheel needs a polish, and the workings would doubtless benefit from a touch of oil, but the needle is still threaded. Carefully, Cath pulls a strand. It snaps in her fingers, perished.

Undeterred, she rethreads it with the new reel she bought a week earlier, carefully leading the cotton between the tension discs, into the take-up spring and down to the fork. She tugs the thread in the bobbin – that seems OK – and she is ready.

But before she sits down, she must check – as she is checking at least every hour – that she has not started spotting. She's glad Rich isn't here to see her; she knows she's being obsessive, but she doesn't know another way to be.

She goes to the loo, examines her knickers.

Nothing.

So far no period, no signs of implantation either. Even if the egg hasn't taken, her body will have to expel it and the hormonally induced lining of her womb somehow . . .

Stop thinking about it! she scolds herself. Hasn't she just decided that today, instead of spiralling into cycles of worry as she has been doing, she's going to follow the advice of the woman from the forum and shift her focus?

She unfolds the pieces of fabric she laid out on Mike and Sukey's living-room carpet and the sketch she made of her final design. Then she takes two of the squares, planned for the top corner, slips the edges face together under the foot, pulls the thread taut and lowers the lever.

'Now work for me, little machine,' she says.

*   *   *

Karen is weeding around the runner beans and Luke is kicking a football, repetitively, irritatingly, against the high metal gate. Lou could offer to go and play with him – she's aware this is what he's angling for – but although she is sympathetic to the fact he is bored, she doesn't like to be manipulated by children, even Karen's. She and Molly are picking blackberries. Molly is down at four-year-old height, Lou at adult level; they each have a Tupperware container, though Molly's is filling more slowly – a lot of her harvest seems to be going in her mouth. The brambles are laden with sweet, ripe berries; time is of the essence.

A row of sunflowers blooms above them; the leaves are scraggy and drooping but the heads are huge and impressive. She and Molly planted a batch at Easter that failed, so they tried a fresh packet at Whitsun, and they have fared better.

There are no guarantees in nature, Lou thinks, and begins to worry about pregnancy again. What if it doesn't work and she needs another round of IVF?

It's a gorgeous day and you're in a lovely place with dear friends; why on earth panic about something that might – or might not – be necessary in several weeks' time, she chides herself. What is wrong with revelling in the moment, making the most of where you are?

But I'm thinking things through, another inner voice protests; always better to be prepared.

Oh, piss off, she retorts, cross at giving in to pessimism. She decides to play a small trick on herself, even though her alter ego is busy arguing the notion is pathetic, mere pop psychology. She visualizes an ancient trunk. She opens the lid, picks up the gremlin of negative thoughts, and pops him – arms and legs beating in rage – inside. Then she slams it shut and locks it.

There, she says to herself, that's sent you packing.

She turns to Karen's son. 'Luke, why don't you join me and Molly?'

'I'm fine here,' he says, and thwacks the ball especially hard against the gate. The wire mesh rattles violently.

Karen glances at Lou and shakes her head in despair.

Oh dear, thinks Lou. He reminds her of herself as a child. 'I'd really like your help,' she cajoles. 'Look, we've no one in the middle. I can reach up high and Molly's down there, but with you we could get a proper conveyor belt going, and there is so much fruit they'll only go to waste otherwise.'

'You can pick them another day,' says Luke.

'They'll go rotten.'

Luke hesitates.

'Here.' While he's in two minds, she picks up an empty ice-cream container from close by. 'Catch!'

Automatically Luke reaches into the air and seizes it. Grudgingly, he makes his way round the brassica bed and over to join them. Soon his fingers are stained purple with juice and his arms are scratched by brambles, just like Lou's.

Several hours later, Cath has the body of the quilt sewn together. It took a while for her to sort the tension; having to adjust the dials this way and that was a test of her patience and determination, but eventually she got the machine working properly. She started by sewing six squares into a strip, alternating floral, striped, spotted, checked, plain and paisley. The next row she started with striped and finished with floral, and so on, using seven strips in total. And so she's watched it grow, square by square, finding it a good distraction from her preoccupation about what might – or might not – be growing inside her. Whilst there's more to do, she now has a real sense of how the quilt will look when it's done.

As she stands back to admire her handiwork, she can feel the presence of her grandmother and her mother standing by her shoulder. My grandmother taught my mother, and mum taught me, she thinks. She can recall Judy making curtains when she was a girl; she had an electric machine, would pretend the long seams were a train journey. 'Now we're going up to Scotland,' she'd say, as Cath looked on, and she'd push the foot pedal down hard, so the motor made a *whoosh* sound as it stitched, fast as an InterCity 125.

It's a shame so many people don't know how to sew any more, Cath thinks. If we have a child, I'll make sure to pass on what I've learnt.

36

'You can drop me off here,' says Cath. The traffic is at a crawl; it's a good opportunity to jump out.

Rich pulls up the hatchback outside Starbucks. As she opens the door he says, 'I thought you were going to the supermarket.'

'I fancy a coffee first,' she says.

He eyes her suspiciously. 'You're not doing another check in the Ladies, are you?'

'No!'

'Good. I'm not sure it's helping.'

But instead of going into the smartly done-up red-brick cafe, once the car is out of sight down Headingley Lane she nips across the street.

The parade of shops on the Otley Road is a reflection of Headingley's mixed customer base: chichi gift emporiums and trendy hair salons butt up against cheap sandwich bars and charity shops. It's studentsville meets suburbia, where youths with a zeal for maximum alcohol intake and minimum expenditure bump shoulders with Leeds's upwardly mobile professionals; and dyed-in-the-wool elderly residents live alongside large, loud Asian families. As such it resists gentrification, and the branch of Boots Cath heads towards is no exception. Its navy glass frontage looks inappropriately modern and cumbersome set into the ancient bricks of grey Yorkshire stone; inside the store is scruffy, in need of a makeover.

Cath picks up a wire basket and goes to the pharmacy section. The woman behind the counter appears tired, in need of some sunshine. As Cath picks over the display, she can feel her watching. She has a sudden urge to poke out her tongue at her but resists. Instead she selects four packs, each a different brand – you never can be too sure – and takes them to another till, by the door.

* * *

Hi Cath and everyone again, I came across these five tips online today, so I thought I'd cut and paste them for all of us to share:

1. **Keep busy.** How about arranging a date with friends or relatives? Meet them for a cuppa or a meal out, go to the movies, take up a hobby – anything to distract yourself.

2. **Schedule 'Obsessing time'.** We pretend we're not, but we're anxious. So schedule 15 minutes twice a day to obsess and make a promise you'll only be 'Two Week Wait Crazy' during that time.

3. **Get support.** Infertility is very difficult emotionally, and it's great to find kindred spirits who've been through it too. So connect online, join a live support group, find a therapist who specializes in infertility.

4. Use relaxation techniques. There are many ways to deal with anxiety, from breathing exercises to meditation. I am a great advocate of yoga and acupuncture.

5. Write out your 'what-ifs'. Ask yourself one of your what-if questions, and then answer it yourself. The idea isn't to talk yourself out of being afraid, but to get to the core of what's worrying you. It's like playing therapist with yourself – you'd be amazed how wise you can be if you take the time to respect yourself.

Mia

Sensible tips, thinks Lou, they sound like they've come from a counsellor. She checks the time. OK . . . so it's 9.45 now, she's been on the forum ten minutes; she's allowed another five of obsessing, and that's her quota.

Afterwards, she returns Adam's call – he left a message earlier.

'You were asking about doing a test? I thought next Monday,' she says. 'Why don't you come here, and we'll do it together?'

'I thought the clinic said to wait fourteen days.'

'You can do a test earlier. Other women do, I've seen online.'

'Though you know the longer you leave it, the more accurate it's likely to be?'

'I do. Still, what do you reckon?'

'OK, let's give it a go. You're best off doing it in the morning, so I'll come on my way to work. Eight a.m.?'

'It's a date,' says Lou. 'I'll see you then.'

She rings off, pleased. Hopefully scheduling definite action will keep Adam at bay. He has been texting and calling her an awful lot. She knows he means well, but she's been trying *not* to focus too much on pregnancy, which is hard enough anyway, and his anxiety only makes her worry more herself.

* * *

'So what do you think?' Cath leads Rich into the lounge. She's thrown the quilt over the sofa. 'I know it doesn't go in here,' she says, before he can say he doesn't like the pastel shades. She is aware that the rich terracotta colour scheme of the room drowns them. 'I just wanted you to see. I finished it today.'

'Oh.' Rich twists his lips; shifts, awkward.

Cath can read him so well: immediately she is hurt, defensive. It's taken her such ages: she had to bind the edges, then turn it inside out to attach first the wadding, then the reverse. She's hand-stitched the opening, trimmed it with ribbon and finally used a contrasting bright thread to create diagonal crosses right across the quilt. She's taken enormous trouble, not permitting herself any short cuts, and she's proud of her creation. 'Don't you like it?' She bites her lip, keen for his approval.

'No, love, it's not that, of course I like it. It's really nice.'

But she knows he is holding something back. 'What's the problem, then?'

'I'm just . . . ' He glances away, as if searching for a response that won't injure her. It only makes Cath feel more crushed.

'Yes?'

'I – er . . . I'm worried, love, that's all.'

'Worried?' However worried he is, he can't be as bad as me, thinks Cath. I'm the one who's dancing to the toilet every hour, who's filling my days with displacement activity so I don't spontaneously combust.

'Mm.' He looks at the floor. Not for the first time she is struck by the likeness to her brother: they deal with difficult conversations in the same way.

'Why?'

'Well . . . it's for a baby, isn't it?'

'Not necessarily,' she says hotly. 'We could use it anywhere.'

'But you just said it doesn't go in here—'

'On our bed, in the spare room—'

'Ah, OK.' His features relax. Then his brow furrows once more. 'Though it's not remotely big enough for a full-size bed, is it?'

'We could lay it along the foot, I don't know. Does it matter?' She can hear her voice rising with frustration.

'I just think you're getting your hopes up, love, that's all,' he ventures.

The remark stabs at Cath with the precision only the truth can. 'I am not!'

'I don't want you to get ahead of yourself. Please try and, you know, take this a day at a time. It'll only make it worse if we're disappointed.'

Cath fights a sudden urge to cry. She pictures the carrier bag of pregnancy tests she bought from Boots earlier, upstairs in the bathroom. She'd been going to suggest they do one together, that evening; there's a packet that claims it will give an early result, six days sooner than the fourteenth day, which would make it worth using right away. She doesn't want to do it on her own. If it's good news she wants to share it; if it's bad she'll need support. But now she is convinced Rich will baulk at the suggestion, there is no point in even asking.

Hi everyone, I could scream! I just spent days making this gorgeous quilt so as to take my mind off the 2WW, and my husband was so unappreciative of it. Normally he's so understanding, and I don't know what on earth he expects me to do with my time. It's all very well for him – he works ludicrous hours and it's not his body that all this depends on. He's not the one constantly feeling his boobs or wondering if he's got the first waves of morning sickness. I'm stuck at home crawling the blooming walls, and when I finally find something to take my mind off waiting – a hobby, just like you suggested, Mia – he has a go at me. I was just going to suggest we do a pregnancy test too, even though it's a few days early. He won't go for it now, I just know it. Hmph! CathM

Dear Cath, No wonder you're frustrated by your husband. I do think he is right though: my advice is to go easy on tests. Some women develop a virtual addiction to them during the 2WW. So if you are thinking about taking a test *way* too early, like five days before the fortnight is up, hold your horses. I understand the idea behind taking early tests – you're hoping that maybe you'll get a positive result, and then the rest of the 2WW will be easier to get through. But it doesn't work that way! The odds of getting a positive result before two weeks are slim. Instead you take a test, get a negative, and feel disappointed – even while telling yourself that you know it doesn't count as it was too early. Best to wait the full fourteen days from ovulation, take it from me. Patience is a virtue, as they say. Mia.

37

'Right, you ready?' says Adam.

They're sitting alongside one another on Lou's sofa. Who is more anxious it's hard to say. Adam has picked up croissants for them both from a delicatessen on St James's Street, but neither can face eating.

'As I'll ever be.' Lou takes a deep breath and removes the plastic stick from its cellophane wrapping.

She's about to get to her feet when Adam grabs her wrist. 'You do know we're more likely to get a false negative result by doing it a couple of days before the clinic said we should?'

'It's been fourteen days since ovulation.'

'Still, I'm just warning you.'

'So if it says negative I still might be pregnant?'

'Possibly. It can take a while for the hormones to build up enough to show. Do you think we should talk about what we're going to do if it is negative?'

'No.' Lou can't discuss anything; she's needed the loo since she woke up half an hour before and has held off specially so they can do the test together.

'Do you want me to read you the instructions?'

'No, I'm fine.' Again she feels a touch irritated; again she reminds herself he means to help. 'I looked before you got here.'

She takes the stick and goes to the bathroom, leaving the door slightly ajar.

'Hold it in the stream for at least six seconds!' calls Adam from the sofa.

'I don't know if I've got six seconds of pee in me,' worries Lou, but unsurprisingly she has.

'Make sure the tip is pointing down!'

Oops, it wasn't. Maybe he is of use after all. 'Now what? I've finished.'

'Seal the absorbent window with the cap.'

She edges her way from the toilet, pants still round her knees, and leans round the door so she can see him. 'Done that.'

'And pull up your knickers,' he says.

She comes back to sit down next to him and puts the stick on the coffee table. 'How long have we got to wait again?'

He squints to read the tiny type on folded paper. 'Five minutes, they advise.'

'I can't bear the suspense!'

'I know. Me neither.' And he flips the stick the wrong way up so they can't stare at it meanwhile.

*   *   *

'I swear my boobs are a bit swollen today,' says Cath, standing naked before her husband. 'What do you think?'

Rich grins. 'Whatever, they look pretty good to me.'

'Could mean either thing,' she says.

'Eh?'

'Period due because I've been taking medicine to thicken the lining of my womb, or pregnant.'

'Ah.'

'So.' She sits down on the bed next to him. Luckily it's a working-from-home day for him: he is still under the duvet, but she is due at the gallery in less than an hour. 'Shall we get this over with?'

'Sure.'

Just as he says this, she feels a faint twinge. Or maybe it's because she needs to pee so badly. It's your imagination, she tells herself. And her mind *is* working overtime – even her dreams are filled with tadpoles, litters of kittens, pushchairs, eggs . . . She's been so apprehensive, waiting for this day, but finally it's fourteen days since their donor's egg collection and Rich has relented and agreed to do a test.

Rich stays where he is while she goes down the hall to the loo. Less than a minute later she is back with the stick.

They both sit there watching, willing the blue line to appear.

Seconds pass. No line.

A minute: still no line.

Two minutes. Is that a faint one Cath can see, just beginning to emerge to make a plus sign on the indicator?

She wills it to sharpen, feeling Rich next to her, willing just as fervently.

'Right. Turn it over,' orders Adam.

Lou flips over the stick.

They both stare at it.

They stare at each other.

Then they stare at the stick again.

Still, neither of them can believe it.

Their jaws are open, a spot-the-difference cartoon of shock and surprise.

Adam reacclimatizes first. He leaps up from the sofa and pumps his fist in the air. 'Yesssssssssss!' he cries.

* * *

'It's really hard to be sure . . . ' says Rich eventually.

'I know,' says Cath.

'There's definitely a faint blue line going that way.' He picks up the stick and peers at it closely.

'Maybe . . . ' She examines it carefully too. she can see what he means. 'Perhaps it's too early to tell.'

'Could be.'

'I know they don't give an accurate reading until after implantation of the embryo. Shall we try another one?'

'Have you got another?'

'Mm,' Cath admits. 'I bought a few.'

'Go on, then.'

She heads back to the bathroom. As she opens the cabinet she feels another twinge. This time, there's no doubt about it.

You can spot a little and still be OK, she tells herself as she sits down on the loo. She knows this from all the forums online.

She tries to pee: only a trickle comes out. How stupid of me to think I could do another test so soon, she thinks. Crestfallen, she goes back into the bedroom, sits down once more next to Rich.

'Can't go,' she says.

'Do it later, then,' he urges. 'Take one with you to work.'

'I suppose I could do that . . .' She picks up the instructions to read how long she would need to wait. Suddenly – 'Ow!'

'What?'

Pain shoots through her belly, familiar. It takes a few seconds to pass. Once it's eased, she reaches down, runs a finger between her legs; it feels damp. She looks closely. It appears as if it is – but her skin is pink, it could *not* be . . .

To be sure, she wipes the dampness on the sheet.

A smear of pink.

No doubt, then. It's blood.

38

'We mustn't get too excited,' says Lou.

'It's very early days,' agrees Adam.

'You can't tell anyone I'm – I mean, we're – pregnant.'

'No, *you're* pregnant,' says Adam. 'I hate that "we" thing.'

'Do you? Phew. So do I.'

He pats his tummy. 'Mine's all food. And a bit of beer.'

Lou laughs. 'Anyway, not a word to a soul. OK?'

'OK.' Adam's expression is serious; he's grasped it. He gets up from the sofa. 'I'd best get to work.' He picks up his bag, pauses on the threshold. 'You going to do another test later, to be more certain?'

Lou nods.

'You have to leave it a few hours. Lunchtime would be good, I guess.'

'Sure. I'll call you.' Lou is too exultant to be annoyed by his interference.

She closes the door behind him, sits down on the sofa; immediately jumps up again, restless. Despite her instructions to Adam, she is desperate to tell someone. The news is too exciting, too big, to contain. She is well aware that most people keep news of a pregnancy quiet until they're through the first trimester; nonetheless, there's one person many women *would* let know this early. Their mother. But the idea of telling Irene? Lou can hear the interrogation already. *How will you manage financially? How well do you really know this man? Who will the child belong to if you and Adam fall out?* Yada yada yada.

The irony is that a lot of her mother's fears are mirrors of her own. But right now she doesn't want to be filled with someone else's vexation; she wants to share her joy, even if it's pre-emptive. Who can she trust to keep it to herself, and who will be nothing but happy?

Ah, yes. Of course. She may well be busy getting breakfast, but with luck she'll be able to spare a minute . . .

Lou picks up her mobile and rings Karen.

*   *   *

By lunchtime there is no need for Cath to do another test. She's bleeding so heavily there's no possibility it is mere spotting.

'This is the most expensive period I've ever had,' she wails to Rich on the phone in her break.

'Oh, honey.'

'I can't believe we spent all that time and money and it came to nothing.'

'I know,' he sighs. 'Me neither.'

She sniffs. 'I don't think it's really sunk in yet.'

'No.'

For so many weeks – months – her focus has been on getting pregnant. She can't grasp that in just a few hours her hopes – and Rich's – have been shattered. She feels as if she's yet to catch up with her body mentally and emotionally; she's disoriented, floundering. Being at work doesn't help: no one is aware of what she's going through, which only makes it more unreal. She's like a horse in a steeplechase without a rider, still galloping keenly alongside the other competitors, but with no chance of winning the race. She thinks of her donor, wonders if she's still in the saddle.

And all the while, even through the tablets she took to numb the spasms of pain, she can feel a dull ache in her abdomen, a nagging reminder.

*   *   *

Rich is at his desk at home, online.

Experts estimate that about 50 per cent of fertilized eggs don't make it, and a further 15 per cent of recognized pregnancies end in miscarriage, so unfortunately this is very common. It is only since pregnancy tests became so sensitive that people have realized how often early miscarriages can happen. In the past, these very early losses might not even have been noticed, and the woman would never have known she had been pregnant.

Gently he lifts Bessie the cat from his lap and puts her down on the floor. Then he gets up from the computer, yawns, stretches, looks out of his home-office window onto the terraced houses opposite. Darkened windows stare back at him – it seems no one else in the entire street is at home.

None of this is really helping, he thinks. Googling the subject has only underlined what a gamble getting pregnant is; even without Cath's medical history there would be no guarantees.

But for once Rich was slightly ahead of his wife. Perhaps it was the conversation with Mike, Cath's brother, which alerted him; perhaps it was a result of his own more cautious nature. Certainly he has been more guarded throughout the last fortnight to balance Cath's optimism. In any event, he had a feeling this might happen; that she might not conceive at the first attempt.

By Cath's own admission it's not hit her yet. When it does, he knows it will knock her sideways. He struggles to consider where they might go next.

'It's a numbers game,' Mike had said.

But the first hurdle that he can see is huge, possibly insur-mountable.

Money.

They haven't any left. The bank loan is spent; they're over-drawn; his job is uncertain at best, in danger at worst; and Cath's earnings are low. As for Judy and Peter – they've been generous enough already. His pride won't allow him to ask them again.

He should be working; the last thing he can afford is to slack off with the record label in such flux, but he'll catch up this evening if need be. While Cath is out he can research this without her being aware of it. He sits back down at the computer and types into Google.

Compare credit card deals, offers the top listing. Rich clicks on the link.

* * *

Karen is making Lou a cup of tea when there's a ring on the doorbell.

'I wonder who that is,' she says.

'Do you want me to get it?' offers Lou.

'No, no, it's fine, you stay there.'

A moment later she returns to the kitchen with Anna in her wake.

'Fancy seeing you here!' says Anna.

'And you,' says Lou. 'I'd have thought you'd have been in London.' Instead of crisp designer wear and high heels, Anna's in mufti – jeans and Breton T-shirt. Even in casual clothes, she manages to look put together, thinks Lou. *How come I can never manage that?*

'No freelance bookings this week. It's all very quiet on the copywriting front.'

'I thought it was usually busy in the summer covering for other people's holidays?' says Karen.

'It is. It's rather worrying.'

'I'm sure you'll get something soon. You always get work.'

'Hmm.'

Lou can see Anna is genuinely concerned.

'Anyway, just thought I'd drop these round.' Anna deposits a large rectangular container on the table. Through the clear plastic it's obvious what the contents are.

'Not *more* blackberries?' says Karen.

'Oh sorry, have you got loads?'

'Look in the freezer,' laughs Karen.

At that moment Molly comes charging into the kitchen. 'Anna!' she squeals, coming to an abrupt halt.

'Hello, Molly,' Anna smiles.

I love the way her face softens in the company of children, thinks Lou. She has a sudden yen to give Molly a cuddle.

'Come and sit on my knee,' she suggests.

Molly doesn't need inviting twice; she bounces onto Lou's lap with unfettered enthusiasm, and continues bouncing.

As she senses Molly's weight pummelling against her, Lou is aware that using her belly as a trampoline might not be a good idea. 'Er, Molly, my love, can you bounce a bit less hard, please? That, um, hurts.'

'Oh, do be careful, Molly!' snaps Karen. Then she adds more evenly, 'Lou's a bit fragile.'

Molly tilts her blonde head up and round to face Lou. 'I thought you were better?'

'Er . . . I am . . . from, er, my operation,' she says. 'It's just . . . '

At once, Anna's face breaks into an enormous grin. 'Oh my God!' she cries, putting her hand to her mouth. 'You *are*, aren't you? How fantastic!'

'You are what?' says Molly.

* * *

Rich isn't convinced that a documentary about children living in poverty is the best choice for them on this particular evening, but Cath has insisted they 'ought' to see it. The camera pans around a flat in Glasgow revealing damp so bad there is no point in the occupants even decorating.

'I've tried to cut the mould off my blind here,' says the little girl, Courtney, and holds a strip close to the camera. Never mind that the blinds are made of a stiff fabric held together by chains – a style Rich would have thought more suited to his office in Milton Keynes than a child's bedroom – they are shockingly contaminated. Black spots of fungi pollute every strip. That Courtney has cut small holes into the material only underlines how futile her attempts to deal with the problem are.

Courtney's mum is doing her best, but the cycle of debt and deprivation has caught her family in a spiral it seems they will never break out of, so much so that the little girl says she never wants to grow up. Throughout the programme statistics illustrate how situations like Courtney's are widespread across the country.

By the time the titles come up, Rich feels a mixture of shame and gratitude. At least their cashflow problems are not this horrendous. He has a niggling sense there is something amiss with the way they are spending money on creating a new life when there is so much need close by. These families are not halfway round the world, there is an estate similar to this Glasgow one only five minutes' walk away. Even so, he can't rid himself of the desire to be a dad; not now it's been awakened in him. Seeing these children, he longs to look after them better.

He turns to Cath to see if she's reacted similarly. Tears are streaming down her face.

'Oh Rich,' she cries, and collapses onto his chest, clasping at his sweatshirt as if it's her life support.

While she sobs, he strokes the top of her head, running the fine wisps of her mousy hair gently through his fingers. The gesture helps soothe him too.

So it's hit her, he thinks, to some extent relieved.

All day he's been carrying grief for both of them.

39

'No thanks,' says Adam, as Lou offers him yet another sweet. 'I don't know how you can still have any doubts you're pregnant – that's your second packet of Fruit Mentos today.'

'I won't believe it till I see the heartbeat,' says Lou.

'But my dear girl, you're eating for England and you've done three positive pregnancy tests.'

'Four,' says Lou. 'There was the blood test at the doctor's too. I know, I know. I'm probably being silly . . .' Her voice trails off. Up until last week, her optimism had been growing by the day. Then she'd got a call from the clinic in Harley Street which upset her deeply.

'So how on earth can you think you're not?'

'I've not been sick.'

'Or had a period,' he reminds her.

But Adam's assurance is probably a mask for his own qualms, Lou thinks. They are sitting in the obstetrics unit at the Royal Sussex County Hospital. What a journey I've come since I was here with Sofia for the scan before my operation, thinks Lou. Nonetheless, she is wary.

'I suppose it's ever since I heard about my recipient,' she admits.

'Oh dear, Lou, not that again. You know you've done everything you can.'

'I guess . . . I just feel so bad for her.'

'It's not your fault.'

Lou sighs. 'In theory I appreciate that. Still, I can't help but feel sorry.'

'You shouldn't feel guilty that you got pregnant and she didn't. That was always a risk with this arrangement.'

Lou nods, but she can't turn off her sense of responsibility simply because Adam has told her to.

'And now you've given permission for them to use your frozen egg—'

'Embryo,' corrects Lou: it was to get her sign-off that Ian, their embryologist, had called.

'Embryo, sorry. Anyway, you've been hugely generous—'

'It's not as if I got nothing in return.'

'Of course you did. But maybe she'll have better luck this next time. At least she still has an option.'

'I suppose . . . '

'It certainly doesn't mean you're not pregnant.'

'Mm.'

'Or that you shouldn't be happy that you are.' He pauses, and his voice softens. 'You deserve to be, don't you *ever* think you don't.' He pats her hand. Not for the first time, she appreciates what a good GP he must be. Then he laughs, 'And, if you don't mind me saying, your tummy is quite a bit bigger.'

'Probably fat from so many sweets,' she says, stretching out her legs and looking down.

The lino beneath her feet is badly worn; the plastic chair she's sitting on is wobbly, coming unscrewed from its base. Now Lou is so far into her first trimester, the clinic's role is over: she and Adam have been referred on to the NHS.

What a marked contrast it all is to the pristine surroundings of the Marylebone Fertility Clinic, she thinks. And we've been waiting an hour already. Still, at least the hospital is only a few hundred yards from my flat.

At last: 'Louise Burgess!' bellows a nurse from a few feet away.

Lou jumps.

'If you'd like to follow me,' the nurse says. But this is the department where she had a scan with Sofia, an experience she remembers vividly, so Lou already knows where to go. She was nervous then, too, and resented being surrounded by pregnant women. Who could have known she'd be back barely eight months later, supposedly one of them?

*   *   *

'Mr and Mrs Morris, it's good to see you back again,' says Dr Hassan, leading them through to his consulting room. 'Though I'd like to take this opportunity to say how very sorry we are that our first attempt at IVF didn't work for you.'

Being here once again brings their situation home to Cath. The doctor's large mahogany desk with its silver-framed photos of what must be his own family, the tall twiddly-stemmed house plant in the corner, the shelves lined with hefty reference books and research papers. She and Rich have even sat in these chairs before. Cath gulps. *Bet you're not as sorry as I am*, she thinks, but says nothing for fear she might break down.

'I gather that you've had a consultation with the counsellor and discussed your options, and this is what's brought you both here.'

Rich speaks for them. 'My wife decided to give her body a rest for a few weeks before we tried again.'

'Always advisable. So, I gather you've been taking the oestrogen and progesterone tablets for a fortnight . . . ?'

'Yes.'

'Which is necessary because this time we're using a frozen embryo, as you're obviously aware.'

'Before we do, can I ask you something?' Cath wishes she could disguise her upset, but her voice is husky. It only makes her feel more vulnerable.

'Of course.'

'It's just I think last time I, um, got my hopes up a bit too high, and this time, I don't know, I don't want to be quite so unrealistic . . . '

'I see . . . ' Dr Hassan folds his fingers under his chin.

'It's very hard trying to be positive whilst at the same time not allowing myself to believe it's going to work.'

'I quite understand. It's a difficult balance.'

'What we need to know is,' interrupts Rich, 'the odds are not as good with frozen embryos, are they?' He and Cath have discussed this ad nauseam. Whilst it's comforting to hear a positive spin, especially from a consultant, this time round they are endeavouring to be more pragmatic. We need to protect ourselves, they've agreed.

'So are you asking me the odds of having success with this particular treatment?'

'Exactly.'

'It's not easy to say. There are so many variables. Just because IVF doesn't take the first time for some patients is no reason for it not to work the second.'

'But surely, if the embryo is frozen—'

The doctor coughs. 'Actually, research shows the outcome from IVF using cryopreserved embryos is uniformly positive, with no marked increase in birth defects or developmental abnormalities.'

'But that's generally,' urges Rich. 'Whereas I thought our embryo wasn't such good quality as the two you implanted?'

Dr Hassan shuffles in his seat. Cath empathizes with him. It must be hard to get it right for a couple like them: he won't want to seem all doom and gloom; neither will he want to give false hope. Ultimately, the procedure is also a gamble for him. Much of this she and Rich have spoken of already in their counselling session, yet it seems no matter how often they go over it, there are no definite answers: only yearning and vagueness and fear.

'All I can say is we've defrosted the embryo, and the embryologist has had a good look at it under the microscope. She's happy, so I'm happy, and if you're both happy we'll go ahead.'

Mention of looking at this specific embryo gives Cath a fresh perspective. She recalls her mother's concern about what happened to those that remained unused. It seems so wrong to throw it away. In that instant, she is clear. She swivels to face Rich. 'I've taken all the medication . . . We've gone to such lengths to find the money . . . ' She grasps hold of his hand. 'But it's more than that – don't you see?'

'Eh?'

'We both know this embryo might not work. Or it *could* be the beginning of a baby, a life.'

'Perhaps . . . '

'There's no perhaps about it.' She smiles reassuringly at her husband then turns back to Dr Hassan. 'No.' She is vehement. 'We have to give this particular life a chance.'

* * *

'And there you are, can you see that?' says the sonographer.

Lou and Adam look at the screen. After so many scans Lou is getting good at deciphering shapes in the black-and-white blur, but even so she is surprised at how easy it is to make out. She can discern limbs, a torso and a comparatively enormous head.

'Oh my goodness!' says Adam. 'He's got his legs in the air!'

'How do you know it's a he?' says Lou. She can't see anything to indicate it is.

'I don't,' says Adam.

'We don't want to know,' says Lou quickly to the sonographer.

'Are you sure?' says Adam. Although they've agreed not to find out, Lou detects he's angling to.

'No, I don't want to, if that's OK.' She explains, 'I think it will help me with the labour, if I'm pushing with a surprise in store.' She's not admitted it to Adam – that would be truly tempting fate when she's been finding it hard to believe she's even pregnant – but the prospect of giving birth terrifies her.

'A birthday surprise.' The sonographer nods. She's a young woman, so skinny her uniform hangs off her. Lou wishes she'd crack a smile. 'We can't tell ourselves at this stage. Not accurately. You'd have to wait till the next scan to find that out anyway.'

'Ah.'

'I'd forgotten he'd be this big,' says Adam, going right up to the monitor. 'It's ages since I saw a scan. But he looks like a real baby.'

'Yes, at ten weeks they do,' says the sonographer. 'I should measure him.'

'Or her,' says Lou.

'He seems to be in a very chilled out position,' says Adam.

'Those are the arms up behind the head,' says the sonographer.

'Ooh yes!' says Adam.

'He's five centimetres from crown to rump. That's a really decent size.'

'Specially since I'm such a short-arse,' says Adam.

'From this I'd have said you're actually more like eleven weeks.'

'Well, I can't be,' says Lou.

'Are you sure? I need to put the date for our records.'

'We had IVF, so yes, we're sure.'

'Hmm . . . ' She sounds doubtful.

'It was Monday 5th August. I can even tell you the time if you want,' says Lou.

'No, that won't be necessary.' But Lou could swear she

sees her make two little lines on the form nonetheless. Hmph, she thinks, irritated.

The sonographer moves the scanner to the right. 'Your ovaries are slightly enlarged,' she observes.

'Really?' At once Lou is alarmed.

'I think it's quite common with IVF . . . '

Think? Lou's anxiety grows.

'Mm . . . ' She moves the scanner to the left. 'They do seem to be. Have you been uncomfortable at all?'

'Well, yes.' Lou is uncomfortable right now. Yet again she's been required to have a full bladder. 'But I've never been pregnant before, so I wasn't sure what I should feel like.'

'I'll just get the senior radiographer in, for another opinion.' The nurse lays down the microphone and leaves the room.

Adam goes over to the machine. 'She's left it on.' He picks up the microphone.

'Adam!' says Lou. 'What if they catch you?'

'Stuff it if they do. They're hardly going to strike me off.' He moves back to Lou's belly. 'Gosh . . . I haven't used one of these since med school, they've changed an awful lot . . . '

'Don't break it, for God's sake.' She is half nervous, half wants to laugh. She feels like a naughty schoolgirl. 'And don't you DARE check if it's got a willy!'

'I'm not going to,' says Adam. 'I just want to check the heart—' He moves the microphone to the centre of her belly, but just then the door opens. Adam thrusts the microphone back before the sonographer sees what he's doing. She has a second uniformed member of staff behind her: Lou is glad to see she is older.

'So.' The older woman swivels the screen with one hand, picks up the microphone with the other, and immediately locates Lou's uterus. 'Anya says your ovaries are a bit enlarged . . . ' She moves the microphone this way and that. 'Ah yes, I see they are. But you've had IVF, I gather?'

'Yes. Ten weeks ago.' Lou grips the side of the couch, bracing herself for bad news. I *knew* it was too good to be true, she thinks.

The woman looks at the form, frowns, picks up a pen, makes a small correction. Lou feels vindicated. Then the woman says, 'I'd say it's nothing to be concerned about, then. It's very common, if you've had fertility treatment. You've a touch of OHSS.'

'Ovarian hyperstimulation?' asks Adam. It's a term Lou knows too. It always sounded so ominous. Perhaps she feels sick after all.

'Yes . . . ' Again the nurse moves the microphone. 'Looks that way . . . '

Lou grips the couch even tighter.

'But you say it's nothing to worry about?' says Adam.

He sounds much calmer than me, thinks Lou.

Adam peers at the screen. 'If the baby is five centimetres long . . . they don't look that big to me. I'm a GP,' he explains.

Bless him, thinks Lou.

'No, they're not, really. They're only two or three centimetres bigger than normal.'

Ah. Lou relaxes. In comparison to a growth the size of a grapefruit like her fibroid, that doesn't sound drastic.

'You feeling any pains?' asks the woman.

'No,' says Lou. 'Just a bit, well, er, bloated.'

'Short of breath? Thirsty?'

'No.'

'Then to answer your question, I genuinely wouldn't worry, no. Just drink lots of water and it should subside as your pregnancy progresses.' She moves the microphone some more. Presently, she smiles. As she does so, like Anna, her whole face changes. She appears to shine with pride and confidence. 'Just look at this little thing! He's perfectly happy. See that?' She points at the monitor.

There, sure enough, is a tiny heart, ferociously beating away.

40

For fourteen days, Cath has had in her handbag the test that they gave her when she left the clinic. This time she's pledged to handle the process as differently as she possibly can. So she's not bought any extra tests, she's not gone on about being pregnant to Rich (well, not much, at any rate), she's even worn black knickers to make checking them hard. She's continued to keep schtum about the treatment at work, instead offering to cover for a colleague's holiday on top of her usual hours, which has helped provide distraction.

'Buddhists say there's a period of negotiation between the womb and the mother,' Sukey had commented on hearing of her lack of success first time round. At the time Cath had been livid – 'Not more bloody Buddhism!' she'd fumed to Rich when she'd come off the phone – but three months on she can appreciate there may be some value in the words, and she's tried to be less bullish in her approach. I can't force myself to be pregnant, she's told herself, so whenever she's felt herself getting excessively preoccupied or fretful, she's developed her own vituperative mantra: *Fuck it*. After all, what will be will be.

But today it's as if all her pent-up energy has come to the surface and, mantra or no mantra, she can't contain herself a moment longer.

It's 5 a.m. and Rich is asleep beside her. It's unfair to proceed without his involvement, she knows. But *if it's bad news I can break it to him gently*, she reasons, *and if it's good he'll be pleased regardless.*

She slips quietly from the room and pads downstairs to fetch her handbag. Then she returns with it to the bathroom, gently closes and locks the door and removes the box. Her hands are shaking as she tears off the cellophane. No need to read the instructions; it's the same brand she used before.

I hope that's not a bad omen, she thinks, and as she pees, she prays.

*　*　*

Rich wakes with a jolt.

The light is on and Cath is virtually sitting on top of him, brandishing something. Bleary, he focuses his eyes, and realizes what she is saying – yelling:

'IT'S-POSITIVE-IT'S-POSITIVE-IT'S-POSITIVE!'

'No!' He sits bolt upright.

'Look!' She waves the stick so close to his face there is not a chance he can read it.

'Hang about, slow down.' He grabs her wrist. 'Let me see.'

She hands it over and he leans on one elbow towards the

light. His eyes take a while to adjust but eventually he can make it out. Whereas before there was perhaps, only possibly, the vaguest hint of a line, this time there is no mistaking it.

'Fucking . . . hell . . . ' he says, slowly.

'I know! Fucking hell, indeed.'

'Did you do it without me?' he asks, though the answer is obvious

She wrinkles her nose. 'I did, I'm sorry.'

'Love, this is fantastic!' He can feel himself grinning.

'Isn't it?'

His mind is whirling, he's so shocked. He needs to ground himself. 'What time is it?'

She checks the bedside radio alarm. 'Nearly five thirty.'

'Ah . . . ' He flops back on the pillows. No wonder he feels so knackered.

She snuggles up to give him a hug. 'Do you think it's too early?'

'Too early for what?'

'To ring my mum.'

Dear Cath, honestly. He laughs, shakes his head. 'Yes, I darn well do. It's too early in the day for a start. But I think it's too early to tell her anyway. It's still only day fourteen.'

'Well, I'm not waiting three months!'

He knows he's onto a loser. 'At least do another couple of tests. Please?'

*   *   *

'Mum?'

'Yes?'

'It's me,' says Cath.

'I know it's you. Is something up?'

'No, not exactly.'

'Oh. But it's pretty early.'

'It's gone half eight, Mum.'

'You don't normally ring me at this time. Where are you? I can hear children crying.'

Cath is in Morrisons in Headingley. 'I'm at the super-market.' She moves away from a woman trailing a distressed toddler and into the frozen food aisle. 'It opens at eight.'

'I see.'

But Cath can tell she doesn't. She'd best be direct. 'I came here to buy something specially.' She tries to keep the excite-ment out of her voice. 'It's a fortnight since we did our egg transfer, you realize?'

'I had worked that out, yes. But I didn't want to bother you. You seemed to be dealing with it all a bit better this time around.'

Cath ignores the implied criticism. She knows her mother finds her difficult when she gets hyper. 'Yes. Well, it seems to have worked.'

'You mean you're pregnant?'

'Yes.'

'Oh, darling! That's wonderful!'

'Thanks,' Cath purrs. 'Rich wouldn't let me tell you till I'd done another test.'

'So, what? You've done more than one, then?'

Cath hesitates. She realizes her actions will undermine the impression she's played it cool and she really doesn't want her mother to say anything that might quash her enthusiasm. Not today. But equally, fibbing to Judy isn't her way. 'I did one first thing this morning, and another one just now.'

'Gosh, darling, you've been busy.'

'I came here to buy another test,' she says.

'What . . . So you did it there? In Morrisons?'

'In the disabled loo,' Cath confesses.

'I see.'

Cath can tell her mother considers the concept most unpleasant.

'So what are you going to do now?' asks Judy.

'I've got to go to work in a minute,' says Cath. 'I'm just buying a sandwich for my lunch.'

'That's a shame.'

'Meaning?'

'Well, it'd be good if you could put your feet up for a bit.'

'Yeah, yeah.'

'Don't overdo it now, will you? It's very early days and you get stressed out so easily. You be careful.'

She sounds just like Rich, thinks Cath. They often echo one another. But Cath knows her mum has her best interests at heart, and the welfare of her unborn baby.

41

'I had some great news this morning,' says Lou.

'Oh yes?' says Karen.

'Apparently my egg recipient is pregnant.'

'That's great!' says Anna. They're in Lou's flat, waiting for friends. Rod, who after six months is officially Anna's boyfriend, is with them. 'How do you know?'

'I rang the clinic today just to touch base, tell them my twenty week scan went OK—'

'Wow, are you twenty weeks already?'

'I am,' Lou beams. 'Well, actually I'm nineteen, but what with Christmas and everything, it was either do one now or not till early January.'

'So the scan was OK?' asks Karen.

'Yup, seems perfectly fine.'

'Lou,' interjects Molly. 'When are you having your baby?'

'I'm due in May,' says Lou.

'But that's *ages*.'

'You're telling me,' Lou laughs. Just then the buzzer goes. 'Ah, that'll be Adam and Howie.' She presses the intercom.

'Don't bother coming up, we'll come down and meet you.' They're gathering here before going to the seafront – it will be too crowded to hook up easily otherwise.

'Come along, folks,' Karen addresses her children. 'We'd best get a move on if we're to get a good view.' She turns to Lou. 'You can tell us on the way.'

'There's not much more to tell.' Lou pulls on her parka. It's getting snug round her middle, but luckily she's never been one for skin-tight clothing. She crouches down to fasten the toggles of Molly's duffle coat – she has to squat, rather than bend. 'They're not allowed to say much, so all I know is she had a second go a few weeks back with a frozen embryo and it was successful.'

'That's amazing,' says Karen.

'I'm so pleased,' says Lou. 'I feel I can really celebrate my own pregnancy now.'

'It's still relatively early days for her, though, I guess?'

'Yes, it must be.' Lou locks the door to her studio and they troop downstairs. The two men are waiting on the pavement outside; Howie in his familiar woollen hat and donkey jacket, Adam in the sort of sweeping tweed coat that reminds Lou of her father. The effect on Adam is more geography teacher than matinee idol, whereas her father cut an imposing figure, broad-shouldered and tall. Howie is stamping his feet to keep warm.

'It's freezing,' moans Anna. She's hardly dressed for the cold – her jacket barely covers her behind.

'You can snuggle up to me,' says Rod, pulling her to him. They walk down the road arm in arm.

At the end of the street they all halt to assess the situation. Across Marine Parade it's thronging with people packed tight against the balustrade who've beaten them to an Upper Circle view over the beach.

'The kids will never get to see from here,' says Karen.

Luke scowls and pouts; Lou picks up his disappointment.

'Some of your friends are in the procession, aren't they?' she says.

'I can lift you,' offers Adam. 'Would that help?'

Luke appears unsure – he's not met Adam before.

'And I could give you a piggyback,' suggests Rod to Molly.

Howie is busy checking his mobile; it seems he'd rather not get involved.

'I think we should head down to Madeira Drive,' says Lou. The road runs parallel to the shore much nearer the display.

'Will you be OK?' asks Adam.

'Sure,' she nods. She's not spending months encased in bubble wrap like a piece of crockery, and as she's well into her second trimester she's feeling positively healthy – almost every day someone tells her she is glowing.

Adam leads the way down the steps, and pushes his way through the crowds with a cheery smile and a "Scuse me – small children – pregnant lady,' until they're near the front. Lou is impressed by his sheer nerve.

'Better?' he says.

'Better,' says Karen as Luke wriggles between a couple of grown-ups to a prime spot close to where the procession will pass. She checks he is still in her line of vision. 'Thanks.'

'Do you want to go piggyback?' Adam asks Molly. Rod is cuddling Anna to keep her warm.

'Yes, please,' Molly says, and Adam scoops her up.

'Ooh, listen,' says Anna. 'They're coming!'

In the distance there is the thump of a drum, like a deep protracted heartbeat. Gradually it gets louder and louder, until there is a flicker of light and to the west the procession heaves into sight, a stately cortege of children and adults brandishing ghostly white lanterns made from willow and tissue paper.

'So what's it for?' asks Rod. 'I get it's winter solstice and all that, but why the lanterns and the bonfire?'

'It's called the Burning of the Clocks because it's to summon in the new sun,' says Lou, watching in awe as a spectral Big Ben and Houses of Parliament are carried right past by a group of ten schoolchildren. Behind it is a homage to the Pavilion; behind that a woman dressed in a large hoop skirt decorated with minutes and hours.

'Oh bless her, she's Mother Time!' says Howie.

There are simple stars and suns and moons, precarious skyscrapers and flamboyant palaces, ghoulish skulls and comic cartoon characters – no two constructions are alike.

'Apparently each lantern is supposed to contain the wishes of the maker,' says Karen, as the procession winds its way towards the shingle, a stream of bright against the dark. The lanterns are then thrown on a fire, one by one, until flames lick high into the sky.

'But really it's just hocus-pocus,' says Anna.

'Brighton PC hippies at it again,' chuckles Rod.

'Well, it makes a bloody good antidote to the commercialism of Christmas, if you ask me,' says Karen snippily. Lou remembers what a tricky time this is for her friend, how upset she was last year, with all the pressures of present-buying and family gatherings without Simon. 'I had to put on a brave face for the children,' Karen had said. Lou watches the burning pyre, symbol of passing seasons, and reflects that a year from now she'll also be putting someone else's needs before her own.

Then, as the fire crackles and sparks and reaches its zenith, the drum stops and the music starts, eerie and magical through giant loudspeakers. So what if it's superstitious claptrap, Lou thinks. This is something the whole city can participate in regardless of faith or creed. She wishes she could bring the kids from work here. What a shame they're so far away.

'This is the best bit.' She nudges Rod. 'Watch.'

She turns to look at Adam. He has Molly's legs held firmly in his arms, a contrast of pink woollen tights and heavy over-coat, small girl and man. A moment later there is a *WHOOSH!* and the fireworks begin.

'Ooooooooh!' the two of them gasp in unison, as several whirls shoot overhead at speed and explode in a tumble of green. Then 'Aaaaaaaaaah!' as before the sparkles fade and drop to shore, an even bigger array of fountains bursts white on white. There's an 'Oh! Oh! Oh!' as rockets go *BANG! BANG! BANG!* like cannons over the water, and an 'Eeeeeeeeeeeee!' as an effervescent rainbow shimmers above the black horizon.

Lou wishes she had a camera, but not for the pyrotechnics. She'd like to capture Molly and Adam's faces lit up by the spectacle, cheeks flushed in excitement, eyes wide with wonder.

* * *

'If we go I'm not staying long,' says Cath.

'We've got to, love, don't be silly.'

'She's still not apologized.' Cath throws the wrapping paper onto the bed.

Rich coughs. 'But if you don't mind my saying so . . . ' He hesitates: can he risk this? For the sake of a happy Christmas, he has to. ' . . . Nor have you.'

'I've got nothing to apologize for!' Cath empties the Toys R Us bags onto the duvet.

She must have spent a fortune, thinks Rich, eyeing the array of presents she has bought for her nephews, but he'll worry about their finances later. 'No, I know . . . but sometimes it can pay to take the higher moral ground.'

'By saying sorry when I'm not?' She waves an arm dismissively and pushes past him. 'Where's the Sellotape?' Seconds later she's back with the roll and scissors from his office. 'Bugger that – she's the one on such a high horse.'

Oh dear, thinks Rich. For the umpteenth time he's forced to tiptoe round his wife, in the hopes of circumventing a hormonal explosion. To say she's been moody is an understatement. She's been sick not just every morning, but noon and night too, and her emotions seem off the Richter scale. Yet he's at least a month to go before they're through the worst of it, according to Internet forums for dads-to-be. He's been sneaking contact with others who've been through it in a bid to keep sane.

He tries a different tactic. 'So what about Alfie and Dom?' he ventures, aware he's standing like the proverbial lemon while she busies herself around him.

'What about them?' She sits down on the bed with a sigh.

'You wouldn't want to miss them, would you? It's been a long while since you've seen them.'

'No . . . of course not.'

'But if we don't go to your mum and dad's on Christmas Day, when are you going to?'

'I thought Mike could bring them here on Boxing Day.' She starts slicing the wrapping paper with alarming vehemence. Any minute now she'll cut through the duvet cover by mistake, thinks Rich.

'I'm not sure he'll be prepared to do that. It's a big ask.'

'Is it?'

He has a sense he's getting to her. 'It'll put him in a very awkward situation with Sukey—'

'I don't give a fuck about Sukey!' Cath thumps the roll of paper on the bedding as if it were a truncheon.

'No . . . but still, it would be a real shame not to have lunch with them all. Your mum always does such a terrific roast—'

He can see her wavering again. Invariably food is a good lure for his wife; even though she's been nauseous she is as keen to eat as ever.

'All right, we'll go,' she relents. 'But we're not staying beyond five, and you're not to get drunk.'

'Of course I won't,' says Rich. Though it would have been nice if he could have for once; Cath can't drink anyway and could have driven them home. Still, he learnt long ago that there are some battles simply not worth fighting.

* * *

'So what are your plans over Christmas?' asks Karen, coming back into the living room having put Molly and Luke to bed.

Lou swings her feet from the sofa so Karen can sit down.

'No, no, you're all right, I'm fine here.' Karen flops into an armchair. At once Toby, the tabby, comes to sit on her knee.

'He's grown so much,' observes Lou. When she first met Karen he was still a kitten.

'I know,' says Karen. 'He's a bit of a thug to look at, but the children adore him.' She tickles him under the chin. 'So, anyway, will you be staying in Brighton?'

Lou stretches out her legs again – after all the standing she's done this evening it's a relief to have her feet up. The others headed off home straight after the fireworks, but it was still early and Lou, conscious Karen might like company, offered to come back to her place.

'I think I'd best go to my mother's,' Lou says.

Karen's face registers surprise. 'Really? That's brave. Christmas with your mum will be a bit of a nightmare, from what you say. I thought you liked to avoid it. Are you sure you don't want to spend it with us?'

'I'd love to. In fact—' She pictures Molly and Luke beneath the tree that's before her now, excitedly ripping open their presents, and contrasts it with her mother's formal handing round of gifts one by one, and careful note-taking of who's given what. 'There's nothing I'd like more. But I can't.'

'Why not? Have you promised you'd be there?'

'It's just . . . well, look at me.' Lou lifts up her top to reveal the distended dome of her belly. Even though she's lying on her back, there's no mistaking she is pregnant.

'Ooh, you look lovely. I remember that feeling so well . . .' Karen sounds wistful. 'When I was expecting Molly . . . I felt fantastic at twenty weeks, actually. Every day I could sense my body changing, it was as if I could hear the blood going round . . .' She smiles. 'And I could feel her kicking by then.'

'I can feel the baby moving too,' says Lou, resting a hand on her lower abdomen and sensing the warmth of her own skin. 'It's quite amazing, isn't it?'

'Almost . . . what's the word? Primordial. I remember getting this sense of a connection going right back . . . this is me, like my mother, like my grandmother . . .'

Exactly, thinks Lou. Karen has hit on something more significant than she realizes. 'That's why I've got to go back to my mum's.'

'Eh?'

'To tell her.'

'Goodness.' Karen's expression is horrified. 'She doesn't *know* yet?'

Lou looks away, sheepish.

'No,' she admits. 'And nor does my sister.'

42

Rich reverses the hatchback into a space outside Judy and Peter's bungalow. There are far more cars in the street than usual, but it's Christmas Day; presumably everyone with family in the Dales has chosen to come out here. Little surprise; the village is pretty to the point of twee. Surrounded by high fells and nestling on the banks of the Wharfe, it has an arched bridge to provide a focal point, a pub that serves cream teas as well as draught beer, a church that still boasts a decent-sized congregation and a main street where every house looks like something from a greetings card. Judy and Peter's is the only modern residence in the vicinity, and even that is appropriately weather-worn and lichen-covered.

I'm glad we decided to come, thinks Rich. This is exactly the sort of place where one should spend Christmas, and being at home with only a hormonal Cath might have been a strain.

'You know, it's funny, but I seem to have stopped feeling sick over the last few days,' she says as they wait for someone to answer the doorbell.

'Really?'

'Yup. A week ago I felt like throwing up all the time. Now, I feel fine. That horrible taste in my mouth has gone too.'

'That's good.'

'Mm.'

At that moment the door opens – it's Alfie, or Dom – he's never been good at telling the twins apart, and the lad seems to have grown a couple of inches since he last saw him. Rich is hit by a smell of cooking – brussels, roast turkey, chestnut stuffing – and his tummy rumbles in anticipation.

'Happy Christmas, Dom!' says Cath, stepping inside with two enormous Toys R Us carrier bags. 'Are we doing pressies before we eat?'

* * *

'Lou, hello!' says Georgia, when Lou finally manages to get all the bolts undone and open the front door. Lord knows why her mother insists on creating such a fortress – compared to some of the vast properties around St Albans, it's hardly as if there's *that* much to steal.

Lou's sister is standing in the porch with her husband, Howard, and their children, Elliot, five, and Annabel, two. Georgia is laden with nappy sacks and presents, Howard is brandishing two bottles of wine, and the children have clearly already been opening gifts this morning: Elliot is dressed head to toe as a pirate and Annabel has a baby doll almost as big as she is clutched to her chest. No gender stereotyping there, then, thinks Lou wryly.

'Come in,' she says.

'When did you get here?' asks Georgia.

'Late last night.' Lou takes their coats and hangs them in the hall closet – she knows how her mother hates anything lying about and getting in the way. 'I came by train.'

She leads the way into the kitchen so Howard can hand over his bottles. Irene, dressed in a pinny over a pale-turquoise skirt suit, is busy preparing lunch.

'Darling, hello!' She greets her daughter with a peck on the cheek. 'You look lovely!' Georgia is wearing what Lou has to concede is a becoming green silk dress and has curled her strawberry blonde hair. As her mother bends down to greet her grandchildren, Lou thinks, *she hardly ever kisses me.* Then Irene smiles stiffly at Howard: that's more like it.

'Can we open our presents?' asks Annabel.

'No, not yet,' says Irene. 'After lunch, if you don't mind.'

And then we'll do it in age order, thinks Lou.

'I'll put these under the tree, then, shall I?' says Georgia.

'Yes, there's a love, that's a good idea.' Irene addresses Howard. 'Would you like a drink?'

'Please.'

'Sherry OK?'

'That would be lovely,' says Howard.

I bet he'd prefer a beer, thinks Lou. She has half a yen for some alcohol herself. She has a flutter of nerves as she considers breaking the news to her family. She's dreading it. *Not today,* she decides. She wants to tell her mother in private first, and anyway she'd hate to spoil the children's Christmas. It's less than two years since she told Irene she was gay; she's ruined a family get-together once already.

* * *

'I hear congratulations are in order,' says Mike, coming down the hall and enveloping Cath in a bear hug.

Cath is taken aback that he knows.

'Sorry.' Judy winces on seeing her expression. 'I let it slip. I assumed you'd have told him already.'

Now there will be no avoiding telling Sukey too, thinks Cath, heart sinking.

They head into the living room. Her father gets up slowly from his favourite armchair to greet them. Alfie and Dom duck under Cath's arm and plonk themselves beneath the tree, impatient to start unwrapping.

'Where's Sukey?' she says.

'Mummy's in bed,' says Alfie.

'She's got flu,' says Mike. 'It's doing the rounds at the boys' school, apparently.'

So the woman who is never ill has succumbed to a virus, Cath thinks, and says sweetly, 'Oh dear. Poor thing. I presume she'll be down for lunch, though?'

'Doubt it,' says Mike. 'She's sick as a dog.'

Behind him Cath sees Rich wink at her.

* * *

'Wine?' Howard gloops burgundy into her glass before Lou can stop him.

'Ah – that's fine,' she says, holding up a hand. Probably best not to refuse completely anyway, lest she arouse suspicion.

Her brother-in-law returns to the head of the table and picks up the carving knife and fork. Her mother is at his elbow, ready to dish out the veg.

'So, who's for breast and who's for brown?' he asks.

Lou eyes her nut roast. Typical: it looks burnt at the edges; she should never have trusted Irene to cook it. 'I'll do mine,' she says, and gets to her feet to reach across the table for the dish.

As she does so she can feel cool air on her midriff. Even though she's wearing her loosest trousers, nothing tucks in easily these days and her top has ridden up.

'Gosh,' says Irene. 'You're getting a bit chubby.'

Lou sits back down with the platter of nut roast, winded by the remark. She can feel herself going red, and wishes she could prevent it. She looks up: Georgia is looking at her through narrowed eyes, which only makes her blush more. She focuses on serving herself, unsure how to handle the situation. Then she has a little sip of wine – if she behaves naturally, with luck it'll throw Georgia off the scent. That her mother should comment critically on her appearance is nothing new, after all. She glances up again. Georgia is still staring at her, if anything more intently.

Lou shifts in her seat, pulls down her top and says, 'I know, Mum, you're right. I haven't been doing as much exercise recently.' She's always been a hopeless liar, but perhaps she can continue to bluff her way out of it.

'That doesn't look like just fat,' says Georgia.

Lou wishes she could reach under the table to kick her, but she is diagonally across and too far away. I really don't want to have this conversation now, she thinks. Can't Georgia grasp that?

'Your stomach looks *hard*,' says Georgia.

Meanwhile Howard is doling out turkey, oblivious. Lou watches as the plates are passed by her down the table, it seems in slow motion, to the children. They are holding their cutlery at right angles, expectant. Elliot is still in his pirate outfit: skull-and-crossbones hat, eyepatch and all. The whole experience would be surreal were it not so excruciating.

She pushes back her chair. 'Sorry, I just need the loo.'

As she rushes from the room she hears Irene say, 'Not in the middle of eating, darling, can't you wait?'

In the bathroom, she stands in front of the mirror, as if to act as her own advisor. Her face appears startled, terrified even. She tries to compose herself. Perhaps a quick rinse with cold water will help. She runs her hands under the tap, splashes her cheeks, then dries herself quickly on the hand towel. She'd better go back; any delay will only make things worse.

She opens the door to the dining room, slides back into her seat, hoping against hope no one will comment, and reaches for the bread sauce.

'So, is Georgia right, then?' asks Howard.

'Eh?' Lou colours again; there's just no way she can prevent herself.

'I said you couldn't possibly be,' says Irene.

'And I said of course you could,' says Georgia. Lou could swear she sounds smug, even gleeful.

For the first time in a while, Lou has a real surge of longing for Sofia. If only she had a girlfriend here with her, to help her through this. They could explain the set-up together.

'I don't understand how.' Irene shakes her head.

'Oh, anything's possible these days, Mum, don't you know?'

All this in front of the kids, honestly. Despite years of experiencing their insensitivity, Lou can hardly believe it.

'But I thought you didn't like men . . . ?' says Irene, lowering her voice at least.

'I don't!' Lou snaps, no longer able to restrain her temper. 'Not that way, anyway.' Her mother seems completely unable to understand that, actually, she likes male company just fine.

'Did you use a turkey baster?' whispers Georgia, as if she is on stage.

Howard splutters on his wine, then laughs.

'No, I did not!'

'Ah, so you *are* pregnant.' Georgia sits back in her chair.

'So what if I fucking am?' No sooner has she sworn than she feels the consternation of two small presences close to her. 'Sorry,' she says to the children. 'But yes, you're right. I'm nearly five months gone.' She glances at her mother, then glares pointedly at Georgia. 'Happy now?'

43

Maybe I've got Sukey's bug, thinks Cath, as she feels herself go hot and cold and clammy. It would serve me right for being so pleased she was ill earlier. I have eaten an awful lot, perhaps that wasn't wise.

She puts down her spoonful of Christmas pudding. Suddenly the room starts to spin, pain sears through her. She almost doubles over.

'Er . . . I think we'd better leave now,' she says to Rich. At least they're nearly at the end of the meal.

'What, now?'

'Yes.'

'I thought you said we'd stay till five?' He frowns, confused. She glances at the clock on the mantelpiece – she can only just read what it says, the hands are blurry. *Three thirty.*

'Oh dear, nothing I cooked, I hope?' says Judy.

'No, no,' says Cath as she cramps again. 'I've probably just overdone it.' She has to get out of there. 'It must be the same bug as Sukey – I'm so sorry—'

Rich is slow to make a move. Come *on*, she thinks, I have to go home.

'You don't look too great,' says Peter.

'Are you sure you wouldn't be better putting your feet up here?' asks Judy. 'You can always use our room.'

With Sukey next door? thinks Cath. No way.

'I'd rather get home, thanks.'

'Can't I just finish this?' asks Rich, dolefully looking down at his pudding.

'Um, I'd rather you didn't.' She flashes him a look to communicate she is not to be argued with, then grips the edge of the table to steady herself.

He takes another mouthful. At last he wipes his mouth on his napkin and stands up.

'Well, thanks for everything,' he smiles. 'That was a truly delicious meal.'

Come ON! Cath has an urge to scream, but she doesn't want to cause a panic.

The entire family rises from the table to bid them farewell, in spite of Cath's protestations that they needn't bother. After what seems like an age, she and Rich have their coats on and are in the hall. She practically pulls her husband through the front door and runs ahead of him to the car. As she rushes down the garden path, it feels as if her whole body is convulsing.

Finally he seems to have picked up that something is wrong; a second later he flings himself into the driving seat next to her and starts the ignition.

'You OK?'

'Take me to the hospital,' she barks.

'Eh . . . ?' But he's realized. Instantly his cheeks are ashen.

*   *   *

At least I managed to curtail an inquisition about my pregnancy over lunch, thinks Lou. Or Howard did, rather. Seeing the atmosphere heat up like a volcano – and realizing what the damage might be – he'd stepped in and said, 'I think we'd best not do this in front of Elliot and Annabel, if you don't mind.' The rest of the meal was permeated by Georgia's fury at being circumvented and Irene's shock, but at least Lou was given dispensation to finish eating.

Next is present-opening. Quite how her mother manages to dampen the joy of such an occasion is no longer the disappointment for Lou it was when she was small. She's come to expect the formality of turn-taking, the 'remember to say thank you, children', and the lack of any gifts that might suggest someone in her family has an understanding of what she might actually like. Once all the still-viable wrapping paper is folded and put away ready for re-use next year, Howard suggests he and the children head outside to play with Elliot's stomp rocket on the lawn.

Lou is just about to go with them – the rocket was from her, so this seems more than reasonable – when Georgia says, 'Um, I think Mum and I could do with a hand clearing up, don't you?' and Lou realizes she has no choice but to stay.

She goes to the sink so she can start the washing-up. She has barely turned on the taps and squirted detergent into the bowl before Georgia says, 'So who's the father, then?'

Thankfully Lou has had a couple of hours to work out a top-line approach to her news. She chooses her words carefully. 'A friend of mine in Brighton. He's a doctor, in fact, called Adam.'

'So not a donor, then?'

'If you mean someone anonymous, then no.'

'So you had sex with him?'

'Bloody hell, Georgia, where do you get off?'

'Sorry, sorry—' Georgia holds up both her hands in innocence and steps back, as if she's amazed to have caused offence.

'No, and no, I haven't suddenly gone straight or anything, though I'm sure you'd both love it if I had.' She turns back round to face her sister and mother. 'We had IVF, if you must know.'

'IVF, really?'

'Yes.'

'What, on the NHS?'

Lou can't bear to hear how Georgia thinks the NHS shouldn't be funding such things. But neither can she face explaining the whole egg-sharing set-up. She'll admit to that later, maybe, but certainly not now. Having to deal with both her sister and mother in one hit is already more than she can handle.

'No,' she says, then lies. 'Adam paid for it.'

'Oh.' Her sister pulls a face as if to communicate she's lucky to have landed such a sugar daddy. Never mind that Howard's been the breadwinner for years, thinks Lou.

'For your information, the whole idea of turkey basters is pretty erroneous,' says Lou. 'Some gay women do inseminate themselves at home, but they use a proper needle-less syringe, not something from the kitchen utensil drawer.' The irony of where she is standing does not escape her. 'But anyway. Adam's a doctor and he has contacts.' Now she's on a roll she relishes bigging him up, even if it isn't entirely truthful. There's undeniably satisfaction to be gleaned from pandering to their snobbery. 'And they helped us sort out doing it properly, privately, through a clinic in Harley Street.'

'Harley Street . . . ' repeats Irene. She sounds almost impressed.

'Well, it seems a bit, I don't know . . . selfish, if you ask me,' says Georgia.

'I didn't ask you.' Lou feels herself flush again, then says, 'But how do you mean exactly, selfish?'

'Bringing a child into this world with two gay parents.'

'What, and your act of procreating was entirely selfless, then?'

Georgia reddens too. 'Well, not entirely, I guess, but – well, did you think about all the implications?'

'Oh for God's sake, Georgia, of course I did! What do you take me for, an idiot? I'm a counsellor, for fuck's sake, I've thought about little else!'

'Ah.'

'And of course I know the kid might have a few problems, but what kid doesn't? Not a single child on earth goes through life without the odd hiccup. Jesus Christ, both you and Mum are so effing uptight sometimes. And you live in each other's pockets, surrounded by nothing but narrow-minded people as conservative as you are. Well, if I was a kid, I know where I'd rather be brought up.' The moment she's said it she half regrets it – normally she manages to hold her tongue. But she's hormonal, and has no one here to support her, so she's also relieved to have let rip.

'Where?' says Georgia. 'In Brighton?'

'Yes,' says Lou. 'Why not?'

'In your little attic?'

'Yes, in my *little attic*. If need be, sure.'

'Well, I don't know what Mum has to say about that. And you can call me narrow-minded if you like, but I know what I think.'

Suddenly, there is a little cough behind them.

'I can speak for myself, you know, Georgia,' says Irene.

'Oh.' Georgia is taken aback.

'Actually, from everything Lou has said it sounds as if she's thought all this through pretty carefully.'

'I have,' says Lou, astonished. 'And believe you me, it wasn't that simple.' She takes a deep breath. 'I didn't have much time, according to the doctors, if I wanted to maximize my chances of a straightforward pregnancy.'

'Really?' says her sister.

Does Georgia think she is exaggerating? 'They said after my fibroid operation I ought to get on with it, so I did a lot of soul-searching and asking around and research, and decided it was something I wanted to do. In fact, I think I might make quite a good mother.'

'Do you now?' says Georgia.

'Georgia! That's enough.' Lou can hardly believe her mother has said this. 'Stop it, both of you, it's Christmas Day.'

Ah yes, of course, Irene won't want the occasion ruined. They're not being polite.

Her mother takes off her pinny and hangs it on the back of the door, checks through the kitchen window that the children are still playing in the garden. And then, instead of resuming clearing up, she turns to face them both. She has two bright-pink spots on her cheeks.

'It might surprise you to hear this, but actually, Lou, I do think you'll make a good mother.' Irene raises her eyebrows pointedly at Georgia. 'You know, Georgia, when your sister told me last year she was a lesbian, I felt like the ground was no longer steady under me. I haven't really talked to you much about it, or you, Lou, or anyone come to that, because I thought my reaction was just old-fashioned and, well, selfish, I suppose.' She pauses, picks up a napkin, starts twisting it round her fingers. 'But as you are both accusing each other of selfishness, perhaps I can admit that yes, I did find it hard. I felt humiliated, embarrassed, trailing behind your announcement, Lou, with a huge amount of catching up to do. I mean, yes, of course I sort of knew you were gay, or suspected, but I'd never been wholly sure . . . And I tried to talk it over, I mentioned it to a couple of friends of mine in the village, but they just said, "Oh well, as long as she's happy . . . ", "Better than living a lie . . . ", "She's still your daughter . . . " Stuff like that.' She sighs. 'So I kept my feelings to myself.'

Lou has a flash of anger, yet she restrains herself. There's something refreshingly honest about the way Irene is talking.

'I'm sorry, Lou.' Irene stops folding and refolding the napkin and glances up at her. 'I kept a lot of this from you because I thought it would just make you annoyed and upset. I felt so guilty, but it was a bit like I suffered a bereavement. I don't mean it was as bad as when I lost your father, but still, it was such a blow. Everything became hard: running this place, seeing people, being with you, Georgia, because your family seemed so *normal* in comparison – sometimes I used to just cry myself to sleep.' She gulps, then continues, 'For months there was nothing in my head but worry. Gradually I recovered, got used to the idea, you introduced me to Sofia – that was nice, you know . . . ' Blimey, thinks Lou, I had no idea. 'Then something would happen to trigger me, and the whole thing would hit me again . . . Like when you split with Sofia, there's an example, and I just couldn't get it out of my head that you'd end up on your own, with no partner, no one to share your life with . . . '

Not dissimilar to you, then, thinks Lou. 'Oh, Mum,' she says, at once feeling tearful herself.

'But after that I gave myself a talking to, I said life's too short, Irene, stop all this self-absorption and blame and worry. Lou's all right, she can look after herself. She's a grown woman, she's got a good job, there's a lot more to her than just who she goes out with . . . '

Hurrah, thinks Lou. Too bloody right. 'Thanks,' she mutters.

' . . . And now you're telling us this, and yes, I admit, I'm completely shocked.' Irene shakes her head. 'I'd kind of thought you might have a child in some way, with Sofia – yes, Georgia' – Lou sees her sister is equally astonished by all this – 'I'm not *that* naive, but then when your relationship ended I assumed there was just no way.'

Lou is finding it hard to keep up.

'And you know what?' Irene puts down the napkin.

'What?' says Georgia.

Irene's brow furrows, just a little, as if she's checking with herself this is in fact the case. Then she nods, and gives a small smile. 'I rather like the idea of another grand-child . . . ' She frowns more intensely, to reaffirm she's right about her response. 'Yes, I am . . . ' Next she laughs, lightly. 'In fact . . . I'm rather pleased.'

44

Cath and Rich are sitting together, struggling to take stock, when a nurse comes and signals to Rich.

'Can I have a quick word?' she says, beckoning him over.

'Sure,' Rich nods. 'Back in a sec,' he says to Cath and pats her knee.

'I think perhaps your wife's not in the best state to take this in,' says the nurse. 'So I thought I'd have a chat with you. Is that OK?'

'Mm,' says Rich. He's no idea what sort of a state he's in himself, but no matter. Cath is his priority.

She checks Cath can't hear, and steps a few paces further from earshot. Rich follows her. He notices the Airedale Hospital label pinned to her grey-blue jacket. *Sister Maureen Ehrlich*, it says. How do you pronounce that? he wonders, then realizes it doesn't matter at all.

'I suppose there's no chance she's not lost the baby?' he says, grasping at hope.

'No, I'm afraid not.' She blows out her cheeks, lets out a rush of air. 'The doctor says she's lost too much blood already

357

for that to be the case. Your wife is miscarrying. I realize this is hard.' She stops and allows him a moment. Rich nods and she continues. 'So . . . you'll need to ensure she has plenty of super-plus sanitary towels to absorb the bleeding. She shouldn't use tampons as they might cause an infection.'

Where on earth am I going to get those on Christmas Day? thinks Rich. He's not even sure what super-plus sanitary towels are.

Sister Maureen seems to realize the problem. 'I can try and see if I can get some to last you a day or so, if that helps?'

'Please.'

'OK, but first let me just run through this with you. We're on a skeleton staff over the next few days so I wouldn't want you to have to come back.'

'No, I understand.' Anyway, they're miles from home, this isn't even their local hospital.

'And unfortunately, with a miscarriage, there's not that much anyone can do.'

'Resting in bed won't help?'

'No. I'm sorry. It really is too late for that.'

'I see,' says Rich. Although he doesn't; not at all, not yet.

'I suggest you just go home, help your wife to rest.'

'I don't need to take her to the hospital in Leeds?'

'Well, you should let your GP know what's going on, when they're open, say, in a couple of days.'

'But Cath seems to have stopped bleeding quite as much now, she says. She was worse on the way here.'

'I'm afraid although it may feel as though the bleeding is

slowing down or stopping, it's an illusion. In reality, the blood collects at the top of the vagina and then drains away when your wife walks or goes to the toilet. So if she's been sitting for a while, that's probably what's happened.'

'I see.' His last vestiges of hope smash.

'If your wife wants to go to bed, that's fine. Just make her as comfortable as you can.'

'She seems to be in a lot of pain.'

'I can imagine.' Sister Maureen winces. 'By all means give her some paracetamol or ibuprofen – even both, if you are careful and follow the instructions. You could also give her a hot-water bottle to ease the cramping.'

'You don't need to keep her in?'

'We don't.'

Rich is unsure if this is because they haven't the beds, it's not an emergency or they don't care. He can't work it out. He can't work out anything.

'You only need to worry if the bleeding becomes so heavy she's getting through more than a pad in an hour, or if there's lots of clotting, because then she's losing too much blood.'

He rubs his brow, as if it will prompt his brain to function and help him remember if there's anything else he should ask. 'How long is the bleeding likely to last?'

'It'll probably tail off in a week to ten days. Usually it stops after a couple of weeks. Bleeding after this time can still be normal but it's likely your doctor will want to check your wife's health, to make certain she's not had an incomplete miscarriage.'

'Right,' says Rich. Though it all feels very wrong.

The sister gives his arm a sympathetic squeeze. 'Otherwise,

just be there for her. Now, if you hold on a sec over there, I'll just get you those pads.'

A few minutes later she returns. 'Here you go.' She hands over a paper bag. She's poised to return to her duties when she stops and says, 'I'm so sorry this should happen to you both, today of all days. That really is tough.'

Yes, thinks Rich. It is. Thank God she doesn't wish them a merry Christmas.

45

It takes a few days for the magnitude of losing the baby to hit Cath. At first she feels OK; she's surprised by her own resilience, proud of herself for holding everything together. The remainder of Christmas passes unremarkably; luckily she and Rich didn't have much else planned. She feels unsteady on her feet and a bit dizzy, and she can't face calling her mum to tell her what has happened. Her family seem to have assumed she's got Sukey's lurgy, so when Judy rings on Boxing Day to check up on her, Rich is able to say she is in bed with flu to give them breathing space.

But come 28th December Cath is due to go in to work at the gallery, and she wakes up in the morning ahead of the alarm and realizes it was a false reprieve. Before she's even out of bed, she knows there's something dreadfully wrong. It's as though she's been hit repeatedly in the head and her brain has been knocked out of her skull, leaving her mind floating in space, such is the sense of disconnection from her own body. She can barely see straight: the numerals on the bedside radio alarm are way too bright, like car headlights on full beam coming straight at her. At once she's scared: she has been here before. She pushes back the duvet, goes to the window, and when she opens the curtains the winter morning is so dazzling she has to shut her eyes, even though the sky is overcast. It's another sign: the world is too much for her, too demanding, intense.

I can't go to work like this. I'm not up to it. I won't cope. The endless visitors to the gallery, asking questions; having to spend the day in public; everyone wishing one another a merry Christmas and happy new year.

She feels a tidal wave of panic, hurriedly closes the curtains. She prefers darkness.

Rich, only just coming to, is confused. 'You OK, love?'

'No,' says Cath, in a small voice. She sits down by his side.

Rich hoists himself up. 'Oh, sweetheart . . . ' He takes her hand.

'I can't go.'

'To work?'

'Mm.' She starts to cry.

'That's OK,' he says gently. 'Though are you sure it wouldn't make you feel better?'

'No. It won't.' Just the idea of getting on the bus fills her with dread.

'It's just sometimes it helps to be amongst other people. And I won't be here today . . . I really do have to go in to the office. I'm the one doing holiday cover.'

'Of course. I don't expect you not to go. But I'm not ready. I can't do it.' The admission breaks the dam. 'Oh, Rich!' she wails. 'We lost our baby, our precious wee baby . . . I can't

362

believe it's not there any more.' She lifts up her nightdress and looks down. Tears plop onto her skin and run in tiny rivulets over her belly. It appears just the same as it did at the end of last week, surely: soft and smooth, a bit round and lacking in tone. Abs of steel I'm not, she thinks ruefully. Her self-admonishment only makes her more miserable; she cries even harder, and as she does so, Rich places his palm on her tummy, rubbing this place close to where the baby was, this chamber of her loss. For a long while she continues weeping, her whole body lurching in accompaniment to her sobs, and he continues rubbing, calming her, saying nothing, for there is nothing he can say.

*　*　*

Lou yawns and rolls over, enjoying the sensation of her own bed after a few days away. She arrived back in Brighton last night and even though she's had a while to process her family's reaction, she's still not completely unravelled it yet. Maybe her brain is slowing down as she enters the second half of her pregnancy; whatever, that her mother ended up not only pleased about it but putting Georgia in her place was completely unexpected. Lou can't imagine not having to deal with her mother's censure. Her disapproval was integral to how Lou saw the future, yet the next day, when it was just the two of them, Irene even asked if she could lay a hand on her tummy and feel the baby kick. Quite extraordinary.

Inevitably the baby refused to move to order, and at this stage in her pregnancy the flutters are really only discernible to Lou herself anyway, but that wasn't the point. Of course

Lou is less delighted with Georgia's response – if she'd been asked to guess beforehand, she'd have assumed Georgia would be positive and her mother negative – but given Georgia's history of wanting to please Irene, she's hopeful her mum will talk her sister round.

Not that I seem able to prophesy anything for certain, thinks Lou. No matter how much counselling experience I have, people will always surprise me.

And *now* you're kicking! she scolds the baby, as she senses movement in her belly.

She lifts up her T-shirt and examines herself: even in the four days since Georgia spotted the bump, her body seems to have changed. Her waistline has expanded some more – it can't just be overindulgence over Christmas, surely; her belly button is beginning to pop out, her tummy feels itchy as the skin stretches.

Apparently the sonographer could glean a clear idea of the baby's sex at the second scan last week, though neither Lou nor Adam could tell from the screen. 'I can't understand why so many people choose to find out,' Lou had said to her – it was the same older woman performing the procedure as the previous time. 'I guess it makes it easier with baby clothes and decorating the nursery,' she'd replied. 'Well, our baby's not going to have the luxury of a nursery, and if he's a boy, he'll just have to cope with the odd bit of pink.' She can imagine some of their friends – Howie, for instance – might help a baby on that score.

Surely wondering about an infant's sex is half the fun. 'Are you a boy or a girl?' she asks her bump. As if in response, she feels another tiny flutter.

*   *   *

Cath is on a strange planet. There is no sun; only the ice-blue light of a spaceship illuminates her way. It looks cold, though she can't gauge the temperature through the giant eiderdown of her spacesuit. It's a struggle to move and her breath keeps steaming up the visor of her helmet. But she's determined to scrutinize the eerie honeycomb formations that seem to stretch in every direction around her; she can just make them out in the semi-darkness. She crouches down: there are hundreds, no, thousands, of ova; bigger than ostrich eggs, the shells are slightly transparent. She examines one up close; inside she can see a larva, pulsing gently with life. She reaches out, scoops up the egg with clumsy giant-gloved hands. But as she stands upright, it falls from her hands, smashes.

'Whoa!' She jumps.

But it's only Rich; she must have fallen back asleep. Disturbed, she tries to shake herself back to reality.

'Cath, I brought you this.' He is standing over the bed with a mug of tea. His hair is damp from the shower, his face pink from having just shaved, he smells of lemon soap. He is dressed and ready to leave. Cath can't identify with his professional persona at all. She half wants him to go so she can be alone, half wants him to stay, reground her, comfort her.

'Promise me you'll get up, love.'

'OK,' she says. But she knows she won't. She can't face engaging with the day. Getting dressed means she intends to.

365

She hears Rich go down the stairs, shut the front door, start the car, drive away. She doesn't envy him, having to go to Leicester. She can't imagine being able to go anywhere. Even going as far as the bathroom down the hall is an effort, as if she has to swim against a tide of treacle to get there. By the time she sits on the loo she is shaking all over.

She is still bleeding, a reminder that the process isn't over yet. Her abdomen contracts, like period pains, but worse.

She makes herself look into the bowl of the toilet. It's not as gory as it was a few days ago, but it's gruesome nonetheless: there's blood, lots of it, speckled with clots. She has a sudden urge to ladle it up, cup it in her palms, force it back inside her, make the baby live again. But that would be mad, she tells herself, like Jackie Kennedy trying to scoop up JFK's brain from the trunk of the limousine. So instead she watches the blood slowly dissolve in the water, turning it pink. Then she flushes it, down the drain to the pipes beneath the street.

Some graveyard, she thinks.

She waits, trying to pee. Minutes pass; she just sits there. It takes an age for her to persuade her body to let go; she seems unable to give any more of herself away. After what seems forever, she manages a pathetic trickle.

She is vaguely aware her mouth feels horrible, stale. She imagines her tongue is green, but she can't face brushing her teeth; she's had enough. She hurries back to the bedroom as fast as she can, gets under the duvet, pulls it right up to her neck and lies there, engulfed.

After a while she realizes she is shaking with upset, like a frightened animal. Her legs and knees are going judder, judder, judder, as though she were freezing cold, but the central heating is on, she can't be. For some reason she can't cry; it's as if she needs a witness to her suffering for the tears to come. Without Rich present to console her, her grief must remain noiseless, silent, just a gut-wrenching sense of loss that echoes the twisting sensation in her lower abdomen.

She feels so guilty, so disappointed, such a failure. She's let everyone down: not just herself, but Rich, her parents, her egg donor, the people at the clinic. Most of all, she's let down the baby. Why wasn't she able to protect it? What is wrong with her, with her womb, with her ability to mother, that makes her incapable of nurturing life?

She rubs her belly. Forgive me, she says.

But she can't forgive herself.

*　*　*

'Judy, I'm afraid I've got some bad news.'

'Oh?'

'It's Cath.'

Judy gasps. 'Is she OK?'

She is always on her nerves' ends about her daughter's health so he'd best cut straight to it, although he'd prefer to soften his words. 'Er, no, it's the, um, baby. I'm afraid she lost it.'

'No-o-o . . . ' A quiet howl of grief, then a long pause. Eventually she says, 'When?'

'Christmas Day, after we left you.'

'What, when she had that tummy bug?'

'Yes, only it wasn't. I'm sorry we didn't ring before but we needed some time to take stock.'

She is silent a moment, then says, 'Oh, Rich pet, I'm so sorry.'

Rich exhales. 'Me too.' He gulps back his own upset. He has just a few minutes before he has to go into the office and meet a supplier: he can't let down his guard.

'I suppose at this stage of pregnancy, it is still pretty common.'

'Mm.'

'What was she . . . seven weeks?'

'Eight.'

'Gosh, that's hard. Not that it's easy any time, but Cath, she's so fragile . . . Is she all right?'

'To be honest, no, I don't think so. I mean physically, yes, they say she should be OK, she just has to take it easy, allow nature to take its course. She's still losing blood, but it's not that . . . I don't know, when I left this morning, just from the way she was acting, I'm worried about her.'

'Oh dear, poor love. I was concerned this might happen – especially after the first time.'

'Were you?' Rich isn't sure if she's referring to the unsuccessful IVF or Cath's previous depression. Not that it matters.

'I did try and say, but you know what Cath's like. She won't listen. But from everything I hear IVF is by no means always plain sailing, and with the health problems she's had, I didn't expect it to work easily.'

Why didn't Judy say all that to me? thinks Rich a few minutes later as he heads back to his desk. Instead I left Cath and Judy to talk it through in private, as Cath wanted to. But of course Judy wouldn't want to interfere, and at the time I would have probably resented it if she had. Cath certainly would.

In truth Rich had wanted to believe the medical world could work its miracles as much as Cath did, although when they failed to conceive at the first attempt he'd been knocked back. But since the pregnancy test he's allowed his hope to grow, a little more every day. His emotional responses trail behind Cath's; he follows along in her wake, always destined to be behind, taking his lead from her. But after this latest fall, he's not at all certain she'll get up again. It's not a race he can run alone, so where does that leave the two of them now?

* * *

Cath is not really asleep, but she is closed down, in limbo. She's not moved for hours. The curtains remain drawn, despite the best attempts of daylight to break through the gap between them, and she's in the same position, curled up on her bed. From where she lies, she can see the bedside clock.

Ten minutes pass.

Fifteen . . .

Seventeen . . .

Time moves unbearably slowly. Bessie is cupped up in the 'c' of her belly, one crescent moon within another. The cat usually sleeps on the duvet at the bottom of the bed, but it's as if she's sensed Cath needs her especially close, so she pushed up the cover with her nose and nuzzled right in. Her warmth and the softness of her fur are a small comfort.

At one point Cath hears the landline ring, but she can't

face answering it. The answering machine clicks on. There's her own voice, requesting the caller leave a message. She sounds so together, grown-up, upbeat, like someone else entirely.

A beep, then her mother. 'Darling, how are you?' A pause. 'Cath, pet, I'm pretty sure you're there. It's Mum. Rich just called me and told me the news. I'm so sorry. Really I am. I know how much you were hoping for this to work – we all were – but, oh love, I don't know what to say. We're thinking of you, me and your dad. I hope you're getting some rest. You look after yourself. I want to come and see you so please call me when you pick up this message. Big hug.'

There's a click, and she's gone. Cath reaches for her earplugs so she won't be disturbed again.

46

06:33. Again Cath wakes before Rich. Once more she is floating, weightless, like an astronaut. This is the third? fourth? day she's been here. She has lost track completely. Her head burns, as if someone has opened her skull and filled it with fire. Yet outside birds are beginning to sing. She can't stand it. Once more she reaches for her earplugs, wedges them in tight-tight-tight, until she can no longer hear. Her brain feels as if it's going to explode. She's sure she can feel chemicals reacting against one another, eating into her grey matter. She'd do anything to be able to block out everything: noise and thoughts and the world, to have some sense of calm.

Rich gets up, gets ready for work, again pleads with her to get up. But once he has gone, she admits defeat to herself: she can't move, go anywhere. Even the cocoon of her familiar bed in this familiar room doesn't feel safe – how on earth could she venture further? She wants, craves, safety, but without it, the most she can hope is to go back to sleep again: if she sleeps she might find peace. For hours she tries; the harder she tries the more sleep eludes her. All she can do is think the same thoughts repeated again and again:

I deserve what happened.

I don't deserve to be a mother.

Childless women are useless.

I'm a terrible person.

I've let everyone down.

I'm a failure.

My womb doesn't work.

I hate my body.

I hate myself.

I don't deserve to be happy.

Round and round and round they go, and as they whirl and crash and explode she feels her personality disintegrating, disappearing, being burnt up in the chemical fire in her brain. All the while she doesn't move; she lies absolutely still, on her side, paralysed, stuck, like one of the dwellers from the city of Pompeii, captured forever by volcanic ash and lava.

* * *

'I still can't seem to get through to her, Rich. She won't pick up the phone. I've tried both the landline and her mobile time and again. I want to see her.'

Rich is standing outside the double doors of his office in Leicester. Even though it's chilly, he's stepped out so they can speak in private. 'Judy, I'm sorry, she says she doesn't want to see anyone, and she won't answer my calls half the time either. She's been like this all week. I gather she's still bleeding a little, but I don't think that's what's laying her up. She's not getting out of bed at all.'

A pause while Judy assimilates. 'You don't think she's headed for another depression, do you?'

'I can feel her disappearing from me.' He doesn't need to elaborate.

'Oh dear, it sounds as if she might be. Is there anything I can do?'

Rich sighs. 'I'm very worried about her, but it's really difficult for me because I have to go to work. The company is going through tough times – there's such pressure. I worry that if I take my eye off the ball they'll bin me off at the first opportunity.'

'Bin you off?'

'Sorry.' Rich has used an in-joke he shares with his colleagues. They are all on edge, concerned whose turn it will be next. 'I mean make me redundant.'

'That must be dreadful for you. I was going to suggest that you take some compassionate leave to be with Cath, but I guess that's not easy.'

'I daren't ask, I'm afraid.'

'No, I quite see that.'

There's another silence. Rich doesn't wish to hurry his mother-in-law, yet can't help worrying that he's been absent from his desk too long. He's not sure he can trust those he works with not to tell tales if he is seen to be slacking.

Judy says, 'Is she eating?'

'I'm not sure. I make her a meal every evening, but when I'm not there I get the sense she isn't.'

'That won't help.'

I know, thinks Rich. But what can I do? He has a crazy notion that he should set up one of those automatic feeders like they use for the cat when they go away for the night. It rotates round over twenty-four hours, slowly revealing food. He could put it on the bedside table, fill it with nuts and nibbles. Then the only thing Cath would have to do is reach out a hand . . . He stops himself. Maybe he's going mad too.

Judy continues, 'Could you hold on a minute? I just want to discuss something with Peter. I'll be back.'

'Yes, sure.' He bites back a mounting anxiety.

Shortly, she returns. 'If you don't mind, I'm going round. I know she says she doesn't want to see anyone, but I can't bear to think of her so miserable, all alone.'

'She might not answer the door.'

'I've a key.'

'So you have.' When Cath was weak from chemo and needed nursing, Judy used to let herself in. 'By all means then, go. It would be a relief for me if you saw her.'

*　*　*

Cath jumps. Someone is standing over the bed.

It's a burglar.

Then she realizes: it's her mum. In the semi-darkness she can just make out Judy's mouth opening and shutting like a goldfish.

'Hang on.' Cath removes the little yellow sponges from her ears. 'What are *you* doing here?'

'I let myself in. What on earth have you got there?'

'Earplugs.' She half sits up.

'Why? This is a perfectly quiet street.' Judy shakes her head. 'No wonder you didn't hear me phone.'

How can Cath possibly explain?

Judy goes directly over to the window and pulls open the curtains. Sunlight streams in; searing white, burning.

Cath shields her eyes. Judy sits down on the end of the bed, her outline dark against the brilliance. 'Darling, I'm worried. Rich says you haven't got up the whole week.'

Cath flinches, ashamed. Somewhere inside, she knows that this is absurd, but the force keeping her pinned to the mattress is enormous. Moving anywhere is terrifying.

'I can't,' she says.

'Are you still bleeding?' asks Judy, more gently. She shifts up the bed so as to be able to squeeze Cath's shoulder through the duvet.

Cath nods. 'A bit.'

'Oh, sweetheart, I really am so sorry.'

'It's all my fault,' murmurs Cath.

Her mum leans in. 'Now why would you say that?'

'Because it is. I should never have tried. I'm clearly not meant to have a baby.'

'Now you're being silly,' says Judy. The words might sound critical, but her tone is kind.

'Am I?' Cath has no idea if she's being silly or not. Her thoughts don't make much sense. 'My stupid womb is totally fucked up after my stupid cancer. It's not surprising a baby didn't want to stay there.' She half sits up, and starts to weep. As before, once she's started she cries and cries and cries, and in between sobs gasps in giant gulps of air, just

375

as she used to when she was very little. Her mother reaches in, takes her in her arms and just holds her. Her bosom is soft and she smells of washing powder. She's used the same brand for decades. Eventually, Cath moves out of her clasp and says, 'Can you get me a tissue?'

'Of course.' Judy goes to the bathroom – no treacle for her to swim through, it seems – and returns with a length of loo paper. 'Here.'

Cath blows her nose.

'Have you eaten?'

Has she? 'I'm not sure.'

'Oh goodness, darling!'

Cath isn't surprised her mum is exasperated; she's beyond exasperated with herself.

'I'll go and make you a sandwich and bring it up to you.'

Cath leans back against her pillows, looking out of the window. She has to squint. The whole world still feels eerily detached. But at least the panic seems to have subsided a little. It's good to have her mum here. She can hear her crashing plates and rummaging with cutlery, then the kettle coming to the boil. It's the first sound she's not wanted to block out for days and days.

Shortly Judy is back with a tray. On it is a cheese sandwich on brown bread and a steaming mug of tea.

'There's sugar in the tea.' It's a family tradition when they are ill.

'I didn't know we had any bread,' says Cath.

'There's heaps of food. Rich has been trying to look after you.' Judy pauses. Cath feels her mother watching her. 'Well, you must be feeling pretty terrible if you're not eating.'

Cath cracks a tiny smile. It feels odd, as if her face is doing something it's never done before.

'Now, love, I've a suggestion,' says Judy.

Cath takes a bite of the sandwich. Her mouth is so dry the crusts scrape the sides of her cheeks. She has a sip of tea in the hope it will help.

'Come home.'

'Home?' Surely she is home.

'To our house, I mean.'

'What, leave Rich?'

'It's not good for you here.'

Her mother can't mean it. 'I'm not deserting him. I've already let him down so much.' I can be so horrible to him sometimes, so selfish and impatient, I'm surprised he's not gone and left me, she thinks. But how can she explain how much she hates herself? They must all loathe her too – her mum, Rich, everyone.

'I don't mean forever, you ninny.'

'Oh.'

'I just mean for a couple of weeks, maybe more. While you recuperate. Let us look after you.'

'I'm all right, really.' Even as she says this, Cath knows it's not true. But the idea of going anywhere is petrifying. She can't move.

'Well, if you don't mind my saying, I don't think you are.'

Cath tries to assess if this is a good idea, but her brain is such a muddle. Finding a rational thought is like trying to locate a single tin in a rubbish tip.

Judy continues, 'It's not doing you any good to be on your own all day.'

Maybe she's right. Cath does feel awful. And she is aware she has felt similar to this once before.

'I've spoken to Rich about it, and he's happy for you to be with us.'

'He wants to get rid of me,' says Cath, and starts to cry again.

'Of course he doesn't!' Judy's tone is brisk once more. 'It's just he's out at work such long hours, it's mad for you to be here alone.'

'What about the gallery?'

'Bugger the gallery.'

'They'll fire me. I've had so much time off already with this pregnancy' – even the word tears her up – 'not to mention when I was ill before. And Rich is worried about being made redundant . . . ' Panic rises in her chest, her head starts whirling again. 'We need the money.' Even as she says this, she knows that however much they could do with her income, there is no way she can go to work. She can barely get herself to the bathroom.

'We'll get our doctor to sort you a sick note. There's no point you worrying about any of that right now. The best thing you can do is to come with me. Let Rich worry about his job; let me and your dad focus on looking after you.'

'You want me to come now?'

'Yes, why ever not? Unless you want Rich to bring you over later, give you time to gather your things?'

Suddenly, the thought of being alone a second longer is heinous. 'OK.'

Impulsively Cath throws back the sheets, stands up, wobbly on her feet.

Gradually, she and her mother assemble her clothes. Clean knickers and socks, comfy trousers, shoes she can actually go for a walk in, jerseys because their house is colder. She's glad Judy is able to make suggestions as she can't seem to remember half of what she might need. Slowly but surely they assemble everything on the bed. Then she yanks down the suitcase from the top of the wardrobe. As she lays it alongside her packing she sees a label attached to the handle. It's from the ski trip she and Rich went on almost exactly a year ago.

What a long and difficult journey they've both been on since then.

47

'Excuse me, excuse me,' says Lou. She edges past some passengers loading bags onto luggage racks, then reaches Anna's side. 'Sorry I'm late. Thought you'd have to give my place away. Phew.'

'I did have to fend off a couple of people,' says Anna, lifting her coat to make room for Lou to sit down. 'But I said I was waiting for a pregnant friend and it worked a treat.'

'I'm still not used to having to come to the station by bus,' moans Lou. 'It's so impossible to time it, compared to my bike.' She's flushed and hot. She grabs a flier from Anna's magazine and fans herself.

'Thanks for getting me one,' she says, as Anna hands over her decaf latte.

'It's OK, I was early. So, how are you? Good weekend?' It's Wednesday, but Anna has been with Rod for the last couple of nights – lately she's been staying there more and more. She says it's because he lives nearer to London which cuts her commute to work, but Lou suspects they're getting ready to move in together.

'Yes, it seems a while ago though, now.' In fact she had a friend to stay and they had a hoot, but she's not in the mood to run through it all. 'The clinic called me yesterday afternoon.'

'The Harley Street one? I thought you were all through there, pretty much?'

'I was – well, I am, I mean.'

'There's nothing wrong, is there?'

'No, um, not with me, anyway. Don't worry, I'm fine.'

'Gosh, good. You look well, I must say.'

Lou rests her coffee cup on her belly. 'You know the woman I gave my eggs to?'

'Sure. She's pregnant too, isn't she?'

At once Lou feels herself well up. 'Well, no, actually. I found out yesterday she lost the baby.'

'Oh no!' says Anna. 'I'm so sorry.'

'Me too,' says Lou. 'Me too.'

For a while they both say nothing.

'Oh, that's such a shame,' says Anna eventually. Lou has been staring out of the window at the landscape flashing past. The sky is clear blue, yet the fields are still covered in frost. On the South Downs it's unusual for it not to melt in the sunshine; it must still be freezing out there today. 'Though it's not your fault, you do know that, don't you?'

'Mm,' says Lou. She picks up the napkin that came with her coffee and dabs her eyes.

'Oh, sweetheart, you're such a generous person, but it really isn't your responsibility. There's nothing you could have done.'

'No, I suppose . . .'

'In some ways I'm surprised the clinic told you. It might have been better if you hadn't found out.'

'I asked them to keep me informed,' says Lou. 'Some clinics won't do that, but this one will, if you request it. And they were my eggs, so I wanted to know.'

How can Lou explain? She tried to make Adam understand the night before; he didn't really get it either. It's not that she feels responsible, exactly, it's that she feels *bound*. There's a connection between her and her recipient and it might be invisible, but it's powerful nonetheless. To find out her recipient miscarried at eight weeks is unfair and cruel, yet that doesn't touch on the half of it. It was Lou's egg she was carrying and in some way Lou feels as if she has lost part of herself.

* * *

'I think I'll go for a little walk,' says Cath. It's just gone eight o'clock. She's come downstairs to make a cup of tea; sun is streaming through the kitchen windows.

'Really, darling? OK. You'll need to wrap up warm, but it is a lovely morning.'

Cath can tell her mum is pleased. She also knows why: it's the first time she's stepped outside the house alone in the weeks she's been here. She's been to see the village doctor on her father's arm, all unsteady and spaced out, and gone for a drive with her parents a couple of times, but that's it. The GP told her she was 'understandably upset' and – yet again – to 'take it easy', so was of little use, other than signing her off work. Aside from this she's been in bed, occasionally surfacing for meals, or, more recently, to join her parents in the living room where she's sat, curled up on the sofa, watching telly. The programmes skate over the top of her, as if she is beneath a lake of ice and they are happening up above, on the surface. She seems to feel vacant and anxious wherever she is, however, so before she gets frightened and changes her mind about venturing forth she says, 'I've got my mobile,' and heads out of the front door.

Her mother is right: it is bitterly cold. Walking is still very strange, but at least she appears to be able to put one foot in front of the other. The grey stones of the cottages on either side of the lane are blurry. Gradually, she acclimatizes enough to focus.

It's not just depression that's making everything appear other-worldly: there's been a hoar frost. In an instant Cath is caught up, rapt, as though she's hallucinating, has taken a drug. It's at once beautiful and agonizing, breathtaking and too much to bear. Who would have thought white could have so many shades? A field of furrowed earth is striped pale silver and brown, delineating the tracks of the plough; trees glisten misty grey, like billowing smoke; a hedgerow sparks platinum and steel. She steps closer and sees a fairy-tale landscape in miniature. The briar is covered in hundreds – no, thousands, of miniature spikes; every berry, every twig is preparing for battle, daggers drawn. The frozen florets of autumn's hogweed are like small umbrellas blown inside out by the wind. Iced cobwebs swoop between the flower heads; Tarzan's ropes through a tiny jungle.

On impulse, she breaks off a couple of the blooms; the stalks snap with ease. She carries them back to her parents' bungalow, mindful of every step she takes, lest they come to harm.

'What have you got there?' asks Judy, as Cath comes through the kitchen door.

She lays the flowers on the table. 'I'm going to draw them.'

'Oh . . .' Her mother sounds surprised. 'They are gorgeous. Do you want a vase?'

'Please.'

Judy reaches into a cupboard and passes her one.

Gently, Cath places the hogweed inside. 'Where's my stuff?'

'What stuff?'

'My drawing stuff.'

'Goodness, darling, I don't know. Isn't it at your house?'

'No. I cleaned out our shed not that long ago. My pots are there, but not my drawing things. It's years since I did any. But I've seen my stuff here, I'm sure.'

'I think it's in the study,' says Peter. 'I'll help you find it.'

He's right. Wedged in amongst the faded hardback books and old magazines that her father saves for only he knows what, is a battered metal box. Although it was originally designed for workman's tools, Cath bought it many years ago to store her art materials.

'Careful!' says Peter, as she grabs it by the handle and tugs it from the shelf. Ancient photo albums topple, sending dust flying. She props them back up again and returns to the kitchen.

'Have you any paper?' Now she's had this idea, she's itching to start.

'Not proper drawing paper, no,' says her mother.

'What have you got?'

'I don't know. There might be some lined paper in my desk.'

'That's no good.'

'There's some plain paper in the printer,' says Peter, and he goes back to his study to fetch it.

Cath sighs. 'That'll have to do.' She knows she's being unfair. Neither of her parents is artistic in the way she is, and she hasn't put pencil to paper in years. How can she expect them to be prepared for this?

'I can get you something proper when I go into town,' says Peter, handing her a wedge of A4.

'Thanks, Dad.' She smiles at him, feeling guilty for not being more appreciative. Her mum and dad have been very good to her, especially during the last few weeks. And maybe they're not so slow; she's too impatient. What a nightmare she is.

'So what are you going to do, then?' asks Judy, peering as Cath clicks open the fasteners of the box.

The lid opens like a butterfly to reveal three tiers of shelving on either side. Each tier is subdivided into compartments, with various coloured pencils and pastels in each. Long ago she clustered similar hues together to make them easier to find, just like the balls of yarn she saw in the haberdashery department of John Lewis a few months ago. Given that she's not used them in such a while, the contents seem in pretty good condition. And at the bottom she even finds a packet of chalk, a rubber, a sharpener and a ruler.

'Dunno . . .' In spite of her sudden burst of enthusiasm, she still feels removed from everything; it isn't so easy to know where to begin. Then she spies a dog-eared cardboard container tucked under the chalks. Yes: it's the shape of the flower and the texture that interest her, not the colour. 'Charcoal, maybe?'

No sooner has Cath put charcoal to paper than she realizes it's far too grainy a medium for such a smooth surface. Charcoal needs texture to bite against, to hold it in place.

Goodness, I'm rusty, she thinks, frustrated. It isn't easy to pick this up again. Needlework was simple by comparison. She eyes the hogweed before her, appraising its scale. Each bloom must be over six inches across, never mind the vase: this sheet of A4 is far too small. How annoying.

She's not well enough to drive anywhere, but there's a faint possibility the village shop will have something, and it opens early. She pushes back her chair, grabs her coat.

'Off out again?' says Judy, trying to keep up.

'Just Chaplin's. Back in a tick.'

She leaves the front door on the latch and within five minutes she returns, clutching a scrapbook. As she comes down the hall, she hears her mum say, 'Well, this is a good sign.'

'Yes,' says Peter. 'She seems a lot better today.'

'I only hope it lasts.'

Cath supposes her parents are right. Nonetheless she resents being talked about behind her back. She makes a loud huffing noise so they are aware she is there, and rejoins them in the kitchen.

'Success?'

'Mm. This'll be much better. It's sugar paper.'

'I see,' says Judy, though Cath isn't sure she does.

She sits back down at the table and cracks open a page.

386

'You know the really spooky thing?' says Anna, scrunching up her napkin and putting it inside her empty coffee cup.

'No, what?'

'You know what day it is today?'

Lou frowns, trying to work it out. Her memory truly isn't what it usually is at the moment.

'Promise me I won't start you off blubbing again if I say?'

Lou looks at Anna, wary. It takes until this remark for her to realize her friend looks tired and worn, too, not her usual perfectly made-up, immaculately dressed self. Her mascara is smudged a little, her cheeks are blotchy. Suddenly she realizes. 'Oh shit.' It's February: the month Karen's husband, Simon, died.

'Is it really two years?' she says.

Anna nods.

'Crikey.' Lou shakes her head in disbelief. But of course: it was a Monday, mid month . . . It figures. Right now they're whizzing through the station at Gatwick Airport – that morning they never made it that far. She and Anna were turfed off the train at a station only a few miles from Brighton, and ended up sharing a taxi into London. It's how they met.

'It's our two-year anniversary,' Anna smiles, and Lou can see that tears are pricking behind her eyes, also.

She reaches over and squeezes Anna's hand. 'And what more apt reminder that good comes out of bad?'

I must remember to call Karen later, she thinks. The realization serves to impel her out of her own self-absorption.

Karen she can do something tangible for; her egg recipient she can't, not directly.

I hope she has people around her to lean on, Lou thinks, and sends a supportive vibe up into the ether, praying it reaches her mirror woman, wherever she is.

*   *   *

'You look exhausted,' says Judy. 'Let me get you a drink.'

Rich follows his mother-in-law into the kitchen.

'It's been a long day,' he says. Work is more full-on than ever; countless redundancies only mean that those left have to make up the shortfall. The drive to the office down south from Leeds is bad enough; on top of that, he's had to come out here to the Dales afterwards.

Nonetheless, as he gulps down a beer, he is glad. He could tell from Cath's smile as she opened the door to greet him that she is in better spirits. And now she seems keen to show him something.

'Look,' she is saying.

He follows her gaze. There, propped up on the kitchen mantelpiece, is a series of sketches.

'Hey, love, those are fantastic,' he says, but his eyes are so tired from the drive that he can't take them in properly. They seem to be drawings of large flowers, like cow parsley.

'You finished that fast,' says Cath. He looks down at his beer: the bottle is nearly empty. It is helping – he can feel himself relaxing.

She passes him another from the fridge and says, 'They're not that good. I'm dreadfully out of practice.'

He sips more slowly, examining the sketches further as he does so.

They look familiar, then he realizes why: they remind him of the patterns on the pottery Cath unearthed in the shed. There's the same eye for detail, the same fluidity of line. It seems she's only used two colours: white and black, yet in a few simple strokes she's captured the essence of the blooms.

48

'Aah, here they are,' says Cath, as the 4x4 pulls up outside the house. The vehicle looks enormous in their narrow street of terraced houses – none of their neighbours has anything remotely this size. She runs to greet them, opens the passenger door. 'Hello!'

'Hello, Auntie Cath,' say the two boys from the back seat.

'How was your trip?' she asks her brother.

'Knackering. Roadworks on the M1.'

'I thought there must be a hold-up. I'm sorry to hear that. Come in, come in.'

While Mike is still yawning, Alfie and Dom unclip their seatbelts and wriggle out of the car onto the pavement.

Cath follows them towards the house. 'Do you need a drink?' she asks them.

'Yes, please.' She fetches each of them a Ribena. She's stocked up the fridge specially.

'What they could really do with is a run in the garden,' says Mike. 'They've been cooped up for hours. Go on, you two. See who's fastest four times round the lawn. Have your juice after.'

Cath opens the back door and out they go without protest – clearly they need to let off steam. She and Mike stand watching them through the kitchen window.

'It looks really lovely out there,' says Mike. 'I'm impressed.'

'Thanks.' Cath is pleased to have his praise: he's not one to go into raptures.

'It's so much tidier than ours.'

Cath's heart twists. She knows he means it as a compliment, but she wouldn't mind exchanging their carefully manicured space for a lawn worn by children playing and a patio cluttered with toys.

'So how are you?' he asks. 'It's been months.'

'I'm OK. Much better than I was.' Cath blinks back tears. Being shown sympathy unlocks her upset. But she's done enough crying over the last three months – she wants to make this visit a happy one.

'So I gather.' Their mother will have kept him posted. 'How long have you been back here?'

Cath says, 'About a fortnight. It's good to be with Rich properly.' In the end she stayed with her parents far longer than the two weeks her mother originally mooted. She needed to return to the womb herself, it seems, to heal.

'I'm so sorry about everything.'

'Thanks . . . Was Sukey OK about not coming?'

'Mm . . . I think she was a bit hurt you didn't want to see her, but she does understand.' Cath can feel him check her expression before he says, 'You know, she isn't always the ogre you make out.'

'I'm sure. It's just I can't face any criticism right now.'

'I think she's mellowed in her stance.'

There he goes again, thinks Cath, brokering peace between us. 'Really?' She tries to keep cynicism from her voice.

'Yeah, really. She was very upset to hear you'd lost the baby. I was surprised myself at the strength of her reaction. She cried when I told her.'

'Oh.' She feels a twinge of guilt at not inviting her sister-in-law as well.

'Still, it's nice to see you just us anyway.' Mike reaches for her and gives her a hug across the shoulders.

'Ditto.' He's right: they rarely get one-on-one time. Maybe he wanted some too.

* * *

'Mum?'

'Lou!' says Irene. 'How are you getting on? Any news?'

'I wish.' Lou is walking along the seafront, on her way to meet Adam for a morning coffee. It's a good moment to call her mother for a catch-up. Since Christmas it seems there is new chemistry between them – there's more warmth to their conversations and Irene appears to enjoy getting regular updates on her pregnancy. 'I'm so uncomfortable it's untrue,' Lou complains. She can't imagine how she ever used to think going to the Meeting Place cafe was a pleasurable stroll; she's exhausted, her feet are swollen and she's not even halfway. She'd do anything to be able to sit on her bike and freewheel all the way there, but her cycling days are over for the time being.

'Not long now, though.'

'It could still be at least a fortnight. They won't induce me till I get to forty-two weeks.' Lou wipes sweat from her brow. For April it feels unseasonably warm.

'I'm sure it appears like forever, but you'll get there, trust me.'

'I hope to goodness it's early. I've had terrible heartburn on and off for days. Anyway, Mum, I wanted to ask your advice.'

'Oh yes?' This is a role Irene clearly relishes. Lou realizes this must be one reason why over the years she's seemed so much closer to Georgia; they've bonded as Irene passed on her experience of child rearing.

'I was wondering about my waters breaking, in case it happens before my labour starts. What happened with you?'

'Gosh, it's hard for me to remember exactly – we are talking over thirty years ago . . . But I think with Georgia it was slower and with you a bit more of . . . well, a gush, I suppose you'd call it.' Irene titters self-consciously at the phrase. 'I believe it's quite common for everything to go faster with a second pregnancy.'

'R-ight. And did your tummy seem less big afterwards?'

'Again, dear, I really can't recall that well. Why don't you ring your sister and ask her? She's been through it so much more recently.'

'Mm.' Lou hesitates. She's more inclined to google it, or ask Karen. On the other hand, she's yet to find a way to connect with Georgia on these issues, and has been avoiding much contact. But perhaps her sister can give her some insight. They are siblings and their bodies might just react in a similar fashion. 'OK . . . ' she relents. 'I might just give her a call.'

*   *   *

'Where are we going again?' asks Alfie.

'Just here,' says Cath, and pushes open the door. Mike and the twins follow her inside. The brightly lit room is more a studio than a conventional retail space. Pale wood shelves line the walls floor to ceiling, stacked high with plain white crockery. In the centre of the space are half a dozen large pine tables. Seated at them are several children and their parents who've arrived for the morning workshop before they have. 'We've come to do some potting, like I said.'

'We've done that before,' says Dom.

'Not like this you haven't,' says Cath. 'Your Dad says you've only done your own glazing.'

'What's glazing?'

'Painting on pottery. Like those plates in the window. See?'

'Oh, yes.'

'But today you're going to have a go at making pots,' says Cath, finding a space at the end of one of the tables alongside a mother and her little girl. 'Come on, sit down here and I'll explain.' The boys scramble up on a stool on either side. Mike is busy looking around, investigating the equipment. 'And we're not going to just do boring old painting. We're doing proper pottery, where we'll fire what you make. Do you know what firing is?'

'When you shoot someone.'

'That's *gun*fire,' she laughs. 'This firing is when you put a pot that you've made in the oven and cook it. Potters have a special oven called a kiln. And it gets really, really hot, much hotter than your oven at home. You see, when you start off, the clay that you use to make your pot will be all soft and squashy, like mud – you remember when you were small you used to make mud pies?'

The boys nod. They'd been wary of making the trip to Pontefract, trying something strange.

She continues. 'Look, that lady has some uncooked clay there.' The teacher, a grey-haired woman in a lilac smock, is unwrapping a giant slab of terracotta earthenware. 'See, it's still wet? That allows you to bend and shape it as you want. Then it's cooked and after it's cooked once it goes all hard. That means you can paint it, and then it gets cooked again and that sets the glaze.'

'You know an awful lot about it,' says the mother nearby.

'I used to make pots,' says Cath. She feels a flush of pride.

'She still should,' says her brother, pulling up a stool. 'Are you going to make anything today?'

'I'm not sure I'll be allowed.' Cath is self-conscious. This is an activity designed for children; the teacher may not appreciate an adult muscling in.

'You can help me,' says Dom.

'And me,' says Alfie.

'I think you're going to be busy enough as it is,' the mum smiles at Cath. 'This is Emily.' She gestures to her daughter. 'So, what are your boys called?'

'Oh, they're not mine,' says Cath. 'Well, not exactly.'

'Right, children,' interrupts the teacher with a clap of her hands. 'Are we ready?'

Alfie and Dom nod seriously.

'First, take your clay and knead it with your hands – like this.' She demonstrates.

Alfie and Dom immediately start thumping their wads of clay with zealous abandon. *Bang!* against the table top, and *Bang!* again.

'Boys,' Cath whispers, not wanting to irritate the woman in charge by interfering. 'If you do it like that you'll create little pockets of air.'

'So?' says Dom. *Bang!* goes the clay again.

'You don't want that or when your pots go in the oven it'll mean they end up with cracks in them. What you're trying to do is make it warm and soft. It's a good idea to keep the clay in a round shape – can I show you?' She moves behind him and wraps her palms around his smaller ones. 'Now, throw it back and forth, gently, like this.' Soon Dom has the sense of it. 'Now you, Alfie.' Cath moves to help him.

He drops his hands. 'Show me,' he says, so she takes the lump from him.

It feels so good, to have clay between her hands again. It comes back to her far quicker than drawing did, but she always was better at working in 3D. To and fro, to and fro, she works it. After a while she senses she is being watched; she looks up. Emily, the little girl opposite, is riveted.

'You OK to carry on now?' she asks Alfie.

'Mm.'

'I told you, you should have a go,' says Mike.

'I'm happy helping these two.'

'Will you show me?' asks Emily.

Cath glances over to check; the teacher is busy with another child. 'Of course.'

Shortly they're all ready to continue.

'Now we're going to roll it into a long sausage,' says the teacher.

'It's more like a snake than a sausage,' Cath murmurs to the boys. 'You want a big flat head for the bottom of your pot, OK?'

'Now, the diameter of your sausage will determine the thickness of your pot's walls,' says the teacher.

'What's a diameter?' asks Dom.

'She means how fat your snake is.' Dom's snake appears somewhat overfed. 'You want to make yours a bit thinner. A fat snake will make a very thick pot and it won't cook as well when we put it in the kiln. Can you put him on a bit of a diet?' She watches as he rolls. 'That's it, make more of a worm . . . ' Eventually he has it right.

Getting their hands dirty, making snakes – both boys seem in their element. But Emily's sausage is very lumpy.

'Do you want me to help you again?' Cath offers.

Emily nods shyly.

'You really are very kind,' says Emily's mum. She nods at the grey-haired lady and leans in. 'You should be doing her job, if you ask me.'

*　　*　　*

Lou leaves calling Georgia till late afternoon. She knows much of her sister's Saturday is taken up with ferrying the children to various extra-curricular activities.

'Is now a good moment?' she says.

'Hold on,' says Georgia. 'Elliot, Annabel. Shush.' She hears the TV go on. 'Sorry about that.'

'It's OK. Mum suggested I ask your advice about something.'

'Really?'

'It's about the last stages of pregnancy, and obviously you've much more experience of it than me.' Lou decides to flatter Georgia's ego, a tactic that usually works.

'Mm?'

'I wondered when you had the children, how did you know when you were about to give birth?'

'What symptoms have you been getting?'

'I've been having those Braxton Hicks contraction thingies in the evenings and think my pelvis must be widening a little – I've been getting a sharp pain up my front when I get out of a chair, especially if I've been walking a bit during the day like I have today.'

'You've been walking?'

'Not far.'

'Blimey,' says Georgia. 'I couldn't go *anywhere*. Still, you always were a bit of a fitness freak.'

Lou ignores the jibe.

'I got this mad desire to nest-build,' Georgia continues. 'I cleaned the house top to bottom, reorganized all our cupboards. You been doing that?'

'There's not much space to reorganize,' says Lou, and immediately wishes she could retract the remark. She has no wish to remind Georgia how small her studio is. 'But I guess I have been a bit obsessive about dusting . . . What about your waters, how did you know they'd broken?'

'How did I know?' Her sister hoots and at once Lou feels silly for asking. 'People were sailing past me in boats, that's how.'

Lou laughs. 'God, really?'

'Really. Though that was with Annabel. With Elliot it didn't happen until I'd gone into labour and was nowhere near as extreme. More like when you have a heavy period, and as I was having contractions there was such a lot going on anyway.'

'I see. That sounds like Mum, too – apparently it was more obvious with me than you.'

'You always did like to make an entrance,' says Georgia. Though really, it's untrue. Of the two of them, Georgia was always the one to elbow her way in and take centre stage, while Lou stood back and waited.

*   *   *

'There's something I wanted to mention,' says Mike. The boys are out of earshot, playing. He and Cath are standing, half watching them, in Meanwood Park. Although they were at the pottery till late afternoon, Mike has explained they'll need to burn off yet more energy before settling down for the evening. It's underlined to Cath what a huge amount of work they are.

'Oh?'

He coughs, awkwardly. 'You know, if you did want to have another go at the IVF, I might be able to help you out.'

Cath is staggered. 'You mean that?'

'Yes, I do.'

'Gosh.' She thinks for a few moments. She wants to make it clear to him what he could be offering. 'It's very expensive. You couldn't possibly afford to fund all of it.'

'Not all of it, maybe, but I could help. How much is it, anyway?'

She exhales. 'About ten grand. We'd have to start right over again, pretty much, with a new egg donor and everything.'

'That's what I thought. You mentioned the figure before, when you came to stay.'

'So I did.' She remembers that evening only too well. 'Would you tell Sukey?'

He focuses on his sons' game in silence, then says, 'Mm, I'm not sure . . . '

'If you didn't, wouldn't she wonder where the money had gone?'

'She doesn't know all the ins and outs of my company finances. So, frankly, no.'

Well I never, thinks Cath. There's no way I could sequester several thousand pounds without Rich being aware of it, or vice versa.

Mike continues, 'But I'd probably tell her. I don't really like having secrets. And she has mellowed a lot on the whole thing, as I said.'

'I appreciate that . . . Still, Mike, there is a pretty big difference between mellowing to the idea of IVF and being prepared to fund someone else's.'

'But you're family.'

'Even so.'

He reflects. 'Well, I'd have to choose my moment, obviously. But supposing, say, I gave you half? Could you find the rest?'

Cath is unable to process this in a hurry. 'To be honest, I thought we just couldn't do it again because there's no way we can afford it. So I'd have to talk to Rich and we'll give it some serious consideration. I've been coming to terms with the fact that it just wasn't going to happen for us.'

'I don't want to push you into it again if it's too much, obviously . . . Not if you're happy to stop. It's just seeing you with the boys today . . . You're so good with children.'

'Thanks . . . ' Again her heart twists. But that doesn't necessarily mean I can have them, she thinks. She's learnt the hard way: no matter how great the medical advances that have been made, or how generous people are, life often isn't that fair or kind.

49

'Look at that,' nudges Howie, jerking his head towards a fringed brown light-shade.

Adam is with his friend, looking at art, in Hove. Or rather, they're pretending to be looking at art; really they are nosing in strangers' homes. At least Howie is, by his own admission. It's May, the month of the Brighton Festival, and they are on an Artists' Trail of Open Houses where members of the public have their work displayed for sale. Some of the paintings are good, many are bad, but this is of secondary importance to Howie, who is using the opportunity to pick up interior design tips.

'Dreadful kitchen,' he says, as they emerge from a basement flat near the cricket ground.

Just then Adam's phone beeps. He couldn't get reception down there; he's missed a call. He's on his nerves' ends at the moment. 'Someone's left a message,' he says, but Howie carries on talking as he tries to listen. 'Shh! It's Lou . . . Oh my God! She's gone into labour!'

'No way!'

'Yup. I'm sorry, but I've got to go.' Adam scans the street for his car. He's so disconcerted he can't remember where he parked it.

'Right this minute?'

'Yes, of course this minute. I'm her birthing partner.' He breaks into a run.

'Ew,' says Howie, panting after him. 'All those lady-bits . . .'

'Oh, for goodness' sake, Howie!' says Adam, annoyed. 'I'm a doctor, you great big wuss. I've seen the odd woman's body before.' He stops at the car, catches his breath. 'Right. I don't mean to be rude, mate' – he squeezes Howie's shoulder – 'but I'm going to have to leave you here.'

Within thirty seconds he is accelerating down Kingsway towards Kemptown, barely slowing as he passes the speed camera on the way.

* * *

When Adam arrives, Lou is bent over by the steps outside her house, trying to breathe the way she's been taught. Her bag is discarded by her side on the pavement. If anyone wants to mug me they'll get my entire pre-packed labour kit, she thinks. But right now she can only grip the railing as the pain starts low and rises in intensity until it radiates over her belly.

'I'm so sorry I missed your call,' he says.

Poof! Poof! Poof! she breathes out as the pain moves to her back. Eventually it subsides and she replies, 'It's OK, honestly.'

'How often are your contractions?'

'Pretty often.'

'You've not been timing them?'

'Yes, I have, hang on . . . ' She grimaces. This is getting worse. She thought that was it. 'Every three or four minutes . . . ' Thank Christ, it's diminishing. She's vaguely conscious passers-by are staring at her – everywhere seems very busy today – oh yes, it's the Festival . . .

'Why didn't you call me earlier?' Adam picks up her rucksack.

'I didn't want to bother you until I was into it properly,' says Lou. 'And I knew you were on alert.'

'You ridiculous woman!' scolds Adam. 'Here, lean on me.'

She grips onto his arm as a support so she can edge to a sitting position on the front doorstep. 'I know, well, I didn't realize it was going to move on so fast—'

'What about your waters?'

'They broke this morning.'

'You should have rung me then!'

'I know, but I don't know, I just thought lots of women have these false labours, especially the first time—'

'And to think you were the one who told *me* we didn't need to do everything on our own!'

'I know, but—' Nonetheless she feels resistant. WE'RE NOT A NORMAL COUPLE! she wants to scream. But right now she can't speak; she just goes 'ARRRRRRRGG-GGGHHHHHHHHHH!' as she feels another contraction build to its peak. Over the road, a woman pushing a man in a wheelchair jumps in alarm, assesses what's happening and leans forward to explain to her charge.

'Breathe,' Adam reminds her.

'I called the midwife at the same time as you,' says Lou, when she can get her voice back once more.

'Good.'

'And she said not to come in until the contractions were three in ten minutes.'

'But they are.'

'Yes, now they are,' she snaps. 'But they weren't when I called. That's why I'm waiting here on the bloody pavement. For you.'

*   *   *

Adam is standing in the porch outside the Royal Sussex eating a sandwich. The midwife has suggested he take a break from the birthing room for a bit, while Lou has a bath to ease her discomfort, and Lou has asked him to call various people and bring them up to speed. She chucked him her mobile and told him to 'for God's sake use this!' when he'd asked for the necessary numbers. She's been yelling at him a lot over the last five hours.

He leans against a pillar and attempts to take stock. Even though he's been preparing himself for months, he can't quite believe it's actually happening at last. Up on level 13 of the tower block a new life is coming into the world – and he will be partly responsible for the growth, development, education of this whole little being. It brings up a whole host of emotions: honour at being allowed to be there, excitement, pride and incredulity.

Support, support, support, he reminds himself. That's what your role is today.

On that basis, who's the first person to call? It should probably be Lou's mother.

* * *

I want to just go home and have a cup of tea, thinks Lou as Adam steps back into the room. Ugh – I can smell food on him. But there's only one way this baby's going to go and that's out of me, so I have to go through with this.

'AAAAAAAAAAAAAAAARRRRRRGGGGGGGG-GGGGGGHHHHHHHHHHHHHHHH!' she bellows as another contraction sears through her. The pain is so intense, so visceral, she feels she's going to die. I'm going to tell everyone labour is absolute agony, she vows.

'I sound like bloody Sharapova,' she gasps. Was it yesterday she was watching tennis in the French Open on telly?

'She's come on a fair bit since you left,' the midwife says to Adam.

'So I see,' says Adam.

'We've given her some gas and air,' she says.

It's very weird, thinks Lou, I can hear all these people talking, but they don't feel quite real. She can hear someone singing a hymn, though it must be her imagination. *Onward Christian soldiers . . .* What a peculiar choice. She hasn't been to church in years. *Marching as to war . . . Christ, the royal whats-it, leads against the . . .* Where on earth has this come from? She doesn't believe in God. She must be high.

Like a mighty army . . . It's my mother, thinks Lou. She used to sing this all the bloody time . . .

Then . . . at long, long last . . .

'He's coming . . . he's coming . . . ' says the midwife.

'SSSSSSSSHEEEEEEEEEEEEEEEEEEEEEEEEEEE!' screeches Lou, in one last yell of defiance.

'I can see the head!' says Adam.

'Now pant!' says the midwife. 'I'm just checking the cord isn't compromised . . . '

I couldn't care what you're doing, thinks Lou. *I'm* giving birth to a bus.

'It's got red hair!' Adam shrieks.

And, good God – it feels the size of a fucking elephant – but that's it, the head is out.

After that, the rest of the body is comparatively quick. It almost seems to slither from her, until out the legs finally slip.

For a few moments, Lou is so relieved and exhausted she almost forgets to breathe, and she can't speak at all.

It's over.

'Congratulations,' says the midwife. Immediately she lifts the baby, and after a swift wipe puts the infant, still covered in blood, on Lou's chest. Not that Lou cares how sticky the experience is.

Her baby boy is here.

50

The door of the ward bursts open, saloon-bar style. It's Molly and Luke, too excited not to race ahead of Karen and Anna.

Oh-oh, I'm not sure I've the stamina for this, thinks Lou. But then Molly is at her side, head barely high as the hospital bed, brandishing flowers. They appear to have been picked at the allotment: the leaves are a touch slug-eaten, the petals are crushed and they're wrapped in silver foil.

'For you.' Molly thrusts the posy at her, arms rigid.

'Thank you,' Lou says. The baby is at her breast; after an initial struggle, she's just managed to feed him.

'Hold on a minute, poppet,' says Karen, reaching the bed too. 'Sorry,' she says to Lou. 'Molly, can't you see, Lou isn't able to take those right now?'

'Oh,' says Molly.

'She's got the baby just there,' Karen explains. 'Oh, Lou, he's gorgeous!'

From Molly's perspective he is probably not easily visible, wrapped in a blanket.

'Can I see him?' says Molly.

Karen lifts her daughter up a little, Lou carefully edges down the cover, and turns the baby, gently, to reveal his face. His skin is all red and blotchy, his brow is damp, yet Lou is overcome with love. Nothing has prepared her for this: if she could bottle the joy she is feeling, she'd overdose on it every morning.

'He's got *lots* of hair!' says Molly, impressed.

'It's really dark,' says Luke.

'I can see red in it,' says Karen. 'Though it's likely to fall out.'

Molly looks worried.

'It'll grow back,' Lou assures her. 'That's what happens with newborns.'

'You had very dark hair when you were a baby,' says Karen. 'And look at you now.'

Molly tosses her blonde curls; she's aware of her assets already.

'You must be wrung out,' says Karen. 'Well done, you.'

'Now he's here, it's all been worth it.'

'He's beautiful,' says Anna, peering, too.

'Thank you,' says Lou. She couldn't agree more: there's never been such a beautiful boy in the whole wide world, ever.

'Look at his tiny fingers,' says Anna, as if Lou hasn't noticed them already. 'They're so small and perfect. And those nails – wow, they're paper-thin, aren't they?' She inhales. 'Ah . . . He even smells new.'

Just then Adam arrives with two cups of tea: he's been to get one for him and one for Lou. Anna turns to him. 'Congratulations.'

Adam beams; he seems almost as euphoric as Lou is. 'Did you want me to get you some?' he asks. 'The machine's down the corridor.'

'No, don't worry,' says Karen. 'We won't stay long – I need to give these two their supper. But they were desperate to see the baby.'

'Has he got a name yet?' asks Anna.

'We think so,' says Adam. 'We're going to live with it for a few days, before we let everyone know.'

Lou suppresses an urge to laugh. They're both heartily sick of everyone putting in their twopenn'orth.

'I met you at Christmas,' says Molly. She frowns. 'Are you Lou's boyfriend?'

Karen shakes her head. 'I'm sorry. I've tried to explain.'

'No . . . ' says Adam, unfazed. 'But I am the baby's daddy.'

Molly frowns, perplexed.

'I blame Disney.' Karen drops her voice. 'She's determined to find a prince for everyone. I'll have another go at helping her understand.'

'It's OK,' says Adam.

'You know, I think he looks a bit like you,' says Anna. 'He has a similar hairline.'

Adam appears as if he might burst with pride and Lou smiles to herself. They've had a few visitors today: her mother, Adam's parents, Howie. Each one has commented on the perfection of the baby's fingers and his resemblance to Adam.

She's not even sure they're right about this last observation; she can't quite see it. To her their baby just looks like himself, but no matter. She imagines that the globe over there are babies being born today, with people commenting just like this. It's just such a terrible shame her egg recipient wasn't one of them.

*   *   *

The phone rings in the kitchen. The only person who regularly dials Cath and Rich's landline is Judy, although it's unusually late in the day for her to call.

'I gather your brother has offered you half the money to try the IVF again, darling,' she says without preamble. 'Your Dad and I have discussed it. We've got a few savings, so we can give you the rest if it would help.'

At once Cath's spirits lift, then fall as she considers the implications. 'I don't know, Mum . . . It's so kind, but . . . '

'Well, think about it.'

'I have been thinking about it already. Ever since I spoke to Mike.'

'Oh?'

'It's only, I'm not sure I can go through it all again.'

'No need to decide now. We'd need to give the bank a bit of notice anyway. I just didn't want you to have to rule it out because you couldn't afford it.'

'Gosh, thanks, Mum, it really is very generous of you.'

Cath puts down the receiver. 'They've offered to pay for it,' she says to Rich. He's been at her shoulder throughout.

'That's good, love,' he says. But his voice sounds flat, steam-rollered.

'We'd have to use a different donor, I guess . . . ' She strives to be positive, yet it feels forced. Something in her heart died with the baby-that-nearly-was.

'Maybe we'd have more luck with someone else,' he says, but Cath isn't convinced he believes it. 'We could always consider going to Spain or something – it's cheaper there.'

'Mm . . . I don't know, a half Spanish baby . . . it wouldn't look as much like us. It's just I felt a real connection with that donor . . . ' She thinks of her mirror woman, wherever she is, although now the woman has a child they are no longer a reflection of one another. Cath sways, knocked by the acknowledgement, leans against the sink unit to steady herself. 'You know, I am glad it worked for her, really I am.'

Rich takes her into his arms. 'Me too.'

'We helped her, didn't we?'

'We did.'

'And without us, her baby might not have happened.'

'No.'

Though of course Cath knows it might well have: a different couple would doubtless have paid for their donor's IVF in return for her eggs. But it wouldn't have been that exact baby, created at that exact moment.

Cath and Rich stand together a moment, holding one another. Then Cath pulls away so she can articulate what's on her mind. 'I truly don't know if I can go through every-thing for a third time. It's so gruelling, building up my hopes, only to have them dashed. I'm strong, but not that strong.'

'They might not be dashed, this time . . . '

'I know, though the odds are they will. There's a 35 per cent success rate on a third attempt; that's what it says on the net.'

'That might not be true for you, though. Those statistics are for everyone.'

'I don't see why they wouldn't be.' She checks his expression. 'What do you think?'

'I'm not sure . . . Though I do agree; it's such a lot to go through, yet again. But you know me, you need to give me a while.' Then he adds, pre-empting her concern, 'I'm doing OK, honestly.'

'You're sure?'

He nods, 'I'm sure.' Then he says carefully, 'I do know that I want you back, love.'

'What do you mean?'

'You go somewhere else when you get down . . . You disappear, away from me.'

'Mm.' She knows he's right. When she's in that deep, dark place, she disappears from everyone; it's all she can do not to disappear from herself. At times she felt that she was losing her personality, slipping away from her essence, completely. To be back up, gasping for air, to have caught herself again, feels like it took every ounce of strength she had. She almost drowned, this last time. But sometimes she forgets: if it's hellish for her when she is in despair, it must also be hellish for Rich, watching from the sidelines, unable to throw her a lifebelt. And he has his own grief too: it's his baby they were making.

Recognizing this only underlines how risky it would be to undertake a third round. They must think it through, properly, and she mustn't rush Rich; it would be easy to bounce him into a decision and she's learnt that his slower, more measured way of working things through is equally – sometimes more – valid.

'Let's sleep on it,' she says.

Thank goodness, thinks Lou. She'd hoped for a tranquil day to start her baby's life; it was not to be. She's so exhausted and emotional, she has absolutely no energy left. But at last the visitors have gone, and Adam too.

It's just the two of them.

She should probably follow the example of the woman in the bed next to her and get some rest – it's gone 10 p.m. – but she can't stop looking at her baby. He's so small, so dependent and vulnerable, she can't bear to turn away.

Instead she lies with her face close to his, studies him. His head is bigger than she expected, but maybe it seems that way because his limbs are so scrunched up, and he has a rash of tiny white spots on his wrists. What a miracle he is: a bundle of potential, a giant question mark wrapped up in a blanket. She can't wait to share news of his birth with the friends she's made on the forum – they've been such a source of support to her. She wonders what profound effect her baby will have on her life – and Adam's. She's amazed that he appears totally alert: his eyes are open, and though she knows his vision is blurry, he seems to be staring straight at her.

'Hello,' she whispers.

And maybe it's wishful thinking, or hormonal euphoria, but she could swear she sees her father in that instant, looking out through the windows of her baby's soul.

* * *

Next morning, Cath wakes very early. The sun is shining through the curtains; a slash of light lands on the bed. Bessie the cat is basking in its warmth on the duvet.

Rich is still asleep. She doesn't want to disturb him before he has to get up for work, so she rises surreptitiously, goes to the window, pulls the curtains apart just a few inches. Mike is right. the garden is pleasingly ordered, the shrubs cut back, the ivy under control, the lawn freshly mown.

At least I achieved something over the last year, she thinks. Mania has its benefits.

She gazes up, as if the clouds might be able to provide an answer from on high to their dilemma. Then she hears Sukey's voice – Sukey, of all people – deriding her so many months ago.

'Have you ever practised acceptance?' she'd said.

Maybe Cath is mellowing, or changing. Whichever, at that second her sister-in-law's words resonate. She has given over so much of her life to treatment – nearly four years. And much of that time she was fighting: fighting cancer, fighting infertility. Has she really got it in her to fight any more?

Again her eyes fall on the garden. There by the back wall is the shed. She pictures the carefully ordered tools and garden furniture inside, and her pots, lined up on shelves. She can envisage the ghostly vases, the cups etched with leaves and flowers, the translucent plates, the teapots, the jugs, the cobweb bowls. It's as if they are beckoning, issuing an invitation.

And she gets a sense – gradually at first, then with more certainty – that there could be more to her future beyond having babies. She could give to the world, perhaps, find her place on the planet, in another way.

It won't be the same as having a child; nothing could be a substitute for that. She'd be a fool to think anything could. But she's had so little control over her own body over the last few years, and this last depression has reminded her how fragile she is. It might be better to wrest back control, to take her life once again into her own hands, but in a calmer, less impatient fashion.

Yes, she thinks it would.

And then she could even – if they were up for it – accept her family's support.

She checks the time. It's too early to ring her mother; she'll only alarm her. And although Mike might be awake, he'll be busy with the children; it's not the right opportunity to share these thoughts with him.

Just then, as if he knows instinctively that she is eager to speak, Rich stirs, opens his eyes, focusing directly on her. 'Hello, love.' His voice is bleary.

'I've been thinking.'

'Mm?'

'Ten thousand pounds . . . That's what another round of IVF would cost here, and I'm really not sure about going abroad.'

Rich eases himself up to a sitting position, props a pillow as support. 'I understand that.'

'It's too much money.' She shakes her head. 'When the odds are so poor.'

'I remember you saying you could never put a price on a baby,' he reminds her.

'That was before we'd been through everything we've been through . . . Supposing we spend another ten grand and end up exactly where we are now? Do we spend another ten . . . and another? When do we stop? We can't forget the money equation completely. No.' She is decisive. 'It's too big a gamble. I'm really not happy spending it again with so few guarantees.'

'We haven't got the money anyway.'

'I meant if we took it, or borrowed it or whatever, from my parents and Mike. If you're happier with a loan – and I think I would be – I've been thinking, maybe we could borrow it to spend on something else.'

'Oh?' His tone is sceptical.

'I've had an idea. Something I feel more certain of, something that might make me happy. Or happier, at any rate.' He frowns. Cath will have to take this slowly. 'The shed.' She gestures through the pane. 'It's pretty big.'

'But what's that got to do with anything?'

'When I was little, in the Dales, my pottery teacher had a studio out the back of her house. And taking the boys to Pontefract . . . it set me thinking. I thought we might do the same . . . maybe.' She checks to see he is keeping pace. He seems to be. 'Convert it, I mean. I think it might be better if we used the money for that – or some of it, anyway . . . That building is pretty sturdy; the walls are concrete. We could adapt it somehow, and buy a kiln.'

'Ri-ight.' Rich nods, very slowly.

'I could teach people to pot,' she continues. 'Kids mainly, I'm thinking. As far as I know there's nothing like that round here.'

'Give up the gallery?'

'Possibly, eventually. Though not till I'm up and running properly. I wouldn't want to put us under that kind of financial pressure while your work is up in the air too. It wouldn't be fair. It would take time.'

'Sounds like an interesting idea.' He smiles.

'Do you think so?' Cath thinks of the train of toddlers on the ski slopes, how the sight of them learning a new skill touched her. She can hear children scampering through the house, headed out to the garden, excited. She can imagine their palms as they work the clay, the slip on their fingers helping to shape and mould it. How she'd like to see them, eyes wide as they carry freshly fired handiwork from the kiln, glazes transformed by heat from dull and muted to the brightest of shades!

She stops. She mustn't get ahead of herself again. It's been her downfall before, getting too hopeful. She's tried to push events, control biology, force timings – and look where it got her. To the brink of insanity, although, thankfully, back again. And perhaps that's what acceptance means, for them, for her: accepting that what has gone is gone, and allowing life to take its natural course, trusting the way forward to be something that emerges slowly, gently.

There is Bessie, asleep in her favourite place, at the bottom of the bed. She could learn from her. 'There's no need to rush,' she says, more to herself than her husband.

After all the pressures they've been through, counting the minutes and hours and days, it'll be a relief not to worry about biology and its clocks, or to have to wait in limbo until someone else gives them news or a directive. This is their decision – and theirs alone. They can take it as fast or as slowly as they want.

'It sounds a great plan,' Rich reiterates. 'Mike said the other day that you were a natural—' But he chokes before the words are fully out, and then, unexpectedly, starts to cry.

'Oh honey,' says Cath. He so rarely weeps; she's only seen him tearful two or three times before. She's been so wrapped up in her own grief she's not thought enough of him. She returns to the bed, sits down beside him. The mattress dips and creaks under her weight. Bessie stirs and stretches, comes to join them, wanting attention.

Rich sniffs, and strokes the cat absent-mindedly. 'Sorry. Stupid of me. Crying.'

'It's not stupid.' She looks at him. His lovely, lopsided mouth is downturned. To see him this way causes her distress, too. She mustn't trample over his wishes. 'Do *you* want me to try again?'

He shakes his head. 'No.'

'Are you sure?'

'I'm sure.' He gulps, and returns her gaze, steady. 'I'm OK, it's OK, honestly. I really do think the pottery is a good idea. You'd be a great teacher; you've so much enthusiasm, so much talent and passion. And I think you're right. We can't go through it again. You can't, and I can't either. It's tearing our lives apart, all this giving of ourselves to hospitals and clinics . . . I'm sick of them. I just want to be able to enjoy our time together, me and you.'

'So why are you crying, then?'

'I'm crying for what we're giving up,' he says.

Epilogue

c/o Dr Hassan
The Marylebone Fertility Clinic
London W1V 2PF

June 10th

Dear Friend,
You don't know me – we have never met, and we will always be unknown to one another. But we travelled a journey together, and it is for this reason I am writing. If this reaches you, I hope you don't mind that I have got in touch – I asked Dr Hassan from the clinic to check if you would like to receive this letter, and if you said yes, he agreed to pass it on.

I was your egg donor. I gather you asked about my pregnancy and already know that I conceived, so I am writing to let you know that a few weeks ago I had a little boy. I understand that you were unsuccessful in your attempts to conceive with my eggs, and I am so sad and sorry to hear that. Dr Hassan tells me he believes you have decided not to try again – which must have been a very difficult decision to make, and I admire your bravery. Should you ever change your mind, I would be happy to donate my eggs to you again, without your needing to pay for my IVF. But I respect your decision and in no way want to interfere with that, so unless I hear back from you through the clinic, I'll assume that you don't wish to pursue it.

The other reason that I wished to write is to thank you. My income is not vast, and for various medical reasons of my own I was advised to have a baby soon and to have IVF if I wanted to maximize my chances of conception. Your incredible generosity made this possible.

I want you to know that I think of you often and I hope that whatever the future holds for you, you are happy. My little boy is called Frankie, after my father, and his middle name is Matthew, which means 'gift from God'. I'm not religious and neither is Frankie's father – this name is in honour of you.

With deepest gratitude,

A Friend x

*   *   *

Lou is struggling to put Frankie into his pram in the hall when the doorbell rings.

Damn, she thinks, tempted to leave it. But through the glass she can see the blur of a blue shirt – it's the postman. So she holds the baby close with one arm, and gingerly opens the door with the other.

'Parcel for Ms Louise Burgess,' he says.

'That's me,' she nods, and he hands her a large Jiffy bag.

I wonder what this is, she thinks, laying Frankie down.

She feels the package: something squashy – baby clothes, perhaps? Most of her friends have sent gifts and cards weeks ago; even Sofia sent a small bouquet when she heard the news. She looks for a postmark – it says *London W1*, so is little help. She checks Frankie, who seems happy enough for a moment, gurgling away with his feet in the air, so she tears open the tape and staples sealing the top of the parcel.

Inside are an envelope and a plastic bag. The envelope – she recognizes the logo – is from the clinic. She opens it, curiosity mounting. It contains a short typed covering letter from Dr Hassan and a short handwritten note. Dr Hassan's letter is mere detail; the note is what captures her.

From your recipient, it says. *This is for Frankie, with love.*

She tips open the bag. A tumble of fabric falls to the floor. She picks it up, shakes it out, and gasps.

It's a beautiful pastel-coloured patchwork quilt.

Acknowledgements

A great big thank you to all those who were generous enough to help me with my research for this novel; who shared their knowledge and opened their hearts, and whose stories were an inspiration. They include Rachel Beaumont, Gillian Aird, Carla Greco, Deborah and Nick Castle, Adrian Baker and John Staples, Rebecca and Vicky Hindley-Jones, Marina and Benoit Ruscoe, Bill Graber and many more.

Another equally deeply felt thank you to the crack team at Sheil Land: my agents Vivien Green and Gaia Banks, along with Virginia Ascione. Then there are those at Picador: my publisher Paul Baggaley, editor Francesca Main, Kris Doyle et al., plus Sam Humphreys, who believed in this book when it was no more than an idea.

Huge appreciation, too, for those good souls who read the manuscript ahead of publication and offered me invaluable feedback: Alison Boydell, Chris Chalmers, Alex Hyde, Nicola Lowit, Pam McLeod and Clare Stratton. Plus a special mention for Jules Harvey and the folk at NWP Creative and Object Source who helped with the birth of the concept.

I must also thank those at the London Women's Clinic, especially Dr Kamal Ahuja for his advice on the clinical aspects of egg sharing, and Emma Smith, who went through the book with a fine-tooth comb. Any remaining inaccuracies are mine, not theirs.

Finally, thank you to my mum, Mary Rayner, and my other half, Tom Bicât, for their wisdom, forbearance, editorial support and encouragement. I could not have written this novel without them.

Questions for Book Groups

1. For the person who chose the book: what made you suggest it to the group?
2. Do the characters Lou and Cath seem real and believable? How do they change over the course of the story?
3. Talk about Sofia, Adam and Rich. Did any stand out for you? And how about Lou's mum, Cath's mum and Sukey? Were there any who you didn't like? Did you agree with any of their points of view about IVF?
4. Has anyone in the group read Sarah Rayner's previous novel, *One Moment, One Morning*? If so, how did you feel about meeting the characters from that novel again? Do you think you need to have read *One Moment, One Morning* to enjoy *The Two Week Wait*? Did you prefer one to the other?
5. What did you think about the structure of the book, and the use of flashbacks and multiple perspectives?
6. What was more important, the characters or the plot? Was the plot moved forward by the characters' decisions, or were the characters at the mercy of the plot?
7. What did you think about the author's use of research? How did it enhance or take away from the story? What did you learn from reading this novel?
8. What about the language and writing style? Was it appropriate to the story? (You might like to have each member read a favourite passage out loud. It's best to warn them ahead so they'll be prepared!)
9. What specific themes did you notice throughout the novel? Did you think the author was trying to get anything in particular across to the reader overall?
10. What do you think your lasting impression of *The Two Week Wait* will be? Are you glad to have read it and would you recommend it? Did it make you want to read more by this author?

One Moment, One Morning
Sarah Rayner

The 07:44 train from Brighton to London. Carriages packed with commuters. One woman occupies her time observing people around her. Opposite, a girl applies her make-up. Across the aisle, a husband strokes his wife's hand. Further along, a woman flicks through a glossy magazine.

Then, abruptly, everything changes: a man collapses, the train is stopped, an ambulance called. And for three passengers that particular morning, life will never be the same again.

'A real page-turner . . . You'll want to inhale it in one breath'
Easy Living

'A story of loss, secrets and lies, family and the enduring friendships between women – life-affirming and insightful'
New Books Magazine

'A great, quirky must-read with a heart'   *Red*